HUNTED

CARO SAVAGE

Boldwood

First published in Great Britain in 2022 by Boldwood Books Ltd.

Copyright © T.I.A. Goddard, 2022

Cover Photography: Shutterstock

A CIP catalogue record for this book is available from the British Library.

Paperback ISBN 978-1-83889-536-5

Large Print ISBN 978-1-80415-441-0

Hardback ISBN 978-1-80415-443-4

Ebook ISBN 978-1-83889-538-9

Kindle ISBN 978-1-83889-537-2

Audio CD ISBN 978-1-83889-534-1

MP3 CD ISBN 978-1-80415-445-8

Digital audio download ISBN 978-1-83889-535-8

Boldwood Books Ltd
23 Bowerdean Street
London SW6 3TN
www.boldwoodbooks.com

For Claire & Edward

1

Senior Crown Advocate Jeremy Westerby had already passed out once from the pain. Now as he came to for the second time, he realised that the agony he was currently experiencing surpassed anything he'd ever gone through before in his life.

Passing a kidney stone. Being stung by a poisonous jellyfish on holiday. Slipping a disc in his back. Those things, while extremely painful at the time, were nothing compared to this.

Having his genitals slowly crushed in a portable vice really did top them all. The pain was absolutely unbearable but he couldn't scream out loud because there was a gag in his mouth.

The whole experience was amplified no end by the sickening fear that also consumed him. To know that someone was deliberately and maliciously subjecting him to this.

He looked up through blurred vision at the man standing over him. The man was tall and gaunt with dead black eyes and a small scar across his right eyebrow. Westerby had never seen him before in his life, but whoever the man was, it was obvious that he did this kind of thing for a professional living.

Westerby himself worked for the Crown Prosecution Service

bringing offenders to justice on behalf of the state. He didn't earn as much as other legal professionals, particularly those in the private sector, but he did it because of his principles. However, he now realised he was paying a high price for holding those moral values for it had become very clear by now that this incursion related to the work that he was doing.

He'd been alone in his house in Ealing, West London, his wife and two children having gone out to the theatre earlier that evening to watch a musical. Much as he'd have liked to accompany them, he'd declined to do so in order to stay in and focus on the casework he was doing for the trial of a major-league drug trafficker that was coming up in a few weeks' time. And it was this very trial that the man was torturing him about.

One minute he'd been sitting in his study tapping away on his laptop immersed in the casework, then something had hit him over the back of the head and the next thing he knew, he'd woken up tied to his desk chair with his hands bound firmly behind his back, a gag in his mouth and a portable vice attached to his nether regions. It hadn't taken him long to realise that the man had broken into his house somehow and in fact had probably been watching and waiting for an opportunity to catch him while he was home alone.

He kept being assailed by a sense of disbelief that this was really happening to him. Although he knew that he was prosecuting some very dangerous people, the idea that they'd go so far as to actually harm him had seemed like an abstract consideration. After all, he'd worked for the CPS for many years and nothing like this had ever happened to him before.

The man repeated the question he'd asked Westerby just before he'd passed out.

'What's her name?' he hissed. 'Tell me the name of the under-cover cop who's testifying in the trial. What's her *real* name?'

Westerby knew that this information was highly confidential. Undercover police officers always testified anonymously in order to protect their security. He knew that the man only wanted this information so that he could harm the policewoman whose evidence was key to securing a conviction at the trial. If he told the man the woman's name then he would be placing her in terrible danger. He would in effect be signing her death warrant.

The man pulled the gag from Westerby's mouth to allow him to answer. Westerby sputtered and gasped, sucking in a huge mouthful of air, sweat running in streams down his face.

'Pl... please...,' he pleaded.

'The name,' repeated the man. 'Tell me her name.'

'I can't. Please. I... I can't...'

The man shook his head and tutted. He slipped the gag back on and leant down to tighten the vice even further, sending an almighty spike of agony through Westerby's body. Westerby felt like he might be about to pass out again, but instead his pain and fear conspired to make him lose control of his bowels, his sphincter opening up to release a hot flatulent gush of foul-smelling effluent.

The man recoiled, his face wrinkling in disgust. He looked down at Westerby scornfully and shook his head in cold contempt. Westerby gritted his teeth and fixed the man with a shaky but defiant gaze.

The man picked up a framed picture of Westerby's family that was sitting on his desk. Holding it in a leather-gloved hand, he examined it with his cruel eyes.

'Nice family,' he whispered nastily. 'Maybe I'll hang round here until they get back. Unless you tell me what I want to know.'

Westerby's eyes widened. The thought of the man harming his wife and kids filled him with insurmountable horror. Better to just tell the man what he wanted to know. Better to cooperate with him.

It was a terrible thing to have to do, but with the lives of his family at stake, he didn't have much choice in the matter.

Knowing that he'd got Westerby by the balls, in a metaphorical as well as a literal sense, the man pulled off the gag to let him speak.

'Her name is Bailey Morgan,' whispered Westerby. 'Detective Constable Bailey Morgan.'

The man smiled sadistically.

'Detective Constable Bailey Morgan.' He rolled the name off his tongue. 'There. That wasn't so hard.' His face tautened to become hard like stone once again. 'Where does she live?'

'I don't know,' said Westerby.

The man shook his head as if that was the wrong answer. He raised his eyebrow at the picture of Westerby's family.

'Please believe me!' said Westerby. 'I don't know where she lives!'

With a snort of contempt, the man straightened up to his full height. He seemed to sense that Westerby was telling the truth. Looking down at him with a cold sneer, he reached into the pocket of his black jacket and pulled out a long thin implement. Westerby recognised it as an ice pick. A heavy black dread descended upon him as he knew now with a fatalistic certainty that the man was going to kill him.

Grasping Westerby's head with a leather-gloved hand, the man inserted the pointed tip of the ice pick into Westerby's right ear. For a brief moment Westerby felt the cold invasive tip of the pick penetrating his ear canal. And then with a shove the man pushed it deep into his head, right into the middle of his brain.

The last coherent thought that Westerby had was that at least the pain would be over.

2

Detective Constable Bailey Morgan woke up suddenly on Wednesday morning. The hangover hit her a few moments later, swamping her with a tidal wave of nausea accompanied by a splitting headache. She groaned softly. How many vodka blackcurrants had she drunk the night before?

Memories of the previous evening started to filter through in bits and pieces. It had been the leaving do of a work colleague, Anthony. He was one of the IT guys, a civilian police worker who'd decided to leave the police to go and get a better-paid job doing the IT for a bank. Bailey's friend Emma, a fellow detective, had invited her along, saying that Bailey didn't get out enough. So she'd dutifully attended. They'd all started off in the pub, then gone to a bar, then there had been some dancing. And then...

She rolled over in the bed. It felt odd. Lumpy. Unfamiliar. This wasn't her bed. She then realised that she was naked. She didn't normally sleep naked.

Her eyes opened a crack. A horrible sinking feeling came over her. She reluctantly turned her head...

...to see that there was someone else lying beside her.

It was Anthony. He was asleep, snoring softly.

Bailey instantly felt overcome with excruciating shame that he'd seen her naked. Her body was disfigured with an extensive lattice of scars and small round burn marks which covered most of her upper torso, front and back, and she was deeply self-conscious about it. Normally the most that anyone saw was the thin white scar running down the left side of her face, and even so, she made a concerted effort to conceal that behind a lock of hair which she deliberately wore loose for that very purpose.

She'd acquired the scars in the course of an undercover operation several years earlier which had gone badly wrong. The trauma of that experience had consequently been the source of profound intimacy problems. For almost three years since then, her life had been devoid of sex, and she'd reached the point where she'd as good as resigned herself to never having those kinds of experiences again. Yet somehow she'd managed to get wasted, sidestep all of that emotional and psychological baggage and sleep with... the IT guy from work. He was someone she barely knew, someone she'd barely even spoken to until Emma had introduced them both properly the previous night.

She sat up, her head throbbing horribly. Anthony made a grunting noise and shifted in the bed. She froze. But he didn't wake up. He was still out for the count. She wondered what the time was. Locating her iPhone, which was lying on the floor next to the bed, she saw that the battery had died. Glancing round the room, she noticed a digital clock on the bookshelf – it was eight-thirty in the morning. Shit. She was going to be late for work.

Stealthily easing herself out of the bed, she gathered up her clothes, which were scattered across the floor, and slipped them on. And then she rapidly made her escape from Anthony's house.

Rather than go straight to work in her current state, she decided to return to her flat first to quickly take a hot shower and have a strong cup of coffee, both of which would hopefully go some way to mitigating her hangover.

Anthony lived in Streatham, not too far from where Bailey lived in Crystal Palace, so it didn't take her long to get home. Just as she was standing in the hallway fiddling with her key in the lock, she heard a door open behind her.

Her heart sank.

Without even turning round she knew who it was.

It was her neighbour Alastair, and, right now in her current state, he was the last person she wanted to have a conversation with.

Alastair Primpton was in his late forties and single, and he occupied the one other basement flat in the building. They both shared a hallway and he always seemed to be finding something to have a go at her about, however petty.

She turned round slowly and forced an empty smile onto her face.

'Hello Alastair.'

He was wearing a yellow polo-neck jumper and a pair of those square-rimmed glasses that seemed to be perennially popular with people who worked in certain sections of the arts and the media. He was standing in his doorway with his arms crossed and an aggrieved expression on his face.

He nodded at the messy pile of letters lying on the floor of the hallway just inside the main door.

'Are you going to pick those up any time soon?'

Bailey glanced down at them disinterestedly. 'Yeah I'll go through them later.'

'I've picked out my ones but you've just left yours lying there. They've been there for ages.'

'They just look like junk mail to me,' she muttered.

'All the more reason to pick them up then. It's just common courtesy you know.'

'Yes I—' she tried to get a word in edgeways.

'Consideration for your neighbours,' he continued. 'It's like that time you didn't bother to take your rubbish out for several weeks. I don't know where you were but it stunk to high heaven. The smell got so bad it was stopping me from getting to sleep at night. I was seriously considering calling the Fire Brigade to knock your door down and remove it.'

Bailey rolled her eyes at his histrionics. 'Look I'm really sorry about the rubbish okay. I just forgot to take it out. I was... away doing something at work.'

In fact Bailey had been working undercover infiltrating a notorious crime family called the Molloys, living for the duration of that job in a different flat in a different part of London as part of her cover. Unfortunately, what with the demands of that particular operation, it had slipped her mind to take the rubbish out before she'd left, and since then Alastair just hadn't been able to let her forget about it.

'I mean, what is it that you do exactly?' he demanded. 'I know you work for the Metropolitan Police. How come you're away all the time? Are you travelling abroad or something? Where were you?'

Bailey didn't reveal to anyone outside the police that she worked undercover, and she would hardly have shared those sorts of details with the likes of him.

She sighed. 'Look Alastair, I'm really sorry,' she said, as she eased herself into her flat. 'I'll try to be more thoughtful in the future.'

She closed the door on his peeved face and breathed out a sigh. Maybe it was time to think about moving house.

She noticed that the light on the answering machine was flashing. Bailey would have got rid of her landline phone and answering machine years ago if it hadn't been for the fact that her mum still insisted on calling her on it. She went over and pressed the button.

Sure enough there was a message from her mother. She must have left it the previous evening when Bailey had been out.

'Hello Bailey, it's Mum here. Hope you're well. Just checking if you're still coming over for Sunday lunch this weekend. Give me a call when you're free. Lots of love. Bye.'

Turning away from the answerphone, she started towards the kitchen to make a cup of coffee when there was a loud rap on the door.

She rolled her eyes. Not Alastair again, she thought. What's he going to have a go at me about this time? That bloke needed to get a bloody life. Taking a deep breath, she prepared a harsh retort in her head, and opened the door.

But it wasn't Alastair.

Standing in the hallway was a smartly dressed black woman in her late thirties who Bailey instantly recognised as Detective Inspector Stella Gates. As an undercover operative Bailey reported into an undercover covert operations manager, or COM-UC. Up until very recently her COM-UC had been Detective Inspector Frank Grinham. Frank, however, had sustained serious injuries during the course of one of Bailey's recent undercover assignments. Fortunately he'd survived and was well on the way to recovery, but it meant that he'd been unable to continue his role managing undercover operations. While he was recuperating, his role as COM-UC had been taken over by Stella.

'Stella,' said Bailey with a puzzled frown. 'What brings you here?'

This visit was somewhat unexpected. For Stella to actually turn up in person at Bailey's flat indicated that something was awry, and by the grave expression on Stella's face, it didn't look like things boded well.

Stella looked Bailey up and down. 'Morning Bailey, you look like shit. Why's your phone not working?'

Bailey scratched her head groggily. 'Uh... the battery died. I need to charge it.' The sense of consternation was rapidly growing inside her. 'Why? What's going on?'

'Walls have ears,' said Stella, motioning over her shoulder at Alastair who was peeking nosily through his open front door. 'It's probably best if we discuss this in private.'

Bailey guessed Alastair must have let Stella into the hallway just after she'd finished talking to him. Whatever was going on, it was certainly none of his business.

'Well I guess you'd better come in then,' she said.

3

Bailey stood aside to let Stella enter the flat and closed the door behind her. Stella stood in the middle of the small living room, her eyes flickering around, automatically taking in the details with the observant gaze of a seasoned police detective.

Stella hadn't been to Bailey's flat before and Bailey imagined she was now using what she saw to supplement her knowledge of Bailey's character. The place was overdue for a clean and, coupled with her somewhat dishevelled appearance this morning, Bailey hoped Stella wasn't judging her too harshly although going by her serious manner, Bailey guessed there were more important things at stake right now.

Bailey gestured at the sofa and Stella sat down whilst she herself took a seat on an adjacent armchair.

They'd only started working together fairly recently and thus didn't know each other too well. Stella had supervised Bailey's most recent undercover operation, the only one they'd worked on together so far, and from that experience Bailey had found Stella to be efficient and hard-edged with a very strong eye on her own personal career advancement. Bailey was still in two minds about whether she liked Stella or not, but then she wondered if she just missed working with Frank who she'd known for ages and who, being of the old-school, was a very different person indeed.

'Would you like a cup of tea?' asked Bailey, but Stella waved it aside.

'There are armed police stationed outside your flat right now,' she said, pointing at the window of the basement flat. 'We got here just a few minutes ago.'

Bailey gulped. 'Why? Am I in danger?' An unpleasant sense of trepidation crept over her, not helped by her hangover.

'I guess you haven't watched this morning's news,' said Stella. 'Senior Crown Advocate Jeremy Westerby was murdered yesterday evening.'

Bailey gasped in shock. She knew Westerby well. She'd been working closely with him on the case of a drug trafficker called Charlie Benvenuto who she'd taken down in her most recent undercover operation. She was due to give evidence against Benvenuto, who was currently on bail, in the trial at the Crown Court in a few weeks' time. Westerby had been assigned as the prosecutor in the case.

'Jeremy Westerby? Murdered?' whispered Bailey. 'What happened?'

'He was found dead in his house by his wife and kids. He'd been tied up, tortured and murdered. A full autopsy hasn't been done yet but it looks like he died from having something long and sharp inserted into his brain through his right ear.'

Bailey blinked as she tried to process the appalling news. She'd liked Westerby, having worked closely with him on a number of cases in the past. He was a cultured hard-working man with a strong sense of moral justice. It made her shudder to think that he had died in such a horrible way.

The ramifications began to sink in. 'You're here because you think it's related to the Benvenuto case, aren't you?'

Stella nodded. 'Files relating specifically to the Benvenuto case were missing from Westerby's house.'

Following a successful undercover infiltration of his organisation by Bailey several months earlier, Benvenuto had been charged with supplying Class A drugs and possession of cocaine with intent to supply. Bailey had caught him on tape selling her twenty-five kilograms of cocaine with an estimated street value of £2.5 million. If found guilty and convicted, he was facing several decades in prison.

'So you think Benvenuto's trying to wipe out anyone who's connected with the trial? First Westerby, as the prosecuting lawyer, and now me, as the key witness?'

'We can't prove anything at the moment,' said Stella. 'But *cui bono* and all that. Who stands to gain? Killing Westerby and you would certainly benefit Benvenuto in a big way. Without your testimony the case against him would be greatly weakened, if not totally unviable. When it comes to hiring a hitman to do his dirty work, he definitely has the right underworld connections and he's certainly got enough cash, not to mention the fact that as he's currently on bail this makes it a lot easier for him to arrange that kind of thing.'

Stella was more than familiar with the ins and outs of the Benvenuto case as she had been the one supervising Bailey's infiltration of his organisation.

Fixing Bailey with a sombre look, Stella continued. 'We think that Westerby was tortured in an attempt to find out details of who'll be giving evidence in the case, namely you. As the prosecuting lawyer, he would have been party to that information. Benvenuto's not stupid. He will have worked out that you were an undercover cop, seeing as he was arrested during a buy that you were orchestrating. And he'll know that your evidence is key to his conviction. However, seeing as your cover remained intact during that operation, he doesn't know your true identity, and he needs to know this information in order to have you killed. That's probably why Westerby was tortured, and it's likely the reason that the killer took the files from Westerby's house – in a bid to try and find out more information about you.'

Bailey frowned. 'Technically there's no way that anyone should be able to identify me or find me from those files. My name and any details that could identify me would have been redacted from any documents that Westerby would have had in his possession. He and I stuck very closely to the security protocols regarding witness anonymity for undercover police officers.'

Stella sighed. 'Be that as it may, Westerby himself knew your real name. After all, you'd worked with him before, hadn't you? We have to assume that he compromised your identity under torture. If so, you're in real danger of being the next target.'

Bailey swallowed and nodded as she digested the unpleasant possibility, her hangover throbbing more painfully than ever.

Stella continued. 'The fact that you're still alive suggests that the killer doesn't know your home address. Yet. However, if they have your real name, it'll only be a matter of time before they find out.'

'I'm very careful with my personal details,' said Bailey. 'Even with my real name they'd have a tough time finding me. I stay off the electoral register and I keep well away from social media. I maintain a pretty low profile generally. As an undercover cop, I figure it's best not to take any chances.'

'Even so,' said Stella, 'we have to assume that this flat is no longer a safe location for you to be in.' She paused. 'The trial is still set for the eighth of October. That's three weeks away. The CPS is currently arranging for a new Senior Crown Advocate to take over the case. He or she will obviously be placed under heavy protection. Seeing as you're the sole witness in this trial, we don't need to worry about protecting anyone else apart from you. We can place you in a safe house under armed guard until the trial commences.' Her eyes then narrowed in a calculating manner. 'Or you can help us catch the killer.'

'Catch the killer?' asked Bailey, a little confused. 'What about the murder investigation team? Isn't that what they're doing right now?'

Stella nodded. 'They've already run a preliminary forensic analysis on the crime scene and managed to recover some fragments of DNA that they think belonged to Westerby's killer. The results came back early this morning.'

Bailey knew that forensic results could be returned within just four hours. The murder investigation team would have referenced the UK National DNA Database, known as NDNAD, and attempted to match any DNA found at the crime scene to the records contained therein. NDNAD contained details of over five million individuals – the DNA either having been recovered from crime scenes, or having been taken from suspects, which encompassed anyone charged with an offence even if they were subsequently acquitted.

Stella continued. 'The DNA doesn't match anything taken by the police from any individual who's been charged with a crime. However it does match DNA samples recovered from several other prior crime scenes. They cross-checked those crimes in the Police National Database and they're down as unsolved cases.'

The Police National Database contained the data records of all of the UK police forces, and enabled a police officer from one force to search the records of another. The data consisted amongst other things of crime scene reports, intelligence information and details of individuals.

'What kind of cases are we talking about?' asked Bailey.

'They're gangland hits by the look of it. We're talking about a professional hitman here, someone who's brutal and ruthless, and very good at not getting caught. This person has never once been charged with any crime which is why there's no name associated with their DNA. This person is little more than a phantom.'

Bailey shuddered. From what Stella was saying, it looked like a professional hitman had tortured and murdered Jeremy Westerby and this same person was potentially targeting her next.

'As you probably know,' continued Stella, 'the problem with contract killings is that the motive is dissociated from the crime. Normally on a murder investigation, nine times out of ten, it's someone the victim knows. But with professional hits, that's just not the case. It's usually done by a complete stranger, purely for financial gain. That's why they're so hard to solve. That's one of the reasons we've never managed to catch this hitman.'

Stella paused. There was an ominous look in her eyes.

'I get the feeling you're building up to something,' said Bailey.

'We're familiar with this set of unsolved cases already. In fact we think we already know who the culprit is.'

Bailey was puzzled. 'You think you know the culprit? I thought you just said this person was a phantom.'

'Based on underworld rumours and intelligence from informants, we believe that the person responsible for this particular set of murders is the contract killer known as Rex.'

Stella waited to let the information sink in.

Rex.

Bailey was more than familiar with the name. Rex was a notorious underworld hitman who was allegedly responsible for multiple murders. The police had long been aware of his existence for he had a well-established reputation on the streets as a brutal and ruthless killer which made him a highly sought-after asset in the underworld. He was known in particular for two things: his utter relentlessness in making sure that he completed whatever job he was hired to do, along with his willingness to go the extra mile if paid a bit more – that usually meant inflicting some form of sadistic torture on the victim before killing them.

Bailey blinked and swallowed, feeling dizzy all of a sudden. If Rex was after her then Benvenuto must be really serious about having her rubbed out.

'Rex?' repeated Bailey weakly. 'Are you sure?' Her hangover seemed to have returned with a vengeance.

'Nothing is for sure when it comes to Rex,' said Stella, 'because we don't really know anything about him. We don't know his real name. We don't know what he looks like. We don't even know if he's a man. Rex could be a woman for all we know... although the general consensus seems to be that he's a bloke.'

Bailey knew that as a top-level contract killer, Rex was the kind of shadowy pro who probably went to great lengths to preserve his anonymity. Indeed, despite his widespread infamy, no one appeared to know him by any name other than Rex – whether this was just a pseudonym or whether it was related in some way to his real name was a total mystery, or at least it was to the police and anyone they spoke to.

'We've been after him for years,' said Stella. 'But Rex has always been one step ahead of us. Up until now, he's mostly killed criminals and informants. But a Senior Crown Advocate... That crosses the line in a big way. Catching Rex has now suddenly become top priority. The fact that Westerby was an old university friend of the Mayor's wife probably plays a part. The powers-that-be are concerned that the murder of a Senior Crown Advocate makes London look completely lawless and that if we don't clear it up soon then it'll reflect particularly badly on the Met. I've been tasked by senior management to do something about it above and beyond the regular murder investigation.'

Bailey was starting to get an idea of what Stella was suggesting.

'So you think Rex killed Westerby and you think he's out to kill me next, and you want to use me as bait to catch him.'

Stella smiled diplomatically. 'Well, it's more a case of you agreeing to collaborate, as the intended target, in a plan to ensnare him. The fact that he's potentially on your tail gives us an unparalleled opportunity to apprehend a notorious contract killer who we've been after for ages.'

'You don't know it's Rex for sure,' said Bailey. 'And you don't know for sure that he's planning to kill me.'

'That's true,' conceded Stella. 'But the circumstances would suggest that it is the case, don't you agree?'

Bailey nodded reluctantly. She had to concur. It certainly did look that way.

Studying Stella for a few moments, Bailey perceived a hungry look in her eyes that betrayed more personal motives for proposing this operation. Bailey knew Stella was thinking of what she stood to gain career-wise – she would no doubt garner a great deal of kudos from successfully capturing Rex especially if the directive to do so had come straight from the Met's top brass. Bailey was touched with the faintly unsettling feeling that she was a pawn in a bigger game.

'It's your choice though,' said Stella. 'You can choose to sit somewhere holed up until the trial date. Or you can participate in the capture of a dangerous criminal. I wouldn't want to force you to do anything you don't feel comfortable doing.'

'You don't need to persuade me,' said Bailey. 'I liked Jeremy Westerby and I want to bring his killer to justice. What's more, if we capture Rex, we may be able to get him to confess that Benvenuto hired him. Conspiracy to murder is a serious crime. That'll add at least another fifteen years to Benvenuto's sentence, maybe more. It'll be a very long time until he sees the light of day again. I want to see Benvenuto punished for this as well.'

Stella swelled in satisfaction at Bailey's accordance.

'But,' continued Bailey, 'I'm not just going to wait passively for Rex to walk into some trap with me as the bait. For one thing I don't think it'll work. I think he's too clever to fall for that kind of thing. There's a reason he's never been caught. That's because he's smart. And for another thing, I'm a police detective and an undercover cop. The kind of work I do is proactive by its very nature. That's where my skills lie – to be out there hunting him just like he's probably hunting me.'

Stella eyed Bailey with something approaching admiration. She nodded in assent.

'If that's how you want to approach it, that's fine by me. After all, you're the one taking the risks. I know we've only worked on one operation together, but from what I've seen of your work so far, I'm very impressed. If anyone can catch Rex, you can.'

'I'll need you to sign it off with my CID detective sergeant,' said Bailey.

'Consider it done,' said Stella, smiling.

Working as an undercover operative, or UCO, was something that Bailey did alongside her regular job as a detective constable. When she embarked on a new undercover operation, she was signed off from her regular job, with all of her normal casework being put on hold or being redistributed to colleagues.

'I haven't had the chance to check your most recent psychological assessment,' said Stella. 'We want to be sure that you're up to this mentally.'

'My last assessment was fine,' said Bailey. 'And I'm due for another routine appointment in the very near future.'

Stella nodded, satisfied. 'You'll report to me for the duration of the operation. You can call me directly on my mobile. I'll be on hand for you day or night. Like I said, catching Rex is now top priority. As for the specifics of the operation, I'll leave those up to you. One thing though... you won't be able to stay in this flat any longer. Do you want us to provide you with an apartment to base yourself in?'

Bailey pursed her lips and gave it some thought. 'Normally, I'd say yes, but in this case I think I'll use a hotel. It'll give me much more flexibility. I'll pick somewhere cheap and suitably anonymous, somewhere that allows me to operate below the radar and stay relatively mobile.'

'Whatever you think is best Bailey. At any rate, we'll keep this flat under surveillance in case he turns up here.' She paused. 'From this point on it's a case of you finding Rex before he finds you. It's our assumption that he has to kill you before you testify at the trial on the eighth of October. That's in three weeks' time. That's how long you've got to catch him.'

Three weeks.

Bailey nodded pensively. The crucial question wasn't just if she could catch Rex in the space of three weeks, it was if she could stay alive long enough to do so.

Either way, she had a feeling she wasn't going to be able to make Sunday lunch with her mum this weekend.

4

The Royal City Hotel was a shabby-looking three-storey building situated in Earl's Court in West London. The white plastic illuminated sign above the entrance bore a large crack on one side and the top was encrusted with what looked like several decades' worth of bird droppings.

The streets had a somewhat seedy feel and the hotel – a three-star – was one of the many budget tourist lodgings that characterised the area. Bailey could have picked any one of them for they were all just as unremarkable as each other, and thus ideal for her purposes. The only reason she'd chosen this particular one was because it possessed convenient on-site parking for her Audi A4.

Entering the cramped lobby, Bailey immediately found herself being enthusiastically greeted by the man sitting behind the reception desk. Probably around thirty years old, he looked South Asian in origin and had a name badge saying 'Ravi' pinned to the breast pocket of his black shirt.

Bailey gave him the fake surname she'd used to make the booking. He studied the computer screen in front of him.

'You are staying for three whole weeks?' he said, with a faint tone of surprise as if this was highly unusual for an establishment such as this.

'That's right,' she replied. 'Hopefully I will have checked out by the eighth of October.'

Ravi grinned broadly. 'If you stay here more than one week then you qualify for our VIP programme.'

'Oh yeah?' smiled Bailey. 'What does that entitle me to?'

He rummaged round in a drawer and took out a small foil-wrapped chocolate. He placed it on the desk in front of her.

'Your VIP welcome gift,' he said with a beaming smile.

Bailey picked it up. The foil round the edges was somewhat scuffed, exposing the chocolate beneath. Her face dropped a little. 'Thanks.'

Following his directions, she hauled her suitcase up a poky stairwell to her room on the first floor. The interior of the hotel was in serious need of redecorating, with peeling paint, threadbare carpets and tired-looking furnishings, and on top of that a strange musty smell permeated the dingy corridors.

Entering her room using the keycard Ravi had given her, she was immediately struck by how small it was. The bed might have been king sized, as advertised, but it was too large for the tiny room, preventing the door of the en-suite bathroom from opening properly.

Looking inside the bathroom, she saw that it didn't appear to have been cleaned very well, noticing amongst other things that there was a length of used dental floss on the floor.

She sighed to herself. Well, she'd wanted somewhere low-key and that was what she'd got. She'd briefly contemplated getting an Airbnb, but had settled on the idea of a hotel because, despite being a little more expensive, it offered her more flexibility in terms of being able to maintain the requisite level of personal security. She could check in and check out as she pleased, and change rooms with relative ease if needed.

Kneeling down, she opened her suitcase and began to unpack her belongings. Seeing as the operation was likely to be of a relatively short duration, she hadn't brought too much with her. A few sets of clothes. Some selected toiletries. A book of cryptic crosswords. Her work laptop. Laying out her items on the bed, she gazed down at them with the disconcerting feeling that she'd forgotten something important, but she couldn't work out what it was.

Her thoughts were interrupted by a trilling sound as her mobile phone suddenly started ringing in her pocket. Taking it out, she recognised the caller's number as that of her friend Detective Constable Emma Broggins. Emma, who was a similar age to Bailey, worked down at the same South London police station where Bailey was based and she was the closest thing Bailey had to a friend there. They played well off each other, Emma being quite gregarious and Bailey being quite the opposite; Emma was always telling Bailey she should get out more which was largely why she'd exhorted her to come out with them on Anthony's leaving do.

She knew Emma was calling to follow up on the series of text messages she'd sent Bailey in the wake of her one-night stand with Anthony. Emma, being the one who'd introduced them both to each other, had been curious to know how it had gone. Swept up with recent concerns, Bailey hadn't yet got round to responding to her.

She chewed her lip, debating whether to answer the phone. Whilst Emma was a good friend, Bailey wasn't in the mood to discuss romantic issues at this exact moment. She was keen to get the operation up and running and every minute counted. Letting the phone ring out and go to answerphone, she made a mental note to call Emma back later that evening.

Sitting down on the bed, she booted up her work laptop and

connected to the hotel's Wi-Fi network. The connection was a bit patchy but it functioned well enough to allow her to log into the Metropolitan Police computer system through a secure VPN.

Her fingers tapping rapidly on the laptop's keyboard, she accessed the Police National Database and pulled up the files relating to the unsolved murders that had been ascribed to Rex. Stella had let her know which ones to look at and they seemed like a good starting point in terms of working out what steps to take next in order to catch him.

Although the unsolved cases totalled just seven in number, Bailey knew that Rex was rumoured to have killed substantially more people than this. She knew that these particular cases only comprised those instances where sufficient DNA evidence had been recovered to tie a distinct culprit to the murders in question. She imagined that for just as many other murders committed by Rex, DNA evidence wouldn't have been available for whatever reasons, and on top of this it wouldn't have surprised her if there'd been situations where deaths might have been disguised as accidents or suicides and thus never even considered as murders in the first place.

She began to read through the unsolved cases, feeling an undeniable chill of foreboding as she did so. They were a veritable catalogue of murder, mutilation and torture-on-request. A gangster who'd been beaten to death and thrown in the Thames. A drug dealer who'd had his brains blown out in the middle of Knightsbridge in his open-topped sports car. Another drug dealer who'd been injected with strychnine and left to die. A Kurdish gangster who'd been riddled with bullets in a social club in Haringey. An informant who'd had his tongue cut out. A prostitute who'd been thrown off the top of a tower block. Another informant who'd been tied up and buried alive.

Finding little to help her in the files, she switched to the internet to see if she could unearth any supplementary insights on the cases that might ultimately lead her to Rex. For most of them it was just the odd local news article here and there, reporting little more than the bare facts of the crime in question. However, one of the cases stood out dramatically for the abundant news coverage that it had received at the time.

The gangster who'd been beaten to death and thrown in the River Thames was a man by the name of Vincent Peck. Peck had been the co-owner of a high-end strip club in Central London called Ruby Red that was popular with a number of big celebrities, and this tinge of sleazy glamour was the reason that his murder had received more news coverage than a normal gangland hit.

According to the police file, Peck had been killed three years earlier, which made his death the first actual hit to be attributed to Rex. His body had been found washed up near Sheerness on the Thames Estuary. The corpse had been in a fairly degraded state, having been in the water for a while, but the murder investigation team had managed to recover DNA from an unidentified individual via some blood spatters on his clothing. It seemed that Peck had put up some kind of struggle before being murdered.

Although the police file gave no indication as to the identity of the murderer, the news articles on the internet provided a tantalising hint as to who might have actually hired him, and Bailey realised that this information itself could provide a potential means of finding Rex.

A number of the more salacious articles alluded to a rift that had taken place between Peck and the other person who owned Ruby Red, a notoriously shady businessman by the name of Jack Wynter. Ruby Red was an extremely profitable enterprise, and it was some kind of financial wrangling over this that had caused Peck and Wynter to fall out with each other, Peck being murdered a short while afterwards. Following his death, Wynter had assumed full control of the club and all of its profits. It appeared that although Wynter was strongly suspected of being behind Peck's murder, nothing had ever been proven.

As a police detective, Bailey was vaguely aware of Jack Wynter by reputation, knowing that although he claimed to be an innocent nightclub operator, he was little more than a gangster at the end of the day.

Looking at Peck's murder in the context of her current situation, an enticing idea occurred to Bailey. One way to trap Rex might be to try and actually hire him. But in order to do so she would need to find out how to contact him. And that was where Jack Wynter entered the picture. If Wynter had used Rex to dispose of his former business partner – and it certainly seemed to look that way – then it was highly conceivable that Wynter knew how to hire Rex. All Bailey needed to do was ask him.

Not that it would be easy by any stretch. For a start, she'd have to approach Wynter in the guise of a fellow criminal for he quite obviously wouldn't reveal that kind of information to a regular police officer. But even so, getting him to trust her would still present a considerable challenge. After all, he'd never met her before, and criminals weren't very trusting people by their very nature.

She tried to think of a plausible means by which she could approach Wynter and gain his trust. Sitting there on the bed, she twisted her loose-hanging lock of hair round her finger and let it slowly uncurl as was her habit when she was contemplating the solution to a problem.

A sudden loud cacophonous racket ruptured the atmosphere. Bailey jumped and immediately tensed, her concentration shattering. She looked round wildly to see where the noise was coming from. After a few moments she realised that it was the sound of someone playing the bagpipes. It sounded like they were right outside her window.

Crossing over to the window, she looked outside to see that, sure enough, standing on the street directly below was a red-headed bearded man clad in green tartan blowing furiously into a set of bagpipes. The din gradually became discernible to her as the song 'Scotland the Brave'.

She realised that the bagpiper was some kind of busker, probably plying the tourist trade emanating from the cheap hotels in the vicinity. She rolled her eyes and then noticed that the window was slightly open. That explained why the noise was so loud. She tried to close the window, but however much force she applied it didn't seem to want to close. It appeared to be jammed open.

With a sigh, she gave up trying to close it and turned her attention back to the matter at hand.

5

It was a sunny Thursday evening at St Katharine Docks, unseasonably warm for mid-September. Well-dressed stylish people sat in the cafés and restaurants round the marina, basking in the laid-back atmosphere, eating al fresco and chatting and laughing, whilst the masts of the nearby yachts quavered ever so gently in the soft breeze.

The hitman known as Rex sat on the deck of his forty-foot luxury catamaran playing Solitaire whilst sipping from a can of San Pellegrino Limonata. He loved it when the weather was like this and he could sit outside.

St Katharine Docks was the most upmarket of the London docks and it was the only marina in Central London. The boats moored here were top of the range. No doubt about that. Sleek and pricey. The top brands: Beneteau, Dufour, Hanse. You weren't going to find any shitty houseboats tied up at these docks.

The marina was located in Wapping very close to the Tower of London and Tower Bridge. In fact Rex could see the distinctive turrets of Tower Bridge from above the tops of the upscale apartments which lined the docks. The architecture here was a mixture of old and new with the former bankside warehouses now remodelled into luxury residential, office and retail space.

He lived here on the catamaran all by himself and that suited him just fine as he loved the feeling of freedom it gave him. He could just uproot whenever he pleased and sail wherever he wanted.

It was definitely a nice boat to live on. This particular model was known as a Lagoon 40. Possessing the distinctive twin hulls of a catamaran, it was white in colour with a teak deck and had a deceptively spacious interior which included a large saloon area with a faux leather sofa, four cabins and a well-equipped galley.

By all accounts it was a very expensive boat to purchase. But then Rex hadn't actually purchased it. It had been more a case of appropriating it. After all, the previous owner hadn't had much use for it... after Rex had murdered him. It had belonged to a gangster by the name of Vincent Peck and it happened to be fitted out with some very useful hidden compartments in the twin hulls which had been designed to hold illicit merchandise.

The boat had originally been called *Eager Beaver*, the previous owner having had a penchant for double entendres. Even though Rex had heard it was bad luck to change the name of a boat, he just wasn't prepared to live on a boat called *Eager Beaver* so he'd renamed it *Aletheia* which he thought sounded a whole lot more sophisticated. *Aletheia* was the name of the Ancient Greek goddess of truth, and for some reason, something about that particular name had struck a chord with him.

Every so often he'd take the catamaran out to sea. A loner by nature, he liked being out on the open water with no one else but him for miles around. He'd always been partial to boats and sailing although he couldn't recall quite where or how he'd picked up the taste for it.

Studying the playing cards laid out on the table before him, he reflexively scratched at the small scar which ran diagonally through his right eyebrow.

He only ever played one card game, and that was a version of Solitaire known as Concentration. The rules were pretty simple. You laid out the entire deck face down on a table and then you had to turn over the cards two at a time. If the two cards matched then you took them off the table. If they didn't then you turned them back over. You just went on like that until you cleared the table. The goal was to do this in the shortest possible number of moves. The game was all about memory because you had to be able to remember which of the face-down cards that you'd already looked at matched the one you'd just turned over. Rex had reached the point where he could complete the game in just thirty-nine moves which was apparently better than most people.

He found the game an infinitely absorbing way to pass the time. But he also liked to play it in order to hone his powers of retention and recall, for having a good memory was a definite bonus when it came to planning and carrying out hits.

Considering that it was a game based on memory, it was ironic that he couldn't remember for the hell of him where he'd learnt to play it.

About to pick up a card, he suddenly froze, his fingers hovering over the table. He sniffed the air. If he wasn't mistaken he could detect the scent of a familiar perfume wafting in his direction. A smile slowly spread across his chiselled face.

'Hello Milena,' he said without turning round.

'Don't you ever get bored of playing that game?' said a female voice with a strong East European accent.

'It helps my memory,' he replied, turning round slowly.

Standing on the pontoon just by the boat was a blonde woman with a sharp, pretty face dressed in a fashionable black trouser suit and designer heels holding a leather portfolio pouch. She looked like she'd just come from, or was on her way to a business meeting... which wasn't surprising seeing as she was a businesswoman of sorts.

Milena functioned as his business manager, brokering contract killings on his behalf, earning a ten per cent cut of whatever he was paid. From Rex's perspective, the good thing about having a business manager was that it insulated him from his clients and helped to maintain his anonymity which in turn served to increase his general mystique. And not just that, for Milena was a born saleswoman who was skilled at soliciting new work for him, a task he was more than happy to hand over to someone else.

She stepped aboard daintily, making her way across the deck to sit down at the table opposite him.

'You know if you ever want to play with someone else, you can play with me sometime,' she said with a flirtatious wink.

He knew she was just teasing though. She liked to tease. Their relationship was and always had been purely platonic.

'I think I'll stick to Solitaire,' he said, turning his attention back to the cards.

Milena shrugged indifferently. 'Suit yourself.'

Out of the corner of his eye he caught her studying him in that strange way that she sometimes did when she thought he wasn't looking. A mixture of curiosity and intrigue, plus something else that he couldn't quite put his finger on... Fear perhaps. People who spent any amount of time round him, getting to understand the kind of things he was capable of, tended to become afraid of him.

He raised his head to meet her gaze, and as always she quickly suppressed the look, once again resuming her brisk and friendly visage.

'You only ever come here for two reasons,' he said. 'When you have a new job for me. Or to hassle me about one I'm in the middle of. And I think I can guess which of the two reasons it is today.'

She raised one eyebrow in disapproval. 'The client specified that this job has to be completed by the eighth of October, *at all costs*. I come here and what do I find? You're sitting here drinking lemonade and playing cards.'

'It's a nice evening to be sitting outside,' said Rex with an offhand smile. 'Anyhow, you know as well as I do that once I've been paid I always finish the job. When have I not? It's a matter of professional integrity.'

And he had been paid well for this particular job.

One hundred and fifty thousand pounds upfront.

Rex always insisted on advance payment. Sometimes the client attempted to wheedle a 'half now, half later' deal. But in his opinion, only the little-league operators settled for that, the kind of workaday killers who just did domestic jobs. Here in the big leagues it was all or nothing. But for that, those who hired him got platinum service. He prided himself on never having once let a customer down. Reputation was everything in this business and he did all he could to keep his as pristine as possible. After all, good word-of-mouth ensured a steady stream of new work.

'You don't need to worry,' he said. 'Everything's in hand. Now that I know her real name, it'll only be a matter of time before I pinpoint where Bailey Morgan lives. The files I got from the lawyer's house didn't contain any information about her so I've had to resort to other slightly more long-winded methods.'

Rex had spent a good part of the previous day utilising a specialist database to which he subscribed. The database aggregated the personal data of millions of UK citizens – their names, addresses, telephone numbers, shopping preferences and much more – making it a very handy reference tool for someone like him. The monthly subscription cost wasn't cheap but he'd found that the return on investment was more than worth it.

He was betting that at some point in the past Bailey Morgan had let her name get onto a marketing list, most likely as a result of an item or service that she'd purchased. She would no doubt be receiving junk mail as a result but what she, like most people, probably wasn't aware of was that her data would have been sold by that very same company to the third party who operated the database which Rex found so helpful.

The only drawback with the database was that it had spat out the results of several Bailey Morgans who happened to live in the London area and Rex didn't know which one was the one he was supposed to kill. Normally he'd have cross-referenced the database results with information from social media platforms in order to match a name and address to an actual face. However, the Bailey Morgan he was looking for didn't appear to be on social media if the physical description the client had given them was anything to go by – a white female, slender in build, in her early thirties, with a thin white scar running down the left side of her face.

'I've narrowed it down to a shortlist of potential addresses,' he said. 'I spent most of yesterday afternoon and today visiting some but none of them were hers. I'll resume first thing tomorrow morning with the next one on the list. It's down in Crystal Palace.'

6

Charlie Benvenuto was sitting at the luxury granite-topped kitchen island in his large mock Tudor mansion in Cobham, Surrey, brooding over his upcoming trial. He rubbed his bald head and glanced at the calendar on the kitchen wall. Three weeks to go. His jaw twitched in an agitated manner as he wondered if the hitman he'd hired would be able to complete the job by the time of the trial date.

A few metres away his petite wife Amy pottered round the luxurious kitchen preparing dinner for them both. It was a Thursday evening and their two daughters were currently participating in after-school lacrosse classes at the expensive private school that they both attended.

Charlie had been spending a lot of time at home recently, what with the conditions that had been imposed as part of his bail. As well as surrendering his passport to the police he had to report to the police station twice a week and he wasn't allowed to drive which was extremely annoying as it meant that Amy now had to give him lifts everywhere. Still, despite the inconvenience, he reflected that it was far better than being remanded into custody. He counted himself lucky to have been granted bail at all. When the magistrates had come to making the decision, the fact that Charlie had never been convicted of a crime before had played strongly in his favour, along with his ostensibly upstanding character as demonstrated by the large donation he'd recently made towards the construction of a new science wing at his daughters' school, plus they hadn't regarded him as likely to abscond, although they'd obviously held him in enough suspicion to feel the need to impose all these conditions restricting his liberty.

A plate of salmon with grilled asparagus and boiled new potatoes appeared in front of him on the granite worktop. He blinked out of his fretful trance to see that Amy had sat down opposite him at the kitchen island with her own plate of food.

She forlornly picked at the delicious-smelling food. Observing her, he couldn't deny that she'd been looking quite drawn recently. In fact, she suddenly looked a good ten years older than her forty-four years. All the stress of his arrest had really put her through the wringer.

Of course he himself wasn't exactly in the best form. The looming prospect of prison was playing inescapably on his mind and the idea of being locked up filled him with unutterable horror. He knew he'd be spending decades behind bars if he was convicted of the crimes for which he'd been charged. It would mean he'd lose all of this. This nice house with its beautiful garden. His expensive cars. And most importantly he'd lose his family. He wouldn't get to see his two daughters grow up, and of course Amy would be devastated... for she had no idea that he'd spent the past several years operating as a high-level drug trafficker, although what with him getting arrested he could tell she was starting to suspect that the man she'd married wasn't quite what he seemed.

'I just can't understand how they could have made such a big mistake,' she said for what was probably the hundredth time since it happened.

'I told you,' he said, rolling his eyes. 'It's all a huge misunderstanding. They got me mixed up with what some other people were doing.'

She looked up at him from her plate of food, her eyes wide and anxious. It looked like she was about to cry. Again. He could tell she desperately wanted to believe him but he could also see there was a tiny glimmer of doubt in her gaze. He sighed to himself. He'd been lying to her for so long that he knew the truth of it would destroy her.

'If you say so,' she said weakly. 'I suppose if you're innocent then it'll all be proven in court. They have to have proper evidence don't they? And if they don't have evidence...' her voice trailed off.

He stared at her circumspectly without saying anything. She swallowed uncomfortably, dropped her gaze and resumed picking at her food.

It had started out small. That was the thing. He'd kind of fallen into it. He'd been working as an estate agent for some years when he'd closed a property deal for a wealthy Spanish client. They'd hit it off, and after a bit of socialising, the man had confided to Charlie that he was a drug importer looking for someone to help him bring illicit drugs into the UK. Lured by the promise of generous financial rewards, Charlie had slipped into the role with ease, discovering that he had an aptitude for organising the illegal importation of large shipments of Class A drugs. He'd soon branched out on his own, starting an import business as a cover for his operation, smuggling cocaine into the UK via lorries from Continental Europe, hidden in boxes of cheapo kids' toys. His business had grown exponentially, snowballing into a very lucrative money-making operation. It had obviously entailed a certain amount of criminal enterprise, but negotiating deals came naturally to him which was why he'd made such a good estate agent – it was just that the deals he was negotiating now were for substantially larger sums with substantially more serious people... with considerably more at stake. The money involved in drug trafficking was on a whole different level, and once he'd got a taste for the profits that could be made he knew there was no going back.

Right from the outset, he'd kept his illicit activities hidden from Amy as he knew she wouldn't have approved. She had a strong moral sensibility which was one of the reasons he'd married her in the first place and it was the reason he'd decided to have kids with her – she was conscientious and she made a good mother. He often reflected that he'd probably been attracted to her because she possessed exactly what he lacked, for he was well aware that he didn't have any such high principles... which is why he found it so easy to lie to people, even to those close to him.

His flair for deception meant that it hadn't been a problem to continue to hide his criminality from her as his business grew larger, until it had reached the point where he realised that it was just not going to be viable to suddenly admit to her over dinner that he was running a multi-million pound drug empire. She would have totally freaked out. Whether she would have gone so far as to inform the police was another matter, but either way he thought it a much safer option to just make sure that she didn't know anything about his drug trafficking activities whatsoever. As far as she was concerned, his import business was doing very well, end of conversation. She rarely asked him questions about it anyhow because she just wasn't that interested in it. Business-related things made her bored. What made her happy was raising the kids, running the household, cooking nice meals and enjoying their nice well-off existence. But now she had been pulled unwillingly into his other secret life. And he knew it would destroy her if he was convicted for, relatively naïve as she was, even she wouldn't be able to deny the final decision of the Crown Court and all the media coverage that would inevitably accompany it.

And it was all because of that fucking undercover cop.

At the thought of her, an acrid bile rose up in his gullet. He couldn't believe how dumb he'd been to trust her. It really stuck in his craw. But with that nasty scar on her face, coupled with the fact that she was a woman, it had never occurred to him that she might be an undercover police officer. She'd come across as so convincing – a wheeler-dealer wholesaler looking to buy a considerable amount of cocaine off him. And then suddenly there he was on camera caught in a sting while in the process of selling her twenty-five kilograms of cocaine. And boom! Just like that he was looking at upwards of twenty years inside.

The first thing he'd done was obtain the services of an expert firm of criminal defence solicitors. They were considered to be one of the best in their field, and their fees certainly reflected it. They'd immediately got to work, arguing in the pre-trial hearing that her evidence had been unlawfully obtained and was thus inadmissible, claiming that it was a breach of his human rights, specifically his right to privacy. However, their application hadn't been successful as it seemed that her actions had been authorised correctly under all the various laws governing that kind of thing. In the forthcoming trial at the Crown Court, his solicitors were going to cross-examine her with the aim of trying to prove that the sting operation had been a case of entrapment, but even so, they'd confided in him it wasn't looking too good on that front either. It would only have constituted entrapment if she'd actually incited him to commit the offence, but all she'd done was merely present him with the opportunity to sell her drugs which he had done so. All in all, it was looking increasingly likely that he would be convicted of supplying Class A drugs and possession of cocaine with intent to supply. And with the quantities of drugs involved, that meant a very long prison sentence indeed.

He was in a pretty tight corner and he'd realised that the only way of avoiding a conviction was to try and scupper the trial altogether. So he'd gone all out and hired a hitman to solve his problem. Killing the Senior Crown Advocate went some way to achieving that, but wiping out the undercover policewoman would really throw a spanner in the works, for his solicitors had told him that her testimony and her evidence were the real key to securing his conviction.

The fact that people were getting murdered didn't really bother him too much. His liberty and his family were considerably more important than their lives. When he'd watched the news about the death of the CPS prosecutor Jeremy Westerby, his main emotion had been a sense of relief that at least one obstacle was out of the way, but he knew he'd only be happy when he was certain that the undercover policewoman was dead as well.

Well aware that he possessed a cold ruthless streak, he knew he was more than capable of committing murder himself should it ever come down to it. But of course he wasn't that stupid. He always got other people to do his dirty work. That was why he'd never gone to prison. That was the whole point of having money. If you had enough you could pay for anything you wanted... including murder.

And when it came down to money, he was determined to make the most of his financial resources now while he was still on bail, because once he was sent to prison all of his assets would likely be confiscated under the Proceeds of Crime Act. His carefully laundered cash was being investigated right now, so he'd had to resort to using bundles of illicit bank notes that he kept stashed in various secret locations. A hundred and fifty grand to hire a hitman was a drop in the ocean compared to what he stood to lose if he got convicted.

Rex had come with solid recommendations from a number of criminal associates and he trusted in him to get the job done. When it came to killing the undercover policewoman, Charlie hadn't been able to provide much information about her – only what she looked like, for he knew that she'd used a false name when she'd approached him and he had no idea what her real name was. Still, if Rex was as good as people said he was, then he'd manage to track her down sooner or later.

The bile in his throat subsided a little with the knowledge that with any luck she would be dead very imminently, his trial would be scuppered, and all of his troubles would be over.

7

Bailey jerked awake, her eyes flicking open. It was the middle of the night. A dark figure was standing at the end of the bed, his face in shadow, pointing a gun at her. She froze in fear, paralysed by the ghastly realisation that Rex had found her. It was too late to do anything now. Numb with horror she helplessly watched as his gloved finger squeezed the trigger...

BANG.

Bailey woke up for real, breathing hard, her muscles clenched, the sweat-soaked sheets twisted round her.

Slowly, shaking slightly, she sank back into the mattress, her muscles gradually loosening, her breathing returning to normal.

It had just been a nightmare.

There was no one else in the hotel room and the door was locked. Outside it was still dark and the background hum of the city at night filtered reassuringly through the jammed-open window along with the gentle sound of light rain.

Nightmares were something that Bailey suffered from on a frequent basis. They were a symptom of the post-traumatic stress disorder that she'd sustained as a result of the ordeal which had left her with the scars that now covered her body. In that undercover operation which had gone so awfully wrong, she'd been infiltrating a gang of professional car thieves when her cover had got blown, and as a result she'd been tortured horribly – cut with a straight razor and burned with a cigarette – and she'd also been sexually assaulted. The man who'd inflicted these violations upon her invariably featured heavily in the dreams she had, but tonight he'd been displaced by the shadowy faceless hitman known as Rex.

She picked up her iPhone to check the time. The illuminated screen showed that it was quarter past three in the morning. Switching on the lamp beside her, she rolled out of bed and made the short journey to the bathroom to get a glass of water with which she could take two beta blockers to calm herself down. And it was then that she realised that in her hurry to leave her Crystal Palace flat she'd forgotten to bring the medication with her. That funny feeling she'd had that she'd forgotten to pack something important... it had turned out to be her beta blockers. She cursed to herself and wondered how long she'd be able to cope without them.

She sat down glumly on the edge of the bed. With little to distract her at this ungodly hour her thoughts were sucked inexorably into a swirling vortex of negativity and paranoia. Rex was out there somewhere. Hunting her. Drawing closer. Every day. Every hour. Every minute. Getting that little bit closer. And then at some point, sooner or later, he'd catch up with her. And when he did... the thought filled Bailey with profound apprehension. Although Bailey was trained in jiu jitsu, she didn't rate her chances too highly against an extremely motivated and probably very well-armed, professional killer who doubtless possessed reams of experience in this kind of thing. If she was to survive she had to get the jump on him. She had to find him before he found her and the pressure was on.

She knew the isolated nature of her situation was only serving to compound her anxiety. Although Stella had emphasised that she would be on hand for Bailey, just a phone call away, Bailey still felt distinctly alone, operating from this shabby hotel. Undercover work tended to be solitary by its very nature, which was indeed one of the reasons Bailey liked it – the independence it gave you and the fact that you didn't have someone looking over your shoulder all the time. But the flipside was that your mental health could suffer if you weren't careful. And that was the reason that regular appointments with a psychologist were mandatory for undercover operatives.

She reflected that a bit of friendly human contact would probably help to balance her mood. With a pang of guilt, she then remembered that she still hadn't called her friend Emma back. Bailey reproached herself for being such a flaky friend to Emma. Hopefully she would understand though. Working in the same police station as Bailey, Emma would be aware that Bailey had been signed off for an undercover operation. Bailey would be sure to explain everything when they talked, resolving to call Emma back later that day.

* * *

It was early morning, not yet dawn, and Rex was unable to get back to sleep, having awoken some time before from troubled dreams about the past. As always the actual nature of them eluded him in his waking state. He emerged only with the sensation that he'd been lost in a suffocating mist, flailing round blindly for some kind of direction...

Lying there in the darkness of the cabin he could discern the soft patter of rain on the hull. He focused on the hypnotic rhythm of the raindrops in a bid to settle his agitated thoughts. That was the thing with the more distant past. At a certain point it all turned into a muddled fog in which he lost all sense of his bearings.

The catamaran, moored firmly in the dock, was a good place to moor his mind. The murder of Vincent Peck over three years ago had been his first proper job and this he remembered as clearly as if it had been yesterday. He'd beaten Peck to death right here on this very boat. There were still faint remnants of bloodstains on the cabin floor and on the sofa. Peck had been a large man and had put up a decent struggle, leaving Rex bruised and bleeding, but ultimately he'd succumbed to Rex's driven rage.

Rex had never been too worried about the police coming here to this boat to investigate Peck's murder. He'd known beforehand that Peck had registered the boat under an alias. Peck had done this in order to dissociate himself from the boat which he used for illicit purposes and the police therefore had no idea that he even owned it. Dumping Peck's body way out in the Thames Estuary had further occluded any link to the boat. In the three years since his death no one had turned up poking round so Rex reckoned he was in the clear. As for the administration at the marina, Peck had paid for a long-term berth booking under the alias which it had been relatively easy for Rex to assume control of.

The client who'd commissioned Peck's murder – a gangster called Jack Wynter – had been so pleased with the result that he'd recommended Rex's services to a number of associates, and the work had come in thick and fast after that. There seemed to be no shortage of people who wanted other people knocked off.

Rex had killed twenty-three people to date. Every moment of each of those hits was imprinted indelibly on his brain, forming part of his very identity, as if by killing those people he'd somehow managed to assimilate them into himself.

He couldn't deny that he enjoyed the sense of omnipotence that came with killing, a feeling that was particularly pronounced on those occasions where he got to look into the victim's eyes right at the very end. And when it was over he was left feeling simultaneously high on the buzz but also spent. One thing he didn't feel was any kind of remorse.

He supposed some people might have labelled him a psychopath. He didn't know what he was. All he knew was that it would have felt wrong doing anything else for a living. It was who he was.

Although he ostensibly killed people for money, what he really lived for was the hunt. The whole process of planning and carrying out the hit was like a sport to him. Although most contracts specified a plain vanilla hit by whatever means necessary, others were more particular in their requirements, designating torture or mutilation, or some special way of killing the victim in order to send a message. He did whatever was asked... and asked no questions. That was one of the reasons people hired him. That and his ability to finish the job come hell or high water.

He wondered now if the reason he'd woken up at this early hour was because he hadn't yet killed Bailey Morgan. It had probably been playing on his subconscious. It was often like that when he was partway through a job. He was never able to fully relax until he was completely sure that he'd successfully eliminated the target.

Bailey Morgan was proving to be more of a challenge than most though. Normally, clients provided enough information to ensure a clear positive identification of the target, along with sufficient details of their daily routine – where they lived, worked, and other places they frequented – enough at least to enable a hit to be planned.

But the information on Bailey Morgan had been sparse to say the least. All he had was her physical description. And that was it.

No home address. No work address. No details of favourite places she liked to visit on a regular basis. But he'd find her soon enough. He was sure of it. He always did. Maybe even today. He hoped so for he had a deadline to stick to and he was acutely aware that it was drawing closer with every second that ticked by.

He got up and began to get ready. By the sounds of it the rain had ceased. The sun would be up soon and once it was light he'd head on down to that next address on the list... the one in Crystal Palace.

* * *

Sitting in her hotel room, Bailey wasn't about to try and go back to sleep again. Now she was awake, she was awake. Might as well do something productive.

She turned her thoughts to the issue that had been occupying her mind the day before. If she was to move forward with her plan to ensnare Rex, she had to think of a credible way of engineering a meeting with Jack Wynter in which he would trust her enough to reveal details of how to hire the notorious hitman.

Racking her mind, Bailey tried to think of anyone she'd encountered in the past who might be of some use. It was then that she remembered a case that she'd worked on around nine months earlier as part of her normal job as a detective constable in South London. It had been a fairly routine case relating to a stolen car. The car had belonged to a woman in Croydon who shared a flat with a girl called Dani who just happened to work as a dancer at Ruby Red.

Visiting the apartment in Croydon to record details of the stolen car, it had taken Bailey by surprise when, on her way out, Dani had furtively collared her, handing her a Ruby Red matchbook with her phone number written on the inside. She'd told Bailey to contact her if she wanted to know any useful information about the clientele of that establishment.

As well as being popular with A-list celebrities, it transpired that Ruby Red was also frequented by a fair number of villains, acquaintances of Wynter for the most part, and Dani, eavesdropping on their drunken, drug-fuelled underworld chatter, had boasted that she was party to a fair amount of information that could be very useful to the police.

As to Dani's motivation for wanting to become an informant, she'd explained to Bailey that writhing naked in front of these boorish men had imbued in her such a sense of contempt for them that she said it would give her a real power kick to betray them to the police. Bailey had asked her why, if she hated being a stripper so much, she didn't just get a different job, but Dani had told her that the money was just too good for her to give it up.

It now occurred to Bailey that she could potentially use Dani as a means to approach Jack Wynter. Typically, in an undercover infiltration, the police utilised informants to vouch for the undercover officer in order to establish that initial trust. With a sense of mounting excitement Bailey realised that Dani just might be able to fulfil this role for her.

However, Bailey had no idea if Dani was still working at Ruby Red, or indeed if she was still willing to work as an informant. There was only one way to find out and that was to call her.

At the time, Bailey had tucked the matchbook away in her pocket with the aim of potentially obtaining an authorisation to use Dani as a CHIS, or Covert Human Intelligence Source, which was the official name for an informant. But she'd never actually got round to filling out the necessary paperwork as the Molloy job had come up and everything else had suddenly taken a back seat to that. As far as Bailey could recall, the matchbook was stowed away somewhere in her flat in Crystal Palace. She just couldn't quite remember where she'd put it. It was probably lying at the back of a drawer somewhere.

She needed to go back to her flat to try and find it. And while she was there she could also pick up her beta blockers – it would save her the hassle of calling her GP to try and get a new prescription and then having to wait for it to be sent to the pharmacy.

Bailey knew that going back to her flat constituted somewhat of a hazard given her current circumstances, but then she also knew that the police had the place under twenty-four-hour surveillance which went some way to mitigating the risk. Either way she thought it a good idea to call Stella to update her on the status of the operation so far.

Picking up her phone, she dialled Stella's number.

After a few rings, Stella answered, sounding grumpy and groggy. 'I know I said I'd be on hand for you day or night Bailey, but this is kind of early. It's half past three in the morning.'

Bailey suddenly remembered that it was still the middle of the night for most people.

'Oh sorry Stella,' she gasped. 'It totally slipped my mind. I was keen to update you on how things were going. I can call you back later if you want.'

'It's okay,' muttered Stella. 'I'm awake now. You might as well continue.'

Perched on the edge of the bed, Bailey outlined her plan to go undercover to find out from Jack Wynter how to hire Rex. She waited tensely for Stella's response.

'Hmm...' said Stella, after a longish pause. 'So you think we could lure Rex out by pretending to hire him?' She sounded intrigued by the concept.

'That's right,' said Bailey eagerly. 'He'll come out of the shadows thinking it's a new job. And when he does we'll pounce on him. But the first step is finding out how to make contact with him. And that's where Wynter comes in. I reckon Wynter knows how to hire Rex.'

'I'm not totally sure about this Bailey.' A doubting tone entered Stella's voice. 'For one thing you're making the assumption that Jack Wynter is responsible for the murder of Vincent Peck. Admittedly, the circumstances imply that this is the case, but even if he is behind Peck's death, he's not going to admit that to anyone, even to a fellow criminal.'

'I don't need Wynter to admit anything of the sort,' said Bailey. 'I'm not going there to try and arrest him for Peck's murder. All I need him to do is to tell me how to hire Rex.'

'Okay...' said Stella, still sounding a bit sceptical. 'If you think you can successfully wangle that knowledge out of him, then it's probably worth a try. If we did have that kind of information then we could definitely be onto a winner.'

'The only thing is,' said Bailey, 'in order to get Wynter to trust me, I need to use an informant to vouch for me. I think I've identified a good candidate but her contact details are lying round somewhere in my flat. So I need to go back there to try and dig them out.'

'We can retrieve them for you. Leave it with us.'

'No, I don't think that'll work. For one thing I neglected to leave you a set of keys to my flat. And for another thing, I doubt anyone else would be able to find what I'm looking for. Even I'm not sure where I put it and my flat is a bit of a mess. It'll be much easier if I just go there myself. Anyhow, I also need to pick up some medication which I left there.'

Stella sighed. 'Okay Bailey,' she conceded. 'It sounds a bit risky but we do have surveillance watching your flat. So far they haven't reported anything suspicious. I'll let them know you're coming so they can be on the alert. When are you planning to go there?'

'I'll go straight there this morning, as soon as the sun comes up.'

8

Rex wasn't particularly enamoured of Crystal Palace. It was a thoroughly unremarkable piece of London and its grubby terraced streets felt somewhat down at heel. But then this was exactly the kind of dismal place he would have expected a low-paid public servant like a police officer to live.

It was early on Friday morning and a cool mist lay over the place. Rex was sitting in a bus shelter around two hundred metres from the flat he had come to visit, carefully and unobtrusively observing the immediate area to check for any suggestion of police who might be hovering round in wait for him.

He knew by now that with Westerby's murder, there was every likelihood that Bailey Morgan would be aware that she was next in line to be eliminated. If that was the case then he imagined there would probably be a police surveillance presence in the vicinity of the flat where she lived.

But the presence of a few police wasn't going to deter Rex from his objective. He hadn't let that kind of thing put him off in the past. There was a good reason why he'd never been caught and that's because he was expert at evading detection. If the Bailey Morgan he was looking for was currently in that flat, he was going to get in there and kill her one way or another. And if it turned out that she wasn't there right now, he was sure that the flat would contain a treasure trove of information about her which would enable him to pick up her trail, no problem.

Deciding to dress down for this particular outing, he was clad in jeans and a black bomber jacket, the pockets of which contained a few useful tools of the trade, including a folding knife with a nasty serrated edge which would do a more than adequate job in gutting her like a fish should he be fortunate enough to encounter her today.

Assessing the street, Rex noticed a white Transit van occupied by two men parked just across the road from the flat. Further up the road he spotted a grey Ford Focus RS with a man sitting in it. To anyone else the vehicles might have seemed relatively innocuous, but to Rex they appeared highly suspect. He knew that the spacious interior and comparative ubiquity of Transit vans made them ideal surveillance vehicles for the police. And as for the Ford Focus, it was a deceptively powerful little car which made it an excellent choice for an unmarked police vehicle. His hackles went up slightly as they always did when he sensed that something was off. They were police, he was sure of it. And that meant that this was indeed the flat where Bailey Morgan lived. He felt a tingle of anticipation at the possibility that he'd managed to successfully locate his target.

Having studied the layout of her street on Google Maps prior to his visit, he knew that her block of flats had a communal garden out the back. Bailey lived on the lower ground floor, a basement flat essentially, which meant that she probably had a back door with access to the garden. Whilst the police might have surveillance covering the front of the flat, he doubted they'd have it out the back, for anyone wishing to gain access to either the front or the rear of the flat still had to approach the property from the front.

But Rex wasn't planning to approach her flat from the front. He was planning to enter the back garden of the property at the far end of her street, and then cut through the neighbouring gardens until he reached Bailey's garden. He would then be able to enter her flat via the back door without the knowledge of anyone watching it from the front.

Standing up, he left the bus shelter and started down the road that ran perpendicular to the one that she lived on, putting him out of sight of the watching police in their vehicles. He paused by the wall which bounded the back garden of the house at the far end of the street. He glanced round to see if anyone was watching. It was early morning and there wasn't anyone around.

He pulled himself up over the wall and dropped down into the garden on the other side. Glancing up, it looked like no one inside the house had seen him. Running in a low crouch, he advanced to the wall of the next garden, and scaled it, repeating the process for the next three gardens until he reached the back garden of Bailey's block of flats. He silently congratulated himself on getting there without being accosted by anyone or getting attacked by any large dogs. A startled-looking fox had been the only thing he'd encountered.

Crouching low in the bushes at the back of the garden, Rex cautiously observed the rear of the old Victorian building that Bailey lived in. In terms of security there were some bars on her windows and back door but he couldn't see any sign of an alarm system. The lights were off indicating that she wasn't up yet or she wasn't in. Either way, he reckoned it was safe to approach without getting spotted.

Emerging from the bushes, he padded rapidly up to her back window. He took a closer peek in and found himself looking into her kitchen. It was empty, and beyond that there didn't appear to be any sign of activity. He was starting to get the feeling that she wasn't in.

He moved round to the back door, examining the Yale-style lock. Taking a small lock-pick set out of his pocket, he selected the appropriate pick along with a small torque wrench. Inserting both tools into the lock he softly raked the pins inside the tumbler with the pick whilst exerting a gentle but constant pressure with the torque wrench. It took him about twenty seconds to pop the lock. Pushing open the door, he eased himself into her kitchen and quietly closed the door behind him.

The flat was silent and dim. There was just the soft humming of the refrigerator. The feeling of her absence was stronger now. Rex was sure that she wasn't here. Not that he was going to take any chances though. Taking out his folding knife, he thumbed open the blade. It gave a soft click as it locked into place. Holding the knife before him, he silently stalked through the small one-bedroom flat, glancing in the living room to see that it was empty, walking down past the bathroom, also empty, to then ease open the bedroom door to see that the bed was unoccupied, the covers pushed aside. There was definitely no one home. It looked like she'd left in a hurry. There were clothes scattered on the bed. A drawer was half open. The place was a bit of a mess.

Satisfied that she was absent, Rex folded the knife blade back into the handle and returned it to his pocket. He felt a little disappointed at being deprived of the chance to kill her. Not to worry. He would make the most of his visit. That was for sure.

He went back into the living room. Located as it was – at basement level – light was filtering down relatively weakly from the morning sky outside, but Rex decided not to turn the light on so as not to draw undue attention to his presence there.

Stepping into the centre of the living room, he slowly surveyed the interior of the small flat, his powers of observation going into overdrive. The place was rich with information about his target and he allowed all of his senses to come into play as he absorbed it like a sponge, registering every tiny detail, filing each one away, cross-referencing them with what he knew about Bailey so far with the aim of fleshing out his picture of her.

Bailey Morgan was an undercover cop – an expert in deception – which made her all the harder to track. But in this flat – her personal space – he was seeing the woman beneath whatever façades she chose to assume as part of her job. Here was the real Bailey Morgan.

On the coffee table, a tabloid magazine lying open at an inter-view with an aging pop star from the eighties. Hanging on the wall, a tacky chocolate box painting of a house in the countryside. Propped on a shelf, a variety of books on cryptic crosswords and Sudoku. Sitting on the mantelpiece, some jiu jitsu trophies. Dotted round the room, a number of potted plants that were starting to wilt from lack of water. Standing on the sideboard, an array of photographs...

Rex focused in on the photographs. He walked over and picked up a picture of Bailey and examined it. The photo matched the description that the client had provided, in particular the thin white scar running down her left cheek. It confirmed that he was definitely in the flat belonging to the woman he was intending to kill.

Peering closely at her face, he memorised every line of her features. Pale skin with some freckles across the top of a small flat nose, straight lips, round ears, thin eyebrows, grey eyes surrounded by dark rings intimating lack of sleep. And of course the scar. He looked into her eyes. There was something haunted about them, the hint of a trauma. He wondered if it was related to her facial disfigurement.

He placed the photo back on the shelf and cast his eye across the others. Bailey with her arm round the shoulders of a much older man... Bailey standing with the same older man and also an elderly woman – Rex guessed them to be her parents. A photograph of a black headstone in a cemetery. Rex peered closer. The name on the headstone was 'Dennis Morgan'. Her father probably. The older man in the photographs. Dead now, it seemed.

Wordlessly registering the information, he turned round. Seeing a small desk in the corner of the room, he crossed over to it and pulled open the drawer. It was stuffed with various papers – utilities bills, bank statements, receipts. He noticed an itemised receipt from Co-op Funeral Care. Scanning it briefly, he saw that her father's headstone was located in Beckenham Cemetery. Rooting round in the drawer a bit more, he found her passport. He flicked it open to the personal details page. He saw that she had been born in Bromley and he saw that she was now thirty years old.

The information that Rex was gathering here would help him to anticipate Bailey's likely next moves and perhaps clue him into ways in which she might try to deceive him.

Experience had taught him that every person had their own individual quirks and peculiarities, all of which contributed to a distinct signature in the trail that they left as they moved through the environment. The more information you gathered about a person, the easier it became to identify this unique pattern.

Leaving the living room, he walked into the kitchen. He opened the fridge, hearing a clatter as he did so. Looking down, he saw that one of the fridge magnets had fallen onto the floor. It looked like a holiday souvenir from Koh Samui. He stuck it back on the fridge door and then proceeded to examine the contents of the fridge.

Rex had found that having some idea of the target's diet could be useful in all manner of ways. Not only could it help him to understand the kind of eating establishments they might frequent, but if he was using poison as a method of dispatch then it could also help him know how best to achieve this. And in addition to these factors, it also gave him an insight into what the target might smell like – certain foods gave a person's sweat a characteristic odour which could in certain situations give them away, and Rex possessed an acute enough sense of smell to take advantage of this.

The fridge didn't have all that much in it. Half a cold pizza on a plate, an unopened tub of hummus, a pack of crème caramels, a carton of semi-skimmed milk...

He closed the fridge and left the kitchen. Walking along a small hallway, he turned and entered the bathroom. Opening up the bathroom cabinet, the first thing he noticed was a packet of beta blockers. So she had mental health issues. Not to be unexpected for a person in her profession. He filed the observation away in his mind as a potential weakness he might be able to exploit at some point. Any type of Achilles Heel was useful in his trade.

* * *

For the sake of safety, Bailey had parked a few streets away from her flat in Crystal Palace and was now carefully approaching it on foot.

It felt strange feeling so wary in a place she usually felt so at home in. She reflected that she'd always liked Crystal Palace as an area to live in. It had a quirky vibe and it wasn't too posh although it had become more gentrified in recent years. Being on high ground it had good views over the capital, it possessed some great little restaurants and shops, and she was a big fan of the indoor market on Haynes Lane where she'd picked up all kinds of bargains from the bric-a-brac that was on sale there.

Aware that she was placing herself in potential peril by returning here, she stopped momentarily at the top of her road to take stock of the situation. The front entrance to her flat lay around two hundred metres ahead of her on the right. Once again she asked herself if it had been a bad idea to come back here. If Rex was going to strike this would be a very good opportunity for him to do so.

Peering down the length of her road she tried to determine if anything looked amiss. On the surface everything looked fine. It was early and there wasn't much activity. Some light traffic. A few parked cars. A cyclist. Two pedestrians – an elderly man and a young Asian woman. Bailey didn't peg either of them as Rex.

She noted the white Transit van parked opposite her flat. Further down the road she spotted the grey Ford Focus RS. She knew that the van contained two plainclothes police officers and there was one in the car, and she knew that all of them were armed. They weren't too obvious, but then they weren't exactly that subtle either, if you happened to be looking out for that kind of thing. Either way, they'd know by now she was coming, courtesy of Stella, and she felt consequently more assured of her safety.

As she drew closer to her flat, she flickered a glance to the two men sitting in the front of the Transit van. They didn't acknowledge her and she didn't acknowledge them, but she knew they'd seen her. She crossed the road to the side that her flat was on. It was around a hundred metres away now.

Rex closed the bathroom cabinet and went back out into the hall-way, continuing down back into the bedroom. Opening up the wardrobe, he noted the white jiu jitsu outfit and recalled the trophies he'd seen on the mantelpiece in the living room. There was a purple belt draped on the coat hanger along with the jiu jitsu outfit; Rex wasn't exactly sure what this signified in terms of Bailey's proficiency in martial arts but reminded himself to be extra wary of her if it came down to a close-quarter encounter at the end.

He shut the wardrobe and turned his attention to the dresser. On top of the dresser were some cosmetics – lipstick, eyeliner, perfume. He pulled open a drawer. Taking out a blouse, he examined the label. She was a size eight. A slight build. He lifted the blouse to his nose, closed his eyes and inhaled deeply, memorising her scent. It wasn't unpleasant. If at some point in this pursuit he encountered her in a disguise so good that even he was deceived, he knew he would be able to recognise her by her smell.

He put the blouse back in the dresser and exited the bedroom, returning to the living room. Taking one last look round, he decided that he'd probably garnered enough information to build a decent picture of her as a real person. At the beginning of this pursuit she'd been nothing more than a name, a cipher, with only the sparsest details attached to her. But by now he had quite literally fleshed her out and clothed her. The next stage would be to get inside her head to the extent that he could accurately gauge her emotional state.

Rex saw the answerphone light flashing by the landline telephone. He pressed the button to play the message.

'Hi Bailey,' said a jaunty female voice. 'This is Emma. I've been trying to call you on your mobile by the way, but you weren't answering. I'm guessing that's because you're on an operation at the moment. But I also thought maybe there was a problem with your phone or something so anyway that's why I called your landline. *But*, to get to the point, I was just chatting to Anthony *and...* he wants your telephone number! Obviously I won't give it to him if you don't want me to, but you know what, I really think you two would make a great couple. So give me a call. Or if you want to have a chat about it in person, which I'd obviously prefer, then I'll be at our regular corner spot in Marzini's. The ciabatta's on me! Bye-ee!'

The answerphone clicked off. Rex smirked to himself. So Bailey Morgan had a love life. It sounded like she should be making a bit more of it considering that she only had a short time left in which to do so.

Standing in the centre of Bailey's living room, he decided that he'd gained as much information as he was going to. There was no reason to stay here any longer.

From what he'd seen in this flat, coupled with the presence of the police surveillance vehicles outside, he was fairly certain that Bailey knew she was a target and had thus temporarily fled her flat to lie low somewhere. The question was where? With the information he'd gathered here, he was confident he'd track her down soon enough.

He walked back into the kitchen with the intention of leaving her flat the same way he'd entered.

* * *

Bailey descended the small set of concrete steps to the outer entrance to her flat. She took her keys out of her pocket and unlocked the front door, entering the hallway that she shared with her neighbour Alastair.

It was quiet and cool in the hallway. Looking down she saw that the pile of junk mail addressed to her had grown even larger. No doubt Alastair would be even more annoyed with it now. But this wasn't the time to start sorting through it.

She walked up to the front door of her flat and inserted her key into the lock.

* * *

Going to the back door, Rex quietly let himself out of Bailey's flat, gently easing the door closed behind him.

'Who are you and what are you doing?' demanded a male voice.

Rex spun round. A man was standing in the open doorway of the back door of the neighbouring flat. He was wearing square-rimmed glasses, a dressing gown and a pair of fluffy slippers. He was holding a mug of tea and he had a meddlesome expression on his face. Rex guessed the man was Bailey's neighbour.

'I'm a friend of Bailey's,' hissed Rex in a low voice.

'Oh? You're a friend of hers, are you?' The man looked a little nonplussed as he took in Rex's appearance.

Rex's hand closed round the folding knife in his pocket. He began to slowly thumb the blade open. He eyed the man's carotid artery and thought about how quickly he could open it up. The man would be dead within minutes. He'd bleed out quietly here on his back doorstep.

'Well... uh...' The man swallowed nervously. 'I was just a little bit surprised to see you walking out of the back door. There is a front entrance, you know. Still, I suppose her personal life is her business.'

Rex just stared at him coldly. The man was babbling. People had a tendency to do that when they were round Rex. It was because they were scared, even if they didn't quite know why. He just had that effect on people.

Eyeing the man, Rex could see that he was an immensely irritating human being. He wondered how Bailey put up with living next door to him. He suppressed the urge to kill the man right now. Doing so could potentially create complications that might prevent him from ultimately dispatching his real target – Bailey Morgan. He relaxed the hold on the knife in his pocket, pushing the blade back into the handle.

The man adjusted his glasses and squinted at Rex curiously as if he seemed to recognise him. 'Do I know you from somewhere? You look familiar.'

'I don't think so,' murmured Rex.

Turning away from Bailey's neighbour, Rex jogged to the garden wall and vaulted over it. As he did so he caught a final glimpse of the man staring at him open-mouthed.

9

Entering her living room, Bailey stopped for a moment to listen. If she wasn't mistaken, she could detect the familiar yacking tones of her neighbour Alastair talking to someone. It sounded like he was standing outside by his back door. She couldn't quite make out what was being said and wondered who he was talking to at this early hour, but then it occurred to her that he was probably just talking on the phone to someone. Either way, it wasn't her concern. She had more important things to focus on.

Scanning the living room for a few long moments, she tried to think where she might have left the Ruby Red matchbook after taking it out of her pocket nine months ago. Noticing that it was a little dim in the basement-level room, she reached for the light switch and turned on the light.

Walking over to the mantelpiece, she prodded round in a saucer where she kept spare change and other small items. No, it wasn't in there.

Crossing to the desk in the corner of the living room, she pulled open the drawer which she used as a dumping ground for just about anything and everything. It was a total mess just as she remembered. She rooted round amongst the various bills and receipts but the matchbook didn't seem to be in there. She frowned to herself trying to think where else it could be.

Then she remembered the milk jug on the kitchen shelf that she'd picked up at a bric-a-brac stall in the market on Haynes Lane. She'd never actually got round to using it for milk, and its main purpose these days was as a repository for random bits and bobs. Maybe the matchbook was in there.

She went into the kitchen. Glancing through the kitchen window, she saw the quiet empty garden and no sign of Alastair by his back door. If he'd been out there earlier he wasn't there any longer.

At the thought of Alastair, she looked down reflexively at the kitchen bin and was relieved to see that she had in fact remembered to take the rubbish out this time. At least he wouldn't be able to complain to her about *that*.

Going over to the kitchen shelf, she took down the milk jug and upended its contents onto the kitchen top. Some drawing pins. A biro. A radiator key. The Ruby Red matchbook.

There it was. She felt a small flare of excitement. Success.

Flicking open the matchbook, she immediately entered Dani's telephone number into the contacts on her iPhone. And then, just to be on the safe side, she secreted the matchbook in the pocket of her jacket.

She turned to leave the kitchen. Now she just had to get her beta blockers out of the bathroom cabinet.

Just as she was about to leave the kitchen, she was struck by the unsettling feeling that something didn't feel quite right. Some tiny detail had subconsciously caught her eye and she couldn't quite work out what it was. Pausing for a moment, she skimmed her gaze across the kitchen. And then she spotted it. One of the fridge magnets was in the wrong place. The one from Koh Samui. It had a habit of falling off the door whenever she opened the fridge, and she always put it back in the same place, pinning down the bottom left corner of a recycling guide that she kept stuck to the front of the fridge with various magnets. But the Koh Samui magnet was now stuck randomly near the top of the fridge door. That meant it must have fallen off and someone else must have stuck it back on the door again because she would never have placed it in that position.

A disconcerting shudder went through her. Someone had been in her flat. She was sure of it. She was certain it wasn't the police as they hadn't had access to a set of keys. Maybe her mum had dropped by, because she did have a spare set of keys to Bailey's flat. But that seemed unlikely. Her mum would never have let herself into Bailey's flat without checking with Bailey first.

The uncomfortable feeling inside her turned into a cold chill as she realised that it could have been Rex who'd been in here. Had he found out where she lived already and managed to avoid the police surveillance to get in here somehow?

If Rex had been in her flat, then he'd no doubt come here with the intention of killing her. But the thought then occurred to her that, thwarted by her absence, he probably would have made the most of his visit by learning as much about her as possible from what he'd found here. She shivered in revulsion at the thought of him poking round in her personal stuff, feeling violated by his intrusion of her privacy. She dreaded to think what kind of insights he might have gained that could bring him closer to her.

Swallowing apprehensively, her heart beating faster now, she walked back into the living room to check if there was any indication that he'd been in there or not. She hadn't noticed anything when she'd arrived just a few minutes earlier. Glancing round uneasily, she still couldn't immediately detect anything amiss. The photographs on the sideboard looked fine. The tabloid magazine on the sofa was as she'd left it. The jiu jitsu trophies on the mantelpiece looked untouched. The desk drawer full of junk... well, it was so messy it would have been impossible to tell if anyone had been looking through it.

Biting her lip in concern, she turned and went into her bedroom and stood there surveying the room for a few moments. Having departed in a hurry without taking the time to tidy, she'd left the bedroom in a bit of a mess, with her clothes and belongings strewn everywhere. It was therefore hard to ascertain if someone had been rifling through her stuff or not.

She took a deep breath to calm herself. Maybe she was just imagining it. Maybe her paranoia was just playing up. But then what about the fridge magnet?

Trying to shake the worrying thoughts from her head, she made her way into the bathroom and pulled open the bathroom cabinet, feeling a profound sense of relief at the sight of her beta blockers sitting there on the shelf. She opened the box to check that the blister pack was all intact. They looked fine. Placing them in the pocket of her jacket, she went back into the living room. She was all done. Mission accomplished. It was time to leave.

Walking back to the front door, she stepped out into her hallway. She had just closed the door behind her when the door of the neighbouring flat clicked open. She turned round with a sinking feeling.

Alastair Primpton was standing in his front doorway clad in a dressing gown and fluffy slippers. He was staring at Bailey through his square-rimmed glasses with a deeply vexed look on his face.

Bailey braced herself and prepared to deliver some harsh words. She wasn't in the mood to talk about junk mail right now.

'I have to say,' he stated sharply, 'your friend was completely out of order. When he was leaving he trod all over my courgette patch at the end of the garden. And then he actually climbed over the garden wall. I can't see why he couldn't have just used the front entrance like any normal person.'

Bailey froze, her eyes widening. 'Friend? What friend?'

Alastair frowned. 'The one who was visiting you just now. This morning.'

Bailey's breath caught in her throat and an icy feeling crawled over her scalp. 'A person was in my flat?' she whispered. *Just now?*'

Alastair nodded, looking puzzled at her reaction. 'Yes, not more than five minutes ago. I bumped into him just as he was coming out of your back door. He said he was a friend of yours, and then he ran off down the end of the garden, trod all over my courgettes and climbed over the wall and disappeared.'

Bailey tried to swallow but it felt like there was a lump of concrete in her throat. It had to have been Rex. There was no other explanation. He *had* been in her flat. And she'd missed him by a matter of seconds. If she'd got there a fraction earlier he would have heard her come in and he would have killed her. She felt dizzy as she realised just how close she'd come to encountering him. And it struck her now just how foolish she'd been to return here in person. What a stupid decision! It had almost cost her life.

An intense fear suddenly gripped her. Was Rex still hanging round outside the flat somewhere? Was she in mortal danger right now?

But then simultaneously she was struck by the realisation that if he was still in the vicinity then they might be in with a chance of detaining him.

She rapidly pulled out her phone and called Stella.

'He was here,' she gasped before Stella had a chance to speak. 'Rex was in my flat this morning. Not more than five minutes ago.'

'What do you mean he was there?' asked Stella. 'Surveillance didn't—'

'He managed to evade them. He must have accessed the property via the neighbouring back gardens so as to avoid the front of the flat.'

'Are you safe?' Stella sounded concerned.

'I'll be fine. He's gone now but he might still be in the area and we might just be able to catch him if we act now.'

'I need a description,' urged Stella.

Bailey turned to Alastair. The affronted expression on his face had now been replaced by one of slight bewilderment.

'What did he look like?' demanded Bailey. Seized by a taut excitement, she realised that this would be the first time that anyone would have been able to provide a proper physical description of Rex.

Alastair looked a little flustered as he tried to recall. 'Er... Tall. Dark hair with grey bits. Probably in his late thirties or early forties I'd say. Oh yes... he had a small scar on his right eyebrow.'

Bailey breathlessly relayed the details to Stella.

She turned back to Alastair. 'What else? Anything else?'

He scratched his head and frowned. 'Er, well... You know, I couldn't help thinking that he was a spitting image of that stand-up comedian, the one you see on that TV show where they have to improvise. Toby whats-his-name. You know.' He clicked his fingers. 'Toby Freeman. That's it!'

A stand-up comedian? Bailey vaguely knew of the programme Alastair was talking about, although she never watched it which is why she had little idea who Toby Freeman was or what he looked like.

'He looks like some comedian called Toby Freeman,' said Bailey down the phone.

'Yes I know the one you're talking about,' said Stella. 'That'll be useful. Okay, I'll get onto the surveillance teams immediately.' She terminated the call.

Bailey immediately opened up the internet browser on her

iPhone and plugged Toby Freeman's name into Google. A selection of images came up in the search results. She scrolled through them, studying his features closely. If Rex did indeed resemble this stand-up comedian as much as Alastair was implying, then knowing what the comedian looked like would at least give her a rough idea of what to be looking out for.

Alastair craned his head to look over her shoulder. 'Yes, that's right. He looked just like that. Maybe not quite as pudgy though. And he had a slightly stronger jaw.'

'Do you think you could come into the office to give a statement and provide a photo-fit?' she asked.

'Er... yes I suppose so. Why? Was he dangerous?' Alastair looked a bit alarmed.

'You could say that,' muttered Bailey. She gave him a brisk smile. 'Thank you for your help Alastair. You've been invaluable.'

She walked towards the outer entrance of her flat to liaise with the armed surveillance officers parked outside.

'Wait a minute,' said Alastair, raising a finger. 'What about my courgettes?'

But the door had closed and Bailey had already gone.

10

Driving back to her hotel a few hours later, Bailey reflected with frustration on how the morning's events had panned out. Despite their best efforts, Rex had successfully managed to evade them. The police search of the area around her flat hadn't managed to net him, and public CCTV hadn't yielded anything useful. The only good thing was that at least they now had a description of him, even if it was based in part on his resemblance to a minor-league TV comedian. She supposed she should count herself lucky that he'd missed the chance to kill her and she wondered if he'd known just how close he'd got.

Heading out of South London, she drove across Battersea Bridge towards Earl's Court, back to her fugitive existence in the hotel. At the thought of her wretched situation, she once again felt a sharp stab of anger at Charlie Benvenuto. There he was sitting in his big house in Surrey, taking advantage of his bail to direct this hit on her which he'd paid for no doubt with his illicit drug proceeds. It made her more determined than ever to take him down, more so than when she'd been on the actual deployment itself.

That operation had been nothing out of the ordinary for her, a relatively short-term deployment organised by the drugs squad for whom Benvenuto was a priority target. Operating at the uppermost level of the supply chain, he was responsible for bringing hundreds of kilograms of cocaine into the UK each year, and they'd been after him for a while. Working under Stella's supervision, Bailey had posed as a wholesaler claiming to have the kind of retail-level connections that were capable of shifting the multiple kilos of coke that she was hoping to buy from him.

He'd fallen for her patter over a series of meetings, several of which had been purely social in nature. As a person, she'd found him to be superficially affable with a shrewd head for business. But she didn't underestimate the cunning and ruthlessness lying just beneath the surface of his personable exterior. Physically imposing with a bear-like frame, she suspected he was more than capable of brute violence, although at no point did she ever witness anything of the sort. He was no mindless thug and, given the high-stakes game he was playing, he was too smart to let himself get into that kind of trouble.

As for his personal life, she knew he had a wife and two daughters. Bailey had briefly met his wife Amy during a social encounter at the horse races. Fairly small in size compared to her husband, she'd come across as surprisingly straightforward and morally upright, quite a contrast to him, and Bailey got the impression that she had no idea what he really did for a living. She wondered how the poor woman was holding up right now.

Bringing someone like him to justice would be an important coup. The UK drugs trade was a dirty business that brought violence and exploitation to communities all across the country, from murders in the inner cities to the county lines gangs who used children to sell drugs further afield. Sitting at the top of the drugs supply chain, Benvenuto played a crucial role in enabling this trade, and putting him away would have a seriously detrimental effect on everyone beneath him.

And as an undercover police officer, she knew that her testimony in particular would exert a strong influence on the outcome of the trial. The judge would clear the courtroom, and she'd testify and be cross-examined from behind a screen. From past experience she knew it always made quite an impact on the jury, really ramming home the dangers of her role, and as a result often made the defendant more likely to be convicted and get a longer sentence. She wondered if Benvenuto was aware of this which was one of the reasons he wanted her dead.

She would have dearly loved to go to his house to confront him but she knew that was out of the question. For one thing, it would adversely affect any legal proceedings, and for another, quite frustratingly, she couldn't prove that he was doing anything wrong. Or at least not yet. No – for the time being, the best she could do was to stay alive long enough to get him convicted of his drugs offences, and with any luck, if they captured Rex, pin the conspiracy-to-murder charge on him as well.

* * *

The receptionist Ravi looked up at Bailey as she entered the reception area of the Royal City Hotel on the way back up to her room.

'Miss Bailey,' he enquired, endowing her with a beaming smile. 'How is your room? Is everything to your liking? As a VIP guest your comfort is our priority.'

She returned his smile. 'It couldn't be better,' she replied without breaking her stride. It was a complete lie but she didn't have time right now to complain about the poor standards of cleaning. She was impatient to make contact with Dani and there wasn't a second to lose.

Through Dani's potential association with Jack Wynter, as a dancer in his club, Bailey was hoping that Dani would be able to provide her with an introduction to the gangster, or otherwise she knew it was unlikely he would trust her enough to confide anything about Rex.

Climbing the stairs to the first floor, she made her way through the dingy corridors to her room. Taking out her keycard, she unlocked the door and went in. The first thing she did was pop two beta blockers out of their blister pack and knock them back with a glass of water, craving the relief they would bring from the tension jacked up inside her by the near run-in with Rex earlier that morning.

She then took out her phone and scrolled through her contacts to Dani's phone number which she'd entered earlier that morning. It had been nine months since Bailey last talked to Dani and she hoped the dancer was still using this particular phone number.

In terms of obtaining an authorisation to use Dani as a covert human intelligence source, Stella had immediately passed the application up to the relevant superintendent who'd granted an oral authorisation. Normally a written authorisation was required but in urgent cases such as this one, an oral one was permitted. Whereas written authorisations expired after twelve months, oral ones only lasted seventy-two hours. Bailey was hoping that would be enough time to achieve what she needed.

Informants, more colloquially known as 'snouts', provided their services to the police for a variety of reasons – financial reward, getting their charges dropped or reduced if they'd been arrested, or other more personal reasons such as revenge for wounded pride. Bailey often found them to be rather unreliable people, and once they'd served their purpose in aiding an undercover operation she did her best to remove them from the picture as they could end up being a liability otherwise.

Bailey wasn't too sure how Dani would turn out in terms of

being an informant, but if she handled it right, there hopefully wouldn't be any problems. She dialled Dani's number, hoping that Dani remembered who she was.

The phone rang for a few seconds and then a female voice with a South London twang came on the line. 'Hello?'

'Hello,' said Bailey. 'Is that Dani?'

'Yeah. Who's this?' Dani sounded faintly suspicious.

'This is Detective Constable Bailey Morgan. We met last year when—'

'Oh yeah I remember you. Bailey. Yeah.' A brief pause. 'You never called me.' There was a distinct tone of dismay in her voice.

'I'm sorry Dani. I did mean to but I've just been so busy recently. You know how it is.' Bailey took a breath. 'Are you still working at Ruby Red?'

Dani's voice brightened. 'I certainly am, and I've got plenty of juicy gossip for you. It's amazing what these blokes are willing to tell a girl after a few drinks. I think they think it impresses me.'

Bailey found herself smiling. 'Well, actually, I was wondering if you could help me out. How well do you know Jack Wynter?'

'I know him very well as it happens,' said Dani with a slightly exclusive air.

'Can you introduce me to him as a friend of yours?'

'Sure. I suppose so,' she muttered, sounding a little disappointed that Bailey wasn't interested in hearing her underworld gossip.

'Great. Well, we'll have to think of a cover story because we can't very well have you introduce me to him as a policewoman. It doesn't have to be too detailed. It just needs to be believable enough that Jack doesn't feel the need to double-check it.'

'A cover story?' Dani sounded intrigued. 'Ooh... okay.'

When it came to situations like this, Bailey found the best approach was to ask the informant a bit about their life until she found something that they had in common that could be used as the basis for a cover story.

'Do you have a criminal record?' asked Bailey.

'No, I do not!' exclaimed Dani.

That was a shame, thought Bailey. Something crime-related would have added extra plausibility when it came to convincing a villain like Jack Wynter of her criminal credentials.

'Okay,' she said. 'Well, where did you grow up then?'

'Lewisham. Born and bred.'

'That's good. I'm from South London too. I grew up in Bromley.' Bailey paused to think what she could ask about next. 'What kind of music do you like?'

'Me? I'm into house music. You know... David Guetta... Calvin Harris...'

Bailey wrinkled her nose in distaste. She couldn't stand house music. She herself was a committed fan of eighties pop. It looked like music was off the table.

'What about travel?' she asked. 'Where do you like going on holiday?'

'Um... Ibiza. Tenerife. Thailand—'

'Thailand? Great. Me too. Have you been to Koh Samui?'

'Koh Samui?' enthused Dani. 'Yeah! I love it. I've been there three times.'

'Brilliant. Okay. Let's say that we met each other at a beach bar in Koh Samui three years ago, got chatting, found that we were both from South London, hit it off with each other, and have been friends ever since. You can say that I dabble in business on the wrong side of the law.'

'Ooh, this is exciting, isn't it?'

Bailey smiled to herself. She wasn't too surprised by Dani's reaction. Informants, particularly first-timers, often got quite a thrill from embarking on this kind of venture.

'You can still refer to me as Bailey. If Jack asks for my surname, tell him it's Smith – that's an easy name to remember, isn't it?'

Bailey had found that it was usually best to use her real first name when working undercover. When it came to interacting with criminals, the less lies you were juggling in your head the better. And with someone as inexperienced in these matters as Dani, Bailey wanted there to be as little margin for error as possible.

'Bailey Smith,' echoed Dani. 'Yes, I think I'll be able to remember that.'

'How soon do you think you can introduce me?' asked Bailey.

'How about tomorrow evening?' said Dani. 'I think Jack will be quite amenable on this particular Saturday.'

'That sounds great,' said Bailey. She was pleased to be making progress so quickly.

They spent a short while longer rehearsing the cover story, just to make sure they were both confident about it, and then Bailey terminated the call.

She sat there for a few moments on the edge of her bed contemplating the forthcoming meeting with Wynter. The cover story wouldn't bear too much examination and she hoped Wynter would buy it... but if he didn't she was sure she'd be able to wing it – working undercover was all about thinking on your feet and that was one thing she was good at.

It was sometime later in the afternoon, following a rather unsatisfying lunch consisting of a meal deal from a local supermarket, that Bailey remembered that she was going to call her friend Emma back.

'I'm sorry I haven't been answering my phone,' said Bailey. 'I'm on a—'

'On a deployment,' chimed Emma, interrupting her. 'I know, Bailey. Of course I understand. You don't need to apologise. It's probably me who should apologise for hassling you when you're busy doing super-important stuff.'

Emma herself didn't do undercover work. Most police officers didn't as most of them just weren't cut out for it. It took a special kind of guts to work undercover and Bailey knew Emma held her slightly in awe because of it. In fact, one of the reasons Bailey enjoyed working undercover was the kudos it brought her from colleagues.

'I just wanted to let you know that I wasn't ignoring you,' said Bailey. 'It's just that things have been a bit hectic recently.'

She refrained from telling Emma that there was a professional hitman out to kill her. Much as she would have liked to confide in her friend, anything related to a live operation was highly confidential. At any rate, she knew it would only have filled her friend with worry.

'I couldn't help myself Bailey,' said Emma excitedly. 'I just had to know how it went with you and Anthony. I even left a message on your answerphone.'

Bailey frowned to herself. She hadn't noticed the answerphone light flashing when she'd gone back to her flat, which meant that someone had already listened to the messages. She realised with a shudder that it must have been Rex.

'Oh did you?' she said. 'I neglected to check it.'

'Well, what I was saying is that Anthony wants your telephone number. He wants to see you again!'

Bailey raised her eyebrows in mild surprise, feeling pleasantly flattered that Anthony was still interested in her, particularly considering that he'd seen the full extent of her scars. On that basis alone she'd assumed that he wouldn't have wanted to see her again. Her acquaintance with him had been fairly limited when sober, and as for the night they'd spent together, she had virtually no memory of it because she'd been too intoxicated. However, from her experience of him so far, he seemed like a nice guy and he wasn't bad-looking either, but what with everything that was going on in her life, she felt it was a bad idea to be embarking on romantic endeavours right now.

'Well it's nice to know he likes me,' she said. 'But... perhaps now isn't the best time for me to be dating someone. I'm tied up with an undercover operation at the moment.'

'Come on Bailey,' beseeched Emma. 'Anthony's a good friend of mine and I can tell you he is a top fella. And he does work in a bank now, you know. That means expensive holidays. Big gifts. I can think of a hundred reasons why you should let me give him your number.'

'Maybe some other time,' said Bailey. She attempted to change the subject. 'How's the office?'

Emma sighed and giggled. 'Andy's really pissed off. You know what he's like. He just keeps going on about the big backlog of cases you've left behind. I keep hearing him muttering and cursing about you under his breath.'

Bailey's CID detective sergeant was a dour Geordie called Andy Jobbins. Andy was a decent enough bloke but he'd never been very keen on her working undercover, as it meant that she inevitably fell behind in her regular work. Her recent assignment on the Benvenuto operation had already caused her workload to mount up, and her father's recent passing prior to that and the subsequent time she'd had to take off work to help out her mother had only served to aggravate the matter. Andy also resented the fact that he didn't have much say whenever he received an authorisation request from her covert undercover operations manager. Covert operations usually trumped regular police work in terms of importance so he had little choice but to sign her off.

'Well I'm sure he'll manage,' said Bailey. 'I'm hoping this operation will be over by the eighth of October. That's not too far away.'

'It would be great to see you before then,' said Emma. 'We could just grab a quick coffee. Are you in London at the moment?'

'Yeah but I can't tell you—'

'You can't tell me exactly where you are due to the rules round operational security for undercover work. Of course not. Silly me. I forgot. I shouldn't have asked.' Emma sighed. 'Still, it's lonely having lunch at Marzini's without you. Our usual spot feels empty.'

Their usual spot in Marzini's was the corner booth by the window where they would spend most of their lunchtime gossiping about work-related issues. The Italian deli, just round the corner from the police station where they worked, was such a regular haunt of theirs that the proprietor knew by heart what each of them liked to eat.

'Uh... things are pretty busy at the moment,' said Bailey. 'Let's wait until this operation is over.'

'Bailey, you're so anti-social,' scolded Emma half-jokingly.

'I'd love to see you Emma, but it's just that—'

'Look why don't you come round my place for dinner?' wheedled Emma. 'We can have a good natter. Put the world to rights. I'll make you dinner. We can share a bottle of wine. I can tell you all about Anthony and why you should be going out with him. Surely even undercover cops have to take an evening off some time?'

Bailey shook her head with a smile of disbelief. Emma was even more stubborn than she was. Bailey couldn't help but feel sorely tempted by Emma's offer. She was a fantastic cook, and given the poor lunch Bailey had just eaten, the prospect of her friend's cooking did seem appealing. And so did the idea of a good chat. However, social engagements just weren't her number one priority right now, not when there was someone out there trying to kill her.

'I'll think about it,' said Bailey diplomatically, not wanting to let her friend down.

'Okay,' said Emma expectantly. 'I'll look forward to hearing from you. And if I don't... well, you can look forward to hearing from me.'

11

From the outside, with its smoked glass exterior and elegant sign, Ruby Red bore the semblance of an exclusive and sophisticated establishment. Located just off Shaftesbury Avenue in Central London, it touted itself as a high-end gentleman's club but beneath the glamorous veneer Bailey knew it was little more than a lap-dancing joint with hugely over-priced drinks, its primary function being to separate the punters from as much of their cash as possible.

Bailey had turned up at six o'clock on Saturday evening, when the club opened, keen to get business squared away before the place got too busy.

The doorman had evidently been informed of her visit in advance.

'My name's Bailey,' she said. 'I'm here to see—'

'Dani, yeah I know,' he grunted, nodding his bald head. 'Go on in.'

Entering the club, she found herself in an expansive grotto-like space dominated by a catwalk-style stage with a mirrored surface and a pole at one end. The décor consisted of dark red drapes and lavish gilt fittings with cut-glass chandeliers hanging from the low ceiling. They were aiming for an atmosphere of decadent opulence and Bailey could see how it might come across that way when it was buzzing at night but right now, this early in the evening, it was completely dead and the whole place just seemed a bit tacky.

There were fifteen or so girls sitting around on the red velvet furniture looking bored, a few of them idly tapping their feet to the rock music that was playing softly over the sound system. Clad in skin-tight dresses, they comprised a range of ethnicities but the one thing they all had in common was that they were strikingly attractive, which probably went some way to explaining why this club was such a hit with A-list celebrities.

They all looked up sharply when Bailey walked in, like sharks smelling blood in the water, but most of their faces fell when they saw she was a woman, probably assuming that she wasn't a proper punter who they could fleece for cash like they normally would. Some of them gave her bitchy judgemental looks, like they thought she might be there for an audition.

A female voice rung out. 'Bailey!'

Bailey turned round to see a statuesque redhead in a white body-hugging dress and heels peel away from the bar and totter towards her. If the girls in here were gorgeous then Dani was in a league of her own and Bailey found herself enviously admiring the stripper's incredible physique.

'You said Jack would be more amenable this Saturday,' said Bailey, keeping her voice low. 'What did you mean by that exactly?'

'Jason Blixen's coming in tonight,' whispered Dani. 'Him and his fuckwit mates'll spend a fortune on the Dom Perignon and private dances.'

Jason Blixen was a Premier League footballer. Although Bailey didn't really follow football, she often encountered mention of him in the news on account of his vast wealth and extravagant party lifestyle.

'I'm Jason's favourite,' said Dani, 'and Jack knows it. If it wasn't for me Jason probably wouldn't even be coming tonight. Jack's dead nervous about it. Wants to make sure it all goes smoothly... and yours truly is key to the whole operation. Jack'll do anything I tell him to keep me sweet and if that means helping you then so be it.'

Dani beckoned Bailey to follow her through a door next to the bar into a small corridor. They stopped outside an office. Dani winked at her and then knocked on the door.

Bailey felt that familiar twinge of nerves that she always felt when encountering criminals for the first time in an undercover context. She'd never met Wynter personally so there was little risk that he would know that she was a police officer, but she also knew that she needed to stay on her guard as you could never be too careful round crooks for some of them were very dangerous people indeed.

'Come in' said a gravelly well-spoken male voice.

Dani pushed open the door and Bailey followed her in.

Jack Wynter was lounging in a luxurious leather swivel chair behind a large antique wooden desk. Probably in his late fifties, he had the craggy look of a heavy smoker, and when he smiled at them both, Bailey saw that he had the stained teeth to match. That said, with his coiffured grey hair and expensive-looking suit, he obviously took pride in his appearance. And he also appeared to take pride in rubbing shoulders with celebrities for the walls of the office were adorned with a surfeit of framed photographs depicting Wynter accompanied by various famous people who'd visited his club in the past.

Dani bestowed a dazzling smile upon him. 'This is my friend Bailey who I was telling you about. She needs a favour and I said you'd help her out.'

Jack flicked Bailey a cursory look, almost immediately turning his attention back to Dani. 'Yeah yeah all right. Just make sure you've got everything ready for Jason tonight. I want him to have a good time and you know what that means.'

A loaded look passed between them and Bailey had an idea what the full extent of 'a good time' might entail.

'Of course Jack,' said Dani. 'I'll make him feel very welcome indeed. Just make sure you take care of my friend Bailey here.'

Wynter nodded dutifully and Dani retreated from the office, leaving Bailey and Wynter alone.

Lounging back leisurely in his chair, Wynter studied her curiously with a hint of suspicion round the edges of his eyes. He nodded for her to sit down in a chair facing him. She did so.

'So you're a friend of Dani,' he said slowly.

Bailey nodded. 'I've known her for a few years. Met her on holiday in Thailand. We've been mates ever since.'

Wynter regarded her silently for a few moments and she wondered if he'd probe any further. From her past experience of working undercover she'd found that some criminals were keen to know every tiniest detail about you... but then she'd also encountered plenty of others who couldn't have been less concerned.

'So what's this favour you need then?' he asked, glancing impatiently at his watch. To her relief she guessed he had larger things preoccupying him this evening than spending time delving into her rather thin cover story.

She took a breath. 'Uh... well it's a rather delicate matter. But Dani said you're the kind of person who can help with things which... how shall we say, sit outside the realm of normal affairs.'

He observed her circumspectly from his chair without saying anything. She took it as a cue to continue.

'I don't know if Dani told you much about what I do, but I like to get my hands dirty dabbling in this and that.'

Wynter's eyes bored into her. Still he didn't say anything. By telling him that she was involved in illicit activity, she was implicitly suggesting that he was too, for why else would she confide in him otherwise? However she was careful not to overtly infer that he was a criminal for she knew that this might offend him, well aware that people such as him often liked to think of themselves as nothing more than businessmen, albeit unconventional ones.

She chose her words delicately. 'I have a problem though. There's a person who's causing me business issues. This person is causing me a great deal of inconvenience.'

He nodded in an understanding manner.

'I need to deal with them,' said Bailey. 'And I've realised that there is really only one way to do that.'

His thick eyebrows raised slightly as he realised what she was saying. He was now looking at her in a new light, understanding the reason she had come to him, and probably understanding that she had done so precisely because of the allegations surrounding him regarding his ex-business partner's death. However she wasn't planning to broach the topic of Vincent Peck's murder in any way whatsoever as she knew Wynter would never openly admit his culpability, especially not to a stranger like her.

She waited tensely for his response.

He gave her an erudite smile. 'The Russians have a saying,' he said. 'No person, no problem.'

Bailey felt relieved that he appeared to be concurring with her. 'Those are my sentiments exactly,' she said. 'It's very important that this gets done properly. So I want to go with the best. I've done my homework and I want someone called Rex to take care of things for me. I just need to know how to get hold of him.'

At the mention of Rex his eyes widened slightly and his face took on a suspicious slant once more.

'What makes you think I know how to hire Rex?'

She shrugged. 'You seem like a very well-connected person. Dani tells me you know everyone in town. She tells me you're the kind of bloke who can get anything done. She tells me that's the reason you're so successful.'

Her flattery seemed to have a positive effect on him. 'I am aware of the existence of Rex,' he said, 'and I am also aware of how he operates... although *not* from any personal experience I should emphasise. Do you understand?'

Bailey nodded eagerly. 'Of course. I totally understand.'

He nodded with a satisfied smile. She knew he wasn't going to say anything to incriminate himself and she didn't want to ask questions in a way that would make him suspect that she was trying to make him do so. Anyhow, she wasn't here to try and prove that he had his business partner murdered, she was here to find out how to hire Rex.

'Rex isn't cheap,' he said. 'But he'll keep his mouth shut if he gets caught. That's all part of the arrangement, you see.'

'Money is no object,' said Bailey.

'You can't be too careful these days, what with Old Bill worming their way into all kinds of places. So he's very careful.'

He took a pen off his desk and wrote down something on a piece of paper. He pushed the piece of paper across the desk to her.

'You just send an email to this email address. Just write "problem" in the subject line and someone'll get back to you.'

She picked up the piece of paper and looked at it. It had an email address on it:

sortmyproblem@protonmail.com

It was suitably innocuous sounding with no indication as to the service that it provided.

'And then?' she asked.

'You'll get instructions to meet somewhere. And it goes from there. Apparently, you just provide details of the person you want rubbed out. And that's it.' He paused. 'Oh yeah. And you have to pay upfront.' He grinned at her. 'And, like I said, I hear it ain't cheap.'

It seemed that Wynter had told her everything she needed in order to move to the next stage of the operation. She felt gratified that she'd got this far so quickly.

'Thank you for your advice,' she said, standing up to leave. 'I'll do my best to return the favour sometime.'

'Just put in a good word for me with Dani,' he said.

Amy Benvenuto watched her husband from the kitchen window as he walked off down the garden and disappeared out of sight round the corner of a large laurel hedge. She knew he was heading to the wooden arbour seat with the trellis which sat right at the end of the garden in a little secluded alcove. It was one of his favourite spots, and since he'd been on bail he'd been spending more time than ever down there, talking on the phone to his lawyers discussing his upcoming court case.

He refused to discuss the specifics of the case with her, not that she minded too much because from what little he'd told her, it sounded like a horrible, complicated mess. He'd explained that the authorities were under the mistaken impression that he was some kind of drug trafficker. At first she'd found the notion completely absurd, and then, as the reality of the trial approached with the very real possibility of him being sent to prison, the disbelief had turned to stress and it was taking a heavy toll on her.

He was insisting of course that he was innocent, and she was a hundred per cent behind him. After all, surely the man she loved wouldn't have been lying to her for so long about something this serious, about something so illegal. But then when she thought about it, she realised that up until this point she'd known virtually nothing about his import business except for the fact that it generated more than enough money to enable them and their daughters to live a very comfortable lifestyle. Now, in retrospect, a tiny gnawing part of her wondered if some of the things about it had been a little odd. Like those trips he took abroad all the time... maybe there was something else to them. And the way that whenever he talked business on the phone, he always insisted on doing so down at the end of the garden, well out of her earshot, almost as if he was determined not to let her hear what he was talking about.

She found these small niggling doubts extremely unpleasant to contemplate. The idea that her husband might actually be involved in something illegal was a complete anathema to her. She herself had always been an extremely law-abiding person, her view being that if there weren't laws to keep things in place then surely the whole world would fall apart. It was perhaps a simple view, but then she knew she was a simple person. Charlie on the other hand, was much more complex, although that was what had drawn her to him in the first place. He was interesting and exciting.

He'd been working as an estate agent when she'd first met him. She'd been looking for a flat to rent and he'd won her over with his charm and patter, for he could be very charming and persuasive when he wanted to be. He'd persuaded her to go on a date... and six months later they were married, with the two girls coming along shortly after that.

She'd been glad to give up her job as a secretary to become a housewife and raise her children. The job had been dull and she'd detested all the office politics. She'd dedicated her life to him and their two daughters and together they'd built what in her eyes was a perfect family existence. But now with all this hanging over their heads it looked like it was going to fall apart.

Already their life was fracturing thanks to the news coverage of Charlie's arrest. Many of their so-called friends were now making an effort to distance themselves, and whenever Amy went out, she saw the neighbours gossiping about her. Even the girls had been affected, subjected to nasty taunts from their schoolmates whose parents had no doubt told them about Charlie's situation. It angered her that everyone was already judging him before he'd even had a chance to prove his innocence in court. It was so unfair. They were acting as if a guilty verdict and a prison sentence were a foregone conclusion.

The thought of him being locked up made her feel nauseous with worry. She could barely bring herself to think about a future without him. Since they'd been married money had rarely been a problem, but she realised now how completely dependent she was on him. Although she managed the household finances, he was the breadwinner, and without him, she wondered how she and the girls would survive. Would they lose the house? If so where would they live? Would they have to move into some crummy rented accommodation riddled with damp and mould? And what about the girls' private school education? She doubted she'd be able to afford that any more. Would they even have enough to eat? She'd have to find some means of supporting them but did that mean she'd have to find a job? Would she have to go back to being a secretary? It was the only thing she knew how to do and the idea of it filled her with dread.

Trapped in thought, she stared out of the kitchen window at their scenic garden, praying and hoping that the authorities would realise what an awful mistake they'd made and that she and her husband could go back to the untroubled life they'd been living before.

* * *

Sitting out on the deck of his catamaran, savouring the unusually warm weather, Rex idly observed the wealthy older couple who owned the Beneteau yacht that was berthed opposite his. Like him, they too were sitting out on deck, reading the papers and enjoying a cool drink. They waved at him in a neighbourly manner, completely oblivious to the fact that he was a professional contract killer. He flashed them a smile and a wave in return.

St Katharine Docks could accommodate around a hundred and eighty-five boats. Rex's catamaran was berthed right at the very end of one of the long floating pontoons, placing him right in the middle of the basin, furthest from the dockside, which was exactly how he liked it. There were around twelve other boats berthed on this particular pontoon and Rex occasionally exchanged small talk with the owners of some of them, though he made sure that it never went further than sailing-related trivia and comments about the weather. As far as they were concerned he was nothing more than a wealthy bachelor with a nice boat.

As he sat there, he contemplated his next move in regard to Bailey Morgan. He'd found out where she lived, and with the information that he'd gathered from her flat, he was one step closer to tracking her down. Right now he was feeling energised by that familiar flush of anticipation that he always got when he picked up the spoor of the quarry. The spoor consisted of the signs and traces of Bailey that he could follow and that would ultimately lead him to her. The nature of the spoor often changed over the course of a pursuit – at the beginning it might be a digital trail, but by the end it could be a set of actual footprints. Whatever form the spoor took, Rex was adept at sniffing it out to decipher the location and movements of his intended victim.

Rex knew a lot about hunting and inside the catamaran he

possessed a small library of books on the subject, many of which he'd had to purchase from specialist book dealers as they were long out of print. At this very moment he was partway through reading *Five years of a hunter's life in the far interior of South Africa* by Roualeyn Gordon-Cumming, a Scottish big-game hunter who'd pursued various large cats, giraffes, elephants and other wildlife in Africa in the mid-nineteenth century. Not only did Rex find it inspiring to read about the lives of such individuals, he also found that the books contained many useful tips on how to track and stalk prey.

Despite the fact that Rex largely operated within a modern urban environment, the principles and ethos of tracking and stalking weren't that different from those used by a big-game hunter on the African savannah. The basic questions were the same: What places does the prey frequent? When does it go there? What measures does it take to protect itself? Where does it like to take refuge?

To that end, Rex would request from the client as much information as possible about the person they wanted him to kill. If you wanted to hunt successfully you had to know the traits, the diet, and the physique of the quarry as well as the habitat that it lived or moved in. Routine and location were key factors in planning a hit. Most people followed a prescribed routine so it was relatively easy to kill them. Others were less predictable. But there hadn't been one so far that he hadn't managed to get in the end. And that's why people hired him.

In an ideal situation the quarry was never aware of the stalker until the final moment when the stalker pounced. Rex found that in most cases he was able to preserve the element of surprise, but with Bailey Morgan it was going to be different. She knew she was being hunted and this made his job infinitely more challenging. But then he liked a challenge because it meant that when he did catch up with her and finally kill her it would be immeasurably more satisfying.

Sitting there on the deck of his boat, he smiled evilly as an idea came to him. Out of all the information that he'd gleaned from Bailey Morgan's flat, one bit now surfaced in his mind as a very promising way to find her.

Bailey sat cross-legged on the bed in her hotel with her laptop open in front of her. It was now Sunday, the day after she'd met Wynter and, with the information he'd given her, she was about to initiate contact with Rex.

Glancing down at the corner of her laptop screen, she saw that it was the twenty-second of September today, which meant that the trial would be taking place in sixteen days' time. It wasn't far off and she was all too aware that time was quickly running out.

The trial would begin on the eighth of October with the opening statements from the prosecution and the defence, and then the prosecution would present its case at which point she would be called to the witness stand to give her evidence against Charlie Benvenuto. Rex would be doing everything in his power to prevent her appearing in that courtroom... unless she succeeded in stopping him. And she was praying that Wynter's information would help her to achieve this aim.

Following her visit to Ruby Red, Bailey had debriefed Stella on what she'd learnt from Wynter, pointing out that, for someone like Rex, email was a good communication option because unlike a mobile phone number, it was much harder to trace the user, and in the case of this particular email provider, almost impossible. That was because Rex was using ProtonMail – a Swiss-based email provider who was renowned for extremely high levels of privacy and security. It took just minutes to set up a free account without entering any kind of personal details, and they didn't keep IP logs of their users, which meant you could remain totally anonymous to them if you so wished. The data was stored in an encrypted format and held on servers located in an underground bunker in Switzerland. Swiss privacy laws were among the strictest in the world, and Switzerland conveniently lay outside of UK, US and EU jurisdiction which meant that there was virtually no possibility of the British authorities gaining access to users' data.

In order to make contact with Rex, Bailey herself had set up an anonymous email account with ProtonMail. She composed a fresh email addressed to:

sortmyproblem@protonmail.com

She entered 'problem' in the subject line, took a deep breath and hit 'Send'. The email went off into the ether.

It seemed very simple. Maybe too simple. But then maybe simple was best.

Now it was just a case of waiting for a response. Would Rex get back to her today? Tomorrow? Next week? She supposed there was always the possibility that he might not get back to her at all. The email seemed like such a slender link to him, but it was all she had and she just prayed that it yielded something before the eighth of October.

Taking a deep breath, she tried to quell the anxious thoughts by focusing on other things. She thought about her family and what a momentous year it had been on that front. It had only been a few months earlier that she'd finally discovered the fate of her older sister Jennifer who'd been abducted off the street as a child over twenty years earlier. The revelation had been truly earth-shattering, and Bailey was still coming to terms with it. And then, not long after that, her beloved father had passed away from cancer. Bailey had always been closer to her father than her mother and had felt his loss most keenly. But on the positive side she and her mother had both grown considerably closer as a result of his death. In the past Bailey had often got annoyed with how her mother incessantly harped on about religion and the way she was always pestering Bailey for grandchildren. But these days Bailey felt an increased sense of protectiveness and concern for her now that her husband was no longer there to keep her company.

Feeling a sudden pang of tenderness, Bailey picked up her phone and dialled her mother's number. It would be good to chat. And talking to other people was always a good way to get out of your own head.

Her mother answered the phone. 'Hello Bailey. It's so good to hear from you. It's a shame you weren't able to come round for lunch today though.'

Following Stella's portentous visit to her flat several days earlier, Bailey had sent her mother a brief text message cancelling their planned Sunday lunch date, which would have been today.

'Yes I'm sorry Mum,' she said, a tinge of guilt creeping over her. 'Something important came up at work and I've had to drop everything else. Anyhow, I thought I'd call just to see how you were.'

'I'm doing just fine Bailey,' her mother replied gently. 'In fact I couldn't be better. I've been doing a lot of work for The Friends recently. They are such a wonderful group of people.'

Ever since Bailey's father had died, Bailey's mother had been ploughing even more of her time into the voluntary work she did for the evangelical Protestant Christian group to which she belonged. They were called The Kindred Friends of Jesus. Not so long ago, Bailey had held particularly disparaging views on her mother's involvement with the group, seeing them as a bunch of cranks at best and a cult at worst. But now she was grateful for their supportive presence in her mother's life since her husband was no longer around.

'Howard really keeps me busy,' continued her mother. 'But then he works harder than all of us combined. He's such an inspiration.' Her voice rang with admiration.

Howard was the trendy young pastor who ran the Bromley chapter of The Kindred Friends of Jesus that Bailey's mother belonged to. Bailey had met him on several occasions when her mother had invited him round for tea.

'Well, so long as you're happy Mum,' she said, warmed by the comforting sound of her mother's voice on the other end of the phone.

Although Bailey would have liked to relieve the strain of her current situation by telling her mother some of the details about it, she knew her mother wouldn't really understand and would only become distressed. Bailey had always kept her parents well removed from her work, particularly from the undercover operations, and they'd only ever had the vaguest idea of what she got up to. It was for their own security and mental wellbeing as much as anything.

'Anyway,' her mother said, 'I'll pop round with a nice lemon drizzle cake that I've made for you.'

'Actually, Mum, I'm not in Crystal Palace at the moment. I'm away for work.'

Her mother tutted. 'You're always away for work, Bailey. Oh... well. I'll pop round anyway. I've got the spare key. I'll give the plants a water.'

A worrying thought suddenly occurred to Bailey. What with her current situation, her flat was potentially still a risky place to visit.

'Actually Mum, don't bother. I'm sure the plants will be fine.'

'Are you sure Bailey? Remember that time they all died because you forgot to water them before going away on one of your jobs?'

'The plants don't matter Mum.'

'Maybe you should buy a cactus instead. I hear they don't need as much water.' Her mother sighed. 'You always seem to be on the road Bailey. Don't you think it's time you settled down, met a nice young man and had some children? There's a dating ads section at the back of Keyways. Do you want me to put an ad in for you?'

Keyways was the name of the printed monthly gazette which was produced by The Kindred Friends of Jesus. It covered various theological issues and served to disseminate the group's ideas, and amongst other things featured a lonely hearts section at the back. One of the main things Bailey's mother did was to distribute Keyways door-to-door on behalf of the group.

'I think you'd be a marvellous catch for any young man,' she said.

Bailey sighed. 'Look Mum I don't have time for that now,' she said. 'I'm super busy.'

'That's part of the problem Bailey. That's why you never meet anyone.' She paused. 'I mean, where are you right now? Are you even in London?'

'I can't tell you Mum. Remember I told you I can't talk about the details of my job? The less you know the better.'

'Of course, I forgot. Sorry dear.'

'I just wanted to say...' Bailey wondered how best to phrase it without alarming her mother. 'I just wanted to warn you to beware of any strangers.'

'Strangers?' asked her mother. Her voice took on a sermonising tone. '"Do not neglect to show hospitality to strangers, for thereby some have entertained angels unawares."' She paused, her voice going back to normal. 'Hebrews, chapter thirteen, verse two.'

Bailey rolled her eyes. She might have known her mother would start quoting the Bible. She'd walked straight into that one.

Suddenly the sound of bagpipes cut through the air. Bailey looked up with a wince of irritation.

'Are those bagpipes?' asked her mother, sounding surprised.

'Yeah,' muttered Bailey. 'This bloody busker starts up first thing in the morning right outside my window, and he plays them all day long.'

'Are you in Scotland Bailey?'

'I can't tell you that information Mum. It's for your own safety.'

'If you are in Scotland, you should go to the Laphroaig distillery on Islay. Your father and I went there on our honeymoon and... and...'

Her voice faltered and started to break. She was still grieving her husband's passing. They'd been married for over thirty-five years.

Bailey heard her mother swallow hard. 'Do you know where I am right now Bailey?'

'No. Where are you Mum?' asked Bailey gently.

'I'm just visiting your father's grave. I've got some fresh flowers with me.'

Bailey recalled then that her mother paid a visit to her husband's grave every Sunday.

'Say a prayer for him on my behalf Mum.'

Although Bailey herself wasn't religious, she knew that asking her mother to do so would make her happy.

'Of course I will Bailey,' she said. 'And I'll say one for you too.'

Bailey nodded to herself ironically, reflecting that at the moment she needed all the prayers she could get.

14

Rex sat on a bench in Beckenham Cemetery in the shade of a large oak tree, the gravestones spread out all round him. He had to admit, he liked it here. It was an oasis of tranquillity in the busy city.

Around fifty metres away lay the headstone belonging to Bailey's father. It was a simple affair. Dark polished granite with a white inscription.

Rex had been staking it out for several hours now. It appeared that someone had been changing the flowers and he knew it would only be a matter of time before this person came round again. He was guessing it would be Bailey or Bailey's mother. Probably the latter given Bailey's current circumstances.

Sitting here waiting around wasn't exactly the most exciting of tasks, but in his profession patience was most important. As was persistence. He'd found that the two qualities often went hand in hand, and he possessed both in abundance which probably went some way to explaining his reputation for always finishing the job.

After visiting Bailey's flat and mulling over what he'd learnt there, he'd decided that her father's headstone would be a good next step in his pursuit of her.

Successfully following a trail was like putting together the pieces of a jigsaw puzzle, one which was spread out over time and space. A good memory was crucial in this respect as you had to be able to remember all the pieces you'd encountered in the past in order to be able to see if they matched up with any in the present. It was similar in many ways to the game of Solitaire that he liked to play, which was one of the reasons he played it.

The key was observation. Observe and remember. And that meant paying attention to detail and using all of your senses. Unlike most people, who let their senses atrophy, Rex lived in a state of heightened awareness.

And thus it was that he noticed the stooped elderly woman walking along the cemetery path towards Dennis Morgan's head-stone. Recalling the photographs in Bailey's flat, he recognised her almost immediately as Bailey's mother. She was holding a bunch of flowers in one hand, whilst her other hand was holding her mobile phone to her ear. Although the cemetery was very quiet she was a little too far away for Rex to make out what she was saying.

His gaze focused in on her like that of a predatory animal and his body imperceptibly tensed, ready to spring. She was small and bird-like and didn't bear much physical resemblance to Bailey, certainly not enough for him to have deduced that she was Bailey's mother if he hadn't seen the photographs of her.

He watched her finish her phone conversation and then kneel down by her husband's headstone to change the flowers.

Rex contemplated his options…

He could follow her home, break in, hold her hostage and then make her call Bailey under the pretence of inviting her round for a visit… at which point he'd kill Bailey, and her mother as well.

Scratching his head, he dismissed the idea. It was too risky. Bailey knew that she was being hunted, and if she smelt a trap, if she detected the slightest quiver of fear in her mother's voice, then she'd alert the police and then the tables would be turned and it would be Rex who'd be in trouble. He'd never liked the idea of kidnapping people anyway. It was too logistically complex and fraught with too many potential issues. His forte was killing people and he figured it was best to play to his strengths.

With that in mind, he supposed he could kill Bailey's mother right now. She didn't look like she'd present much of a challenge on that front. It would be easy to walk up to her and snap her neck like a dry twig. But what purpose would that serve? He couldn't see how it would bring him any closer to finding Bailey.

No. Bailey Morgan's mother would be much more useful alive. For the time being. And the most productive thing he could do was to have a nice innocent conversation with her.

From his position on the bench, he watched her finish changing the flowers and get to her feet. She stood there motionless at the graveside with her eyes closed. Peering at her more intently, Rex could see that her lips were moving. She was making some kind of utterance. A prayer perhaps.

After a minute or two she opened her eyes and turned to leave, trotting off back down the cemetery path the way she'd come.

Rex stood up and followed her.

15

Monday made for a frustrating day. Waiting around for a response to the email, Bailey found it hard to settle to anything. Although she'd only sent the email the day before, she was acutely aware that time was of the essence. She was almost a week into the operation and with every minute she waited here in this hotel room Rex drew that little bit closer to her.

Once again she tried to envisage him as a person, but even though they now possessed a physical description of him, she found it hard to formulate any idea of what he was really like. In her head he was still little more than an anonymous man-shaped void – a phantom killer with a superlative prowess in murder.

Towards the middle of the afternoon she received a text message from Emma.

Let's have dinner soon. Lots to catch up on ;) xx

Stuck alone in her hotel room, the idea of having dinner with Emma seemed more tempting than ever to Bailey as she debated with herself whether it might actually be beneficial for her mental health to catch up with her friend. However, she didn't feel like making a decision about it right now so she opted for a non-committal response:

Sure. Would love to see you. Will let you know xx

She'd been suffering from the nightmares again, although at least she now had the beta blockers to mitigate their effects. Her current isolation obviously didn't help, but then that was something that she was used to as an undercover operative. The isolation, coupled with the high-risk nature of the job and the necessity of maintaining a false identity, could often lead to serious mental health issues amongst undercover police officers. As such, they were monitored very closely and were required to attend regular appointments with a psychologist who was specially vetted to work with the police.

Bailey herself had an appointment with the psychologist coming up in just under two weeks, although given her current circumstances, she wondered if she'd have to cancel it. So saying, she'd missed the last two appointments already and if she missed this one as well then it could affect her future eligibility to deploy on undercover operations.

All in all, she wasn't feeling in the best state of mind at the moment, and she knew the longer she was trapped in this situation, the more her mental health would deteriorate, and the worse it got the less capable she would be of catching Rex. It was a vicious spiral downwards and it was something she had to try and avoid at all costs if she was to be in with any chance of succeeding... and surviving.

16

Rex paused by the entrance to the community hall in Bromley and examined the notice pinned to the door. It stated that The Kindred Friends of Jesus met there every Tuesday and Thursday at six o'clock in the evening.

Today was Tuesday and Rex had been covertly shadowing Bailey's mother ever since encountering her in the cemetery two days earlier, his endeavours eventually having brought him here to this community hall which he'd just observed her entering. Looking at the notice on the door and realising that this was some kind of religious meeting, it occurred to him that this could be the ideal opportunity to talk to her directly under a seemingly innocent guise.

Pushing open the door, he entered the hall. He was confronted by the sight of twenty or so people – men and women of varying ages – milling around, conversing cordially. A number of chairs had been set up to face a stage at the end of the hall on which there was a high stool and a microphone stand. To his right, next to the wall, was a folding table holding some plates of biscuits alongside a plastic stand displaying copies of a small magazine called Keyways.

Rex eyed the people in the hall with cold contempt. In his opinion religion was nothing more than a crutch for the weak.

A few heads turned in his direction shooting him looks of amiable curiosity. Almost immediately a man detached himself from one of the clusters of people and strode confidently over to Rex. Probably in his early thirties with a hipster beard, he was wearing slim-cut blue chinos, a baggy green cardigan and a pair of beige loafers.

'Hello. My name's Howard,' he said with a warm welcoming smile. 'I'm the pastor here. Welcome to The Kindred Friends of Jesus. Are you interested in joining our congregation?'

Rex affected a meek and slightly needy air. 'I... I'm looking for a bit of spiritual guidance.'

Howard's large brown eyes shone with compassionate zeal. 'Well I can tell you, you've certainly come to the right place.'

Rex smiled hesitantly. Howard beckoned for Rex to accompany him and they walked together side-by-side towards the rest of the group.

'We believe in the power of the Holy Spirit and the gifts that it endows us with,' explained Howard. 'We practise prayer to invoke the Holy Spirit in order to transform the world as we know it into the Kingdom of God on Earth. We're fighting a spiritual battle against the cosmic forces of darkness and we need as many people in our army as possible.'

Scanning the other people in the room, Rex soon spotted Bailey's mother. She was sitting on a chair by herself eating a biscuit. Rex veered away from Howard and sat down in an empty chair next to her. Howard looked round quizzically to see where Rex had gone. He changed direction to come over and join them.

'I'm glad you've decided to start socialising already.' he said. 'This is Janet. She's one of our long-time members.'

Bailey's mother smiled at Rex maternally. Both she and Howard waited with expectant expressions on their faces. Rex realised that they wanted him to introduce himself. He plucked a name randomly from thin air.

'I'm Eric,' he said.

They both beamed.

Janet Morgan offered him a plate of biscuits. 'Would you like a chocolate Hob-Nob, Eric?'

'Why thank you,' he said, taking one from the plate.

'I always prefer the dark chocolate ones,' she said conspiratorially. 'Don't you?'

Rex smiled as he munched on the biscuit. 'Indeed. The dark chocolate ones are by far the best.'

'I'll leave you in Janet's very capable hands,' said Howard with a benevolent smile, retreating to chat with some other members of the group.

Janet Morgan observed Rex enquiringly. 'Do you have any family Eric? A wife? Children?'

Although lying to her was simple enough, Rex found that her question perplexed him. That was because, like it or not, it made him think about the past, and whenever he tried to think too much about the past he was touched by that bewildering foggy state that always descended upon him when he did so. He tried to shake off the disconcerting feeling.

'No,' he said. 'I don't have a wife and I don't have any children. I don't have anybody. How about you?'

Her eyes lit up. 'I have a daughter. Her name's Bailey.'

'How wonderful,' said Rex. 'Do you see her often?'

Janet Morgan smiled broadly, manifestly pleased that someone was taking an interest in her daughter of whom she was so clearly proud.

'She's a police officer you know. Working to keep the streets safe and uphold the law.' Her face took on a dismayed cast. 'But she's so busy with work though. That's why she's single you see. If only she would meet a nice handsome young man and settle down.'

She eyed Rex hopefully. He got the impression she was sizing him up as a potential partner for Bailey.

'A police officer?' replied Rex. 'How fascinating. What kind of things does she get up to?'

Bailey's mother gave a wary glance over her shoulder then leaned in furtively.

'Well I can't really talk about it,' she whispered, 'it being secret police business and all, but I think she's in Scotland at the moment.'

Rex frowned to himself. Scotland? Could that really be possible? Was she lying low north of the border?

'She's not technically allowed to tell me where she is,' she continued. 'But the last time I was talking to her on the phone, there was a bagpiper playing right outside her window. A real bagpiper, not someone off the TV. And I put two and two together.'

She looked pleased at her powers of deduction. Rex gave her a congratulatory nod.

'I do miss her, you know.' She sighed wistfully. 'But I'm lucky enough to have a second family here.' She gestured round the hall at the other members of the group. 'That's why we have the word "Kindred" in our name. "Kindred" means "family". Because that's what we are – a family. If you have no one else Eric, we can be your family.'

Rex gazed round at the rest of the group. More of them were now paying attention to him, giving him welcoming smiles and glances. He saw one or two of the younger women looking at him admiringly.

Bailey's mother gave another longing sigh. 'I just wish my daughter would settle down and have some kids. More than anything else in my life I just want to see some grandchildren.'

Rex smiled coldly and nodded. 'Yes. Wouldn't that be nice?'

There was a loud electronic tapping noise. They all looked up. Howard was now sitting on the stool on the stage with a guitar propped across his knee. He was flicking the microphone with his finger to get their attention.

'Right everybody,' he said with a strum of the guitar. 'Let's start with our old favourite, "Kumbaya".'

17

Bailey was feeling increasingly skittish. Time was bearing down on her and still she'd heard nothing back from Rex. It was just after half past seven on Tuesday evening and she was lying on the bed in her hotel room watching EastEnders on BBC1 in a bid to try and distract herself from the anxious thoughts that were consuming her.

For what must have been the tenth time in as many minutes, she picked up her phone and again checked her ProtonMail inbox for any sign of a response from Rex.

There was a message from:

sortmyproblem@protonmail.com

She sat upright sharply. He must have sent it literally just now. With a tremor of nervous anticipation, she opened the email and began to read through it.

I will meet you at 2pm on Thursday 26th September by the Gandhi memorial in Tavistock Square, Bloomsbury, London.

Carry a bunch of white flowers with you.
I will ask you a question: Did you know that white flowers symbolise purity?
You will answer: Yes and they also symbolise death.
Please confirm your attendance

Bailey chewed her lip pensively, feeling a strange contradictory mix of relief on one hand at having finally made contact with Rex, and apprehension on the other at what it might entail next.

The instructions were clear enough. They brought to mind the world of espionage with its clandestine meetings and coded questions, and Bailey supposed that this kind of guile was more than appropriate for Rex's activities. The use of sign and countersign – the question and answer routine – was an old-fashioned but time-tested method of anonymously confirming identity between two individuals who'd never met before.

The email contained no enquiry as to the intended target, nor did it give any mention of fees, and she presumed that all those elements and any other information necessary to conduct a hit would be discussed following successful confirmation of identity.

She immediately replied to the email to confirm her attendance at the meeting.

There. It was done. A shiver of excitement went through her at the thought that she was now one step closer to catching Rex.

She immediately contacted Stella to update her on this latest development in the operation.

'That's excellent work,' said Stella breathlessly, barely able to conceal the elation in her voice. 'Thursday huh? That's the day after tomorrow. It's not much time but it's enough for us to put together a plan.'

'I just hope it will be Rex himself who turns up,' said Bailey. 'That's what I'm banking on.'

'Well at least we've got some idea what he looks like, thanks to your neighbour, so we'll know what to look out for.' Stella paused. 'Obviously though, it would be stupid to have you making the meet. He'd probably recognise you immediately and might even try and kill you there and then. We'll have another UCO in place.'

'Sure,' said Bailey. 'That makes sense. But I want to be present. Watching. Out of sight.'

'Of course,' said Stella. 'You more than anyone will want to see us take him down. You know, I have a good feeling about this Bailey. I think we're finally going to nail this bastard.'

They said their goodbyes and hung up. The call had ended on a high note and although Bailey felt thrilled at the prospect of Rex's imminent capture, her buoyant mood was tempered by an undercurrent of apprehension because she knew from experience that even the most straightforward of operations could go tits-up quite easily.

There was a knock on the door. Her train of thought broke and she looked up sharply.

Ever since she'd found out that Rex was hunting her, and especially following her near encounter with him at her Crystal Palace flat, Bailey's paranoia had been operating on overdrive. Staring at the door, she now wondered if he'd beat her to the mark and was now standing on the other side poised to kill her.

She stood up softly and padded over to the door. Unfortunately there was no spyhole in the door so she couldn't see who was on the other side. Breathing softly, she placed her head gently against it to listen.

'Who is it?' she asked.

A throaty female voice replied. 'Cleaner.'

Bailey relaxed a little as she remembered that earlier that evening she'd mentioned to the receptionist, Ravi, that the standards of cleanliness in her room, particularly the bathroom, left a lot to be desired. He must have instructed the cleaning lady to come up and sort it out.

She opened the door. Standing in the corridor was an over-weight elderly woman with a trolley full of cleaning products. Bailey had noticed her lumbering round the hotel corridors at various points during her stay.

'Come in,' said Bailey with a welcoming smile.

She stood aside to let the woman enter the room. Taking some cleaning spray and a sponge from the trolley, the cleaner waddled in, wheezing unhealthily as she did so. She reeked of stale cigarettes.

'Bathroom needs a clean, right?' she said hoarsely.

Standing in close proximity to her, Bailey could see that she had milky cataracts over her eyes. She was almost blind. That did at least explain the poor standard of cleaning.

'Well... uh... do your best,' said Bailey.

* * *

Later that Tuesday evening, after having returned from the meeting with The Kindred Friends of Jesus, Rex sat in the cabin of his cata-maran drinking a lemonade and contemplated what Janet Morgan had told him about her daughter.

Scotland. Was Bailey Morgan really in Scotland?

Some part of him instinctively rejected the idea. His intuition told him she was much closer than that. She was a Londoner. She felt at home in this city. It was a terrain she was familiar with. Going to some foreign place would only make her feel more vulnerable.

But how was he going to go about finding her? He felt like the trail was in danger of growing cold and that vexed him no end. He had just under two weeks within which to kill her and he was deter-mined to meet the deadline. It was a matter of pride more than anything. He'd never once failed to meet a client's requirements and he didn't see any reason why Bailey Morgan should present an exception to that.

He closed his eyes and tried to put himself in her shoes. The more Rex found out about her and the more he pursued her, the more able he was to get inside her head and predict her behaviour. It often got like this when he was hunting someone. He'd reach a tipping point where he'd be able to 'tune in' to his quarry and thus anticipate their next move.

It was some primal hunter's instinct, evolved over millennia, lying latent and forgotten in most people, but alive and functioning in those such as himself. The ancient hunters used to dress up as animals, wearing the skins and antlers, and perform ritualistic dances, all in the belief that it would help them get into the minds of the beasts they were hunting. In some of the books he owned, there were pictures of cave paintings depicting these rituals, daubed in ochre on the walls of rock shelters twenty thousand years ago. Rex wasn't about to dress up as Bailey Morgan and do a funny dance but he was certain now that he'd gained enough insight into her thinking to be confident that she was still in London which meant he would tailor his pursuit of her accordingly.

Pausing his thoughts, he tilted his head, his super-sensitive hearing recognising the familiar assertive rhythm of heels on the slatted wooden surface of the pontoon decking. A short while later, just as he expected, Milena appeared on the catamaran, letting herself into the cabin. Tossing her blonde hair, she took a seat on the sofa at right angles to him. She sat there silently scrutinising him for a few moments.

'There's a new job coming up.'

Rex raised one eyebrow. 'A new job?'

Milena nodded. 'I've set up a meeting for this Thursday. The sooner you wrap up the Bailey Morgan job,' she said, 'the sooner you can get on with this new job.'

'She'll be dead soon enough. I said I'd kill her by the eighth and I will.'

There was a brief hiatus in the conversation. Rex took a sip of his lemonade while Milena studied him in that curious way of hers.

'Rex...' she murmured. 'Tall, dark and mysterious.'

He gazed coolly at her, placing his can of lemonade back on the table with a faint clink. She was teasing him, as she liked to do every so often. It usually indicated that she was in a good mood. And that usually coincided with the prospect of a new job and the thought of all that forthcoming cash.

'Women like mysterious men,' she continued. 'But I know your secret...'

She winked at him and tapped the side of her nose. He frowned to himself. She'd mentioned his 'secret' before, and quite what she was referring to he had no idea. He chalked it down to the fact that she was a woman, and they weren't really very logical creatures at the end of the day.

'I have no idea what you're talking about Milena,' he muttered.

'Just like you have no idea where we first met,' she said, with a taunting smile.

That was another thing she liked to tease him about – she knew that however hard he tried, he was never able to recall the occasion of their first meeting. Considering that he was so good at playing Concentration, it confounded him that he couldn't remember such a significant encounter, for there was no question that Milena had subsequently gone on to play a critically important role in his life.

'You always bring that up,' he said. 'And you know I'm never able to tell you.'

'Maybe one of these days you'll remember,' she said. 'And when you do I'll buy you a drink as a reward.' She eyed the lemonade. 'Oh yeah… you don't drink, do you?'

It was true. He was completely teetotal. He couldn't quite recall when he'd decided to quit alcohol, or if he'd even ever drunk it at all. He just knew that sticking to lemonade kept him in full control of his faculties at all times. And that was perhaps the one thing he regarded as more important than anything – staying in control.

18

Bailey peered anxiously through the binoculars at Tavistock Square. It was ten minutes to two on Thursday afternoon.

Tavistock Square was a serene tree-lined public park in the middle of Bloomsbury in central London. Bloomsbury was the cultural and intellectual heart of London and it was where the University of London and the British Museum were based.

Being late September, the leaves on the trees had changed colour, giving the park a distinct autumnal feel. There were a few people walking round and several others dotted about on benches, but by and large it wasn't very busy at all. Relatively secluded, quite spacious and not very crowded, Bailey could see why this particular park made a good location for a meeting. So far though, she hadn't spotted anyone who looked like they could be Rex.

She was standing alongside Stella in a small room on the second floor of a university halls of residence which stood on one side of the square giving them a direct line of sight to the Gandhi statue which sat right in the centre of the park. It was one of several observation points that had been set up discreetly early that morning in various locations round the square.

Both of them were dressed in plainclothes – jeans, T-shirts and trainers – supplemented with black Kevlar bulletproof vests and police-issue chequered baseball caps. Stella, additionally, had a Glock nine-millimetre pistol strapped to her hip.

Bailey herself wasn't equipped with a firearm. She'd never really been that keen on guns and had never undergone the necessary training to learn how to use one. When it came to undercover work, which was all about deception and infiltration, carrying a gun just wasn't necessary and that suited her just fine.

'Seems kind of ironic doesn't it?' she muttered.

'What's that?' murmured Stella, scanning the park intently through her binoculars.

'A hitman wanting to meet next to a statue of the most famous proponent of non-violence in history.'

Stella grimaced. 'Yeah but wasn't Gandhi assassinated by someone at close range?'

'That's a good point,' conceded Bailey. She felt a further twist of the tension in her guts as she continued scanning the park.

It seemed unbelievable that they were already in the arrest phase of the operation only a week after it had started. Things had moved fast and the very idea that they might actually succeed in apprehending Rex today almost seemed too good to be true. But Bailey wasn't going to count her chickens just yet...

She'd spent much of the previous day planning the arrest with the operational team in a temporary covert HQ that had been set up in an anonymous suite of offices a few blocks away. The various teams involved had been briefed that the target could be armed and should be considered extremely dangerous. A photo-fit of Rex had been distributed; the physical description had been provided by Bailey's neighbour, Alastair, and had been supplemented by the hitman's apparent resemblance to the stand-up comedian Toby Freeman. The photo-fit wasn't great but it would have to suffice.

The emphasis had been on the scar on Rex's right eyebrow as a means of positive identification.

From a logistical standpoint, a number of different teams were engaged in the operation. There was a surveillance team observing from various vantage points and there was an arrest team which included armed officers from a tactical firearms unit in an unmarked Mercedes Sprinter van. In addition to that, police marksman were in place on nearby rooftops, and there were armed plainclothes officers sitting in three unmarked cars – a Vauxhall Insignia VXR, a BMW X5 and a Skoda Octavia – parked at strategic points in Tavistock Square. She knew that there was also a police surveillance helicopter on standby. When planning the arrest, they'd had to take into special consideration the security of the general public because the meeting point was in a public space. They'd had to cut a fine balance between having manpower close enough to safely detain Rex, but not positioned so prominently as to prematurely alert him to their presence.

'Senior management are very excited,' said Stella. She'd briefed them the previous day as to the date and location of the arrest. 'There's a lot riding on this.'

Bailey could see that Stella was already anticipating the inevitable commendations that would come with a successful take-down. Her innate ambition had come to the fore and she was clearly itching for a conclusive outcome today, her foot tapping impatiently as she observed the park. Holding her binoculars in one hand, she clutched a two-way radio in the other, poised to give the appropriate command. Stella, heading up the operational team, was the one who was ultimately responsible for calling the strike.

Bailey peered through her binoculars at the UCO who'd volunteered for the task. He was muscular and thuggish-looking with a shaven head, his tattooed forearms bursting out of a Stone Island T-shirt. To his credit he couldn't have looked less like a police officer, although he did look a little awkward holding the bunch of white flowers. His primary role in the operation was to identify the target and give the appropriate signal for Stella to order the arrest team into action.

He was hovering furtively next to the Gandhi statue. The stone pedestal beneath the memorial possessed a cavity in which people had deposited various floral tributes so Bailey guessed it didn't look too odd for him to be hanging around carrying flowers in the vicinity. And she supposed that, given the setting, the question and answer routine wouldn't have sounded particularly odd to anyone who happened to be overhearing the conversation.

'I hope he remembers to answer the question correctly,' she said.

Bailey had drilled him repeatedly during the briefing the previous day.

'It was pretty simple,' said Stella. 'I think he should be able to manage it.'

As soon as the verbal exchange was complete, the plan was for the UCO to drop the flowers on the ground as the signal they'd pre-agreed in the briefing the day before. At this prompt Stella would instruct the arrest team to make the swoop and apprehend Rex... if indeed it was Rex himself who turned up today. They were all desperately hoping so, Bailey more so than any of them.

Glancing at her watch she saw it was five minutes to two. She swallowed nervously, her throat suddenly parched. The tension was killing her. She just wanted it to be over and done with. She scanned the park for the umpteenth time. A family of tourists meandering about taking photographs. Two academic types sitting on a bench eating sandwiches and conversing. A smartly dressed blonde woman trotting along by herself. A homeless man shuffling around with a green sleeping bag draped over his shoulders. Not

many people. And no sign of anyone who might resemble
Rex... yet.

The UCO was the only police officer within the park itself.
Because it was a relatively uncrowded environment, and not a
particularly large place, they'd decided that any supplementary
police presence might look obvious, particularly to a pro like Rex.
At any rate, each of the exits from the park were well covered and
if Rex did turn up and then try and make a run for it, Bailey
doubted he'd get very far, given the manpower ranged against
him.

She just hoped that the van and the cars themselves weren't too
conspicuous. Given the fact that Rex had successfully evaded
surveillance when breaking into her flat, she had to contemplate
the possibility that he had a knack for spotting unmarked police
vehicles.

The sky was overcast and there was a muggy electric feel to the
air. Bailey could sense that a rainstorm was imminent. In fact, if she
wasn't mistaken, a few droplets had started to fall already.

'Do you see the man on the bench?' hissed Stella. 'Just to the
right of the memorial. He just sat down. He entered the park just a
minute ago.'

Bailey swung the binoculars round sharply to focus in on a lone
man sitting on a bench about ten metres away from the memorial.
He more or less fitted the photo-fit description of Rex. Clean-
shaven, with dark hair, probably in his late thirties, he had a pale
angular complexion which was currently set in a blank almost
vacant expression.

She swallowed and squinted hard through the binoculars.
'Could be...' she murmured. 'I can't quite make out if he has a scar
on his eyebrow or not. He's a bit too far away.'

The UCO must have been thinking along similar lines as he was
now peering at the man on the bench as well.

'Stop looking at him,' hissed Bailey, trying to telepathically communicate with the UCO. 'Wait for him to approach you.'

The UCO wasn't wearing an earpiece as that would have been obvious to anyone approaching him. But that also meant that Bailey was unable to talk to him directly.

Although the various teams had been given Rex's description, Bailey knew from experience that this kind of pre-knowledge could sometimes be detrimental to an undercover operation if UCOs displayed recognition of the target before they were supposed to.

Given the significant and highly dangerous nature of this particular target, Bailey knew that everyone in the operation was especially on edge and therefore prone to jumping the gun if they weren't careful. She prayed they wouldn't for this was too good an opportunity to mess up.

The man on the bench was now looking disconcertedly at the UCO. He seemed to have realised something was up.

'Shit,' muttered Stella. 'Do you think we've spooked him?'

The UCO moved a little closer to him, the bunch of white flowers in his hand. The man on the bench fidgeted uncomfortably. Then he stood up abruptly.

The UCO stopped in his steps, his eyes flickering uncertainly up to the observation point occupied by Bailey and Stella.

The man started to walk away, in the direction of the east exit on the far side of the park.

'Fuck!' hissed Stella. 'He's getting away.'

'Wait,' urged Bailey. 'We don't know for sure that it's Rex.'

The UCO began to walk after the man. The man looked over his shoulder at the UCO and began to walk a little faster. The UCO upped his pace correspondingly. The man glanced back once more and broke into a brisk trot. He was now only a few metres from the exit.

At that point, the UCO dropped the flowers onto the ground.

Stella's eyes widened. 'Go! Go! Go!' she shouted into her two-way radio.

Tavistock Square suddenly erupted into activity.

The back doors of the Mercedes Sprinter burst open and armed police poured forth, clad in black, wearing helmets and Kevlar body armour, equipped with Heckler and Koch MP5 submachine guns and Glock nine-millimetre pistols. They raced into the park, their movements highly coordinated as they convened upon their target.

With the screech of a siren the unmarked BMW X5 appeared out of nowhere to skid to a halt in front of the exit that the man was heading for. The two plainclothes officers inside leapt out, brandishing their firearms.

The few members of the public in the park were looking round wildly, alarmed and bewildered by what was going on.

Bailey bit her lip in trepidation as she watched the chaos unfold. The plan had gone out the window and all she could do was hope and pray that they were chasing the right man.

On seeing the BMW blocking the east exit of the park, the man hastily switched direction, veering sharply towards the south exit. The UCO took up the pursuit in full, pelting after him. Throwing a panicked look over his shoulder, the man didn't see the pretty blonde woman who'd been walking casually through the park a short while earlier. He barrelled into her, knocking her to the ground. Bailey winced at the sight of an innocent member of the public getting hurt.

Recovering his balance, the man dashed towards the south exit, pursued by a cohort of heavily armed police, several plainclothes officers, as well as the UCO who was leading the charge.

The unmarked Vauxhall Insignia drove up onto the pavement to block the south exit of the park. The man hesitated for a fraction of a second... just enough time for the UCO to catch up with him and rugby-tackle him to the ground. Moments later the two of them were overwhelmed by the arrest team.

Bailey heard the distinct shout. 'Armed police! Don't move!'

'I think we've got him,' said Stella triumphantly.

Bailey gulped, her mouth dry. She hoped so. Leaving the observation point, they both sprinted down to the foyer of the building.

'You should stay out of sight,' said Stella, gesturing Bailey back with her hand. 'Just in case.'

Bailey hung back reluctantly in the foyer. 'I need to see him,' she shouted after Stella. Even though she'd never encountered Rex before, she knew in her gut that when she met him she'd know if it was him or not.

Peering out impatiently through the windows of the foyer, she watched Stella march over to the large cluster of armed police in the park. It was starting to rain a little more noticeably now, large droplets splatting down on the pavement outside.

She observed apprehensively as the man was escorted out of the park surrounded by an array of police officers. His hands were cuffed behind his back and he was stumbling along with a wide-eyed expression on his face. His mouth was moving in evident protestation at his predicament.

Bailey approached him as soon as he'd been brought into the foyer of the building.

'I asked you what the hell is going on?!' he was demanding in a loud voice. 'Why can't someone tell me what the hell is going on?!'

Standing next to him, Stella was examining a small rectangular piece of plastic.

'Your student ID says your name is Philip Riddenfell,' said Stella. 'It says you work in the Computer Science Department of UCL. Is that correct?'

'Of course it's bloody correct!' he spluttered. 'That's what it says, doesn't it? I'm a post-doctoral student at UCL. I specialise in machine learning. Now can you please tell me why you've arrested me?'

Stella handed the ID card to one of the plainclothes officers. 'Can we verify this?'

Bailey pushed through the crowd of police officers to get an up-close look at the man. Studying his right eyebrow, she couldn't see any evidence of any kind of scar. The man stopped complaining for a moment to regard her with an angry frown. By now Rex would have a good idea of what she looked like, if he had seen the photos in her flat, and if so there would surely have been some glimmer of recognition in his eyes. But all she saw in this man's face was a look of indignant bewilderment.

'It's not him,' said Bailey, sagging a little in disappointment. 'There's no scar on the eyebrow.'

The man stared at her like she was crazy. 'I'm not who?' he demanded. 'Who am I supposed to be? Why have you arrested me?'

Bailey turned to Stella, pulling her aside. 'We should have waited. We blew it. We acted too soon.'

Stella gritted her teeth in exasperation. 'Fuck!' she muttered. 'I guess we were just a bit too twitchy.'

She turned back sharply to the man. 'Why were you running away?' she asked brusquely.

'That man with the flowers kept staring at me. So I got up to sit somewhere else. Then I saw him walking after me, so I thought I'd just leave. And the faster I walked, the faster he walked, and then when I ran, he ran, and then suddenly there were all these police everywhere pointing guns at me. I can't understand what's going on. I was just sitting in the park trying to relax on my lunch break. I'll never be able to go there again now knowing if the police could jump on me at any minute!'

Bailey sighed. It had all been a horrible misunderstanding. The whole thing had turned into a shitshow. She turned to look out through the windows of the foyer at the rain falling down on the aftermath of the operation in Tavistock Square. If Rex had been anywhere in the vicinity then he surely knew by now that this had been a trap.

With an abrupt chill, she wondered if he was still hanging around close by observing events from some concealed location. She drew back from the window a little, suddenly feeling vulnerable despite the heavy armed police presence round her.

Gazing through the window, Bailey noticed the blonde woman who'd been knocked over in the commotion. She was now standing up, holding her wrist, wandering round the park looking a bit disoriented. She was clearly injured and somehow she'd been overlooked.

Bailey glanced over to Stella. She was standing with the thuggish-looking UCO, talking to him in low tones with a stern look on her face, presumably berating him for being a bit too gung-ho in his actions. He was bearing a somewhat rueful expression.

Raising her hand, Bailey hailed her attention. 'Stella, look. There's that woman who got knocked over in all the ruckus. It looks like she might be injured. She needs help. We should bring her in here out of the rain.'

Stella broke off from her conversation with the UCO to look out of the window where Bailey was pointing. She nodded and went over to explain to some nearby police officers who went outside and guided the blonde woman out of the park and into the foyer, sitting her down on a seat to one side. Feeling somewhat responsible for what had happened, Bailey walked over to her.

The woman, probably in her early thirties, had a sharp pretty face and was dressed in a stylish black trouser suit with Dior heels and a Prada handbag looped over her left shoulder.

'Are you okay?' asked Bailey gently. The woman did look a bit peaky.

The blonde woman looked up at her with a wince of pain. 'I think I might have broken my wrist.' She had a distinct East European accent.

'I'm really sorry you got caught up in everything,' said Bailey. She tenderly took the woman's wrist in one hand and did her best to examine it with the basic medical training that she had. 'I think it might just be a strain,' she said. 'But we'll get a paramedic to have a look at it.' She turned round to address her colleagues milling around in the foyer. 'Why are the paramedics taking so long?' she demanded.

She turned her attention back to the woman to see that the woman was studying her intently. She had a strange sly look on her face. The look evaporated almost instantly, to be replaced by an innocent expression of concern.

'What was going on out there?' she asked. 'It all happened so suddenly.'

'You don't want to know,' muttered Bailey.

'You're very kind,' said the blonde woman. 'What's your name?'

'Bailey.'

The blonde woman nodded slowly with the infinitesimal flicker of that odd look. She looked at the watch that was strapped to her uninjured wrist. It was a fancy gold Tissot. 'You know, I'm late for a meeting. I have to go.'

'What about your wrist?' asked Bailey. 'Don't you want the paramedics to have a look at it?'

'I think I'll be fine. Like you say, hopefully it's just a strain.'

'Make sure you get it looked at,' said Bailey. 'Check that it's not a hairline fracture or something.'

The woman nodded impatiently. She suddenly seemed in quite a hurry to leave.

Frowning to herself, Bailey watched the blonde woman stand up and walk out of the foyer and out of sight. Something about the encounter had slightly perturbed her but she couldn't quite put her finger on what it was. Chalking it up to her recent state of stress, she shook her head and dismissed it from her mind.

Milena scurried along the pavement away from the crowds of police. Her wrist hurt like hell and the rain was ruining her hair but those were the least of her concerns at the moment.

On reaching the end of the road, she turned the corner so that she was out of view of the police. She stopped and took a deep breath to calm her racing heart.

That had been a close call. A very close call. But there was no time to lose.

She glanced round surreptitiously. There wasn't anyone in the close vicinity. Taking her phone out of her Prada handbag, she dialled Rex's number.

'It was a trap,' she hissed.

'What do you mean?' he asked.

'Bailey Morgan is here right now. The whole thing was a set-up. I guess they were expecting you to turn up, rather than me. I was just about to approach this guy who was holding the flowers when suddenly all these police appeared out of nowhere. They jumped on the wrong guy. I think they thought he was you. There were loads of them. They had guns and everything.'

'You said Bailey Morgan was there,' said Rex, a tone of urgency in his voice.

'I saw her. I talked to her. She's got the scar on her face, just like you said. She's still here. You need to get here now, before she goes.'

'Stay there. Stay on her. I'll be there shortly.'

* * *

Rex terminated the call and took a second to ponder the news. Despite the alarming ramifications of what Milena had told him, he felt pleasantly vindicated in his notions as to Bailey Morgan's whereabouts. It had at least confirmed that he wasn't required to make what would have turned out to be a fruitless trip to Scotland. All he had to do now was get to Tavistock Square in time to catch up with her.

Standing up in his catamaran, he strode into one of the cabins, knelt down and levered off one of the wall panels to reveal the secret cavity that had been used by the previous owner to carry illicit merchandise. He reached in and took out a shoulder holster containing a Sig Sauer P320 Compact – it was a lightweight nine-millimetre semi-automatic pistol with a stubby four-inch barrel that made it an ideal concealed-carry weapon. When it came to weapons, Rex had contacts who could supply him with just about anything he needed.

He hurriedly pulled on the shoulder holster. Then, drawing out the gun, he drew the slide back with a click to load a round into the chamber and then re-holstered it. Replacing the wall panel, he then turned to one of the storage units. Opening it up, he took out a crash helmet with a tinted visor and a black leather motorcycle jacket. He pulled on the jacket and zipped it up. Clutching the crash helmet, he rapidly made his way out onto the deck and vaulted onto the pontoon, sprinting along it to the dockside, where he headed out of the marina into a side street where he kept his motorbike.

It was an 1100cc Ducati Streetfighter – a high-performance motorbike with a muscular chassis, bright red livery and a grey frame. Leaping astride the bike, he pulled on his crash helmet and started the ignition. He revved the powerful engine and it growled aggressively. He flicked up the bike's kickstand and took off at speed down the road, leaving a smear of burnt rubber behind him.

* * *

Standing in the foyer, Bailey watched as they took the handcuffs off the man they'd mistakenly detained in the belief that he was Rex.

His student ID had checked out. The Computer Science Department was located on Gower Street just a short distance away from Tavistock Square and unless Dr Philip Riddenfell led a double life as a top-level contract killer, it looked like he was off the hook.

'I hope he doesn't try and sue us,' muttered Stella, eyeing him with a chary expression.

'I feel sorry for him,' said Bailey. 'It sounds like he's been going through a bit of a hard time lately.'

Dr Riddenfell had explained to them that he'd recently been undergoing therapy for anxiety and depression, and that he was prone to mood swings and paranoia, which was why he'd got agitated by the UCO looking at him.

'I'm not looking forward to debriefing senior management on this cock-up,' said Stella, looking somewhat deflated. 'I was so sure we were going to bag Rex.'

Bailey sighed glumly. 'Back to square one I guess.'

Stella lifted one eyebrow. 'So does that mean you still want to help us catch him?'

Bailey snorted. 'I'm not going to quit just because things loused up today.'

'People told me you were the stubborn type,' said Stella, smiling. 'I guess they weren't wrong there.'

'The situation hasn't changed. Rex is still out to kill me. And we still want to catch him. I'm sure there must be some other way to find him. I just have to work it out before the eighth of October. That gives me just twelve days.'

The news that Bailey was still committed to the job at hand seemed to put a bit of bounce back into Stella's step.

'Are you going to be okay getting back to your hotel?' she asked.

Bailey glanced out of the window of the foyer, noticing that the rain appeared to have eased off a little. 'I'm sure I'll be fine. If Rex was here to begin with, it'll have become pretty apparent to him right away that this was a trap, and so I imagine he's disappeared by now.'

Telling Stella that she'd be sure to stay in touch regarding her next moves, Bailey made to depart. Pausing for a moment in the front entrance of the building, she scanned Tavistock Square one last time for anyone who might potentially be Rex. She reassured herself that at least she didn't much resemble a copper any more, having swapped the police-issue baseball cap and Kevlar bullet-proof vest for her own *de rigeur* casual outfit of LA Dodgers baseball cap and suede-fringed cowboy jacket.

Deciding that the coast looked clear, she pulled the Dodgers cap down low over her face, and slipped quietly out of the front entrance of the building, making her way rapidly out of Tavistock Square to a neighbouring street two blocks away where she'd parked her car.

She was just opening the door of the car when she noticed the blonde woman standing on the other side of the road around thirty metres away. The woman was chatting on her mobile phone. Their eyes met for a moment. Bailey attempted a small smile, but the woman didn't smile back, too engaged in conversation it seemed.

Bailey shrugged it off, unconcerned, and idly wondered if the woman had already finished her business meeting, and if she would actually end up bothering to get her wrist looked at.

Getting into her car, Bailey started the engine and pulled away from the kerb, heading off in the direction of Earl's Court.

* * *

Rex arrived in Bloomsbury twenty minutes after Milena had called him. He'd made good time on the bike. It had cut through the traffic like a knife through butter.

Milena's voice addressed him through the hands-free Bluetooth headset fitted inside his crash helmet.

'It's a silver Audi A4,' she said. 'She's leaving right now. From Herbrand Street.'

Manoeuvring the bike through the narrow streets of Bloomsbury, Rex spotted Milena standing on the pavement with her phone clamped to her ear looking somewhat bedraggled, her hair hanging in lank strands down her face.

Ahead of him, he saw the silver Audi at the end of the road, indicating to the right, just about to disappear round the corner. Immediately memorising the Audi's license plate number, he twisted the throttle and gunned the bike forwards, determined not to lose sight of his prey.

* * *

The windscreen wipers twitched back and forth as the raindrops pattered down. The gloomy weather mirrored Bailey's mood as she reflected on the botched operation in Tavistock Square. It had been a disappointing turnout, no doubt about that.

Steering the car through Russell Square onto Montague Street, Bailey reached down to the stereo system to put some music on in an attempt to lift her mood.

A few moments later, the song 'Rio' by Duran Duran was pounding out of the car's speakers. Bailey had been a fan of eighties pop ever since she could remember, and recently, before this current problem with Rex had arisen, she'd been reassessing Duran Duran's back catalogue. She'd been pleasantly surprised to find that some of their lesser-known, later work was actually pretty good, most notably their 1997 album 'Medazzaland'. But ultimately she knew that nothing they'd done could ever match their 1981 album 'Rio' with its awesome title track of the same name. In her opinion every single track on that album was perfect and that was the reason she went back to it again and again.

Drumming her fingers on the steering wheel, and singing along to the song, she drove along Shaftesbury Avenue. Down to Piccadilly Circus onto Haymarket, turning onto Pall Mall...

The traffic wasn't too bad for a Thursday afternoon. It was getting towards four o'clock and rush hour hadn't yet hit.

She glanced in the rear-view mirror, registering a motorbike about two cars behind her. The rider was wearing a black leather motorcycle jacket and a helmet with a tinted visor. She realised with a faint whiff of consternation that he'd been there since leaving Bloomsbury. Was he something to be concerned about? Or was she just on edge?

Keeping half an eye on him whilst still singing along absently to the music, she turned off Pall Mall onto St James's Street, turning left at the top onto Piccadilly, going past Green Park and then Hyde Park Corner, and on into Knightsbridge.

The traffic lights ahead of her turned red just as she was passing Harrods. Bringing the car to a halt, she looked out at the expensive designer clothes and accessories that were displayed in the windows of the famous department store. On a detective constable's salary most of them were items she could only dream about owning unless she wanted to get herself into debt.

The 'Rio' album had now reached the track 'Hungry Like the Wolf'. Tapping her fingers on the steering wheel in time to the music, Bailey was singing along to the lyrics when she became aware of a heavy rumbling noise close by. Turning to her right, she saw with a jolt that the bike that she'd noticed behind her on Pall

Mall was now positioned right next to her driver's side window, the powerful engine idling as the rider waited for the lights to change.

She looked up at him, feeling slightly unnerved. The dark tinted visor meant that she couldn't see his face. He slowly swivelled his head to look down at her. Droplets of rain studded the surface of the visor. When she looked into it, all she could see was a convex black reflection of the side of her car. An icy shiver went through her. Even though she couldn't see his eyes she got the feeling he was looking right into hers.

Swallowing nervously, she tried to suppress the sudden fear that had gripped her. Was he more than he seemed or was she just imagining it? Was that actually Rex behind that visor or was she just projecting her fears onto the blank slate of this sinister-looking but totally innocent motorbike rider? Either way, she was acutely aware of just how vulnerable she was right now sitting here in her car stuck in the traffic.

A horn hooted behind her. She blinked and turned her attention back to the road to see that the lights had gone green.

Rex pulled up right next to Bailey's silver Audi just outside Harrods. He glanced down at her through the side window of the car to see that she was looking the other way, over to her left. She was drumming her fingers on the steering wheel and if he wasn't mistaken she appeared to be singing along to something. She turned her head to look up at him, and he saw the scar on her face. It was definitely her – the woman he'd been paid very handsomely to murder.

For a moment their gazes locked, although he knew she couldn't see his face through the tinted visor. She looked scared, a bit like the proverbial rabbit caught in the headlights, and that made him feel good. It made him feel powerful.

He contemplated shooting her right there and then. The lights were red and she was stationary in the traffic. She was a sitting duck. He felt the tempting weight of the loaded gun nestled in the shoulder holster beneath his left arm. His fingers were itching to pull it out and empty several bullets into her head and finish the job for good right now.

It wouldn't be the first time he'd killed someone in Knightsbridge. A year and a half earlier he'd killed a drug dealer not far from this very spot. Blown his brains out with a sawn-off shotgun whilst the guy was sitting in his open-topped sports car... at a red light. The client had specified something messy and public for that particular job. Rex had used a motorbike for that one as well. But that had been a stolen vehicle which he'd subsequently ditched. The Ducati, however, was his own bike, and he *never* used his own vehicle to carry out a hit. It was one of his primary rules of operation.

No. It would be unwise to shoot her right now. Better that he tailed her to wherever she was living... and then he'd be able to dispatch her at his leisure. That would be much better. That would be much cleaner.

The lights turned green. There was the hoot of a horn behind. She sped forwards with a rev of her engine and he continued onwards after her. He fell back a little in the traffic though, deciding that he didn't want to alert her suspicions. His intention was to get her exactly where he wanted before he killed her.

* * *

Bailey drove tensely along Cromwell Road, her eyes flitting nervously between the rear-view mirror and the wing-mirror, trying to ascertain if the bike was still behind her. But he now seemed to have disappeared. Maybe he'd turned off somewhere.

Perhaps he hadn't been anything to get alarmed about. Still, he'd put the wind up her.

She tried to assuage her jitters, reflecting that on a major thoroughfare like this in a big city like London there were so many vehicles going in the same direction that any one of them could be following her and she wouldn't know it.

But that said, she was now in the vicinity of Earl's Court, and she figured that this close to her hotel it would be a wise idea to take a few precautions just to be on the safe side. As an undercover police officer, her training had included a module on vehicle-based counter-surveillance manoeuvres, and she now decided to put those learnings into practice.

She noted a large lorry in front of her on the dual carriageway. Assessing the road ahead, she saw that there was a turn-off to the left approaching fast. Moving out into the right-hand lane, she put her foot down, accelerating rapidly ahead to overtake the lorry. She cut back sharply into the left-hand lane, the lorry momentarily obscuring her from the vision of anyone who might be following her. Almost immediately she pulled off rapidly to the left into the turn-off she'd spotted just a few moments earlier.

Barely reducing her speed, she zipped down the small street, putting some distance between herself and the road she'd just been on. She gradually slowed down, moving through the quiet side streets of Earl's Court. If anyone was following her she'd be able to spot them more easily in the sparser traffic.

Looking in her rear-view mirror she couldn't see any sign of the motorbike, or of anyone else who might be following her. But she wasn't done yet.

She indicated left, then suddenly pulled a sharp right instead, turning down yet another quiet side street. Then from there, she did three consecutive right turns which brought her straight back to where she'd just been. She knew it would have made no sense for anyone else to have made that kind of manoeuvre unless they were quite definitely trying to follow her.

Once again examining the street behind her, she was satisfied at last that there was no one on her tail.

Maybe she had just been imagining it. Still, better safe than sorry.

She proceeded on towards her hotel.

* * *

Watching her from several car lengths back, Rex saw the silver Audi pull out to overtake a large lorry. For a brief moment his view of her car was blocked by it.

Cursing softly to himself, he twisted the throttle to push the bike ahead, keen not to lose sight of her for even just a second. Speeding along the right-hand lane of the dual carriageway, he rapidly caught up with the lorry, riding past it...

...and saw that the Audi was no longer there.

He swore aloud, realising that she must have pulled off sharply to the left during the short window in which she'd been out of his line of sight. He sensed that she'd done it deliberately to throw a tail. It was just the kind of thing an undercover copper would do. Maybe she'd got suspicious of him after all...

Circling back at the first opportunity, he turned off into the maze of side streets that she'd entered. But he knew it was too late to find her. She was gone. He'd lost her.

He ground his teeth in anger. Fuck.

19

Evening had fallen over St Katharine Docks and the rain had now stopped. The bars and restaurants lining the marina were busy with outdoor trade in the unusually balmy night, the tables on the dockside abuzz with conversation accompanied by the clink of glasses and cutlery.

Rex and Milena sat on one of the tables outside eating dinner. The restaurant was one of Rex's favourites and he was enjoying a large steak, nice and bloody, as was his preference. Milena – wearing an elasticated support bandage on her wrist – was having a chicken salad.

It had only been a few hours since the abortive meeting at Tavistock Square and Milena was still agitated about it so Rex had bought her dinner as compensation... paid for in cash of course. He only ever used cash.

'It's a shame you lost her,' said Milena. 'It sounded like you were really close.'

'She gave me the slip on Cromwell Road,' he said. 'Earl's Court. I drove round the area for a bit but I didn't have any luck.'

'Earl's Court?' asked Milena. 'Do you think that's where she's living? Lots of cheap hotels round there.'

Rex shrugged. 'She might be. It's hard to know for sure. She could be anywhere in London.'

'I reckon she was behind that whole police trap in Tavistock Square. The fact that she was there in person proves it. It worries me that she knows how we operate. That email address is compromised for one thing. I'll have to create a new one.' She shook her head in frustration. 'I can't believe how close I got to getting busted.' She massaged her bandaged wrist. 'How do you think the police found out about us?'

'Word-of-mouth I guess. It's what happens when you do your job too well Milena.'

For once he was teasing her. Her brittle expression started to crumble as she began to relax a little. She grudgingly allowed a small smile to creep across her face.

'I guess she's hunting you Rex. Just like you're hunting her.'

Rex tilted his head thoughtfully. 'Have you heard of a famous hunter called Jim Corbett?'

Milena shook her head.

Rex continued. 'He used to hunt man-eating tigers in India back in the 1920s. In his memoirs, he talked about how one time he was tracking this tiger, following its trail through the jungle. The tiger's trail took him back to his own tracks and that was when he realised that the tiger was actually stalking him rather than the other way round.'

Milena's eyes widened. 'So what happened?'

'He still managed to kill it.'

She frowned. 'So you're saying you're not worried that she's making an active effort to try and catch you?'

'I wouldn't expect anything else from a police officer, especially an undercover police officer. It's in her blood. And a leopard doesn't change its spots that easily.' He smiled at his use of a big-game analogy. 'Anyhow all it means is that the closer she gets to me, the closer I get to her.'

Milena regarded him admiringly. 'I'm glad you're so confident.'

'And if it does all go wrong,' he said, 'I have certain contingency plans in place.'

'What contingency plans?'

'I'll scuttle the boat for one thing.'

'"Scuttle"?' asked Milena quizzically. 'I do not know this word.'

Although Milena's English vocabulary was generally excellent, unfamiliar words would occasionally arise during their conversations and she'd insist on Rex explaining them to her.

'"Scuttle"?' said Rex. 'It means to deliberately sink a boat.'

Milena looked shocked. 'Why on earth would you deliberately want to sink a beautiful boat like that?'

'I like to be prepared for all eventualities.'

* * *

It was Thursday night and Bailey was sitting on the bed in her hotel room watching TV although she wasn't really concentrating on it as her mind was on other things, most notably the botched operation in Tavistock Square that had taken place earlier that day.

She had been staking so much on the operation and she felt both dismayed and frustrated that it had failed. Reflecting on what steps to take next, she doubted that repeating the same tactic again would work. All the furore in the park and the subsequent police presence would surely have alerted Rex to the fact that they were onto him and that his contact email address was now compromised. Anyhow, she knew Stella wouldn't dare risk the wrath of senior management by trying the same thing again, only for the operation to fail once more.

No. She had to think of some other way to locate Rex, but the problem was that she had no idea what to do. In terms of progress, she was right back at the very beginning, but now with substantially less time to find a solution, for there were only twelve days left until the trial. Twelve days for Rex to kill her. Twelve days to catch him. Twelve days to stay alive.

Her iPhone pinged on the bedside table. Picking it up, she saw that it was a message from Emma. It was the second text message Emma had sent her following their phone conversation the previous week. Once again Emma was badgering her to come over for dinner.

How's next Wednesday for dinner and drinkies? xx

Bailey smiled and shook her head at her friend's persistence. Given that there was a ruthless hitman hunting her, Bailey still felt reticent about the idea of accepting social invitations. Anyhow, there was the distinct possibility that she might not even be alive next Wednesday. But on the other hand... the thought of some decent home-cooked food was a very tempting proposition to Bailey for the restaurants near the hotel left a lot to be desired. And she did crave a good chat, even if she knew Emma would be pestering her about Anthony. The more she thought about it, the more she came round to the idea that having a bit of social contact with her friend would stop her from spiralling completely into a nosedive of paranoia and gloom.

She tapped in a response to Emma's message:

Okay let's do it! xx

The phone pinged a few moments later with Emma's response.

Yaay!! 8pm?

Bailey responded:

Perfect xx

Bailey's smile grew. She could tell Emma was delighted and she was pleased to have made her friend happy. She imagined that Emma was already starting to plan the menu.

Turning her attention to the TV, she idly flicked through the channels trying to find something entertaining to watch.

She found her interest piqued as she came across one that was showing back-to-back re-runs of the comedy improvisation show that her neighbour Alastair had mentioned – the one featuring the stand-up comedian Toby Freeman.

She observed the TV show with a droll expression on her face. The host provided the panellists with various scenarios round which they had to build improvisation routines. She supposed it was fairly amusing although it wasn't making her laugh out loud or anything. She'd never really been that into improvisation comedy, although she reflected that it wasn't a million miles away from undercover work with its emphasis on being able to think on your feet.

It appeared that Toby Freeman was a regular panellist on the show. He seemed to specialise in a particularly acerbic type of humour full of nasty put-downs directed at fellow panellists, the host and just about anyone else he could think of.

Staring at the TV, a crazy thought then occurred to her. What if Rex and Toby Freeman were one and the same person? A comedian moonlighting as a hitman... or a hitman moonlighting as a comedian. It wasn't necessarily the most far-fetched of ideas – she'd seen the film *Confessions of a Dangerous Mind*, based on the autobiography of the TV host Chuck Barris who'd claimed that he worked on the side as an assassin for the CIA.

Her neighbour Alastair had said that Rex was slimmer than the comedian, and had a stronger jaw, but then she knew that people often looked different on TV than they did in real life. Peering closer at the TV, she tried to make out if the comedian possessed a small scar on his right eyebrow, as Alastair had described Rex as having, but she was unable to make out if he had one or not – it was hard to see for sure on TV, and in any case make-up could quite easily have concealed it.

What she really needed to do was see him up close, meet him in person. Then she'd know for sure. Plugging his name into Google, she soon found a list of his upcoming comedy gigs.

Picking up her phone, she called Stella and explained her latest theory.

'The stand-up comedian?' said Stella, sounding highly dubious. 'I think you're scraping the bottom of the barrel here. I know you're keen to catch Rex. So am I. But don't you think you're getting kind of desperate?'

'Have you seen *Confessions of a Dangerous Mind*?' asked Bailey, undeterred.

'That's fiction Bailey. I know it's supposed to be true but—'

'I'm going to check out one of his gigs,' interrupted Bailey. 'There's one in Wimbledon tomorrow night. If he does turn out to be Rex, I doubt he'll try and kill me in the middle of a room full of people. And if it is him then I'll let you know immediately, so it would be good if you're on hand to take my call.'

Stella let out a long sceptical exhalation. 'Okay,' she said reluctantly. 'I'll be on hand. Just don't take any unnecessary risks though.'

20

Bailey sat in the shadows at the end of the bar sipping a vodka blackcurrant, the alcohol helping to take the edge off the grim truth that there were now fewer than eleven days left until the trial commenced. Time was passing worryingly quickly, and with each day that went by, she could sense Rex drawing inexorably closer to her. They were pitted in a race against each other with her life as the prize... and she was just hoping that he wasn't in the lead.

It was Friday night and the room was packed with people who'd turned up for the weekly comedy night that this particular pub in Wimbledon was famous for.

She'd sat through two acts already and was now waiting for the compère to finish his short interlude and introduce Toby Freeman who was advertised as being third on the bill.

Once again, it occurred to her that coming here was probably a bit of a last resort, but seeing as she had no other leads to go on in terms of resolving her situation, it seemed like a better option than stewing in her hotel room doing nothing.

She'd made a point of sitting right at the back of the crowd, well out of the line of fire. Experience had taught her never to sit in the front row when you went to a stand-up comedy gig unless you didn't mind the performers picking on you.

With a flourish of his arm, the compère welcomed Toby Freeman onto the stage. Dressed smartly in a silver-grey suit that caught the spotlight, he swaggered forward, grasped the microphone confidently and launched into his routine. Leaning forward on her bar stool, Bailey strained to look for a scar on his right eyebrow but from where she was sitting she couldn't see any evidence of one.

He had a pretty slick delivery and was the most professional of the acts she'd seen so far. He mercilessly laid into the people in the front row, picking on one couple in particular – the girl had a longish face and slightly protruding teeth and Freeman was telling her male companion that she looked like a horse and was asking him if he'd rode in on her this evening. The audience was cracking up but the girl looked like she was about to cry and the man himself looked very uneasy.

'Where are you going for dinner after this?' Toby asked. 'Somewhere that serves oats presumably.'

Even though she didn't want to, Bailey found herself laughing along with the rest of the audience at his cruel humour. Once again she contemplated the possibility that he might be moonlighting as a hitman. He clearly possessed quite a mean and ruthless streak, but did that mean he was capable of killing people?

He finished his set to uproarious applause. Bailey noticed the couple he'd been picking on leave. The girl was in tears. Bailey felt sorry for her. As someone with a physical disfigurement, Bailey sympathised with anyone who got flak because of how they looked. She wondered what Toby would have said to her had she been sitting in the front row.

Bailey observed him as he melted into the shadows to re-emerge moments later at the bar just a few metres away from where she was sitting. He bought a drink, positioned himself on a bar stool and turned to watch the next set.

Bailey's cap was pulled down low over her face and Toby didn't seem to have registered her.

Nudging her stool out of the shadows, she edged along the bar a little closer towards him in order to get a better look at his right eyebrow. At this proximity she could see that he didn't possess a scar. He wasn't the same man who Alastair had encountered at her flat. Toby Freeman wasn't Rex.

Bailey felt somewhat relieved but she also felt a little disappointed that this whole Toby Freeman thing had turned out to be a red herring. Still, at least it had got her out of that grotty hotel for the evening.

He casually glanced at her. Then he stood up from his stool and sidled along to her, a faint smirk on his face. She guessed he thought she was trying to pick him up.

'What's your name?' he asked. 'Guess you already know mine.'

'Bailey,' she said, trying to be polite. There wasn't much point in hanging around here any longer and she didn't see any particular need or have any particular desire to talk to him.

She turned away from him to finish her drink and leave. He adopted an aggrieved expression.

'Wait a minute. First you give me the eye and then you give me the cold shoulder.'

'Thought you were someone else,' she muttered.

'Well, people often mistake me for my better-looking brother,' he said jokingly.

A strange tingle went through Bailey. She turned back to face him. He looked at her hopefully.

'Your brother?' she asked. 'Does he have a small scar on his right eyebrow?'

Toby frowned. 'Yeah. How did you know that?'

She felt a cold chill of realisation. Toby Freeman's brother was Rex.

'Your brother,' she said carefully. 'What's his name?'

'His name was Carl. Why?'

'His name was Carl Freeman?'

He nodded, looking slightly baffled.

Bailey memorised the name. She then frowned, registering that he'd used the past tense. 'You said "was".'

'He's been dead for three years.' Toby paused. 'He was murdered. Died in the line of duty.'

'What do you mean he died in the line of duty?' she asked, the shocking implications already beginning to dawn on her.

'He was a copper,' said Toby. 'He was an undercover copper.'

21

Her head reeling at what she'd just been told, Bailey stumbled out of the pub leaving a mystified-looking Toby behind her at the bar. Fumbling her phone from her pocket, she called Stella's number, her fingers shaking with excitement.

Stella picked up immediately. 'So are you going to tell me it *is* the comedian?'

'No,' said Bailey breathlessly. 'It's a bit more serious than that.'

'What are you talking about?' said Stella, her voice a mixture of puzzlement and concern.

Bailey took a deep breath. 'I think that Rex is a police officer. An undercover police officer. Or at least he used to be.'

'What?!' gasped Stella.

Bailey recounted the details of her conversation with Toby Freeman, glancing round furtively and keeping her voice low to ensure that the smokers hanging round outside the pub weren't overhearing what she was saying.

'The only thing is, Toby says that his brother is dead, that he's been dead for *three years*. Carl Freeman fits the description of Rex, and we know that Rex is very much alive. So that must mean that Carl Freeman is still alive.'

'Wow,' said Stella after a short, stunned silence. 'That's quite a lot to take on board.' She paused a moment. 'Carl Freeman. Hmm. The name rings a bell. I do recall hearing about his death at the time. He was well-regarded, quite highly decorated. I think he was a detective sergeant. I believe he was actually murdered whilst on an undercover operation, although I don't know the specifics of it as I wasn't working on anything undercover-related at that time.'

'I can't believe I haven't heard about this,' said Bailey. 'If he was an undercover cop who died on a deployment, surely I would have known about it.' And then she snapped her fingers as she realised just why she hadn't heard about it. 'Of course...' she muttered to herself.

Three years ago Bailey had been heavily immersed in a deep cover deployment with a gang of professional car thieves. But then her cover had got blown and she'd been horribly tortured. As a result, she'd ended up spending over nine months off work. She'd been totally out of the loop during that whole period, trying to recover from a serious trauma. The whole Carl Freeman thing had completely passed her by.

'Did you know him?' asked Stella. 'As a fellow UCO? Had you ever met him before?'

'No, I've never even heard of him,' said Bailey. 'But then you know how it is with undercover work. It's all part-time. You volunteer for a deployment, it's all kept top-secret and then it finishes and you go back to your regular job. I guess I never got round to encountering him because I was never directly deployed on an operation with him.'

'That makes sense,' said Stella.

'Do you have access to a computer right now?' asked Bailey.

'Can you check the details of the job that Carl Freeman was working on when he died?'

'Sure. Just a minute. I'll pull up the logs and the DMR.'

The policy/decision logs detailed the operational objectives for an undercover operation, while the DMR, or Deployment Management Record, contained information on the operation's briefing and debriefing process. Bailey knew that Stella would also be looking at any UCO notes that would have been submitted by Carl Freeman during the course of the deployment; these UCO notes, along with any covert recordings, would have functioned as evidence in subsequent court proceedings.

Bailey paced up and down impatiently outside the pub, her phone clamped to her ear, awaiting Stella's response. Although it was now late September, it was a muggy evening and there were a fair few people milling around nearby clutching drinks, smoking and chatting to each other. Bailey moved away from them further down the pavement where it was quieter. On the other end of the phone she could faintly hear the sounds of Stella's fingers skittering over her computer keyboard.

'Well, well,' said Stella after what seemed like a long pause. 'This is very interesting. Very interesting indeed.'

'What?' demanded Bailey. 'Interesting? What do you mean?'

'The objective of Carl Freeman's last operation was to charge Jack Wynter with conspiracy to murder.'

Bailey raised her eyebrows in surprise. 'Jack Wynter?'

'The one and same individual who you were talking to just last week.'

'Conspiracy to murder?' Bailey frowned to herself, trying to work it out in her head. 'In what capacity was Carl Freeman approaching Jack Wynter?'

There was a disbelieving snort from Stella. 'You're going to like this. Carl Freeman was posing as a hitman.'

Bailey's breath caught in her throat. 'A *hitman*?' she whispered. 'You're joking.'

Her mind raced frenetically. Things seemed to be coming together fast now. In his final undercover operation Carl Freeman had been pretending to be a hitman in order to charge Jack Wynter with conspiracy to murder. But then he'd died and somehow come back to life as an actual genuine hitman... the notorious Rex no less.

'Something very strange is going on here,' said Bailey.

'You're telling me,' said Stella. 'But this documentation is pretty thin. There's not a lot in here. I guess that's because the operation was aborted when Carl Freeman died. If you want to find out more details about it, I'd advise talking to the COM-UC who was running the operation. Detective Inspector Frank Grinham. I believe you know him well.'

Bailey allowed herself a small ironic smile. She'd been meaning to catch up with Frank for a while. Now she had more reason than ever to see her former undercover covert operations manager.

'It's high time I paid Frank a visit,' she said. 'I'll go to his house first thing tomorrow.'

'Just one thing Bailey,' added Stella, a note of caution in her voice. 'If Rex is indeed a former undercover police officer, then you realise that this adds a whole new dimension to everything. We need to be really sure about this before telling senior management. If you think that Rex really is Carl Freeman then you need to build a solid case for it. This is no small thing to be telling top brass, especially given how importantly they're taking this current operation to apprehend Rex. It could change its entire direction.'

Bailey knew that Stella was covering her own back for if she went out on a limb and dropped a bombshell like this on senior management only for it to turn out to be baseless, then she would look pretty stupid, and it certainly wouldn't do her career prospects much good.

'Don't worry,' said Bailey, knowing how seriously Stella took her career. 'I'll make sure I'm a hundred per cent on it. Or as close as...'

22

Detective Inspector Frank Grinham offered Bailey a pretzel from the bowl in front of him.

'Don't mind if I do,' she said, taking one and popping it into her mouth.

'They're sour cream and chives flavour,' he said. 'I highly recommend them.'

Bailey munched on the pretzel. It tasted pretty good. She scrutinised her former undercover covert operations manager.

'I think you might have put on a bit of weight Frank. All this sitting around at home eating snacks.'

Frank, in his late forties with greying red hair, had definitely developed a bit of a paunch since the last time Bailey had seen him. He'd been at home convalescing for the past six months or so, recuperating from gunshot injuries sustained during the course of one of Bailey's recent undercover operations.

That Saturday morning Bailey had driven up to the small semi-detached house where Frank lived in Enfield in North-East London and they were now sitting in his living room.

'It's good to see you Bailey,' he said. 'I'm getting a bit stir crazy sitting here at home watching TV and eating crap.'

'I miss you too Frank,' she replied, feeling a warm rush of affection for him. 'It's not the same without you.'

'You're reporting to Detective Inspector Stella Gates now, aren't you?' he said, rubbing his chin thoughtfully.

Bailey nodded. 'I've done one operation with her so far. She seems very capable. But I haven't totally made up my mind about her yet.'

'I hear she's the ambitious sort,' he remarked with a faint tone of disapproval. 'I imagine she'll probably end up as Commissioner one day.'

'How's Isabel?' asked Bailey.

Isabel was Frank's five-year-old daughter, custody of whom he shared with his ex-wife. During the events that had seen Frank seriously wounded, Isabel herself had come perilously close to being killed, and only Bailey's intervention had prevented that from happening.

'She's getting on well,' nodded Frank. 'No signs of mental trauma. As yet.'

'That's good to hear,' said Bailey. 'Let's hope it stays that way.'

Frank picked up a pretzel, pausing to study Bailey briefly with his watery blue eyes.

'So what brings you here then Bailey? Job talk? Or is it just a social visit? I sense it's more than that. You seem... agitated.'

She deliberated for a few moments. 'There's a contract out on me Frank.'

His eyes bulged. He dropped the pretzel he'd been holding back into the bowl.

'Jesus, Bailey,' he muttered. 'That's not good news.'

'Tell me about it,' she said. 'And to make it worse, the hitman out to fulfil the contract is none other than Rex.'

'*Rex?* That psycho?!' Frank's look of concern grew even more pronounced. 'Shit. That's even worse news. Shouldn't you be in a safe house somewhere?'

Bailey explained the nature of the operation that she was currently deployed on. Frank listened attentively, nodding intermittently as she laid out the progress of the operation so far. By the time she'd finished, he was sitting there looking slightly ashen as he digested what she'd told him.

'This truly does beggar belief,' he murmured. '...that Rex is actually Detective Sergeant Carl Freeman.' He paused pensively. 'But I can see now how it might be possible.'

'How?' demanded Bailey. 'That's what I don't understand. Carl Freeman is supposed to be dead, isn't he?'

'It wasn't quite that simple,' said Frank. 'Carl Freeman didn't die exactly. He went missing.'

'*Missing?*' murmured Bailey. 'Now that changes everything...'

'Let me explain what happened,' said Frank. 'We'd had word from an informant that a gangster called Jack Wynter wanted to kill his business partner, a bloke called Vincent Peck who was himself a villain. As you know, Wynter runs a strip club called Ruby Red. He basically wanted to get rid of Peck so he could take control of the club.

'We thought we could get Wynter for conspiracy to murder. So with the help of the informant, we introduced Carl Freeman to Wynter as the solution to his problem – a ruthless underworld hitman who would happily dispatch Peck.

'It started off promisingly enough. Carl attended a preliminary meeting, set up by the informant, where he was introduced to Wynter. He was wired up and recording everything. At that stage though, Wynter didn't say anything incriminating enough for us to be able to charge him. I think at that point he just wanted to get the measure of Carl and to establish Carl's fees. And it seemed that

Carl impressed him, as Wynter subsequently contacted him and told him to come to a second meeting where he would lay out the exact details of the hit, the name of the target, the location and so on, and that was also where he'd pay him. A professional hitman would insist on being paid upfront, which was how Carl played it in the first meeting. The details of the target along with the payment for the hit were exactly what we needed in order to nab Wynter.'

'So what went wrong?' asked Bailey.

Frank sighed. 'Well that's it. We don't really know. Carl went off to this second meeting by himself and never came back. He literally disappeared right off the face of the earth. They never found his body. Nothing. We presumed he'd made some kind of slip-up, or his cover had somehow got blown, and he'd been murdered by Wynter, or associates of his. Gangland being what it is, if someone disappears suddenly like that, you tend not to hold out much hope of ever seeing them alive again. Body secretly disposed of. Dissolved in acid. Fed to pigs. Thrown down a well. Encased in concrete.

'We did our best to try and find out what happened to him. But there wasn't much to go on. We found his car abandoned in a side street in Wapping in the vicinity of Tower Bridge, close to St Katharine Docks. We checked CCTV but there wasn't any coverage on those particular streets, but we did make sure to scour footage from cameras all across the area... and we couldn't see any sign of him. But then it was night-time and on that particular evening it was raining quite hard which didn't help with visibility. Plus there was a good chance he could have changed his appearance for the purposes of his cover role, which meant we could quite easily have missed him.'

'How about his phone?' asked Bailey.

'He was using some pay-as-you-go disposable burner for the job, as was his habit. We didn't know what the number was so we couldn't track it or access the call logs. The phone itself was never recovered. As is normal practice, he'd left his regular phone at home along with his wallet, warrant card and anything else relating to his real identity.'

'So what happened next?' she asked.

'Well, much as we tried, we weren't able to pin it on Wynter. To all intents and purposes we thought he'd got away with killing Carl. Then, later, when we subsequently heard that Peck had been murdered, we assumed that Wynter had found some other hitman to do the job. But at no point did we consider the possibility that Carl might have gone rogue, faked his death and actually gone ahead and done the hit on Peck.'

'Well, that's what it looks like,' said Bailey. 'Rex first appears on the scene at exactly the point that Carl Freeman goes missing. It looks like Rex killed Peck and it looks like Carl Freeman is Rex.'

'Now you mention it,' murmured Frank, his eyes widening in realisation, 'it's kind of been staring us in the face all this time.'

'What do you mean?' asked Bailey with a puzzled frown.

'For this operation, Carl Freeman was using the cover name of Carl King. For this particular job we didn't deem it necessary to run up any supporting identity documents. For a job like this with only one or two meetings, it wouldn't have been worth it, plus hitmen are supposed to remain relatively anonymous anyhow. I mean, I can't imagine he would have even used his full cover name. He would have used a nickname. And it just so happens that—'

Bailey snapped her fingers. '"Rex" is Latin for "king", isn't it? Carl *King*. King. Rex. The nickname is a play on his cover name.'

Frank nodded slowly with a smile. 'You were always good at word games Bailey. Must be all those cryptic crosswords you do. I guess Carl liked to play with words as well.'

Frank pensively stroked his greying red moustache, an expression of disquiet on his face.

'What is it?' asked Bailey.

'I simply can't believe that Carl Freeman just caved in for the money and actually did the hit.'

'How much was Carl supposed to get paid for the hit on Peck?' asked Bailey.

'I think he was planning to charge Wynter around fifty grand or so. From Wynter's perspective, that would have been a bargain considering how much he was going to make from taking control of the strip club business.' He paused and frowned. 'But would that really have been enough for Carl to fake his death and leave a family behind?'

'He's got a family?'

'A wife and young son.' Frank paused. 'He never struck me as the type to go rogue. He was a real straight arrow. Highly decorated. Very experienced.' He sighed. 'But then who knows? Sometimes you think you know someone, and there's a whole other side to their personality. A dark side they've been concealing for years.'

Bailey chewed her lip. 'Do you think maybe he'd been harbouring long-term resentments, been planning to jump ship for a while? After all, we know that working for the police isn't a perfect job. And there are many temptations the underworld can offer. And like they say, everyone has their price.'

Bailey knew all too well that working undercover exposed you directly to the lure of the criminal lifestyle – the wads of money, the fancy restaurants, the designer clothes, the flash cars. It was easy to be seduced by it, particularly when you hung round all day with criminals, letting their twisted morality leach into your own psyche until your standards came to resemble theirs. In some ways you had to let them into your head for how else could you survive and be authentic in that environment without some kind of empathy towards their way of thinking. It was a corrosive world to work in and one that could very well have eaten away at

Carl Freeman on the inside without him realising until it was too late.

Well,' said Frank. 'With the skillset that he had, Carl Freeman was very well placed to pivot into working as a high-level hitman. Did you know that he was a top marksman? He won a whole load of shooting trophies. And what with his knowledge of how the police operate, he would have been in a very advantageous position to commit murders and evade detection. And as an experienced undercover cop, he would have been expert in concealing his existence.' He raised one eyebrow. 'And what's more, police officers are not required to submit their DNA so his DNA isn't going to be on the Police National Database, so there was never any way of matching him to all those unsolved hits.'

Bailey was finding herself increasingly intrigued by Carl Freeman. At the beginning Rex had been nothing more than a prolific, shadowy killer, but now she was starting to get an idea of the man lurking behind the notorious reputation. She knew that the more she understood him as an individual, the better her chances of tracking him down... and the better her overall chances of survival.

'What was your experience of him as a person?' she asked. 'You probably knew him better than most people. I never met him myself. Up until yesterday, I'd never even heard of him.'

'It's a shame you never met him,' said Frank. 'You probably could have learnt a few things from him. He was very good at his job. Extremely conscientious. Very serious. Intense to the point that you sometimes felt uncomfortable round him. He was very fastidious about his cover story and would go to great lengths to build up his "legend". He would make a huge effort to get into character just like those method actors who really get into their roles. You know, like Robert De Niro in *Raging Bull* where he put on an extra sixty pounds for the role and got really good at boxing.'

'Haven't seen it,' said Bailey.

'You've never seen *Raging Bull*?' said Frank, looking a bit shocked.

'I'm more of a *Rocky* fan myself.'

Frank shrugged. 'Well, anyway, Carl once told me he used to read books by Stanislavski, the guru of method acting. He would get into the mind-set where he would literally become the role. I actually found it quite unnerving when I encountered him like that. It was like he'd totally transformed into his cover identity.'

Bailey knew how crucial it was to project total belief when it came to your cover story. Crooks had a nasty habit of being able to smell if anything was off in even the slightest way. The tiniest chink of self-doubt could spell doom for an operation and pose a very real risk to the physical well-being of the undercover operative.

Frank continued. 'For the Wynter job, Carl was posing as a ruthless hitman. A stone-cold psychopath. He was developing him as a really nasty character, the kind of individual who would stop at nothing to achieve his ends. I mean, after all, that's what he'd have to be if he was to be authentic in that deployment. Knowing Carl, he would have really immersed himself in that way of thinking.' Frank sighed grimly. 'But in this case, it looks like rather than acting a role, Carl was rehearsing for the real thing.'

23

Charlie Benvenuto closed the kitchen door behind him and walked out into the large back garden which lay behind his sumptuous mock Tudor house. It was autumn now, right at the end of September, and the leaves on the trees were turning red and brown, but Charlie wasn't able to appreciate the picturesque scenery because his head was too full of anxious thoughts about his upcoming trial.

The eighth of October was looming large in his mind as the date when he was due to appear in the dock. On that first day he would hear the prosecution and the defence deliver their opening statements. The prosecution would then present its case where they would call on the undercover cop to anonymously give her evidence against him, and where his lawyers would have the chance to cross-examine her. Then, following that, his lawyers would present the defence case, calling on him to testify on his own behalf in order to present his side of the story. Knowing how weak his legal position was, he wasn't looking forward to being cross-examined by the prosecution, but his solicitors had advised him that if he chose not to testify then it might make him look even guiltier in the eyes of the jury. Either way, he was gripped by the horrible feeling that they would be delivering a guilty verdict against him anyway. He'd thought about engaging in some form of jury intimidation but had then dismissed the idea as being too tricky to arrange – there were just too many factors and too many people to consider. Better to just focus on hiring a hitman to kill the key witness in order to sink the trial altogether.

Glancing over his shoulder, he saw his wife looking at him through the kitchen window. He threw her a forced smile and continued on his way, moving out of her sight round the corner of a large laurel hedge, heading in the direction of the wooden arbour seat at the end of the garden. He liked the arbour seat because its secluded location made it an ideal place to conduct private conversations, particularly those of an illicit nature, without danger of anyone overhearing.

He stopped for a moment next to an old beech tree. Scanning his surroundings, he was fairly confident that no one was observing him. The closest neighbours lived some distance away and their house didn't overlook his garden. He furtively squeezed his hand into a knothole in the tree trunk and withdrew a zip-lock plastic bag containing a mobile phone.

The police had taken away his regular mobile phone when they'd arrested him so that they could examine its contents for possible evidence to use against him. They still had it in their possession and it looked likely that they would retain it until after the trial was concluded. In the meantime he'd been using Amy's phone to communicate with his lawyers, and although he was pretty certain the police wouldn't be tapping that, he kept this simple unregistered burner phone hidden inside the tree trunk for the purposes of conducting conversations that were overtly criminal in nature... like the one he was about to conduct right now.

Clutching the phone in his hand, he proceeded onwards down

the garden path to the little alcove where the arbour seat was and sat down beneath its trellis. The trellis was covered with Japanese wisteria, the leaves of which were now turning an autumnal yellow. Switching on the mobile phone, he dialled the telephone number that the blonde woman had given him. He drummed his fingers impatiently on the wooden seat and waited for her to answer.

After he'd given her the hundred and fifty thousand pounds to hire Rex, the blonde woman had supplied him with a contact number, probably a burner phone much like the one he was holding in his hand right now. She hadn't told him her name and he hadn't asked. And as for Rex, Charlie hadn't met him or even talked to him. The blonde woman appeared to be the sole conduit of communication between the hitman and anyone who wanted to hire him. Although Charlie knew it was safer to keep contact with them to a minimum, it was getting uncomfortably close to the trial date, and he wanted to know if they were any closer to completing the task he'd paid them for.

A female voice answered the phone. 'Hello.'

He recognised the blonde woman's East European accent immediately.

'It's me,' he said. 'I'm calling for an update. It's the twenty-ninth of September today. The trial is on the eighth of October. That's nine days' time. I've paid you a hundred and fifty grand and the job's only half done. If the undercover policewoman testifies then I'm done for. She needs to be dead by the eighth. That was what we agreed, remember?'

Charlie knew that a refund was out of the question if they didn't succeed. It just didn't work like that when it came to this kind of thing. You paid upfront and took your chances. His fate was in their hands completely.

'It's okay. Relax,' purred the blonde woman soothingly. 'The undercover policewoman will be dead by the eighth. I guarantee it.

Rex always completes the job. You hired the best and that's what you'll get.'

Charlie felt slightly mollified by her reassurance, but not much.

'All right,' he grunted. 'If you say so. I'll call back later this week for another status update.'

'Sounds great,' she said. 'Look forward to talking to you soon.'

He was about to terminate the call when a thought suddenly occurred to him.

'Oh, wait a minute,' he said.

'Yes?'

'Did you ever find out her real name by the way?'

'Why yes,' said the blonde woman. 'Yes we did. Her name is Bailey Morgan. Detective Constable Bailey Morgan.'

'Detective Constable Bailey Morgan...' murmured Charlie, rolling the name around his mouth with distaste. At least he knew her real name now, and that made him feel a little bit more in control.

24

Milena ended the call and placed the phone down on the table in the cabin of the catamaran.

'He's getting impatient,' she said with a warning tone.

Rex studied the game of Solitaire he'd been playing. 'I'm working on it,' he muttered.

'You've got nine days to kill her,' she said. 'Your brand depends on it.'

He looked up at her with a raised eyebrow. 'My brand?'

'Your reputation. When a client signs up to your service they have a certain degree of expectation. And I want to make sure we meet that expectation.'

'I'll kill Bailey Morgan one way or another. You don't need to worry about that.'

Milena tilted her head philosophically. 'You know, when I used to work in Sales my job title was Client Success Director. That's how you should think of me.'

Rex gave a dubious smile. 'As my Client Success Director?'

Milena rolled her eyes as if he was missing something obvious. 'It's all about customer relationship management, see? Like this.'

She gestured at the cheap burner phone she'd just been talking on. 'The client even has his own dedicated phone line to talk to me on. I'll dispose of this when the job is over. Like I always do.'

Brand. Service. Client success director. Customer relationship management. It all sounded like marketing gobbledygook to Rex.

He must have looked sceptical because Milena gave a weary sigh. 'Look,' she said, 'you stick to your job and I'll stick to mine.'

Rex shrugged and turned his attention back to the game of Solitaire. Now where was he...? He'd come to the conclusion that playing Concentration was akin to Zen meditation. It completely engaged his conscious mind whilst allowing his subconscious mind the freedom to whir away in the background coming up with solutions to problems... like what his next move should be in regard to Bailey Morgan.

He was a bit stuck on that front. Bailey Morgan's mother had proved to be of little use in terms of locating Bailey and Rex knew he needed to find another means by which to pick up her trail. But what should this new angle be? He had no idea. A sense of urgency pressed in on him, exacerbated by Milena's call with the client just now. Knowing full well that the passage of time typically degraded the quality of the spoor, Rex knew the longer he sat here doing nothing the colder Bailey's trail would become.

'Solitaire is a very unsociable game,' remarked Milena. 'I suppose the clue's in the name. Did you learn to play it at school because you didn't have any friends?'

Rex looked up from the cards to see her observing him with a mischievous twinkle in her eye. She was teasing him again. He didn't respond.

'Don't remember?' she said. 'For someone who's so good at a card game based on memory, you don't have a very good one.'

Quite annoyingly, she was spot on, and she knew it. It was true – he couldn't remember if he'd had any friends at school because he couldn't remember going to school. When he tried to think back that far, he just found himself once again floundering in the opaque fog of the past. He ground his teeth in frustration. She stared at him, bemused, almost as if she was fascinated by the position he was in.

'Ahh... poor Rex,' she murmured, feigning sympathy. 'No friends eh? I'll be your friend. In fact, I already am your friend. Your only friend.'

She was right about that too. In terms of the people Rex knew, Milena was the closest thing to a friend that he had.

The talk of friendship suddenly caused something to click in Rex's mind. An impasse had been broken.

A friend.

That was the new angle by which he could pursue Bailey.

He thought back to his recent visit to Bailey's flat. There had been an answerphone message from a woman called Emma. She'd sounded like a good friend of Bailey's. What was that old saying...?

'A friend in need is a friend indeed,' he uttered to himself.

Bailey was certainly in need. But had she been desperate enough to confide her whereabouts to this friend Emma?

'What's that?' asked Milena quizzically.

'Nothing,' he murmured, with a crafty smile on his face.

25

With just nine days left until she was due to appear in court, Bailey found herself standing outside a modest new-build house located on an unassuming housing development in Watford. It was just after three o'clock on Sunday afternoon.

The place felt like a goldfish bowl. Everybody watching everybody else from behind net curtains. Living somewhere like this was Bailey's personal idea of a nightmare.

Frank had mentioned that Carl Freeman had a wife and son, and with his help, she'd tracked them down to this place. The wife was called Bridget and the son was called Jack. Apparently Jack would be around eight years old by now.

By visiting them, she was hoping to gain some further insight on Carl Freeman that would better position her to find Rex before he found her. Time was running out and Bailey was feeling the pressure now more than ever. She just prayed that today's venture would yield something of value.

Coming here on a Sunday, Bailey was hoping that Bridget Freeman and her son would be at home. It was a clear afternoon, and here and there people were outside the front of their houses, cleaning their cars, mowing the lawn, playing with their kids.

Standing on the pavement in the tranquil suburban street, Bailey wondered if Carl's family had any inkling that he could still be alive, and if so, whether they had any idea where he might be. There was only one way to find out the answers to the questions filling her mind.

She walked up the short driveway and rang the front doorbell, hearing it echo inside the house, followed a few seconds later by the muted voice of a young child shouting excitedly that there was someone at the door.

The door was answered by a slender pretty woman wearing an apron. Almost immediately Bailey was assailed by the mouth-watering aroma of gingerbread wafting out of the house.

The woman had a cheerful but slightly harried expression on her face. Drying her hands on the corner of her apron, she tossed her long brown hair aside and appraised Bailey enquiringly.

'Bridget Freeman?' asked Bailey.

The woman nodded. Bailey flashed her warrant card. The woman sagged, her expression changing to one of weary dismay.

'Is this about Carl?' she said.

'Yes. I just had a few questions about him that I'd be very grateful if you could help me with.'

'I can't see what more you can possibly want to know.'

'Just a moment of your time if you please,' said Bailey with a cordial smile. 'I promise it won't take long.'

Bridget sighed at the inconvenience. 'I'm halfway through cooking. We're making gingerbread men.'

'I'll be no more than ten minutes, I promise.'

Bridget took another look at Bailey's warrant card, studying it more closely this time, her lips silently moving as she read the details to herself, her eyes flickering between the little photograph and Bailey's actual face. Bailey patiently waited. As the former wife of an undercover police officer, it didn't surprise Bailey that Bridget was more diligent than most when it came to checking this kind of thing.

After satisfying herself that Bailey was indeed a police officer just as she was claiming to be, Bridget stepped back to let Bailey into the house, directing her into the front room. Bailey caught a glimpse of a little boy in the kitchen at the end of the hallway, peeking curiously round the corner of the door at her. She knew it must be Carl's son, Jack. Whilst Bailey took a seat on the sofa, Bridget briefly went into the kitchen to issue instructions of some kind to him regarding the baking that was taking place.

Bailey took the opportunity to scan the front room, taking in all the details with a detective's eye. Numerous toys lying around on the floor. A large television. A PlayStation with a stack of children's computer games. A series of framed photographs on the mantel-piece, conspicuous by the lack of any which depicted Carl Freeman – there were only pictures of Bridget and her young son. Was that odd, or was Carl's loss so sensitive a subject that she couldn't bear to have any reminders of him around?

Bridget came into the front room, pulling out a wooden chair from the dining table and sitting down. She raised an austere expectant eyebrow at Bailey.

'What did you want to know about Carl?' demanded Bridget. 'I haven't got all day.'

'Of course,' said Bailey. 'Sorry. I just wanted to know a bit more about him. Get some insights into his character. That kind of thing.'

Bridget frowned. 'Why? He's been dead for three years? What good is that going to do?'

'It's related to an ongoing investigation linked to the undercover operation he was working on at the time of his death.'

'Undercover,' muttered Bridget with a dismissive roll of her eyes. 'He took all that cloak and dagger bullshit so seriously. And look where it got him.'

'It must be hard to explain to your son,' said Bailey. 'That his father is missing rather than deceased.'

'I just tell him Carl's dead,' stated Bridget bluntly. 'That's because he is. Although he's technically missing, I know he must be dead. I mean, what other explanation is there? I filed a claim for presumed death which was upheld by the court which means I'm entitled to his police pension. Although you can't normally claim unless someone's been gone for more than seven years, the court ruled in my favour... probably because they saw I had a young child to raise.'

Unless Bridget was concealing it very well, Bailey sensed that she really did believe that her husband was dead, which meant that Carl Freeman had indeed completely given up his family when he'd gone rogue.

'I don't like to talk about him with my son though,' said Bridget. 'I think it's better if we just put Carl behind us. It's been over three years now. I just want us to be able to move on with our lives.'

Bailey nodded sympathetically. That explained the dearth of photos depicting Carl.

'Can I see a picture of him?' she asked. 'The most recent one you have.'

With a reluctant sigh, Bridget stood up and went over to a bureau standing in the corner of the room. Pulling open one of the drawers, she took out a large photo album and leafed through it. She stopped at one of the photos and handed the album to Bailey.

'That was the last one I ever took of him,' she said.

The picture showed Carl standing on what looked like some kind of boat, wearing a yellow life jacket, a smile on his face, his dark hair blowing in the wind.

'Is he on a boat?' asked Bailey.

'He's got...' Bridget corrected herself. 'He *had* a skipper's license. He'd got it about a year before he went missing. He was very proud of the fact. He had to take all these exams and everything, which he passed with flying colours of course. He'd always been into the outdoors and latterly he'd got quite into sailing. We used to go down to Portsmouth every so often and hire a boat to take us out to sea.' She nodded at the photo. 'That was what we did the weekend before he died.'

The memory cast a melancholy slant across her features.

'Is there a larger picture of him?' asked Bailey.

Bridget reached over and turned the page to reveal a large portrait of Carl in his police uniform, a row of medals pinned to his lapel. His chiselled clean-cut face bore a sober earnest smile. The scar across his right eyebrow was overtly visible.

'How did he get that scar on his eyebrow?' asked Bailey.

'Oh that?' shrugged Bridget. 'He got that when he was a uniformed police officer, before he started working undercover. He'd gone to deal with a pub brawl that had got out of hand and someone threw a pint glass at him. He needed a few stitches for it.'

Bailey stared into Carl Freeman's eyes trying to fathom what lay behind them. Had this wholesome image been nothing more than an empty façade? Just what had been going on inside that head of his to turn him into what he was today?

A shudder of disquiet went through her. She closed the photo album and handed it back to Bridget.

'What was he like as a person?' asked Bailey.

'I really don't see the point of your questions,' said Bridget. 'They're not going to bring Carl back to life, are they?'

'Please indulge me,' persisted Bailey gently. 'You're being super helpful. I can't tell you how grateful I am for your insights.'

Bridget softened slightly, somewhat assuaged. 'Well... he took his job very seriously. Too seriously in my opinion. Everything was about the job. If only he'd spent a bit more time with us instead of the bloody job.'

'You say he took it seriously. In what way?'

'Well, he never drank for one thing. Refused to touch a drop of alcohol. Ever. Even when he was off-duty. He just used to drink lemonade. He said that alcohol could impair his judgement on an operation. Said it was dangerous to drink.'

Bailey understood his rationale. Drinking when working undercover was never a wise idea. Alcohol tended to loosen your inhibitions, giving you a falsely inflated sense of self-confidence that could cause you to overstep the mark and accidentally blow your own cover.

'I always felt like he was judging me whenever I wanted to have a glass of wine,' continued Bridget. 'I felt like I wasn't quite up to his standards. But then he set very high standards... for himself most of all. I sometimes wonder if that was part of the problem.' She pursed her lips thoughtfully. 'I guess he was what you'd call a control freak. In fact I used to joke with him that his initials could stand for "Control Freak" just as much as "Carl Freeman".'

Bailey gave a small smile and nodded encouragingly for her to continue.

Bridget sighed sadly. 'I wished he would just relax. I know he was under a lot of pressure at work. I don't know much about undercover stuff – he never used to talk about it – but I imagine it can be pretty stressful. I suggested he try and do something to help him wind down. Do some yoga or some meditation or something. He told me he didn't have time for that "airy-fairy bullshit".' She shook her head with a humourless laugh.

Bailey knew that stress management was key to coping with undercover work and was emphasised strongly during training. You had to be able to identify when you were stressed and then you had to be able to force yourself to wind down accordingly, using the techniques and processes that worked best with you. It didn't sound like Carl had a very healthy approach to it.

'Did he have many friends?' she asked, thinking of her own current isolation and the importance of social contact in taking you out of yourself.

Bridget shook her head. 'Not really. I think he was quite a solitary person at heart.' She paused. 'That's probably why he enjoyed playing Solitaire so much.'

'Eh?' Bailey's brow creased in puzzlement.

Bridget smiled wistfully in recall. 'When we were on our honeymoon, we were staying on this Greek island called Paxos. One evening there was this horrendous thunderstorm. It was pouring with rain and we were stuck indoors. So we started playing cards. But the only card game that I knew was this version of Solitaire called Concentration. It's unbelievably simple, which is probably the reason I remembered how to play it. You can play it with yourself or with other people. I taught him how to play it that evening and we played it all night while it poured down outside. Later on he told me he sometimes used to play it by himself when he was stuck at work staking out some place for hours on end.'

Bailey paused to reflect on what she'd learnt so far. She was definitely building up a more three-dimensional picture of Carl Freeman. But so far, Bridget had said nothing to indicate that her husband had been on the verge of going rogue. Bailey decided to probe a little further.

'Did Carl ever mention that he was dissatisfied working for the police?' she ventured carefully.

Bridget frowned as if it was an absurd question. 'No. Quite the opposite. He absolutely lived for the job.' Her eyes then narrowed suspiciously. 'What are you implying exactly?'

'Oh nothing,' replied Bailey airily. 'It's just something we ask as a matter of course.'

She wasn't about to inform Bridget Freeman that her suppos-edly deceased husband was now making a living as a professional hitman. For one thing it would probably upset her hugely, if she was even able to accept the idea, and for another thing, Bailey couldn't actually prove it. If and when it came to it, if they success-fully managed to apprehend Rex a.k.a. Carl Freeman, then specially trained family liaison officers would break the news to his wife.

'The evening that he went missing,' said Bailey. 'Did you notice anything odd?'

Bridget smarted as if Bailey had touched a raw nerve. 'I don't want to talk about it!' she blurted. 'I don't like to think about it.'

Bailey scrutinised her closely. Was it just that the memory was too painful to think about, or was Bridget hiding something? Not wanting to upset Bridget, Bailey decided to steer the conversation back onto safer ground for the time being.

'How about his brother?' she asked.

Bridget's eyelids fluttered slightly. 'Toby?' she asked. 'What about him?'

'Do you know him at all?'

'I don't see what Toby's got to do with any of this,' responded Bridget tartly. She stood up abruptly. 'I need to go and check on the gingerbread. Please excuse me for a moment.'

She left the front room to go into the kitchen. Bailey sat there on the sofa, slightly perplexed at the way Bridget had reacted to the mention of Toby. More than ever Bailey was starting to get the impression that there was something Bridget wasn't telling her. But what exactly was it? And was it important? Bailey pensively curled her loose-hanging lock of hair round her finger and let it uncurl slowly.

Her train of thought was suddenly broken by the appearance of Carl's son Jack standing in the doorway of the front room. He was examining Bailey with a curious expression on his face. He had dark hair like his father along with the same strong cheekbones and jaw.

'Hello,' said Bailey gently, smiling at him.

There was a slightly awkward silence. The boy took several tentative steps into the room.

'Are you in the police?' he asked.

Bailey nodded. 'I just had to ask your mum about a few things.'

'I heard you talking about my dad,' he said. 'I heard you say that my dad was missing. Does that mean he's still alive?' He had a hopeful look on his face.

Feeling a burst of sadness, Bailey dropped her gaze to avoid having to look into his expectant eyes. She didn't know what to tell the little boy. She could hardly tell him the truth.

She looked up at him again. 'I don't know,' she said. 'I really don't know.'

'Did you know my dad?'

Bailey hesitated a moment. 'No. I never met him.'

Jack lifted up his right hand and Bailey saw that he was holding something in it. He unfolded his fingers to reveal a small silver music box resting on his open palm. He smiled at her proudly. She got the impression it was a treasured possession of his.

'That's nice,' said Bailey. 'What tune does it play?'

Jack cranked the tiny handle, a metallic tinkling emanating from the music box. Bailey instantly recognised the melody. It was the song 'Over the Rainbow' from *The Wizard of Oz*.

'That's from *The Wizard of Oz*, isn't it?' said Bailey. She hadn't seen the film in years.

Jack grinned broadly. 'It's my favourite film. I like the Munchkins. Dad used to call me his little munchkin.'

Bailey tried to recall the story. 'If I remember correctly, there was a big tornado and then Dorothy banged her head and went to Oz.'

'That's right,' nodded Jack. 'But then she wakes up at the end and it's all okay.' He looked proudly at the music box. 'Dad bought it for me, for my birthday when I was five, because he knew *The Wizard of Oz* was my favourite film. When I couldn't sleep at night, he used to play the music box. Whenever I play it I think of Dad.' He suddenly looked sad. 'But Mum won't let me watch *The Wizard of Oz* any more because she says it reminds her of Dad.'

Bailey observed him sympathetically. However Carl Freeman might have conducted himself in other aspects of his life, it appeared that he'd had a good relationship with his young son.

Jack walked up to her and offered her the music box. 'If you see my dad will you give him this?'

Bailey awkwardly accepted it. 'Sure. Okay.'

She studied the small item for a few moments and then placed it in the pocket of her suede-fringed jacket.

Jack's eyes started to fill with tears. 'I miss Dad,' he said.

'I bet you do,' said Bailey, gently patting him on the shoulder.

At that point Bridget re-entered the living room. Her face creased into a troubled frown at the sight of her son's tears. 'Why's he crying?' she demanded.

'He asked me about his father. He said he'd overheard us talking about him.'

Bridget rolled her eyes. 'Now see what you've done!' she snapped. 'That's why I try not to mention Carl. It only makes him upset. This afternoon was supposed to be fun. We were supposed to be making gingerbread men. Now look at it! It's ruined! Because of you! If you hadn't have come here we wouldn't have been talking about it.'

Bailey swallowed guiltily. She felt it was probably time to be leaving.

'I'm sorry to have disturbed you,' she said, standing up.

Making her way out into the hallway, she opened the front door and, with a final thank you and apology to Bridget, she left the house.

Heading off down the street towards her car, she felt both a little disturbed by today's encounter, but also intrigued at what she'd learnt. Although she'd greatly increased her understanding of Carl Freeman, Bailey felt there was still a considerable way to go in terms of discovering who he really was and how he'd changed from a highly decorated cop into a ruthless contract killer. She needed to gain further insight, and she already had a good idea of who to talk to next.

* * *

Bridget Freeman peered through the net curtains and watched the policewoman walk away. She felt her simmering disquietude subside a little. Carl was dead. Why couldn't they just be done with it? Why couldn't they just leave her alone instead of stirring up all those old painful feelings from the past?

The smell of gingerbread men wafted through the house, and coming from upstairs Bridget could hear the faint sound of Jack crying in his room, where he'd retreated to following the policewoman's visit.

Standing by the window, Bridget waited until the policewoman had got into her car and driven off and then she picked up her mobile phone, dialling a number she hadn't called in quite a while. The phone was answered after a few rings.

'Hello,' she said stiffly. 'It's me.'

'Hello Bridget. It's good to hear from you.'

The male voice on the other end of the line elicited a whole host of conflicting emotions within her. She swallowed hard and pushed them away.

'Look Toby,' she said firmly. 'The reason I'm calling is because I wanted to warn you. There's a policewoman asking about Carl.'

'A policewoman?' Toby didn't sound particularly concerned. But then that was just his manner. He'd always been laid-back. About everything. 'What was she asking about?'

'This and that. She said it was something to do with an ongoing investigation or something. She didn't specify what it related to exactly. I just gave her a bit of background on Carl like she wanted and then I sent her on her way.'

'What did she look like?'

'Young. Maybe thirty or thereabouts. Quite pretty I suppose... although she's got this ugly scar running down one side of her face.'

'Oh. *Her.* I've already met her. I didn't know she was a police officer though.'

Bridget's eyes widened in surprise. 'You've already met her?! What do you mean you've already met her? When?'

'She came to one of my gigs. Down in Wimbledon.'

'She came to one of your gigs?' Bridget was suddenly seized by a nervous worry. 'What did you tell her?' she demanded, picking at the net curtain anxiously.

'Nothing much. I didn't tell her about *us*, if that's what you're asking.'

'Good,' said Bridget. 'I don't want her knowing. And if she does contact you again, I want to be told about it.'

There was a sigh on the other end of the phone. 'I don't see what you're getting so het up about. What difference does it make if she knows?'

Bridget ground her teeth in agitation. 'It makes a difference to me Toby! I just don't want her knowing. I don't want *anyone* knowing!'

She ended the call without saying goodbye. Staring moodily out of the window, she once again wished that the past would stay in the bloody past.

26

Rex lounged unobtrusively in a booth in Marzini's Italian deli sipping from a can of San Pellegrino Limonata. If you were going to drink Italian lemonade this was the place to do it. It was midday on Monday and the deli was starting to pick up with lunchtime traffic.

The woman, Emma, who'd left the answerphone message in Bailey's flat, had mentioned 'their usual corner spot'. There was indeed a booth located in the corner by the window, and if the message was anything to go by, it sounded like she and Bailey came in and sat there on a regular basis. He had no idea what this woman Emma looked like, but he would sit here all day, all week if he needed to, and monitor that booth closely for any potential contenders who sat down there.

As it turned out, he didn't need to wait for very long. Approximately forty minutes after he'd got there, a young woman clad in a grey trouser suit entered the deli chatting loudly on her mobile phone. Momentarily breaking off from the phone, she ordered a mozzarella and rocket ciabatta from the counter and then went and sat down in the corner booth.

Rex observed her closely, casually eavesdropping on her phone conversation which wasn't too hard as she was talking in quite a loud voice.

'Look Anthony,' she was saying, 'I definitely think that Bailey's interested in seeing you, but she's currently busy on an operation and I've got no clue where she is at the moment. You know how it is. You used to work for the police.'

Rex tautened at the mention of Bailey's name. It sounded very much to him like this woman was the Emma he'd been waiting for. He subtly craned his head to listen more closely.

'But don't give up hope just yet,' she was saying down the phone. 'Bailey's coming round my place for dinner at eight on Wednesday evening. I'll ask her again about giving you her number. Obviously I could just give it to you myself, but I wouldn't want to piss her off as she is my friend. You do understand, don't you?'

Rex gulped down the last mouthful of Limonata. Eyeing Emma coldly, he crumpled the empty can in his hand as he contemplated what he'd overheard. Bailey Morgan had a dinner date the day after tomorrow at eight o'clock in the evening. All he had to do next was find a way to invite himself along.

27

Bailey tried to take her mind off the troubling fact that there were now only seven days left until she was due to testify against Charlie Benvenuto.

Seven days. One week. It wasn't long at all now. Where on earth had the time gone?

'Cheer up,' said Toby Freeman as he moved his bar stool closer to her. 'I hear that smiling and laughter are good for the health. As a stand-up comedian I guess I'm kind of like a doctor in that respect. By making people laugh I improve their health.'

Bailey blinked and turned her attention to him once more. By the eye-watering amount of cologne he was wearing, she supposed he thought they were on a date. After all, she had called him up insisting that they meet, having obtained his number before leaving the pub in Wimbledon, so here they were on Tuesday evening sitting in a bar in Fulham not far from her hotel.

She herself was under no such illusions and, as such, hadn't bothered to make any kind of effort for the occasion, being clad in her regular casual garb of jacket, jeans and baseball cap... and as for make-up, well, she'd never been a big one for that anyway.

Moving closer to her still, Toby placed a hand on her knee. 'I like a girl who doesn't feel the need to dress up to the nines every time she goes out,' he said with a leery smile. 'But then as a police officer I imagine you have more important things to think about than mere fashion.'

She politely removed his hand from her knee. 'How did you know I was a police officer?' She hadn't overtly stated the fact at any point during this or their previous encounter.

He smiled coyly. 'Just an educated guess.'

It sounded to her like he'd been talking to Bridget... and that didn't totally surprise her. She wondered what Bridget had told him exactly.

'I'm interested in learning about your brother,' she said.

He pretended to look hurt. 'What about me?'

'We can talk about you in a minute.'

He scrutinised her for a few moments. 'Why all the interest in Carl all of a sudden? Has he come back from the dead or something?'

Bailey studied him closely. Was he just joking or was he alluding to the truth in some way? By the stupid grin on his face, she got the idea he was just joking.

'It relates to official police business,' she said.

He groaned. 'Police business eh?' He assessed her distastefully. 'I never understood the appeal of the police. You have to enjoy catching people. It's like being a traffic warden or a tax inspector.'

'There's a little more to it than that,' muttered Bailey, trying to keep her patience with him. His attitude was already starting to get on her nerves.

His eyes widened in realisation. 'Oh wait a minute. I get it. "Police business".' He made quotation marks with his fingers. 'I know what that means. You're a copper and you had some kind of workplace crush on him.' He sighed. 'Typical! But then girls always liked Carl. I bet you liked the fact that he was all serious and aloof. Women really fall for that shit, don't they? It's the Mr Darcy effect. Me on the other hand, I have to resort to stand-up comedy to pull girls... and even then I'm still living in the bastard's shadow despite the fact he's been dead for three years.'

Bailey sensed a seething resentment borne of a long-standing sibling rivalry between them.

'It sounds as if you didn't like your brother very much,' she said.

'Who? Mr Perfect?' he said with a barely concealed contempt.

'Why'd you call him that?'

Toby's face twisted into a sneer. 'Oh... you know. He was always so bloody good at everything. Anything he set his mind to, he'd always get it done, always follow it right through to the very end to the best of his ability, and he'd invariably do it better than anyone else, including me. He was an obsessive, that's what he was. It was unhealthy if you ask me.'

What Toby was saying made Bailey think of Rex's reputation for always finishing the job. That trait now seemed obvious in retrospect as a manifestation of Carl Freeman's obsessive personality.

'Were there any things he was particularly good at?' she asked.

Toby rolled his eyes. 'Find me something he *wasn't* good at. He was a top-class swimmer. Dedicated marathon runner. Expert marksman. Keen sailor. Skilled hunter.'

'Hunter?' she repeated with a shiver going through her.

Toby nodded. 'Our dad was a gamekeeper. We grew up in the countryside, on the North Wessex Downs. Dad taught us how to read animal tracks, creep up on animals, that kind of thing. I was never very good at it. I don't think I really cared enough about it. But Carl... he excelled at it, to the point where he was planning to follow in Dad's footsteps and become a gamekeeper too. But he moved down to London and became a copper instead.'

Bailey stroked her chin with interest. An aptitude for hunting made a lot of sense in the context of what Carl now did for a living. Everything that Toby was telling her was serving to further cement her conviction that Rex and Carl Freeman were indeed one and the same person.

'I visited his widow yesterday,' she said.

'Yeah I know. She told me. Called me up straight afterwards.'

So he *had* been talking to Bridget.

Bailey nodded slowly. 'I got the impression she wasn't telling me the whole story though.'

His face gave nothing away. He seemed more guarded now, the jokey demeanour having receded somewhat. Presently he shrugged. 'That's her business.'

Bailey got the impression that whatever Bridget was hiding, Toby was in on it as well. An understanding of what that might be was starting to form in her head.

'Are you two close?' she asked. 'I mean, seeing as you're Jack's uncle, do you visit them at all?'

'Not as often as I'd like to,' he said.

There was a brief tell-tale flicker of something in his eyes. It took a few moments for Bailey to pin down what it was. Yearning. That's what it was.

'What did she tell you about Carl?' he asked in an apparent bid to change the subject.

Bailey could see that the deeper she tried to dig, the more intransigent Toby was going to get. She decided to fall back a little and accede to his question.

'Bridget told me that Carl was a bit of a control freak.'

Toby seemed to loosen up, emitting a small snort of laughter. 'She wasn't wrong about that. Carl was the kind of kid who didn't like different bits of food touching on his plate. Everything had to be his way.' He shook his head. 'I sometimes wonder if that was his downfall.'

Bailey leaned closer. 'What do you mean?'

He sighed. 'Carl was wound too tight and he took things way too seriously. With someone like that, someone that inflexible, the smallest thing can send them right off the rails.'

Toby suddenly looked a bit downcast. It seemed out of character for him, considering what Bailey knew of him so far.

'I'm not sure I understand what you're saying,' she said, hoping he would elucidate on the matter. 'So what do you think happened to him?'

Toby fixed her with a bleak gaze. 'I think he fucked up on a job and got himself murdered.' He smiled mirthlessly. 'And that's one good reason to be a stand-up comedian rather than a copper.'

28

Standing in the kitchen of her flat, Detective Constable Emma Broggins was singing along loudly to the music emanating from the Bluetooth speaker on the worktop. The song 'Happy' by Pharrell Williams was playing. It was one of her favourite tracks and she was listening to it on repeat.

The song reflected her mood, particularly this evening. She was quite a happy person generally but tonight she was in an especially good mood because her friend Bailey was coming over for dinner and she was really looking forward to it.

Emma had pulled out all the stops to treat Bailey to a proper feast tonight. For starters, she'd prepared smoked trout soufflés with dill cream sauce. For main course, she was making a garlic and herb pork loin roast with apple sauce, accompanied by steamed vegetables. And for dessert, she'd made a triple-layered meringue cake festooned with an abundance of strawberries and cherries.

She knelt down and opened the oven to check on the roast. The delicious smell of cooking meat wafted out. It looked like it was almost ready. She would take it out in another minute or so, or else it would burn. Anyhow she knew it was good to let a roast stand for a bit before serving it. She'd chosen a pork roast because she knew Bailey didn't like lamb and she herself wasn't that keen on beef.

Closing the oven and standing back up, she checked the apple sauce that was cooking in a saucepan on the top of the stove. Stirring it round with a wooden spoon, she saw that the apples had nearly completely broken down. It was almost ready. Just a few more minutes needed.

She realised that it was getting a bit steamy in the kitchen. The extractor fan was on but it never seemed to work that well. Crossing over to the other side of the kitchen, she pushed open the sash window to let some air in. It was a balmy evening outside even though it was now early October.

Turning back to the kitchen top, she finished prepping the vegetables but she wasn't planning on putting them in the steamer just yet otherwise they'd be mush by the time Bailey got here. At any rate, the two of them were going to have some pre-dinner snacks and drinks before sitting down to eat.

She looked at the kitchen clock. It was seven-fifteen. Bailey was supposed to come round at eight o'clock. It looked like everything was on track for a great evening.

Reaching up, she opened one of the kitchen cupboards to take down a small bowl to transfer the apple sauce to when it was finished cooking.

The song finished... and then immediately started again because it was on repeat. As she sang along to it, she tried to think how she could persuade Bailey to give Anthony her telephone number.

* * *

Rex lifted his wrist to check the time on the Hamilton military-style watch that was strapped to it. The small hands, glowing in the dark, told him that it was seven-fifteen.

The sun had gone down around forty minutes earlier and he was standing on a street in Camberwell, lurking in the shadows just beyond the pool of light cast by the nearest lamppost. Around a hundred metres away was the block of flats where Bailey's friend Emma lived. It was one of those old-fashioned mansion blocks that were dotted all over the city. He'd followed Emma from Marzini's to the police station where she worked. And then he'd waited until she'd finished work. Then he'd followed her from there to this block of flats in Camberwell.

With a little bit of digging around online using his favoured methods, he'd pinpointed her exact address. It was located on the third floor of the block.

From what he'd overheard in Marzini's, Bailey was due to come here for dinner at eight o'clock. He'd decided to get here early just to be on the safe side. He now just had to determine the best way to go about killing her.

Scanning the immediate area, he noticed that the front entrance to Emma's block of flats was directly opposite a busy pub. Because it was unexpectedly warm weather for early October, there were more people than usual standing outside the pub chatting and smoking. That presented a problem when it came to killing Bailey as Rex preferred not to have any witnesses. He didn't know from which direction she would arrive, which meant that if he wanted to kill her on arrival, the likely place to do it would be right outside the front entrance of the flats in full view of the pub. In addition to that, he'd noticed that there was a public CCTV camera attached to one of the lampposts nearby, and he wanted to avoid appearing on that if possible. He could of course kill her when she left, but he had no idea what time she would be leaving, or even if she might be staying there overnight.

Weighing up the options, he decided that the best bet would be to enter the block of flats covertly and kill her when she was inside. That would give him much more control over the situation.

As he stood there watching, he noticed a man come out of the front door of the block holding a black bin bag full of rubbish. The man walked down the road towards him, then turned off down a side alley around fifty metres from where Rex was standing. A minute or so later, the man reappeared from the alley, minus the bin bag, walked back up the street and re-entered the block of flats.

Rex's interest was piqued. It seemed that the side alley led to some area utilised by the residents of that particular block of flats. It occurred to him that it might present some means of entering the building without having to go anywhere near the front entrance. Keeping to the shadows, he slunk along the pavement and slipped down the alley.

It was dark and there was a ripe smell in the air. The alleyway took him round to a small concrete area at the rear of the block of flats. It quickly became apparent that the smell was coming from a set of large communal bins there that the man must have just deposited his rubbish in.

Turning to look up at the block of flats, Rex was emboldened to see that there was a metal fire escape snaking up the back of the building. These old mansion blocks often had these types of fire escapes. This particular one was conveniently recessed into the back of the block, meaning that it lay largely in shadow and wasn't overlooked by any surrounding flats.

Moving forwards in the dimness, he clambered up onto the fire escape and began to ascend.

* * *

Pulling on her jacket, Bailey once again questioned the wisdom of partaking in a social engagement given her current circumstances. It was now the second of October and there were only six days to go until the trial started. In some ways she wondered if it was better just to wait until all this was over before catching up with Emma.

But then it was only one evening, and like Emma said, it would probably do her the world of good. Living like a fugitive all alone in this hotel wasn't exactly great for anyone's mental health. A bit of social contact with a positive person like Emma would no doubt help to recharge her batteries and prevent her from letting herself get completely ground down by the whole Rex situation.

At any rate, cancelling now would sorely disappoint Emma. Knowing her friend as she did, Bailey imagined she had probably gone to a lot of trouble to make a nice dinner tonight.

Talking of which, the more Bailey thought about it, the more she was looking forward to some of Emma's superb cooking. She wondered what Emma was making for dinner. Whatever it was, she was sure it would be good. Her mouth began to water at the prospect.

And as for security, she figured she'd be fine. She couldn't think of any reason that Rex would even know who Emma was or where she lived, and certainly she couldn't imagine that he'd be aware that she was going round for dinner tonight. Still... she'd be sure to be vigilant all the same.

She looked at her watch. It was seven-thirty. She reckoned it would take her half an hour or so to drive from Earl's Court to Camberwell.

A thought suddenly occurred to her. She took out her iPhone and typed out a text message to Emma.

Shall I pick up some wine? Red or white? xx

She sent the message and waited for a response.

* * *

Treading softly on the metal grilled steps of the fire escape, Rex came to a halt on the third floor. On ascending the rickety metal structure, he'd discovered that that the residents of the block accessed the fire escape via a door in their kitchens.

He now stood concealed in the gloom directly outside the kitchen of Emma's flat. Peering in through the window, he watched her as she bustled round the kitchen absorbed in food preparation activities, completely oblivious to the fact that a professional contract killer was standing just a few metres away from her.

The kitchen window had been pushed open several inches and he could smell the seductive aromas of cooking food wafting out. He could also hear the sound of pop music playing and he could see her singing along heartily to the lyrics.

He guessed she was in the process of making dinner for Bailey. Silently moving closer, he examined the back door of the flat. He'd brought his set of lock picks with him but he realised that he probably didn't need them because the kitchen window was open. The window was right next to the door so all he needed to do was to reach in carefully to the door handle on the inside and open the door. He just had to make sure that she didn't notice him.

He moved right up to the window, keeping to one side to minimise the risk of her seeing him. Peeking in, he watched her intently, waiting for an opportune moment to act.

Walking over to the stove, Emma turned off the hob under a saucepan that was on there, and then took the saucepan over to the kitchen worktop where she proceeded to carefully ladle its contents into a small bowl. From where he was standing, it looked like some kind of sauce, possibly apple. The important thing was that she now had her back to him and he decided that it was the time to act.

Quietly pulling on a pair of black leather gloves, he slipped his hand into the small gap of the open window, gingerly avoiding a potted plant on the window sill just inside. Slowly he fed the rest of his arm in, all the while keeping a watchful eye on her as she fiddled with the saucepan.

Operating blind, his fingers groped for the door handle. Very slowly, very gently, he pressed it down and pulled inwards, hoping that the door hinges didn't creak.

But the door didn't move.

It was locked.

He silently cursed to himself. Releasing the door handle, his fingers probed a little further beneath it. He felt a small burst of satisfaction as they closed round the end of a key that was inserted in the lock.

He froze as Emma turned to one side to place the saucepan back on the switched-off hob having finished scooping out its contents into the bowl. She then turned her back to him again as she opened the kitchen cupboard and began to root round inside.

Very carefully, he twisted the key, feeling the bolt slide back as the door unlocked. He winced at the small clunking noise it made. Watching Emma, it seemed she hadn't registered it though, most likely because the pop music was playing too loudly.

Grasping the door handle once more, he pressed it down and pulled open the door a few centimetres. There was a very slight creak as it opened, but yet again she didn't hear it. Withdrawing his hand, he stood up to full height and eased the door the rest of the way open.

Because it was a warm evening, there was no breeze, no sudden gust of chill air to warn her of his presence. Standing there silently in the open doorway, just a short distance away from her, he reached into his pocket and drew out a length of paracord. It was extremely tough, virtually unbreakable... and ideal for what he was about to do next.

Wrapping it round his knuckles, he softly padded across the kitchen tiles until he was barely a few centimetres away from her. She'd taken down a jar of olives from the kitchen cupboard and was now spooning them into a small dish, singing along to the music, jiggling her shoulders in time with the beat.

Brandishing the taut length of paracord between his hands, he gingerly lifted it until it was just above her head. He braced himself and then, with a quick motion, he looped it down in front of her face and yanked it tightly round her neck.

She gasped and jumped in shock, the jar of olives flying from her hands to shatter on the floor. With a choking noise, she batted at the paracord biting into her throat, trying to get a purchase on it with her fingers, but to no avail for it was already too deeply enmeshed in her flesh. She kicked and flailed, trying to scream but only managing to gasp. He stood firm, his jaw set, his face hard and mean, winding the paracord ever tighter, feeling her resistance slowly wane until she finally went limp in his grasp.

Unlooping the paracord, he let her body fall unceremoniously to the kitchen floor. Pocketing the cord, he looked down at her lying there amidst the scatter of olives and broken glass, her glazed dead eyes half open and her tongue protruding from her mouth. He gave a cold snort of contempt. He'd hardly broken a sweat.

The music was still playing loudly from the Bluetooth speaker, its upbeat tone now grotesquely incongruous with the macabre tableau before him.

All he had to do now was wait for Bailey to arrive. But for her he wasn't going to use paracord. He'd only used the paracord to kill Emma because he hadn't wanted the neighbours to hear. For Bailey on the other hand, he would just shoot her, and then get out of here as quickly as possible.

He pulled the Sig Sauer P320 Compact from his shoulder holster and drew back the slide to load a round into the chamber. Just as he was about to re-holster it there was a faint ping.

Turning round, he saw that the sound had come from Emma's iPhone which was lying at one end of the kitchen top. The small screen was glowing, indicating that she had just received a message. Peering down at it, he saw that it was a message from Bailey.

Shall I pick up some wine? Red or white? xx

Rex's eyes narrowed in a calculating manner. It might look odd if Emma didn't reply. It might make Bailey suspicious. He placed his gun on the kitchen top and picked up the iPhone. The phone was locked preventing him from responding to the text message.

Not a problem.

Holding the phone, he knelt down next to Emma's lifeless body. He picked up her limp dead hand and pressed her thumb against the iPhone's button to activate the touch ID. The phone unlocked.

Rex paused for a moment to consider what he would write. Red or white wine? He chuckled to himself and glanced at the oven. Standing up, he went over and opened it. A warm gush of air came out. Peering in, he determined that it was a pork roast. It certainly smelt like one. Everyone knew red wine went better with red meat... although obviously Bailey wouldn't be around to enjoy it.

He typed in a response to Bailey's message.

Yes please! Red would be great.

As an afterthought he added a smiley face emoticon.

A few seconds later a response came through.

Sure will do. Looking forward to seeing you xx

Rex smiled coldly. Yes, looking forward to seeing you too, he thought.

* * *

Bailey pulled her Audi up by the kerb around a hundred metres from the block of flats where Emma lived in Camberwell. She switched off the engine and got out of the car clutching a carrier bag containing the bottle of red wine that she'd picked up in a small supermarket in Earl's Court just prior to leaving.

It was a very mild evening indeed and she almost felt over-dressed wearing her jacket. She took a moment to cautiously assess her surroundings. Although the sun had gone down and it was now dark, the streetlights were on and the road itself was reassuringly busy. Just a short distance away she saw there were a load of people milling around on the pavement outside the pub that lay opposite Emma's flat. She and Emma had been there on a number of occasions when she'd visited Emma in the past.

She didn't sense anything particularly untoward, and once again reminded herself of the importance of not letting her paranoia spiral out of control to the point where it made her lose all sense of proportion. If things looked okay right now, they were probably okay. Relaxing a little, she made her way along the pavement towards the front entrance of the block of flats. The buzz of conversation from the people outside the pub grew more pronounced as she approached. It was a convivial atmosphere and she supposed it was due in part to the unusually balmy weather for this time of year.

Walking up the short set of steps to the front entrance of the block of flats, she rung the buzzer on the intercom and waited for

Emma to answer. The prospect of seeing her friend imminently had raised Bailey spirits and she was now glad that she'd agreed to come and visit her tonight after all.

After a short delay the intercom clicked on. The first thing Bailey heard was the faint sound of pop music emanating from the tinny little speaker. She recognised the song as 'Happy' by Pharrell Williams. She smiled to herself. Emma loved that song.

She leaned into the speaker. 'Hey it's me,' she said.

She waited for Emma to reply but the only response was the clicking sound of the door unlocking as Emma buzzed her in.

Bailey frowned. Emma was such a chatterbox and it was unlike her not to actually say anything, but then Bailey reasoned that maybe Emma had a mouthful of snacks or perhaps was talking to someone on the phone when Bailey had rung the buzzer.

She shrugged it off, pushed open the door and entered the foyer of the apartment block. Straight ahead of her was a lift but she decided not to bother with it. Emma's flat was only on the third floor and the exercise would do her good. Walking to the stairwell, she pulled open the swing door and climbed the triangular flight of stairs up to the third floor, her footsteps echoing on the tiled steps.

Pushing open the swing doors on the third floor, Bailey walked along the quiet carpeted corridor to Emma's flat. Just like her, Emma lived in a one-bedroom flat. Having been here on several occasions before, Bailey was always reminded what a pleasant block of flats this was, a bit nicer than hers she thought.

Turning a corner in the corridor, she walked a short distance to the front door and stopping outside, she glanced down at the bottle of red wine she was holding. Hopefully Emma would approve. It was a Cabernet Sauvignon.

With a pleasant smile on her face, she raised her hand to knock on the door.

* * *

Rex pressed the button on the intercom system to buzz Bailey into the block of flats. Holding his gun in his hand, he stood in the hallway of Emma's flat and waited for her to come to the third floor. She was right on time. It was eight o'clock on the dot.

Reaching down, he put the door on the latch so he could pull it open more swiftly when the time arose, and also so he could re-enter the flat should he have to step out into the corridor to kill her.

In the background music continued to blare from the Bluetooth speaker in the kitchen. That same song must have played at least ten times since he'd got here and he was starting to get really sick of it, but he'd left it playing because he didn't want to disrupt the atmosphere in any way that might make Bailey think something was amiss before he got the chance to kill her.

He sniffed the air, detecting a distinct burning odour, and realised that it was the roast in the oven. Hopefully the burning smell wouldn't raise her suspicions. He mentally berated himself for not having switched off the oven earlier, but it was too late now.

There was a brisk knock on the front door. He leant forward to peer through the spyhole.

There she was. His target. Finally.

Bailey Morgan.

She was standing there not more than fifty centimetres away from him on the other side of the door. And she had only seconds to live.

He held the gun ready to shoot her directly between the eyes. With his other hand he pulled open the door.

* * *

Standing in the corridor holding the bag containing the bottle of wine, Bailey could hear the muted sound of pop music coming from the inside of Emma's flat and now that she was standing right by the door she could also smell the aroma of food cooking.

She crinkled her nose slightly. It smelt like something was burning. She frowned to herself. That didn't seem right. Emma was a bit of a perfectionist when it came to cooking and she wasn't the kind of person to let food get to the point where it burned.

She felt a sudden jab of alarm. First there'd been the intercom thing where Emma hadn't actually spoken to her, which had seemed out of character for her friend. And now there was the burning food, which was also out of character. Considered separately, each of these things might not have raised a red flag for Bailey. But together like this, they signalled that something was off. As an undercover cop, she'd developed a finely-tuned sixth sense for danger and it now kicked in powerfully to tell her that she was in great peril.

The door swung open.

Time seemed to slow right down, almost to the point of stopping completely.

Bailey found herself looking directly into the face of a man who she clearly and indisputably recognised as Detective Sergeant Carl Freeman.

He was tall, with dark hair and a pale complexion with that distinctive scar across his right eyebrow. His firm angular jaw was set in a cruel slant and he now fixed her with the crazy dead-eyed stare of an incorrigible killer.

Physically he was the same man that she'd seen in the photos at Bridget Freeman's house. But whereas in the photos he'd been a smiling clean-cut police officer, the man standing before her was something else completely.

Her body froze with a paralysing chill of fear and she was

almost unable to register the ghastly truth that he'd finally caught up with her and was about to kill her.

Momentarily mesmerised, she couldn't do anything but watch him level a handgun at her, pointing the black mouth of the barrel directly between her eyes. As he did so his lips peeled back to reveal his teeth and she realised he was smiling at her. He was death incarnate and he knew it.

His finger tightened on the trigger.

And at that exact moment she dodged aside, endowed with an infinitesimal head start on him thanks to her presentiment of danger. Every minute reflex of her being conspired to pull her body out of the path of the bullet just as it left the barrel of the gun.

BANG.

The bullet slammed past her into the wall of the hallway behind her.

Reeling away from the door, she saw him emerge from the flat into the corridor, swinging the gun round at her for a second shot.

In a swift fluid motion, she hurled the bag containing the bottle of wine at him. It hit him square in the face just as he pulled the trigger. The impact of the bottle threw his aim off and the bullet whizzed past her left shoulder, the sound of the gunshot deafening in the small corridor. The bottle of wine smashed on the floor at his feet, its contents splashing all over the carpet.

Bailey's mind moved at lightning speed as she assessed their physical juxtaposition. Although he was temporarily disoriented, he was a fraction too far away for her to attempt to disable him with a jiu jitsu move, which even if it had been possible would have been an extremely risky manoeuvre considering he was armed with a gun.

Instead, she decided to take advantage of his momentary distraction to turn and flee. Years of jiu jitsu training had made her incredibly lithe and nimble. She pelted down the corridor, zig-zagging as she did so to try and avoid a bullet in the back.

BANG.

A third bullet narrowly missed her.

And then she was round the corner of the corridor, out of his line of fire. But not for long for she knew he'd be pursuing her with all his energy.

She hurled herself through the swing doors at the top of the flight of stairs she'd just ascended, jumping down the stairs three or four at a time, her footsteps echoing in the stairwell, adrenaline pouring through her veins driving her onwards in the primal urge to survive.

As she bounded down the stairs, she heard the doors slam open above her as he cannoned through them in hot pursuit of her.

Thoughts raced desperately through her head. She realised that her best chance for safety was to get out of the block of flats and into the pub across the road. He wouldn't risk following her in there and shooting her. There were too many people. Too many witnesses.

Glancing up through the triangular centre of the stairwell, she saw him and for a brief instant their eyes locked. He stopped and aimed the gun down at her.

She wrenched herself sideways against the wall.

BANG. The bullet hit the tiled step in front of her, throwing up a spray of splinters.

Continuing her manic flight, she reached the bottom of the stairs, tumbling through the swing doors into the foyer of the building. Breathing raggedly, she burst out of the main entrance of the block of flats. Jumping down the steps at the front, she vaulted across the bonnet of a parked car and sprinted across the road almost getting hit by a bus in the process. She barged through the group of people standing outside the pub to finally crash through the door and collapse against the bar.

The crowded place fell silent as everyone turned to look at her in surprise.

The slightly nonplussed barman gathered himself. 'What'll it be?' he asked.

'Call the police,' she gasped.

And then, and only then, was Bailey able to try and compute the fate of her friend Emma. With a deeply distressing and dreadful certainty, she knew that Rex must have killed her.

* * *

When he saw that Bailey had got out of the building, Rex immediately ceased his pursuit of her. If she had half a brain she'd go straight into that pub where she knew he wouldn't follow her.

He cursed aloud. Killing her tonight had seemed like a sure thing. But she'd got away again. Somehow.

He rubbed the bruise on his forehead he'd got when she'd chucked the bottle of wine at him. With an acidic bite of anger he realised that he was starting to develop a distinct hatred of Bailey Morgan.

This job had started out like any other with her being nothing more than a target to be exterminated. But he now felt personally affronted by the fact that she had once more managed to evade him. Well, she wouldn't succeed again. No one got away from Rex. No one.

He pushed the bitter thoughts aside to concentrate on his immediate priority. He had to get out of here as soon as possible, before too many people started coming out of their flats... before the police got here.

He turned and sprinted back up the flight of stairs, back to

Emma's flat with the intention of going back out onto the fire escape to leave the same way he had come in.

Reaching Emma's front door, which was still on the latch, he was just about to re-enter her flat when something caught his eye on the floor of the corridor. Lying in a puddle of red wine, surrounded by fragments of broken wine bottle, was a receipt from a supermarket. It was half poking out of the carrier bag that Bailey had thrown at him. Realising that it was the receipt for the wine that Bailey had purchased, he focused in on the name and address of the supermarket that was printed at the bottom of the receipt, and saw that it was located on Earl's Court Road. Feeling a quickening sense of anticipation, he knelt down and picked up the wine-soaked receipt to check the time of the transaction. It appeared that Bailey had purchased the wine little more than half an hour earlier. His thoughts moving rapidly, Rex deduced that Bailey had probably bought the wine somewhere local to where she was staying just prior to coming out this evening. And if he was right about that, then that meant Bailey was staying in Earl's Court... just as Milena had speculated.

Standing up with a satisfied smirk, he pocketed the receipt. He might have missed the opportunity to kill Bailey tonight, but she wouldn't get away from him for very long.

Although he only had less than six days in which to kill Bailey Morgan, at least he now knew where to look for her.

Earl's Court.

Hearing some clicking noises, he looked up to see that doors up and down the corridor were now opening cautiously, heads peeking out here and there to see what had been making all the noise.

It was time to go. Now.

Rex pushed open the door of Emma's flat and strode through it, into her kitchen, past her dead body, and out onto the fire escape back into the darkness to make his getaway.

Amy Benvenuto waved goodbye to her two daughters as they left for school and closed the front door. Walking back into the kitchen, she proceeded to clear away the various breakfast-related items that lay on the kitchen top and began to load up the dishwasher.

Glancing out of the kitchen window, she saw her husband's bulky figure disappearing round the corner of the laurel hedge, no doubt on his way to the arbour seat at the end of the garden to have a catch-up with his lawyers.

She sighed glumly. He'd been getting increasingly tetchy recently, snapping at her and the girls for the smallest thing, but she could hardly blame him as she knew his upcoming trial was weighing heavily upon him. It was Thursday today and the trial was next Tuesday. The closer it got, the tenser he'd been getting.

She noticed with a small frown that her mobile phone was lying on top of the kitchen island. Since the police had confiscated Charlie's mobile, he'd been using hers to communicate with his lawyers. If he'd gone out into the garden to talk to his lawyers, then it meant he'd forgotten to bring her phone with him. She imagined that all the stress he was under had made him forgetful. Picking up the phone, she opened the back door and went out into the garden with the intention of giving it to him.

Trotting down the garden path, she rounded the corner of the laurel hedge and made her way towards the little alcove where the arbour seat was. As she drew closer she made out the sound of her husband's voice. *That's strange*, she thought. It sounded like he was already talking to someone on the phone, which meant that he must have had some other phone in his possession. The thought of some other secret phone sent a small warning twinge of suspicion through her that, once again, not everything about him was quite as it seemed.

'Remember I said I'd call you back later in the week?' he was saying. 'Yeah, well, it's time for an update.'

She wondered whether he was talking to his lawyers or talking to someone else.

Something inside her told her to keep quiet and to continue listening. Swallowing nervously, she tip-toed closer. Her heart was beating hard all of a sudden as she was assailed by a sudden guilty feeling that she was doing something awfully wrong. She'd never before dared to eavesdrop on her husband's private business matters. But then, on the other hand, never before had his business matters affected her in such a detrimental way.

Creeping to one side of the alcove, she approached the arbour seat from an angle where he was less likely to spot her, her petite figure shielded from his view by the hanging branches of the Japanese wisteria that grew down over the trellis.

His voice was clearer now and there was a harsh brutal edge to it that she'd never heard before.

'I paid you good money to get rid of two people for me,' he said. 'Jeremy Westerby is now out of the picture. Great. One less lawyer the better. But as far as I understand Bailey Morgan is still alive. I haven't noticed anything on the news telling me otherwise.'

A shiver went through Amy as she tried to make sense of what she was hearing. If she wasn't mistaken, it sounded very much like her husband was paying money to have people murdered. Standing there just a few metres from him, her mouth suddenly dry, she listened with rapidly growing unease as he continued the conversation.

'Rex came close? Well "close" isn't good enough. I want that bitch dead. The trial's on Tuesday. That's only five days away.'

Backing away from the arbour seat, not wanting to believe what she was hearing, Amy Benvenuto silently turned and retraced her steps, and headed back into the kitchen. Her hands braced on the cold granite worktop, she took a few deep breaths to calm herself as she tried to think what she should say to him when he came back in, or if indeed she should say anything at all.

A few minutes later he reappeared from round the side of the laurel hedge and re-entered the kitchen with a dark preoccupied look in his eyes.

She regarded him fearfully. When he saw her his face softened.

'What's the matter darling?' he asked. 'You look terribly upset.'

Amy felt the overwhelming urge to question him about what she'd overheard him saying, but she found herself stymied by the prospect of how he might react if she did so. He would no doubt get angry at her for eavesdropping on his private conversation. He might even shout at her... possibly even hit her, not that he'd ever done anything like that before. But then things were different now, for if she wasn't mistaken she'd heard him actually talking about *killing* people.

'N... nothing,' she said with a tremor in her voice. 'It's nothing.'

He studied her curiously for a few moments. A tiny hint of suspicion edged onto his features. But then it was gone. He smiled and held out his arms. She hesitated for a second and then stepped forward to enfold herself in his bear-like embrace.

'I love you Amy,' he murmured in her ear, his voice warm and gentle. 'Both you and the girls. Don't forget that.'

Tears filled her vision as she was overcome with a rush of emotion, and for the time being whatever misgivings she had were eclipsed by her love for him.

30

Bailey awoke in her hotel room the next day, and a fraction of a second later the events of the previous evening crashed down on her like a ton of bricks as she remembered what had happened to her friend Emma.

Following the arrival of the police in Camberwell, her worst suspicions had rapidly been confirmed. Emma's lifeless body had been discovered lying on the floor of her kitchen. It appeared she'd been strangled to death with a ligament of some sort.

A crushing all-consuming guilt pervaded Bailey for she knew that Emma would still be alive were it not for her and the contract that was out on her. She couldn't escape the conviction that she was to blame for Emma's death. Racked by grief and by her own sense of culpability, Bailey now felt at her lowest ebb since embarking on this operation.

If having a hitman after her wasn't already bad enough, the death of her friend had made her position inestimably worse. A bitter anger seized her when she thought about Rex... or rather, Carl Freeman. His murder of Emma had made this situation personal and she was gripped more forcibly than ever by the desire to take him down and see him punished.

Overcome by emotion, she lay there in bed staring up at the ceiling crying, the room around her splintered by the tears running from her eyes. The outpouring eventually ran its course leaving her feeling spent, and she knew it would be counter-productive to lie there any longer wallowing in self-recrimination and feeling upset. With a wrench of effort she pulled herself out of bed, a plan starting to form in her head for what to do next.

She took a shower and then pulled her clothes on. Just as she was lacing up her trainers there was a knock on the door. She tensed and froze. Was it Rex? Or was it just the cleaner?

'Bailey?' came a muted voice from the other side of the door.

Bailey instantly recognised the voice as belonging to Stella. She frowned in surprise. She hadn't been expecting Stella to turn up here. Standing up, she walked over and opened the door.

Stella stood there in the dingy hallway assessing Bailey with an expression of concern. The normally hard-edged tinge to her features had been supplanted by a hitherto hidden glimmer of compassion.

'I wanted to see you in person,' she said. 'I was worried about you. Coming back here all alone after your friend's murder.'

Bailey swallowed and nodded in acknowledgement. She ushered Stella into the room and closed the door behind her.

'How did you know which room I was in?' she asked.

'I described you to the receptionist,' said Stella, making a scar gesture down the left side of her face.

Stella glanced round the small poky room. 'Not exactly the most homely of places.'

'I wanted to stay low-key.'

Stella scrutinised Bailey's eyes, noticing that they were still swollen and red-rimmed from a recent bout of crying. 'Don't beat yourself up over Emma's death,' she said. 'It wasn't your fault.'

Bailey shook her head. 'Emma would still be alive if it wasn't for me.'

'Rex is the one who killed her and he's the one who's to blame. And that's the other reason I came here this morning. I wanted to update you on the status of the murder investigation. They've been working through the night on it. As you know, Rex more or less got away clean but we did recover some forensic evidence from the crime scene. The preliminary results came back early this morning. The results basically confirm what we already know by now – that this murder was committed by the same person who killed Jeremy Westerby, the same person who was behind those seven unsolved hits. It confirms that Emma was killed by Rex.'

'*Carl Freeman*,' said Bailey. 'Like I told you last night, I saw him with my own eyes. Standing there right in front of me. It was definitely him. One hundred per cent. Rex the hitman is Detective Sergeant Carl Freeman.'

She reiterated to Stella what she'd learnt over the course of the previous few days from talking to Detective Inspector Frank Grinham, and from her conversations with Bridget Freeman and Carl's brother, Toby.

Stella listened solemnly, with intermittent nods of her head, as Bailey explained the background to the situation.

'You see,' said Bailey, 'the fact that Carl Freeman's body was never found makes it all the more plausible that he is in fact still alive... that he faked his death in order to become a hitman.'

Stella chewed her lip, looking bugged. 'When you first told me about the idea, I didn't want to believe it.' She sighed. 'But if you're right about it, then this opens up a whole can of worms. A Met police officer gone rogue working as a high-level hitman. If this gets out the Met will look even worse than they already do. Senior management will not be pleased to hear about this.'

'When are you going to tell them?' asked Bailey.

'As soon as I manage to think of a delicate way to broach it to them. They'll have to know about it sooner or later as it'll obviously come out in the wash if we ever do catch him.'

The bagpiper suddenly started up outside, the shriek of the pipes uncommonly loud courtesy of the permanently jammed-open window. Stella winced and frowned. 'What on earth is that awful racket? It sounds like a cat being tortured to death.'

Bailey gave a weary sigh. 'Some busker. He's playing the bagpipes. He's the last thing I want to listen to right now.'

Stella turned her attention back to Bailey, eyeing her with parental concern.

'Maybe it's best to terminate this operation now and move you into a safe house until the trial commences. What happened last night was too close for comfort. We both knew this operation would entail a certain amount of risk, but you just managed to escape by the skin of your teeth, and an innocent woman ended up dead. I think this has become too dangerous to continue. Rex is running out of time, with the court case only five days away, and he may get desperate and more innocent parties may get caught up in the crossfire.'

Bailey gritted her teeth and shook her head vehemently. 'I'm not going to give up now. I'm not going to give in to him. If anything it's made me more determined than ever to catch him. He killed a friend and a fellow police officer and I'm going to make sure he pays the price for it. Five days may not be long to go but I'm going to make sure every one of them counts. I'm going to get him before he gets me.'

'I'm worried about your mental health Bailey. You know as well as I do that you shouldn't let an operation become personal. When things get personal, people are prone to make bad judgements.'

'You're the one who came to me with this operation in the first place. I said I'd do it and I'm going to see it through to the end.'

Stella gazed at her with a mixture of admiration and disbelief. 'You really do live up to your reputation Bailey. You really are quite stubborn.'

Bailey shrugged. She decided to take it as a compliment. 'Now I know for sure that Rex is Carl Freeman, I need to understand more about him. I need to get inside his head. Once I do that I reckon I can catch him. I'm sure of it.'

Stella frowned, looking puzzled. 'Get inside his head? What are you talking about? How are you planning to do that?'

'I have a strong feeling that Bridget and Toby weren't letting on about everything they know. I think that there's some other angle to this whole thing, something we're missing. The real truth about how and why Detective Sergeant Carl Freeman became Rex the hitman. I just need to find out what it is.'

31

Sitting alone at a table in the corner of the Costa Coffee shop in Watford, Bridget Freeman bitterly observed the two young mothers sitting a few tables away. Gossiping and rocking their infants in their buggies, they seemed so naïvely happy, just as she herself had been when she'd been at their stage of child-rearing. Little did they know what troubles awaited them in the future. But then were either of them married to an undercover cop like she had been? She doubted it.

She looked at her watch and wondered when Toby would arrive. Timekeeping had never been a strong point of his. It was five minutes past five on Thursday evening. After finishing in the healthcare administration office where she worked, Bridget had picked up Jack from school and dropped him off at her mother's house nearby before coming back out to meet up with Toby.

Toby had wanted to come to her place but she'd nixed the idea. It would have brought back too many memories... memories of a time when he'd come there before, when things had been different between them. And also, maybe, one part of her was worried that she'd cave in to what she knew he wanted, and she just couldn't allow herself to do that, not after what had happened to Carl. No. Meeting here in this coffee shop made much more sense.

The affair between them had lasted two years. It hadn't been something she'd ever expected to happen. After all, she'd known Toby for many years, almost as long as she'd known Carl, and never once had she found herself attracted to him. She'd only ever viewed him as a slightly defective version of Carl. He was strikingly similar in looks, but not quite as handsome, not quite as tall, not quite as slim or athletic and not quite as successful or focused. Yet somehow, he was warmer, funnier, more relaxed, more relatable, and much more of a normal human being, and maybe, ultimately, that was what Bridget had needed.

With Carl increasingly absent on his undercover operations, Bridget had begun to feel neglected, slowly withering inside like a plant dying from lack of water. Toby had stepped into the void and had awoken something within her and all of a sudden she'd come alive again.

Looking back on those early years, she realised that the seeds of it had been there all along even if she hadn't been able to see them at the time. That look on Toby's face – that desire for her – had been present since the very beginning, from the first moment he'd set eyes on her. Always that same look, when he'd been there at the family barbecues, at Jack's birthdays, and the many times he'd come over to visit for no other reason it seemed than to just drop in and say hi.

She knew that his rivalry with his brother played an important part in his pursuit of her. Carl had always pipped Toby to the post at everything in life, ever since they'd been kids, and Toby hated him for that. His jealousy of his brother had fuelled his desire for his brother's beautiful wife. For Toby, she was the ultimate prize, the one thing that would finally and unequivocally put him ahead of Carl. He had even told her as much, as they'd lain side-by-side in bed, soaked in sweat after a bout of passion. It hadn't bothered her. It had made her feel desired. And that was what she'd craved – to feel desired.

But it was all over now. She had ended it when Carl had died. Despite her strong feelings for Toby, she'd forced herself to stop seeing him for she was tormented by the terrible knowledge that it was their very affair that had caused her husband's death.

The door opened, sending a brief gust of air into the coffee shop. She looked up. It was Toby. Her heart gave an involuntary lurch. He was wearing that brown leather jacket of his, the one he knew she'd always liked. He scanned the shop, his face lighting up in a smile as he spotted her. Before she could stop herself, she found herself responding in a similar manner, but then just as quickly she squashed the reaction and forced her mind to focus on the actual reason they were meeting here today – she'd told him to tell her if that policewoman contacted him again, and it turned out that she had.

Watching him as he strode over to her table, she couldn't help thinking to herself that he looked as good to her as he ever did. It had been more than a year since she'd last seen him in person. He leant down to kiss her on the cheek, placing a hand on her upper arm. His touch sent an electric quiver through her, and she had to force herself to pull away from his kiss.

'We're in public,' she said, trying to quell her beating heart.

He sat down opposite her looking faintly dismayed at her response. 'Carl's dead. What does it matter? We don't have anything to hide. Not like we did back then.'

'We're not together any more,' she said stiffly.

But as she looked at him sitting across the table from her, she couldn't deny that there still existed inside her some remnants of those old urges, flickering embers of the intense passion they'd once shared for each other. It had been more than just a fling and part of her was still in love with him, and she knew he felt the same way too.

'You could have just called me you know,' she said. 'We didn't need to meet in person.'

'I wanted to see you.'

She swallowed and tore herself away from his questing eyes.

'So?' she said, trying to be brisk and business-like. 'What happened with the policewoman?'

'I went on a date with her last night,' he said.

She swung her face sharply back to his, feeling a stab of jealousy. 'A date? Last night?'

By the triumphant look on his face, she saw that he was trying to elicit exactly that response in her, and he had succeeded. She immediately felt angry with herself for rising to it so easily.

'That was how she was playing it,' he said. 'She made out like she wanted to go on a date with me, but it soon became pretty obvious that she just wanted information about Carl. Just like you said.'

'Did you tell her anything?' she asked. That gnawing anxiety had seized her once again.

'What is there to hide?' he asked.

'Did you?' she hissed.

He sighed loudly and shook his head. 'I didn't tell her about us, if that's what you mean. I just told her about Carl. She was very interested in knowing about him. And you know what? It felt good to talk about him. To someone else. Afterwards I felt like... like I'd got something off my chest.'

'And that's all?'

Toby hesitated, pursing his lips uneasily. A bubble of dread surfaced inside her.

'She suspects something,' he said. 'She thought you weren't telling her the whole story.'

Bridget cursed angrily. 'What business is it of hers to go poking around in other people's lives? What the hell does she want?'

'Who cares what she wants?' he murmured soothingly. He slid round onto the seat next to her and placed his hand on her knee. 'I want to be with you again, Bridget.'

She knew this would happen. He still desired her. More than ever it seemed.

But that was all finished now. She bit her lip hard, so hard that she thought she'd drawn blood.

'No!' she asserted. 'I can't. Not after what we did.'

'What did we do?' he protested. 'We didn't do anything.'

'You know what we did!'

He shook his head. 'Stop blaming yourself.'

She wrenched his hand from her knee and skewered him with an accusatory stare. 'If anyone's to blame, it's you! You should never have come round that evening.'

He sagged in dismay, the spark of longing in his eyes now dampened if not completely extinguished by her indictment. She noticed that other people in the coffee shop had now paused their conversations to look at them. Tears began to well up in her eyes as she was overcome by a wave of frustration, disappointment and sadness. She hadn't wanted their meeting to turn out like this but somehow it had.

Standing up abruptly, she grabbed her coat and bag and swept out of the coffee shop, leaving Toby behind her. She cried all the way home.

On getting back to the house, she immediately went straight into the kitchen to make a cup of tea. That would help to sort things out. She was glad she'd decided to leave Jack with her mother this evening. She wouldn't have wanted him to see her like this.

Just as she'd switched on the kettle she heard the doorbell chime. She looked up in aggravation. Who on earth could that be?

Stepping into the hallway she could see an indistinct figure through the frosted glass of the front door.

Hoping that it didn't look too obvious that she'd been crying, she walked up to the door and opened it... and found herself face-to-face with the last person she wanted to see right now.

It was that bloody policewoman again.

32

The first thing that Bailey noticed when the front door opened was that Bridget Freeman had been crying. Her eyes were puffy and red-rimmed. At the sight of Bailey her pretty face dropped and she went to close the front door, but Bailey jammed her foot in it.

'Do you mind?' said Bridget sharply.

'I just need to talk to you,' pleaded Bailey.

'We already talked. There's nothing more to talk about.'

'It's really important,' said Bailey. She swallowed. 'My life depends upon it.'

Bridget frowned. 'What do you mean your life depends upon it? I don't believe you! Now please remove your foot from my door.'

'It's really important that we talk. *Please.* When I said my life depends on it, I meant it. An innocent woman, a good friend of mine, has just been murdered. And I'm going to be next.'

Bridget gaped at her, her face torn with conflict. She spent several long moments deliberating but then reluctantly, to Bailey's immense relief, she capitulated and let her into the house.

Bailey followed her through into the front room. Bridget gestured at the sofa and Bailey took a seat there in exactly the same spot she'd sat the first time she'd visited. Bridget herself pulled up a wooden chair from the dining table, just like she had before. There was no sign of Jack and Bailey guessed that he was either upstairs or out of the house.

'Are you okay?' asked Bailey gently. 'Has something upset you?'

Bridget emitted an incredulous half-laugh half-sob. 'I can't believe that you're even asking that question. I wouldn't be in this sorry state if it wasn't for you.'

'I apologise for causing you upset,' said Bailey. 'I really mean it.'

Crossing her arms, Bridget stared resentfully at Bailey through her red-rimmed eyes. Bailey shifted uncomfortably on the sofa.

'So what is this all about?' demanded Bridget. 'What do you mean a friend of yours has been murdered? I think it's time you provided an explanation.'

Bailey knew it was time to let Bridget in on a little more information, although she still wasn't planning on telling her the truth about her husband Carl.

'My friend was murdered by someone,' said Bailey. 'And this person is now planning to kill me. I'm working on an investigation to apprehend them.'

It wasn't a lie. Bailey was just being economical with the truth.

'And what's that got to do with me?' asked Bridget with a perturbed frown.

'Your husband's disappearance plays an important role in this investigation. It is inextricably linked to the undercover operation that he was working on at the time. Understanding the circumstances surrounding his disappearance would help me immensely.'

Bridget spent a few moments in troubled thought, then looked up at Bailey with a piqued expression. 'I don't see what else there is to tell you. I already told you everything.'

Bailey took a deep breath. 'I don't think you did actually. I know you're hiding something Bridget. I could tell it when I talked to you. And I saw it when I talked to Toby.'

Bridget eyed her mutely, her face once more bearing that resentful expression.

'I think I know what you're hiding...' said Bailey carefully. 'You and Toby. But it's not for me to judge you. You're both adults.'

Staring hard at Bailey, Bridget still didn't speak, her jaw clamped firmly shut.

Bailey continued, choosing her words delicately. 'But... I think there's something more than that isn't there? Something about that evening Carl went missing. Something that you know that you're not telling me.'

The atmosphere in the small living room was thick with tension. Observing Bridget closely, Bailey detected a slight wobble in her lower lip. Something was giving way. Bridget's chest convulsed as she suppressed some violent flux of emotion inside her. Bailey moved to the edge of the sofa, certain now that Bridget was on the verge of breaking her silence.

Bridget's voice emerged in a strangled moan. 'Why can't you just let me forget about it? No one needs to know about it. Do you understand? No one! It's past history. It's gone. It's too late now and there's nothing anyone can do about it!'

Bailey was both puzzled and intrigued by Bridget's outburst. 'I don't quite understand,' she said.

'You don't need to!' said Bridget, her face twisted in anguish.

'Please,' beseeched Bailey. 'It could save my life. I have to know.'

Bridget broke down sobbing, her body heaving, tears running down her cheeks. Bailey reached inside her handbag for a tissue. She held it out to Bridget who plucked it from her grasp and noisily blew her nose into it. Bridget looked at Bailey tearfully, her eyes filled with torment.

'I'm the reason Carl's dead,' she whispered.

'How's that?' asked Bailey, somewhat baffled. She hadn't quite been expecting this.

Bridget swallowed back a sob. 'Carl always seemed to be on some undercover job. It felt like I hardly ever saw him. I got lonely. Toby was there for me and well... we started seeing each other.'

Bailey nodded sympathetically. That much, at least, she had ascertained for herself.

'Carl was so serious,' continued Bridget. 'So uptight. Toby was so much more easy-going and fun to be round. It started out with just catching up with him when Carl was away on these long operations. But then... then it became more than that.'

Thinking about Toby's resentment of his high-achieving better-looking brother, Bailey wondered if sleeping with Carl's wife was a way for Toby to get back at him.

'You said it was your fault,' probed Bailey gently. 'The reason he died.'

Bridget sniffed loudly and blew her nose again into the tissue she was clutching in her hand.

'He didn't have his lucky rabbit's foot with him. That's why he died.'

'His lucky rabbit's foot?'

'Carl was very superstitious about his undercover work. He always had to have his lucky rabbit's foot with him whenever he went on a job.'

Bailey knew exactly where he was coming from. That kind of superstition was commonplace with undercover police officers. Operating in such a risky environment, they often placed faith in protective talismans. Bailey had known UCOs to have lucky hats, lucky pens, lucky watches... even lucky underpants. She herself tried to avoid relying on anything like that... for she knew that forgetting or losing the item could potentially put her in a negative state of mind during an operation thus making her more likely to make a mistake, in turn transforming any subsequent screw-up into a self-fulfilling prophecy.

Bridget sniffed. 'That evening, the evening he went missing, he'd gone out on one of his operations but he'd forgotten to bring his lucky rabbit's foot with him. He'd left it here on the living room mantelpiece.' She paused and wiped her eyes. 'The problem was that he came back for it.'

'Why was that a problem?' asked Bailey.

'Because as soon as he'd left, Toby turned up. I'd mentioned to him earlier that Carl would be out all evening, and Toby had insisted on coming round. So I'd left Jack with my mother, telling Carl that I was planning to spend the evening with some of my girl-friends. Anyway, Toby and I were getting intimate with each other in the living room when suddenly Carl walked in. I didn't even hear him open the front door. When he saw us, his face...' She shook her head tearfully. 'I could see he was completely devastated. He ran out of the house, got into his car and drove off.'

Bailey nodded slowly. Now it was all becoming clear.

Bridget continued. 'I couldn't understand why he'd come back. And then I saw his lucky rabbit's foot on the mantelpiece and I knew he must have come back for it.'

'Did you tell the police any of this?'

Bridget shook her head. 'I was too ashamed. And I told Toby not to say anything either.' She fixed Bailey with a pained guilt-filled expression. 'I don't know exactly what happened to Carl. All I know is that he must have been very upset when he went off to that meet-ing. And he never came back. I think he was in the wrong state of mind and that caused him to make some slip-up... and he got murdered as a result. And it was all because of me. Me and Toby.'

Bridget slumped down in the chair, spent, emotionally exhausted, staring down at the carpet with a distant haunted look on her face.

Bailey observed her sympathetically, feeling somewhat conflicted. On one hand, she wanted to tell Bridget that her husband was alive, that the poor woman hadn't been responsible for his death. But on the other hand, she knew that telling her the truth about him right now was out of the question and could potentially make her feel even worse.

Sitting there in the living room of the small suburban house, Bailey reflected on this new revelation about Carl's disappearance. She realised that it put a completely different spin on the situation.

It occurred to her now that perhaps he wasn't a calculating corrupt copper who'd decided to turn rogue for the money. Maybe he'd suffered some kind of serious mental breakdown triggered by the discovery that his wife had committed a major infidelity with his brother.

Given what she'd learnt about Carl's personality so far, the more this explanation seemed to make sense to her. With his obsessive level of focus on his undercover role, Carl would have been operating at such a high level of intensity that a betrayal of this magnitude, revealed in such a sudden way, could have had a nuclear effect on his mental state, especially if he had been particularly stressed at the time.

But would it really have been enough to tip him over the edge into becoming a vicious hitman? That was the question that needed to be answered. But who could help her answer it?

33

It was Friday morning and there were now only four days to go until the trial began. The cloying sense of urgency inside Bailey was at stark odds with the quiet tranquil atmosphere of the psychologist's waiting room that she was currently sitting in.

She glanced round for something to distract her from her doleful preoccupations. Noticing a lifestyle magazine that was lying on a small table next to a vase of flowers, she picked it up and began to read an article about interior decorating, memorising a few tips for improving her flat... assuming she ever managed to make it back there.

The psychologist's office was located in a large Victorian house on a quiet residential street in Clapham near the Common. The psychologist, Janice, was approved by the College of Policing which meant that she'd been vetted to SC, or Security-Check, level to deal with police officers, including those in undercover roles.

Bailey was supposed to attend appointments with her at least every six months, and also at the beginning and at the close of any large undercover operation. These ongoing assessments were designed to detect any psychological issues that might have presented a risk to her welfare, and which might impact the efficacy or security of an operation. The psychologist was obliged to report any concerns about Bailey's mental health and fitness to operate back to both her undercover covert operations manager and her regular line manager.

Bailey had been close to cancelling this appointment what with the fact that there was a contract out on her, but she was now glad that she hadn't as she had some pertinent questions about Carl Freeman playing on her mind and she was hoping Janice could help her with them.

The buzzer rang and Bailey closed the magazine, dropped it back on the table, stood up and entered the psychologist's office.

Janice was in her mid-fifties with long grey hair, gold-rimmed glasses and a woolly jumper adorned with a large cat-themed brooch. On the desk in front of her was a box of tissues and a laptop. Hanging on the wall behind her was a framed certificate stating that she, Doctor Janice Upton, was a chartered clinical psychologist who was registered with the Health & Care Professions Council.

Janice gave Bailey a warm smile as she entered. 'Bailey how are you? Take a seat please.'

Bailey sat down in a slightly threadbare chair on the other side of the desk facing Janice.

'Would you like a cup of tea and a biscuit?'

'No thanks.'

Janice peered at her laptop. She then gave Bailey a stern look over the top of her glasses.

'Bailey you haven't been to an appointment with me for quite some time. In fact you missed the last two altogether. You know that if you don't attend regular psychological assessments with me then that can affect your eligibility to deploy.'

Bailey nodded earnestly. Normally, the only reason she bothered to attend these appointments was to get the psychologist to tick the necessary boxes in order to allow her to continue working undercover. Without Janice's official approval, Bailey could find herself withdrawn from doing undercover work altogether, and seeing as Bailey lived for undercover work, she couldn't allow that to happen.

It was ironic really, that she'd heard undercover colleagues complain that the box-ticking was part of the problem, that it was too easy for the police force to pretend that they cared about the welfare of their employees by providing them with a psychologist, when in fact it was little more than a thin exercise in covering their backs from any potential litigation from officers who might have suffered mental issues as a result of their work.

For Bailey, on the other hand, this set-up was ideal. The superficial nature of the assessments meant that it was quite easy for her to mislead Janice as to the real state of her psychological health. If Janice had known the truth about Bailey she would never have permitted her to do undercover work.

Although offloading their problems onto a psychologist might have been beneficial for some of her colleagues, Bailey just couldn't bring herself to open up to Janice about the post-traumatic stress disorder that she'd suffered as a result of her torture at the hands of the car theft gang. It was a very dark place that she didn't want to visit. Undercover work was the one thing that helped to distract her from those bad thoughts, and thus she was determined to continue doing it, even if that meant lying to Janice.

'I'm sorry I missed the last few appointments,' said Bailey. 'My father passed away recently and I've been helping my mother to downsize.'

Janice's eyes widened in sympathy, brimming with concern. 'Oh Bailey I'm so sorry to hear that. This must have been devastating for you. Would you like to talk about it?'

Bailey shook her head. 'That's okay. I'm working through it.'

'Okay, well, before we start, is there anything at all you'd like to get off your chest?'

Bailey contemplated telling Janice about Emma's murder and the subsequent grief she'd been feeling, along with the general stress she was under as a result of being hunted by a contract killer, but she didn't want to get side-tracked into talking about herself. She'd come here with an ulterior motive in mind and she was keen to move onto it as soon as possible.

'Everything's fine,' lied Bailey. 'Nothing particularly amiss.'

Janice smiled, apparently pleased. 'Okay, well let's run through the usual questions then.'

These were the mandatory boxes that had to be ticked in order to permit Bailey to continue working undercover. The two of them went through the same questions in every session more or less. They were basic yes or no answers.

'Are you suffering from flashbacks or nightmares?'

Following her infiltration with the car theft gang, Bailey's PTSD had been giving her flashbacks and nightmares for years.

Bailey shook her head. 'I sleep like a baby.'

Janice nodded contentedly and tapped away on her laptop, presumably entering Bailey's response.

'Do you suffer from feelings of persecution or paranoia?' she asked.

Bailey glanced out of the large bay window, wondering if Rex was out there right now, hiding in the bushes or waiting in a car to put a bullet through her head the moment she walked out of here.

'Nah,' she said. 'Not at all.'

Janice smiled, her fingers tapping on the laptop keyboard. She looked up.

'Do you ever have suicidal thoughts?'

Given Bailey's current situation, suicide would have been a luxury.

Bailey shook her head. 'Suicidal thoughts? No. Never.'

Janice dutifully tapped in Bailey's answer.

She asked a few more questions about whether Bailey was self-harming, using illegal drugs or drinking too much, and if she was depressed or having overly morbid thoughts. Bailey responded in the same way that she always did – that there was absolutely nothing for Janice to be concerned about.

'Are you feeling anxious in the least?' asked Janice. 'About anything?'

'Not remotely.' Bailey forced a wan smile. 'I've never felt better.'

Janice squinted at her laptop. 'Well then maybe we should take you off the beta blockers? It sounds like you don't need them. Would you like me to talk to your GP to review your prescription?'

Bailey gulped apprehensively. 'Uh... no, that won't be necessary.' She definitely did need her beta blockers. Without them she'd seize up like an old car on a freezing morning. 'Perhaps I should keep the beta blockers for the time being. You know... just in case.'

Janice frowned, looking a little bothered. 'Are you sure you're being totally open with me about everything Bailey?'

'Would I lie to you?' smiled Bailey.

Janice smiled and relaxed. 'No of course you wouldn't.' She paused. 'Okay we'll let you keep the beta blockers for the time being. Just as a precautionary measure.'

She tapped in something on the computer, then looked up at Bailey with a satisfied expression on her face.

'Well, I'm pleased to say Bailey that your responses to my questions mean that you can carry on working undercover. I'm quite happy to sign you off. You sound like you're in tip-top condition.'

Bailey gave Janice a grateful smile. The requisite boxes had been ticked. It was that easy. This was how it went most sessions.

She looked at her watch. The whole session had taken less than fifteen minutes.

'Well you're free to go now Bailey. Let's book in another appointment, in say three months' time?'

Bailey nodded but made no effort to stand up. Janice gave her a quizzical look.

'I did have one other question,' said Bailey slowly.

'Oh yes?' said Janice, tilting her head amenably.

Bailey took a deep breath. 'Was Detective Sergeant Carl Freeman ever a patient of yours?'

34

Janice assumed a troubled expression.

'I can't talk about my other patients Bailey. You know that. It's a matter of professional ethics.'

Bailey nodded. 'Yes, of course.'

Janice had been working in this role for years and Bailey was certain that Carl Freeman had been a patient of hers even if she wasn't prepared to admit to the fact.

'I mean I'm sure you wouldn't want me discussing your psychological details with other people,' said Janice.

'If I was dead I wouldn't particularly care,' said Bailey. 'Carl has been dead for three years.'

Janice gave Bailey a stern look. 'Well, dead or alive, all of my patients have the privilege of confidentiality.'

Bailey was disappointed by Janice's reluctance to discuss Carl directly. Getting some psychological insight into Carl's character was really the only reason she'd come here.

'Why do you want to know about Carl Freeman?' asked Janice with a curious frown. 'Not that I'm willing to discuss him personally,' she quickly added.

Chewing her lip, Bailey tried to think of some other angle from which to broach the subject she was interested in.

'I was concerned about stress management,' she said, thinking of what Bridget Freeman had told her. 'I heard that Carl didn't have much time for that kind of thing.'

Janice frowned. 'Well he always seemed very balanced to me.'

Bailey wondered if Carl had been as evasive with Janice as Bailey was herself. With his disdain for stress management techniques, coupled with his intense obsessive personality, had he been getting increasingly tightly wound without realising it, the inner tension ratcheting up and up until, like a mechanism that can be wound up no further, the tiniest incremental pressure snaps the spring and causes the whole thing to fly violently apart? Total mental breakdown.

'But like I said,' added Janice, 'I don't want to discuss Carl Freeman.'

'That's okay,' said Bailey. 'But I did have a question. If someone did happen to be, say, very tightly wound, then could some kind of emotional shock push them over the edge into a full-blown mental breakdown.'

Janice nodded. 'Most definitely Bailey. Now if you'd like some tips on how to wind down, I can give you some links to some really good mindfulness videos on YouTube, and a—'

'What would be the symptoms of that?' interjected Bailey.

Janice looked a bit put out. 'A mental breakdown? Well, it would be indicated by a complete inability to cope with anything.'

Bailey scratched her head, somewhat perplexed. From what Janice was saying, it sounded like someone in that state would be little more than a gibbering useless wreck. Rex didn't come across like that. Quite the opposite in fact.

'But what if the person can cope?' said Bailey. 'Is it possible to suffer a mental breakdown but still be able to function?'

'Yes,' replied Janice. 'It is possible that the person deals with the breakdown by compartmentalising their identity in order to continue functioning.'

'You mean... they assume a different identity?' said Bailey. That familiar tingling feeling was starting to creep over her, the one she got when she felt she was onto something. 'Do you think that working undercover is conducive to this kind of thing?'

'The personality splitting apart under conditions of extreme stress?' Janice paused thoughtfully. 'Yes I would say so. Working undercover is by its very nature quite schizophrenic. Maintaining two or more identities over extended periods of time can place great psychological stress on an individual. You might say it's almost the first step towards living with dissociative identity disorder... more commonly known as split personality. Survival is contingent upon maintaining adequate compartmentalisation between the different identities. We in the psychological profession know that working undercover long-term can lead to identity issues.'

Bailey understood exactly what Janice was talking about. The more extreme the immersion in the cover identity, the more pronounced the division became between the real personality of the police officer and the individual they were pretending to be. Carl Freeman, with his heavy interest in method acting, had adopted a particularly extreme form of immersion in his cover identity. Could it be that a perfect-storm scenario had arisen whereby an emotional shock had tipped him over the edge into permanently and irrevocably assuming his own cover identity?

It barely seemed believable. Yet it explained everything.

The idea of it scared Bailey immensely for it was a form of insanity, and there was no reasoning with people who'd entered that realm.

'Is it conceivable that a person could remain in this other personality permanently?' she asked.

Janice studied Bailey for a few long moments, then nodded slowly. 'It sounds to me like you're describing a fugue.'

'A fugue?' echoed Bailey. The word meant nothing to her.

'A fugue is a clouded mental state in which the person suffers a complete loss of memory triggered by a deeply traumatic emotional occurrence. It comes from the Latin word *fugere* which means "to flee". The person is basically fleeing from the traumatic event by retreating into the fugue state.'

'So what happens in this fugue state?' asked Bailey.

'Well,' explained Janice, 'whilst in a fugue state, the person assumes a completely different personality. It's a form of defence mechanism which allows the person to completely separate themselves from the traumatic emotional event and anything associated with it. A fugue is, in essence, a form of dissociative identity disorder. The sufferer doesn't realise that anything is wrong. That's because they lose all memory of anything that happened before the fugue, including the traumatic event that precipitated it.'

Bailey pondered Janice's words. 'So it's like they've got amnesia?'

Janice nodded. 'Exactly. It's a form of amnesia known as retrograde amnesia. That means that the person cannot recall things that occurred prior to the triggering event.'

A nonplussed expression descended on Bailey's face. Rex had built up a very solid reputation as a highly efficient hitman. She was puzzled as to how he could operate so successfully if he had amnesia.

'But surely a person can't function at all if they can't remember anything,' she said.

'Aha, well that's an interesting point,' said Janice, gesturing excitedly with a finger. 'A fugue constitutes a selective memory impairment, which means that the person only forgets certain things. And what they forget tells us a lot about how the personality is constructed. You see, in a fugue state, procedural memory is unaffected. That means that you remember how to do things that you learnt prior to entering the fugue state. For example if you learnt to speak Italian, then you'd still be able to speak Italian.'

'Or shoot a gun?' suggested Bailey, thinking of Rex's numerous murders.

Janice nodded. 'Shoot a gun. Drive a car. Make an omelette. Any of those things would be unaffected.' She paused. 'It's episodic memory that's affected when you enter a fugue state. That's where the amnesia occurs. Episodic memory is basically the history of your life. You see, your personal identity has a temporal element... that is, it's linked to time. So in a fugue state you might remember how to ride a bike but you won't remember the experience of actually learning to do it. You won't remember that it was your father who taught you on the driveway of your family house on a series of sunny Saturday afternoons twenty-five years ago.'

Bailey meditated on what Janice was telling her. As Rex, Carl Freeman would have retained all of the skills he'd acquired prior to the fugue, but none of the knowledge of how he'd actually acquired those skills... or who he had been.

'We are our memories,' said Janice. 'Our identity is anchored to our personal experiences. If you give up the identity then you give up the memories. Or, to look at it the other way round, if you completely repress the memories then you completely lose the identity.'

'This fugue state,' asked Bailey. 'How long does it last?'

Janice shrugged. 'That depends. Although fugues often just last for a few days, or sometimes a few weeks, it has been known in some cases for patients to "come to" months or even years later.'

Bailey nodded with interest. What Janice was saying seemed to suggest that it was possible for Carl Freeman to have been occupying a fugue state for the past three years.

'When you say "come to", do you mean that it's possible to snap someone out of it?' she asked.

'Certainly. Just as an emotional event precipitated the fugue, some kind of emotional trigger will break the fugue. It could be a smell or a sound, or perhaps an image. It's very difficult to say as it depends completely on how deeply engrained that trigger is within the mind of the sufferer. It really is very specific to the individual.'

'And once they wake up, they're back to normal?'

'Yes. Their past identity and past history come back to them. The interesting thing is that once they emerge from the fugue they remember nothing of the fugue state itself or what took place whilst they were in it.'

'Fascinating,' murmured Bailey.

'I should remind you though that a fugue state is a very rare phenomenon and probably not something you should be worrying about Bailey.' She smiled brightly. 'After all, the answers to your questions indicate that you're a glowing picture of mental health.'

'That I am,' said Bailey. 'And I feel even better after coming to see you Janice.'

35

Rex was in a foul mood, aggravated partly by his lack of progress in tracking down Bailey Morgan. It was Friday evening now and he'd spent the whole of that day, and the previous day as well, cruising the streets of Earl's Court in an attempt to find out where she lived, but to no avail. Using the address on the receipt that he'd picked up in the hallway outside her friend's flat, he'd located the small supermarket on Earl's Court Road in which Bailey had bought the bottle of wine that she'd thrown at him during their encounter. He was certain that she was staying somewhere in the vicinity of the supermarket, but the question was where? Was she in one of the many cheap hotels in the area, was she in a rented flat, was she in an Airbnb, or was she staying with friends or family? He had no idea.

He'd mainly been keeping an eye out for her silver Audi, whose license plate he'd memorised after following her from Tavistock Square, but he hadn't spotted her car parked anywhere. Although he sensed that he was closing in on her, his fruitless searching was making him impatient for he was keenly aware that time was running out. He had less than four days left in which to kill her.

He now stood on the bow of his catamaran, brooding darkly as the sun set above the tops of the surrounding buildings. Although Bailey Morgan was seriously irritating him, the main cause of his negative disposition this evening lay on a fundamentally deeper level. He'd made the mistake of trying to think a bit too hard about the past and whenever he did that it inevitably plunged him into a state of chagrin. However much effort he made, there was a certain point beyond which he couldn't remember anything whatsoever, and this made him angry and frustrated.

Standing there on the bow of the boat, he once again raked over that pivotal point in his memory – that very first episode that he was able to confidently recall with any kind of clarity. It had been the evening and he'd been driving along the M1, heading into London to see a man called Jack Wynter about a hit. Rain had been pelting down on the windscreen and the wipers had been going furiously. He'd just passed the Brockley Interchange at Junction 4, hurtling by in the fast lane, the headlight beams cutting through the driving rain before him, the sky dark and stormy above. But as for where he'd set out from, how long he'd been driving, or indeed anything that he'd been doing before that point, he had absolutely no idea. He knew that, in the other direction from London, the M1 went up to Watford, Hemel Hempstead, Luton, Milton Keynes... right up to the north of England. But at what point had he joined the M1? What had been his place of origin?

The memory both puzzled and perturbed him. If only he knew the answer to the enigma that it presented. But everything prior to it was obscured by the fog, and, hard as he tried, he was never able to penetrate through to see what it concealed.

From that point onwards, after Junction 4 on the M1, everything was crystal clear and he remembered it perfectly. He'd got into London perhaps an hour later, meeting Wynter in the back room of a small fish restaurant in Limehouse in East London, just as they'd arranged. Somehow, despite the massive deficit in his memory, that information was in his head, along with everything about who he was, what he did and how he did it. Wynter had sat there over a plate of mussels telling him all about Vincent Peck's catamaran. Where it was berthed. How it was registered under a false name. How it had secret compartments in the twin hulls. And most importantly, the fact that Vincent Peck was likely to be there that very same evening, for he was expecting Wynter to pay him a visit in order to discuss some business... but of course, it wouldn't be Wynter he'd be meeting, it would be Rex. Wynter had slipped Rex an access card to the electronic gate that would allow him onto the pontoon where the catamaran was berthed. And then he'd given Rex the money, passing it under the table to him. The briefcase containing fifty thousand pounds in used bank notes. And as for what had happened after that? Well, that was history...

A large seagull landed on the deck a few feet away from him, breaking his train of thought. It strutted around defiantly, fixing him with its beady eyes. He lashed out with a vicious kick and it flapped away with a loud squawk.

'That's not very nice,' said a voice behind him. He turned round. Milena was standing there on the pontoon watching him. He'd been so deep in thought that he hadn't registered her arrival.

'I hate fucking seagulls,' he muttered.

'You hate seagulls?' she asked as she stepped aboard the catamaran. 'Why? I've always liked them myself.'

'I don't know. I just do. I don't like the way they look at me. I feel like they know something about me that I don't.'

'Maybe it knows your secret,' said Milena with that familiar teasing twinkle in her eyes.

But Rex wasn't in the mood for her teasing tonight. 'You keep going on about my secret,' he snapped. 'What secret?'

She winked and tapped her nose. 'That's for me to know and you to find out.'

'What do you want?' he demanded. 'Why are you here?'

'I thought you might appreciate a bit of company,' she said. 'It is Friday night after all.'

* * *

Later that Friday, after returning from her appointment with Janice, Bailey went out for an early dinner in a cheap Lebanese restaurant near to her hotel. It was one of the more preferable choices in the immediate area and the proprietor was a friendly sort. On entering the place at six-thirty, she found that she was the only patron in there. As the sun went down outside, she sat by herself in the corner of the restaurant eating a chicken shawarma, ruminating on what she'd learnt over the past two days.

Although it was currently impossible to prove, Bailey felt a deep inner conviction that Carl Freeman was operating in a fugue state just as Janice had described. Something about it rung true with her given what she knew of his personality and what she'd subsequently discovered about his personal life from Bridget. The question was whether these newfound insights about Carl the policeman would help her get any closer to successfully apprehending Rex the hitman. At the moment she couldn't see any direct way that they could. Time was running out and she was still no closer to catching him.

Either way, she knew it was important to let Stella know what she'd found out. Finishing off her chicken shawarma, she took out her phone. Glancing round the restaurant, she saw that she was still the only patron in there. The proprietor was hovering around at the front by the grill, gazing out the window, nodding his head to the Lebanese pop music that was playing in the background. She reckoned it would be fine to talk to Stella if she kept her voice low. She dialled Stella's number.

'Good timing,' said Stella, answering almost immediately. 'I was just about to call you. I've got an important update for you.'

There was a portentous tone in Stella's voice. Bailey felt a faint quiver of apprehension. 'Oh yeah?'

'I informed senior management that we are now almost certain that Rex is in fact a former Metropolitan Police officer by the name of Carl Freeman.'

Bailey swallowed tensely. 'And?'

'They were none too pleased, as you might expect. They didn't want to believe it at first but when I laid out all the evidence, including your eyewitness encounter with him, they didn't have much choice but to accept what I had told them.'

'Does this change anything?' asked Bailey.

Stella breathed out uneasily through her teeth. 'Yes and no. They still want to stop him. In fact, if anything, this makes them want to stop him even more. However the emphasis of the operation has now shifted to damage limitation.'

'Damage limitation, huh?' said Bailey raising her eyebrows cynically.

She understood only too well the implications of what Stella was saying. Senior management wanted to do their utmost to avoid a high-profile trial and the accompanying media shitstorm that would ensue. The best way to achieve this would be if Rex ended up dead with some kind of convenient cover-up in place to conceal the fact that he'd once been a Metropolitan Police officer. Of course, neither they nor Stella would ever openly admit to this for it basically amounted to murder. But Bailey knew that there were ways and means of subverting the outcome of the operation so that it would end legitimately in this manner if those in charge desired it so.

'Well, I'm not sure things are quite so simple any more,' said Bailey.

'What do you mean?' asked Stella, sounding perplexed.

Bailey recounted the details of her recent conversation with Bridget Freeman, along with what she'd learnt on her subsequent visit to the psychologist. She elaborated on the strange psychological phenomenon that appeared to afflict Carl Freeman.

After finishing her explanation, she waited with bated breath for Stella's reaction.

'Interesting...' murmured Stella. 'A fugue, huh? That's the first time I've come across that concept. Whilst it might explain a lot about what's happened to him, it's not really something you can prove is it? It's just speculation really, and I think you'd have a very tough time getting senior management to buy it.'

Bailey smiled mirthlessly. Stella's response didn't exactly come as a surprise to her.

'As a theory, I know it sounds pretty far out,' she said, 'and I don't expect you or them to just blindly accept it. But I feel inside myself that this is where the truth lies. The more I've come to understand Carl Freeman, the more credible this explanation seems.'

'You're basically telling me he's got amnesia,' said Stella, sounding doubtful.

'More or less,' said Bailey. 'Carl Freeman was a bit too diligent in creating the persona of Rex. In keeping with his obsessively conscientious approach to building a believable cover identity he created a monster. Now he inhabits that monster. But deep inside, somewhere in the recesses of his brain is the real Carl Freeman, locked away, unable to emerge. But...' she added excitedly, 'it might just be possible to wake him up.'

'Wake him up?' Stella sounded deeply sceptical. 'How on earth are you planning to do that?'

Bailey sighed. 'Well, that's the problem. I have no idea what kind of trigger possesses the right emotional associations to reach through to the real Carl Freeman.'

'Well, even if you did,' said Stella, 'it sounds like a supremely risky thing to attempt. I think he'd probably shoot you before you got the chance to do anything of the sort.'

'True,' admitted Bailey. 'But don't you see what all of this means? If I'm correct about him being in a fugue state then surely it begs the question whether Carl Freeman the policeman is fully culpable for the crimes of Rex the hitman. Surely that's something only a judge and a panel of doctors can decide... if and when we ever capture him.'

Stella went silent for a few moments and Bailey could tell she was chewing over the quandary. Presently she spoke.

'This doesn't change things that much, Bailey. If Carl Freeman was driven mad by stress then the Met would still be to blame. They worked him too hard and he had a mental breakdown and turned into a psychotic killer. Whether this is actually the case, or whether he is just a rogue cop, it's a stain on the Force whichever way you look at it. Either way he's a huge embarrassment to the Met.'

Bailey pursed her lips pensively. Stronger than ever now, she got the impression that those at the top were determined that this operation conclude in one way and one way only – with Rex's death.

Stella seemed to sense the nature of Bailey's thoughts. 'Don't forget, Bailey, Rex is a highly dangerous individual who is responsible for multiple murders, including a well-respected lawyer and a police officer who also happened to be a good friend of yours. Right now, he's very much focused on trying to kill you, and if we don't stop him then he might very well succeed.'

Bailey nodded glumly. In that point at least, Stella was right. Whatever the truth of the matter with Carl Freeman, the reality was that in his incarnation as Rex the hitman, he was still dead set on exterminating her. And she was still no closer to stopping him.

36

Charlie Benvenuto awoke on the morning of Saturday the fifth of October seized by an intense concern about his upcoming trial. There were three days to go and as far as he knew Bailey Morgan still wasn't dead which meant he was a hundred and fifty grand down and looking at a long stretch inside.

Lying there in the emperor-size bed next to his sleeping wife, the luxury mattress and the expensive bed sheets made of 800-thread count Egyptian cotton seemed more comfortable than ever when he contemplated the grim prospect of prison life. He'd be sleeping on some narrow iron-framed bed with a crappy mattress and cheap scratchy sheets, sharing a cell with some other bloke who would be lying a few feet away snoring and farting. And that's what it would be like for the next twenty years.

He turned his head to look at Amy beside him. She looked peaceful in sleep, not troubled like she did when she was awake. He knew that when she woke up, that aged demeanour would descend upon her, and now, unlike before, a glimmer of fear and distrust would appear in her eyes whenever she looked his way. Something had altered the way that she perceived him, as if he'd somehow let the mask slip and she'd seen him for what he really was. Despite his attempts to cajole her with declarations of love, he sensed that something had permanently changed between them, and not in a good way.

He felt both sad and angry that it had come to this. And once again the focal point of his animosity centred in upon the under-cover cop that had caused all of this to happen in the first place.

Bailey Morgan.

He wanted her dead more than ever now. Getting her out of the way for the purposes of scuppering the trial was one thing. But increasingly, he'd been relishing the thought of her death as a form of revenge for all the trouble she'd caused him.

Bailey Morgan had to die because if she didn't then Charlie Benvenuto was as good as dead because a life inside just wasn't worth living.

37

Bailey woke up bleary-eyed on Saturday morning. She hadn't had a great night's sleep. Once again she'd been tormented by nightmares about Rex. Not only was he hunting her in real life, he was hunting her in her dreams as well. Asleep or awake, there was no refuge from his relentless pursuit.

The trial was three days away now and she knew Rex must be feeling the pressure, insofar as someone in his peculiar state could feel pressure. She knew that Charlie Benvenuto must also be feeling the pressure, for if she wasn't dead by Tuesday then she would testify against him and he would likely be sent to prison as a result. But would any of this be over even when he was locked up? She doubted it. From what she understood of how Rex operated, Benvenuto would have paid him in advance and from what she'd heard about Rex, once he was paid he always finished the job for his very reputation depended upon it.

She'd had enough of living in this hellish limbo. Rex had to be stopped. The sooner that happened, the sooner she would be free to go back to her old life.

Lying in bed in the grotty hotel room, she stared up at the cracks in the ceiling, racking her mind for a possible solution to her dilemma.

She thought back to the undercover operation that Carl Freeman had been working on at the point when he'd made the calamitous transformation into Rex. Something about it had been niggling at her ever since Frank had told her about it. She possessed the irksome feeling that she was overlooking something obvious.

What was she missing?

She frowned to herself, running through every possible angle in her head. And then it hit her…

The snout.

Of course.

She'd somehow neglected to consider the role of the informant in what had happened to Carl Freeman. Despite her extensive discussion with Frank about Freeman, she'd left Frank's house without asking him about the role of the very person who'd introduced Carl to Jack Wynter in the first place.

The informant would have known Rex as Carl Freeman the undercover police officer. But, more importantly, would this person also have known Freeman as Rex the ruthless hitman after he turned to the dark side? If so, how did this person figure in all of this?

The more Bailey thought about it, the more she became convinced that the informant was a vital link in getting to the bottom of this situation. She wondered with growing excitement if they would even be able to provide some clue as to where Rex currently was.

In the documentation relating to the operation, the informant had only been referred to by their codename, 'Seagull'. This was standard operating procedure in order to protect the informant's identity.

Gripped by a sudden impatience to know more about this

person, she sat up in bed and picked her iPhone up off the bedside table. It had just gone seven-thirty. She knew Frank well enough to know that he was an early riser and she was sure he would have got up by now.

She dialled his number and lay there in bed waiting for him to answer.

He answered the phone through a mouthful of crunching. 'I'm relieved to hear that you're still alive Bailey.'

'I'm sorry to disturb you midway through your cornflakes Frank.'

'They're Coco Pops actually.'

She couldn't help but smile to herself. He really did need to stop eating junk food.

'I had a question about the Jack Wynter operation,' she said, getting to the point. 'I neglected to ask you about the snout who introduced Carl Freeman to Jack Wynter. In the documentation relating to the operation, this person is referred to by their code-name of "Seagull". I should have asked you about him but it slipped my mind in all the excitement.'

'Ah yes. Seagull.' Frank paused to swallow his mouthful of Coco Pops. 'Well, for starters, Seagull was a woman, not a man.'

Bailey raised her eyebrows. 'The informant was a woman? Can you tell me her name?'

'Yeah it was an unusual name. Foreign. Her name was Milena Roksander.'

Bailey rolled the name off her tongue. 'Milena Roksander...'

Reaching over to the bedside table, she picked up a pen and the small complimentary notepad. 'How do you spell that?' she asked.

Frank spelled it out and Bailey wrote the name down on the notepad.

'She'd been on our payroll for a while,' said Frank. 'Feeding us titbits of information here and there. Nothing too spectacular. But enough to constitute a decent little revenue stream for her, courtesy of the UK taxpayer.'

Bailey knew that the police paid decently for good information, and although money wasn't the only reason people turned informant, it often played a strong motivating factor.

Frank continued. 'She'd had dealings with Wynter on several occasions and he'd grown to trust her. Enough to ask her if she knew anyone who'd be willing to murder his business partner. As soon as she reported back to us on it, we knew it was something we had to act on.'

'You told me she introduced Freeman to Wynter as this ruthless hitman who would kill Peck.'

'That's right. She was essentially acting as a broker for the hit.'

'So what happened after Freeman "disappeared"?'

'Well, after Carl went missing, we brought her in for questioning. We were desperate to know what had happened. And we did contemplate the possibility that she might have betrayed him. As you well know, informants tend to be treacherous people by their very nature. But she insisted that, just like us, she believed that Freeman had gone to this second meeting with Wynter, and had been murdered and his body disposed of. And that was that. There was no evidence to prove that Wynter killed Carl so we had to leave it at that.'

'This Milena Roksander... do you know if she's still working as an informant?'

'My last contact with her was three years ago. I have no idea if she's still a snout. You'd have to check her authorisation record.'

Bailey thanked him and hung up the phone, leaving him to continue eating his breakfast.

She looked at the name she'd written down on the notepad. Getting out of bed, she went over to her laptop and switched it on. Logging into the police computer system, she accessed the

CHIS authorisation record for Milena Roksander, codenamed Seagull.

The information contained within the record was minimal, displaying just her name, her codename, and the dates on which her authorisation was granted, renewed and... cancelled.

Looking at the record, Bailey saw that the authorisation was no longer in effect. The date of cancellation indicated that Milena Roksander had not been working as an informant for almost three years. It looked like the last time she'd worked for the police had been the Jack Wynter operation.

The authorisation record was accompanied by some supporting documentation outlining the reasons why she was of value as a CHIS, and the circumstances under which she'd been assigned her various tasks. From the relatively sparse information in front of her, Bailey gleaned that Milena operated as a kind of criminal fixer who had a knack for insinuating herself into organised crime groups.

But Bailey wasn't getting much idea of her as a person – how old she was, where she was originally from, or what she looked like. Knowing that many informants were themselves criminals, Bailey accessed the Police National Computer to check if Milena Roksander had a criminal record. Whereas the Police National Database held operational and intelligence information, the Police National Computer was where criminal records were held, containing details such as cautions, arrests and convictions.

Bailey was vindicated to see that Milena Roksander did indeed possess a criminal record. It turned out that she'd been convicted of fraud several years prior to becoming an informant. Scanning through her personal details, Bailey saw that she was thirty-two years old and was of Serbian nationality.

Because the Police National Computer was a text-only system, there were no photographs associated with the criminal record. If a custody image, or mugshot, had been taken upon her initial arrest, it would have been uploaded onto the Police National Database. Logging into the PND, Bailey entered Milena's name to see if any custody images existed of her... and as it happened they did.

When Milena's picture came up on the screen, Bailey immediately gave a sharp intake of breath for she recognised the face instantly. It was the blonde woman she'd encountered in Tavistock Square, the one who'd hurt her wrist. Although she looked somewhat younger in the photograph, and her blonde hair was styled differently, the sharp devious set of her pretty face was unmistakeable.

Momentarily stunned, Bailey took a moment to ponder the significance of this revelation.

She realised that the reason Milena Roksander had been in Tavistock Square was because she must have been brokering the hit on behalf of Rex. There was no other explanation. *She* was the contact they were supposed to meet, not Rex.

Bailey shook her head in disbelief. She couldn't believe how close they'd come to catching Milena without realising it. Had they left it a minute or two longer, instead of rashly pursuing the wrong man, they would probably have apprehended her. Bailey reflected with bitter irony that she'd actually talked to this woman, totally oblivious to who she really was. Thinking back, she now recalled that odd expression on the woman's face. It made perfect sense now. The woman had recognised Bailey. With a chill, Bailey realised that the motorbike that had been following her might actually have been Rex after all. Maybe the blonde woman had put him onto her after she'd left Tavistock Square. Bailey stared at the photo on the screen, looking at the woman with an increased sense of wariness. This Milena Roksander was a dangerous individual indeed.

By this point it had become abundantly clear to Bailey that something very odd was going on. The informant who'd been pretending to broker hits for the fake hitman played by Carl

Freeman now appeared to be doing the same thing for Rex... but for real.

Bailey was convinced that Carl Freeman had lost his mind and become Rex, but she wasn't willing to accept that the same thing had happened to Milena Roksander. No. There was something else going on here and she was determined to find out what it was. More importantly, she was sure that Milena Roksander was the key to finding Rex. A buzzing surge of anticipation went through her. She felt like she'd made a major breakthrough. She just needed to find out where Milena lived.

Bailey knew that the address on Milena's criminal record was potentially several years out of date. In terms of finding out her current address, Bailey would normally have checked the electoral register, but she figured that as a Serbian national, Milena wouldn't be on there. So, hoping that Milena held a UK driver's license, Bailey went back to the Police National Computer and checked the Drivers File – a database containing the driving license details for every single person holding a UK driving license, including their current address. It turned out that Milena did indeed hold a UK driving license.

Bailey excitedly scribbled down Milena's address on the notepad beneath her name. She lived in Bethnal Green in East London.

Picking up her iPhone, she called Stella and explained what she'd discovered.

'This is getting weirder and weirder,' remarked Stella.

'You're telling me,' said Bailey.

'This is excellent work Bailey. It's a solid lead and we need to act on it immediately. Normally we'd place her under surveillance and let her lead us to him, but that means applying for a warrant, plus we could be waiting around for a while before she leads us to him. Time is of the essence here. We need to bring her in immediately for questioning. Do we know her current whereabouts?'

Bailey read Milena's address off the notepad.

'Leave it with me,' said Stella. 'I'll let you know when we've detained her.'

38

Rex jogged along by the River Thames, passing in front of the Tower of London, heading back towards St Katharine Docks. He'd got up early that Saturday morning to go for a run in the hope that it would focus his mind on the rather pressing matter of Bailey Morgan. He had three days in which to kill her and he still hadn't worked out how to do so.

As a last resort he'd considered the possibility of killing her as she entered court on Tuesday, but he regarded the chances of succeeding in that as pretty slim as he imagined security would be extremely tight, not to mention the fact that she'd probably be ushered inside the building through some hidden back entrance with the utmost secrecy. If he was to be honest with himself, he knew that his only realistic option was to locate her and dispatch her before she got anywhere near court. The burning question was how?

The footpath he was on was already busy with tourists, bumbling around taking pictures of each other in front of the Tower of London. Standing on one side of the path hoping to earn some money from them was a swarthy-looking man playing an accordion. He was there almost every day, this little spot being his regular pitch. Every time Rex passed him, he gave Rex a jovial smile, and every time he did, Rex returned him a cold glare. Rex hated accordions. They were almost as bad as the bagpipes.

And then it hit him.

Bagpipes.

He stopped mid-stride to mull it over. His mind went back to Bailey's mother and what she'd told him.

A bagpiper playing right outside Bailey's window.

Rex was sure that Bailey was probably staying somewhere in Earl's Court, but if there was a bagpiper playing outside her window then that could only mean one thing...

A busker.

And surely there couldn't be that many buskers in Earl's Court who played the bagpipes. Buskers liked to stick to certain pitches, as the accordion player demonstrated.

What he needed to do was start looking for buskers who played the bagpipes in the Earl's Court area, and with any luck it would lead him to Bailey Morgan.

Rex felt a sharp twinge of annoyance with himself for not making the busker connection earlier. Still, better late than never. And there was no time to lose.

Sprinting back to the catamaran, he fervently reflected that soon enough Janet Morgan would be visiting two graves in the cemetery.

39

Bailey walked into the interview room to be confronted by the sight of Milena Roksander sitting behind the table with her arms crossed and her pretty face twisted into a defiant sneer. Her blonde hair was tangled and she was wearing jeans and a tracksuit top, as if she'd been roused unexpectedly and forced to throw on whatever clothes lay to hand.

Stella, clad in plainclothes with her warrant card on a lanyard round her neck, was standing up leaning against the wall. She flickered a nod to Bailey. Stella, along with some uniformed officers, had picked up Milena an hour or so earlier from her Bethnal Green apartment and brought her here to this Central London police station for questioning.

Milena's expression changed the instant she recognised Bailey, the arrogant mask momentarily slipping to reveal a flash of something akin to fear, but then just as quickly she gathered herself to reassume her prior demeanour.

Bailey eyed the elasticated support bandage that Milena was wearing. 'How's the wrist?' she asked dryly.

Milena rolled her eyes and emitted a derogatory huff. 'You can't just keep me here for no reason.'

'We can hold you for up to twenty-four hours before we have to charge you with something,' said Bailey.

'I haven't done anything wrong.'

Bailey shrugged. Sitting down at the table opposite Milena, she switched on the audio-recording equipment. She stated the place, date and time of the interview as well as her name and rank. She nodded to Stella who then stated her name and rank.

Bailey then outlined to Milena the capacity in which they were questioning her. 'You are being interviewed because you are suspected to be responsible for brokering contract killings on behalf of a professional hitman.'

She then recited the mandatory police caution. 'You do not have to say anything. But, it may harm your defence if you do not mention when questioned something which you later rely on in court. Anything you do say may be given in evidence.'

'I'm not saying anything,' declared Milena, jutting her jaw indignantly.

'You have the right to private legal consultation. You may do this in person or by telephone.'

Milena raised her eyebrows. 'Thanks for reminding me. Yeah, I want to talk to a solicitor. I've got rights you know.'

Bailey swapped glances with Stella. She leaned into the audio recorder. 'We are stopping the interview because the suspect has requested legal consultation. The time is ten thirty-five.'

She switched off the recorder with a click. They were not legally permitted to continue the interview until Milena had received the legal advice that she had requested.

Milena gave her a smug grin. Bailey responded with a grim smile of her own and fixed Milena with a steely gaze. With the interview currently on hold and the recorder switched off, any subsequent conversation was not going to be admissible as evidence in court, however that wasn't going to deter Bailey from achieving her aims.

'You used to work as a registered informant for the Metropolitan Police, didn't you?' she said. 'I was looking at your details just this morning.'

Milena's eyes darted nervously. 'I don't do that stuff any more.'

'Once a rat always a rat,' said Bailey. 'If you don't cooperate with me then I will do my best to spread it around to all and sundry that you were an informant.'

'You wouldn't do that,' scoffed Milena disbelievingly, a note of panic entering her voice.

'Oh yes I would,' said Bailey. 'Someone called Rex is trying to kill me so I don't really give a fuck what happens to you. I don't think you would last very long out there if the whole of the London underworld knows that you used to be a rat. I know some of the people you stitched up. I wonder how they'd feel if I let them know it was you who was responsible.'

Milena fixed Bailey with a rancorous stare. Bailey gazed back at her firmly, unblinking.

'I know that you work hand in glove with the contract killer commonly referred to as Rex.' Bailey paused. 'I happen to know the real identity of Rex. At one time he was an undercover police officer called Carl Freeman and you were the informant who introduced him to Jack Wynter.'

Milena's eyes widened, betraying her surprise that Bailey had managed to find out this information. Her mouth puckered slightly in concern but she didn't say anything.

'I want you to tell us where we can find Carl Freeman a.k.a. Rex,' said Bailey. 'And then I want you to explain how all of this came about in the first place. I want to understand exactly what happened on the night that Carl Freeman went missing and I want to know how Rex came into being. And I want to know the role that you played in all of this.'

Milena tossed her head, flicking her hair down over her face to hide behind it, her darting rodent eyes peering out sullenly from behind the blonde strands.

The interview room fell into a tense silence as Bailey waited for her to speak, but still Milena said nothing. Bailey glanced up at Stella. Stella bore a stern inscrutable expression. Bailey turned back to Milena.

'Rex murdered a good friend of mine,' she said. 'I will go to any lengths to get him. And if that means dropping you in the shit then so be it. Don't think I won't.'

Stella pushed herself off the wall and took a few steps forward to hover over Milena menacingly. 'I'd pay attention to her if I was you. Once Bailey gets it in her head to do something there's no stopping her.'

Milena looked up at them from beneath her hair, her gaze flickering between them both. Bailey sensed that some kind of calculation was taking place inside her scheming blonde head. She could almost hear the cogs furiously whirring. Milena's eyes narrowed slyly and she tossed her hair back out of her face.

'I will cooperate with you if you agree not to charge me with anything.'

Bailey swapped glances with Stella. Stella chewed her lip pensively.

'This is not a negotiation,' said Bailey. 'Remember what I said. I'll tell everyone I know that you're a rat. Now tell us what we want to know.'

Milena gave her a cold reptilian smile. 'Rex is going to kill you in the very near future. He has to kill you by the eighth of October. Did you know that?'

Once again Bailey and Stella looked at each other, both of them realising simultaneously that this confirmed that it had to be Charlie Benvenuto who was behind the hit, just as they'd suspected all along.

Milena caught the look that passed between them. 'It looks like you already know,' she said. 'I guess you have your suspicions about who hired Rex to kill you. Well I can help you to prove those suspicions. If you drop the charges against me.'

'Tell us the name of that person now,' demanded Bailey.

'I don't know the client's name. I didn't ask. I never do. But I'm sure I can help you find him.' She paused and raised one eyebrow in a cautioning manner. 'But just remember though. Rex has never failed to fulfil a contract. He will kill you by the eighth. Have no doubt about that. He's your immediate problem. And I know as well as you do that you need to stop him as soon as possible. And I can help you do that. I can help you right now.'

Bailey ground her jaw in annoyance, but she knew that Milena was right. Milena had read the situation well and was now manipulating it to barter Rex for her own freedom.

Slippery self-serving bitch, thought Bailey. *Typical informant.*

Milena smiled at her smugly, confident in the knowledge that she held a strong hand.

Bailey glanced once again at Stella. Stella gave her a tiny nod of assent.

'Okay,' said Bailey. 'We haven't officially charged you with anything yet. And we can't do so until we complete your interview under caution. If you agree to cooperate with us in every way that we specify, we won't interview you and we won't charge you.'

Milena eyed them both suspiciously. 'I want it in writing.' she said. 'On headed notepaper. Signed by the both of you.'

Bailey glanced at Stella who sighed and rolled her eyes.

'Fine,' said Stella grudgingly. 'If that's what you want, that's what you can have.'

40

Traffic rumbled past Rex as he prowled through the streets of Earl's Court, his gaze scanning from side to side. Dressed casually in his black bomber jacket and a pair of jeans, he also carried a small innocuous-looking day pack on his back. A few moments later he stopped in his tracks, his finely tuned sense of hearing detecting the distant but unmistakeable sound of bagpipes. Feeling a jolt of anticipation, he quickened his pace, heading in the direction of the sound.

Turning onto a side street, he saw the busker up ahead of him. A red-haired, bearded man dressed in full highland garb of green tartan kilt, knee socks, sporran and cap, he was blowing furiously into his bagpipes in an attempt to render the song 'Scotland the Brave'. As Rex drew closer he noticed a Campbell's Pure Butter Shortbread tin sitting on the ground in front of the busker with a few coins in it.

The busker tried to make friendly eye contact with Rex as he approached but Rex ignored him, concentrating instead on the hotel outside which he was playing. It was called the Royal City Hotel and was one of many of a similar ilk in the area. It was pretty shabby in appearance, and it looked just the kind of place where Bailey Morgan might be living on a temporary basis. A bit out of the way. Probably not too expensive. Convenient on-site parking... not that he could currently see her Audi.

He peered up at the bird-shit-covered façade wondering if this was where she was staying, and if she was in there right now. The trail was hotter now than it had ever been and Rex felt the familiar accompanying prickle of excitement. But he also knew the closer you got to the quarry, the riskier the hunt became, for a cornered animal could be the most dangerous. And from what he knew of Bailey Morgan she had the potential to be a very dangerous animal indeed. Still, wasn't that all part of the sport?

Rex entered the hotel, walking through the poky lobby up to the reception desk.

'Welcome to the Royal City Hotel my friend,' said the South Asian man sitting behind the desk. He gave Rex a gleaming smile. 'You have a reservation?'

Rex shook his head and switched on the fake charm 'A friend of mine is staying here,' he said, refraining from mentioning Bailey's real name in case she was staying in the hotel under a pseudonym. 'She has a scar on her face.' He gestured down his left cheek. 'You know her?'

The man's smile grew wider still. 'Ah yes! Bailey. One of our VIP guests.'

Rex suppressed a victorious smile. So Bailey *was* using her real name, or at least her real first name. This confirmed beyond all doubt that she was staying here. He'd successfully found her.

'That's right,' said Rex. 'Bailey. Is she here now?'

The receptionist shook his head. 'No. She went out a bit earlier today.'

Rex had already prepared for this eventuality. Slipping his day pack from his shoulder, he unzipped it, reached inside and took out a sealed white envelope.

'Bailey has been ill recently,' he said. 'And I have a "Get Well" card for her.'

The receptionist's face morphed into an expression of sympathetic concern. 'She has been ill? Oh dear. Ah yes… now you mention it, she has been looking a little under the weather recently. I think she has been stressed about something.'

'She has a lot on her mind at the moment,' said Rex. 'Anyhow, I'd like to push the card under her door. You know… as a special personal touch. If that's okay with you? Do you know which room she's in?'

The receptionist smiled conspiratorially. 'Well, normally I wouldn't say, but seeing as she is one of our VIP guests and I want her to be happy…' He glanced furtively round the empty lobby. 'Room fifteen my friend. You go up the stairs to the first floor.' He pointed to a dingy-looking stairwell on one side of the lobby.

Rex gave him a dead-eyed smile. 'You're a diamond.'

Ascending the stairwell, he made his way along the dimly-lit corridors to room fifteen, wrinkling his nose at the unpleasant musty smell pervading the place. Stopping outside Bailey's room, he took a moment to look up and down the corridor. No one around. Good.

His plan was to get inside Bailey's room where he would lay in wait until she returned, at which point he'd kill her. Rex wasn't too worried about the receptionist wondering where he'd got to. The man had probably already forgotten that Rex had even come up here, or else when Rex didn't reappear he'd probably assume that he'd left the hotel without him noticing.

Rex assessed the door. It opened by means of a keycard which meant that he couldn't pick the lock. However it didn't look particularly sturdy. He would kick it in and then prop it closed so that when Bailey returned she wouldn't immediately notice. Of course, she'd notice as soon as she did try to open it, but it would be too late by that stage. In that fractional second of disorientation he would have killed her.

He took a step backwards and readied himself to kick the door in.

At that precise moment a cleaning lady wheeling a trolley appeared at the end of the corridor.

Rex froze. For the moment he couldn't do anything.

He studied her with annoyance as she approached him. Heavily overweight, she was wheezing as she pushed the trolley which was piled high with bed linen and cleaning paraphernalia.

He impatiently followed her with his gaze as she laboriously lumbered to the other end of the corridor. Stopping outside the last room, she knocked on the door, waited a few moments, then took a keycard from a box on the top of the trolley and let herself in, leaving the trolley standing unattended in the corridor.

Rex's eyes narrowed as a clever idea occurred to him. Padding rapidly up to the trolley, he peeked into the room she'd just entered to see her with her back to him pulling the sheets off the bed.

Turning to the unattended trolley, he saw the keycard lying in the box on top. He knew it would open every door in the hotel. Plucking it from the box he darted back down the corridor and unlocked Bailey's door. He placed the 'Get Well' card between the door and the doorjamb to stop it locking again. Then he nipped back up the corridor and returned the keycard to its box with the cleaning lady none the wiser. Going back to Bailey's room, he slipped inside and eased the door closed behind him.

Doing it this way was much better. Bailey would never suspect anyone was in here until it was too late.

Casting his gaze round the markedly small room, he saw that the bed, which took up most of the space, looked like it had already been made which conveniently meant that the cleaner wouldn't be disturbing him. He noted a suitcase lying on the floor in one corner, and on the bedside table a book of cryptic crosswords and a notepad. Although it smelt like air freshener had recently been sprayed in the room, his powerful sense of smell could detect the stale odour of takeaway food lurking just beneath it. Coming in from outside was the invasive sound of the bagpipes and the drone of traffic, but other than that he could hear no discernible noise emanating from the neighbouring rooms.

Now it was just a case of waiting. But he was a patient man. Opening up the day pack, he started to take out the various weapons he'd brought with him and tried to decide which one would be best for the job at hand.

41

Sitting at the table in the interview room, Milena scrutinised the signed statement from Stella and Bailey swearing that she would not be subject to any criminal charges so long as she fully cooperated with them.

Seemingly satisfied with the contents of the document, she folded it carefully and slipped it into the pocket of her tracksuit top.

She looked up at them both with a triumphant smile on her face. 'So where do you want me to begin?'

'How about the beginning?' said Bailey.

Milena leaned back in her chair, almost appearing to relish her captive audience as she began to speak.

'It all started in the foyer of the Ritz hotel on Piccadilly. That's where I first met Carl Freeman. He was a policeman back then. Not a hitman. The meeting had been set up by my police handler as the result of a tip-off I'd provided about a gangster called Jack Wynter.

'I'd known Wynter socially for a while and he trusted me quite well because I'd previously helped him out by putting him in contact with some people who could launder cash for him. I'm a good networker, you see. I know a lot of people. So Wynter came to me asking if I knew someone who could kill his business partner, a man called Vincent Peck. He wanted to take over Peck's share in a strip club they both owned. I passed on this information to the police, and they in turn decided to mount an undercover operation to catch Wynter. Carl was the man they chose for the job. He was going to play the part of the hitman who would murder Peck.

'In the meeting in the hotel foyer we discussed how I would introduce him to Wynter. I would pretend to be a "broker" for the hit, taking a ten per cent cut of whatever he was paid. Talking to Carl, I could see immediately that he took his work very seriously. Not just his work but also himself.

'The next time I met him was at the meeting with Wynter. I couldn't believe the transformation. Carl had completely and totally become this psychopathic hitman who referred to himself as "Rex". I was actually a bit scared of him, but then I remembered he was just a policeman who was acting. But I tell you, he could have won an award for his performance.

'I guess it did the trick though because Wynter was very impressed by him. He told me so after the meeting and asked me to set up a second meeting, which I did.'

'Where was the second meeting?' asked Bailey.

'It was in the back room of a small fish restaurant in Limehouse.'

'Were you present at that second meeting?'

Milena shook her head. 'I didn't need to attend. I'd done my part to introduce them. All that remained was for Wynter to explain the ins and outs of the hit and to pay Carl the fifty grand that we'd agreed upon as Carl's fee in the previous meeting. Apparently, giving Carl the money and providing him with the details of the target would be enough to charge Wynter with conspiracy to murder, so for this second meeting Carl was going to be wearing a hidden camera and microphone. Everything seemed like it was going to plan, but little did I know that things were going to change in such a big way...'

Milena paused momentarily, her face taking on a more sombre cast as her eyes flickered back in recall.

'So there I was in my flat wondering how the meeting had gone. Carl had said he'd call me afterwards and update me.' She sighed and swallowed. 'Well he did call me. But it wasn't quite what I was expecting.'

'What do you mean?' asked Bailey.

'He called me and told me that he'd done the job. And then he asked if I wanted my cut of the money. At first I didn't understand what he was talking about. But then I thought maybe this was all part of the operation. He told me to come and meet him on a boat at St Katharine Docks.'

'Go on...' urged Bailey.

Milena's voice was coming out more ragged now, punctuated by fast little breaths. 'It was raining hard that night, and it was really pissing it down by the time I got to the docks. He met me at the electronic gate at the entrance to one of the pontoons. At first when I saw him I didn't think that anything was wrong. But then he took me to this boat, a fancy catamaran that was berthed right at the end of the pontoon. When we got inside I immediately saw that there was a body lying on the floor. It was Vincent Peck. He was dead. There was blood everywhere. It looked like he'd been beaten to death. It was the first time I'd seen a murdered body.' She swallowed. 'And then when I looked at Carl more closely, seeing him more clearly in the light, I saw that there were splatters of blood on his face and his hands and his clothes. I realised that he had killed Peck. He had actually gone ahead and done the hit. When I looked into his eyes I realised something was very wrong. I couldn't see any trace of Carl Freeman. All I could see was this Rex person. For a moment I thought he was going to kill me. After all, he knew I was an informant. But he didn't. It was as if he'd completely forgotten that I was working for the police. He seemed to believe that I was exactly what I was pretending to be – a person who brokered hits for him. That's why he wanted to give me my cut of the money.'

Bailey's heart thumped in excitement as she listened to Milena reveal the truth about what had really happened to Carl Freeman on that fateful night.

Milena continued. 'So I played along with it. I had no choice. I didn't want to try and tell him that he was a policeman, or that I was an informant. He might have tried to kill me. So, I played along. He took out a briefcase. He opened the briefcase and it was full of money. Fifty thousand pounds. He gave me my money. Five thousand, as agreed. Ten per cent.'

Perched spellbound on the edge of her seat, Bailey glanced up at Stella to see that she was similarly rapt. She turned back to Milena. 'And?'

'I asked him how it had gone down. He told me he'd gone to the meeting with Wynter, as arranged. In the meeting Wynter had laid out the details of the hit. He'd told him that Peck would be on the boat that very evening – he was apparently expecting Wynter to visit for a business meeting. He'd told him how the boat belonged to Peck and that it was registered under an alias because Peck liked to use it for illegal purposes. After telling him everything he needed to know in order to do the hit, Wynter had paid him the fifty thousand pounds, just as they'd agreed. Carl had then gone straight to St Katharine Docks and killed Peck. He'd beaten him to death with his bare hands that very same night.'

Milena gave a little snort of laughter and shook her head in disbelief.

'It seemed really crazy to kill him with his bare hands. But then by that point I knew something wasn't right with Carl.' She pointed at her head and made a 'crazy' gesture with her finger. 'And I could see that he seemed agitated. He told me he couldn't remember where he lived. And he didn't have a wallet or anything with his address on it to check. I knew of course that was because his cover identity was totally fake.'

Bailey interjected with the crucial question that was dominating her mind right now. 'Why didn't you subsequently inform the police that something was wrong with Carl? Why did you let them believe that he'd been murdered?'

Milena turned to look at her reflection in the two-way mirror. She absently flicked her hair. Bailey fidgeted impatiently. They'd reached the very nub of it and she was itching to fill in the final pieces of the puzzle.

Milena turned to face her once more. 'Maybe it was the five thousand pounds. It felt good holding that much money in my hand. It gave me an idea. I saw an opportunity. It was a wild opportunity but I had the funny feeling I could make it work.' She paused. 'I decided to take control of him.'

'You decided to take control of him...?' echoed Stella in a tone of disbelief.

Milena raised one eyebrow. 'In the state that I found him, he seemed almost vulnerable... even though he'd just killed a man with his bare hands. I could see that he needed some kind of guidance. So that's what I gave him. I told him to stay put on the boat for the time being. He'd told me it was registered under an alias, and I reckoned that meant there was no way for the authorities to connect Peck to the boat if Peck was reported dead or missing. All Carl had to do was get rid of the body.'

'How did he do that?' asked Bailey.

'The next day he took the boat out along the Thames towards the sea and dropped the body overboard. He seemed to know how to operate a boat.'

Bailey recalled how Bridget Freeman had mentioned that Carl

had a skipper's license. If he was indeed in a fugue state then his sailing skills – acquired before he'd entered the fugue – would have been retained as part of his procedural memory.

'So what happened next?' asked Stella.

'I told him he couldn't use his car again. So he just left it there in the side street where he'd parked it.'

Again, Bailey cast her mind back, remembering how Frank had told her that the police had found Carl Freeman's car abandoned in a side street in Wapping near to St Katharine Docks.

'He was still wearing a wire' said Milena. 'A hidden camera and microphone.' She laughed. 'But he hadn't even switched it on! He didn't understand why he was wearing it so I told him he'd worn it just in case he'd wanted to record the meeting as a kind of insurance policy. I told him he didn't need it any more. I took it from him and disposed of it along with his phone. I dropped them both in the river.'

'And then?'

'Jack Wynter was so pleased with Carl's work... or should I say *Rex*'s work... that he endorsed Rex to various underworld acquaintances. Seeing as I was the one who'd first introduced Rex to Jack, I became known as his main point of contact. I became his business manager, his liaison with the outside world. Rex liked it that way. He liked to have a buffer between himself and the clients. It helped to keep him anonymous. And the more murders he committed, the more important it became for him to remain anonymous. He proved to be very good at his job and he quickly came to be in high demand. In the underworld your reputation is everything.'

'That email address. "Sort my problem". Was it you who thought that up?' asked Bailey.

Milena gave a tinkling laugh. 'You like it? I think it's kind of neat. Yes, the email was my little touch. I used to work in Sales and Marketing you know. Branding is very important, even for hitmen. I wanted to position "Rex" as a solution to people's problems. After all, the main reason you have someone killed is if they're causing you a problem, right?'

Bailey and Stella swapped incredulous glances. Milena was talking about murder-for-hire as if it was nothing more than a regular run-of-the-mill business.

'But on a more serious note,' said Milena. 'I didn't want my name and phone number floating around out there. Using the anonymous email as a means of contact provided me with an extra layer of security. When Jack Wynter told me that he knew people who wanted to hire Rex, I gave him the email and told him to use that as a way to get in touch. It's easy to remember and simple to use.'

Bailey studied Milena with a twisted fascination. It seemed utterly perverse that Carl Freeman was being exploited by the very informant who'd infiltrated him in the first place. As a detective Bailey knew you had to beware of the crafty and duplicitous character of many informants, but this took it to a whole new level.

'So only you knew his secret?' she said.

Milena nodded with a coy smile. 'It was a strange feeling. Kind of like a feeling of power almost. And all this time I've been wondering if he'll suddenly change back.'

'Carl Freeman had a mental breakdown,' said Bailey. 'And you've been taking advantage of him.'

Milena snorted in contempt. 'Give me a break! He enjoys what he does. That's why he's so good at it. Don't they say, follow your passion and the money will follow? And let me tell you, there's been plenty of money.'

'You've been killing people for cash,' muttered Stella derisively. 'Don't you feel any kind of remorse?'

'Most of them were criminals,' said Milena with a dismissive shrug.

'Who made you judge and jury?' growled Bailey, thinking of Emma and thinking of Jeremy Westerby.

'I'm just making a living,' said Milena defensively.

Bailey gazed at her with revulsion for a few moments. A thought then occurred to her. 'Was there ever anything between you and him?'

'You mean, like, *romantic*?' Milena snorted a laugh. 'You must be joking! He's handsome, yeah, I'll give you that. But he's got... how should I say... a few too many issues for my liking. Anyhow, I like to keep things professional when it comes to business.'

'Did you know that Carl Freeman has a wife and son?'

Milena raised her eyebrows in surprise. 'Really?! A wife and son? Well, I don't think he'll be going back to them any time soon. He can't go back to any of it. Ever. Not after what he's done. He's not a policeman any more. He stopped being a policeman that night he killed Vincent Peck.' Milena paused and tilted her head philosophically. 'He's obsessed with memory, you know. He's always playing this card game that tests your memory. I think he's neurotic about it. It's ironic really. I guess it's a symptom of his condition. He must have some kind of amnesia or something, and he sort of half knows it. I tease him about it sometimes.'

Once again, Bailey found herself empathising with Carl Freeman, almost feeling sorry for him. But then she remembered just how many people he'd killed in cold blood as Rex. She remembered that he was planning on killing her in cold blood.

'So where is he?' demanded Stella. 'It's time to give him up.'

Milena tossed her blonde hair. 'He lives on a boat on St Katharine Docks. The name of the boat is *Aletheia*. It's the same boat that belonged to Vincent Peck. But he gave it a new name.'

'Wait a minute,' said Bailey, intrigued. 'Are you meaning to tell me that Carl Freeman has been living on Vincent Peck's boat all this time?'

Milena nodded and shrugged. 'He likes boats. What more can I say?'

'Will he be there now?' asked Stella, a vein of urgency in her tone.

Milena shrugged. 'Maybe. I'll need to call him and check.'

Stella rubbed her jaw pensively. After a few moments, she appeared to come to some kind of decision. 'I think we should strike while the iron is hot. I think we need to move on him today.'

On hearing Stella's pronouncement, Bailey felt an innervating bolt of anticipation go through her. This was it. This was where they finally nailed Rex.

Stella turned and left the interview room, returning a short while later with Milena's mobile phone which they'd confiscated from her when they'd arrested her.

She placed it on the table in front of Milena.

'I want you to call Rex now. If he's not on the boat then tell him you want to meet him there at three o'clock.'

Milena swallowed nervously as she picked up the phone. Her pretty blonde face suddenly looked drawn.

She tapped the phone's screen a few times and then put it to her ear and waited for Rex to answer.

42

Although he had his pistol with him, Rex decided that a silent approach would be the best option under the circumstances as it would enable him to make his getaway before anyone had any idea that Bailey was dead.

He came to the decision that he would hit her over the head with his lead-weighted sap as soon as she came through the door, and then he'd follow up with several well-placed thrusts from a razor-sharp stiletto dagger.

It would be quick and quiet and she'd be dead before she knew what was happening. The room was incredibly cramped, so they would be in very close quarters, and he was mindful of the fact that she possessed jiu jitsu skills. But he had the element of surprise and he knew from experience that it made all the difference.

Pulling out the sap, he positioned himself by the door, pushing himself right up against the wall so she wouldn't notice him until the last moment, if indeed she noticed him at all before he hit her.

Standing there, he casually surveyed the depressing shabby room as he wondered just how long he'd have to wait here for her to appear... and found his attention drawn to some writing scribbled on the notepad lying on the bedside table. Faintly curious as to what it said, he stepped over to take a closer look. It was a name and address. His eyes widened as he recognised the name.

Milena Roksander.

What were her name and address doing written on a notepad in Bailey Morgan's hotel room? He realised with a powerful consternation that the police must have sussed her. But had they detained her yet?

At that exact moment, he felt the tell-tale vibrations of his mobile phone ringing on silent mode inside his pocket.

He pulled it out. The caller ID showed that it was Milena calling him.

He accepted the call and placed the phone to his ear.

'Hello Milena,' he said carefully, listening hard for any hint that things might be amiss.

'Hey Rex,' she said. 'How's the job going? Any closer to finding Bailey Morgan?'

He instantly detected something slightly forced about her cordial tone. Something was off. Tendrils of suspicion wormed through him.

'I'm making pretty good progress,' he replied in a soft dangerous tone.

'Are you on your boat?'

'No. Why?'

'I have something important to discuss with you,' she said. 'But not over the phone.'

'Is everything okay?' he asked.

'Sure. Why wouldn't it be?' she replied breezily.

She was lying to him. He was sure of it. His near-clairvoyant survival instincts told him so. And if she was lying to him, then that meant she'd been detained by the police already. And it meant that she was probably cooperating with them.

Milena was a rat.

He felt a prickling sensation of loathing crawl up his back and neck. Rex absolutely detested rats. He'd killed a fair few in his time. They tended to be popular candidates for liquidation in his line of work. But for his very own business manager to be one...

That dirty traitorous...

'Can I meet you today?' she said. 'On your boat?'

'Sure,' he murmured, doing his utmost to try and keep the bile out of his voice.

'How's three o'clock this afternoon?'

'Sounds good. See you then.'

He terminated the call and stared down at his phone in disgust. It was quite obviously a trap.

A cunning smile spread across his face. Well, no one caught Rex that easily.

43

Bailey stood by the second-floor window in the empty office peering through binoculars at the expensive boats moored in St Katharine Docks.

Standing next to her clutching a two-way radio, Stella pursed her lips pensively as she scanned the marina through her own set of binoculars. She was clad in plainclothes plus a black Kevlar bullet-proof vest, chequered police baseball cap and Glock nine-millimetre pistol. Bailey was dressed in much the same way, minus the pistol.

'It's been a real Indian summer,' remarked Stella. 'But much as it's nice to have good weather, it means that there are more members of the public around. More risk of innocent people getting involved.'

Looking through her binoculars, Bailey could see what she meant. It was a bright sunny afternoon, unseasonably warm for early October, and the tables outside the restaurants and bars lining the marina were occupied by more people than one might expect for this time of year. The fact that it was a Saturday after-noon didn't help, although Bailey reflected that at least the lunchtime peak was over for it was now getting close to three o'clock.

The office they were standing in belonged to some fashion company, but because it was the weekend there was no one at work. Rows of empty computers stretched out on either side of them. Stella had commandeered the space as it offered the best vantage point in terms of Rex's catamaran.

As soon as they'd received the intelligence from Milena as to the existence and location of the catamaran, the boat had immediately been placed under close observation. After calling him up to arrange a rendezvous, Milena had confirmed that he wasn't on board the boat. He hadn't made any attempt to approach it so far which meant that they were now lying in wait for him to arrive.

The *Aletheia* was berthed at the far end of one of the marina's pontoons, the pontoon itself containing berths for around thirteen vessels in total. The location of the catamaran was fortuitous in terms of planning the execution of the operation. Once Rex had stepped onto the pontoon and walked to his boat, he would be conveniently isolated and distanced from any members of the public, thus reducing the risk of collateral damage when they swooped on him.

Given the need to act so urgently, they'd had to put the operation together with the utmost haste, the various teams involved having been mobilised and briefed barely two hours earlier. With the cooperation of the marina authorities, the teams had now been deployed in various strategic spots in and around the docks.

A small, hand-picked team of officers from a tactical firearms unit dressed in plainclothes had inconspicuously boarded a yacht berthed on the same pontoon as the *Aletheia*, concealing themselves inside the cabin, ready to emerge when the signal was given. Like the office in which Bailey was standing, the yacht had been quietly commandeered for the purposes of the operation just a short while earlier.

More armed officers, clad in full black combat gear and Kevlar body armour were waiting inside the back room of a retail unit close to the pontoon gate poised to provide extra support should it be necessary.

Marksmen had slipped into place on several surrounding rooftops, and the entrances to the marina were covered by surveillance teams and further armed officers, although the presence of unmarked police vehicles had been kept to a minimum in case Rex potentially recognised them.

Due to the fact that it was the middle of the day and there were members of the public around, the emphasis had been on keeping the operation as focused and low-profile as possible. If the public weren't aware of what was going on then there was much less likelihood that Rex would sense that anything was amiss when he got there.

'Once he steps through that pontoon gate he'll be ours,' said Stella. 'I just hope no one jumps the gun. I know everyone's twitchy on this one but they need to wait until I give the signal.'

From their vantage point in the office, Bailey and Stella had a direct view of the pontoon gate that would allow Rex through onto the decking leading to his catamaran. Bailey would provide visual confirmation of his identity through her powerful binoculars. Stella would then call the strike only at the point at which Rex had passed by the yacht containing the team of tactical firearms officers. When they emerged from the yacht Rex would find himself trapped between them and the end of the pontoon. There would be nowhere for him to run to, and no members of the public for him to take hostage or get in the way for the yachts berthed in the immediate vicinity had been stealthily evacuated beforehand.

The only person who would be around would be Milena.

'Does Milena really need to be on the boat?' asked Bailey.

'It's best if she is,' said Stella. 'There's always the chance Rex might call beforehand and ask her to randomly confirm something on the boat, even if it's just to check what's in the fridge or something. If she's not able to do so it might alert him that something's up. And we can't risk that happening. Sure we're placing her in a certain amount of danger by having her there, but if all goes to plan we will have taken him down before he even manages to step on board the catamaran.'

She patted the Glock on her hip. 'They're using nine-millimetre hollow points. Real man-stoppers. They flatten on impact and don't over-penetrate which should hopefully minimise the chances of any members of the public getting hit by a stray bullet.'

'The use of lethal force should only ever be a last resort,' said Bailey, chewing her lip in concern. The operation felt more like an ambush than an arrest and she had the nasty feeling she was going to witness a cold-blooded execution in which she herself would play a pivotal part. Rex might be a top-level hitman but he would be no match for the firepower levelled at him here.

'We'll obviously attempt to apprehend him in line with our established code of ethics,' said Stella. 'But as you well know, we have to be prepared for a worst-case scenario and if that entails the use of lethal force then so be it.'

Bailey shot her a sideways glance. Stella's jaw was clenched and she had a hard determined look on her face as she peered through her binoculars. Bailey could tell she was extremely anxious about the outcome of the operation, not least because of its implications for her career. The Commissioner himself had been present at the briefing and Bailey had seen the veiled look that had passed between him and Stella and it had put her in no doubt of mind that there was an unspoken agreement between them to ensure that Rex did not emerge from this operation alive. Bailey's conviction was further compounded by the fact that the various teams participating in the operation had been deliberately kept in the dark regarding the knowledge that Rex was a former police officer – the stakes were far too high for this kind of information to be widely known, especially if a cover-up was being planned. For most of the officers taking part in the operation, Rex was just an extremely dangerous criminal who'd already murdered one police officer and was in the process of trying to kill another.

Stella looked at her watch. 'It's ten to three,' she said. 'And there's still no sign of him.'

'There she goes,' said Bailey, watching through her binoculars as Milena appeared on the dockside heading towards the catamaran just as they'd instructed her to.

Panning their binoculars, Bailey and Stella followed her as she trotted along in her sunglasses and designer suit looking like any other well-groomed affluent young woman of the type who hung around in this marina. They'd let her get changed into something more appropriate for the purposes of the operation; everything had to look just as Rex might expect it to be for they hadn't discounted the possibility that he might already be here hovering around the dockside somewhere watching her right now.

Stopping at the pontoon gate, Milena reached into her handbag and withdrew an access card. She'd told them Rex had given it to her some time previously because she visited him here so often. Tapping it on the electronic card reader, she pushed open the gate and stepped onto the pontoon.

Bailey scrutinised her face through the powerful binoculars. If Milena was nervous she was hiding it well. And Bailey gave her credit for that for she was in the process of betraying a very dangerous man.

44

Milena stepped aboard the *Aletheia* and walked to the cabin door. Reaching into her Prada handbag she withdrew a key and let herself inside the boat. Rex trusted her enough to allow her access to his catamaran, although to be honest, seeing as she'd been the one who'd more or less set him up here, she felt a certain degree of entitlement to come and go as she pleased.

She settled herself on the comfortable sofa and looked at the elegant gold Tissot watch attached to her slender wrist. It was almost five minutes to three. Not long to go. Rex was the punctual type and she was expecting him to be here on the dot.

She took a deep breath. She felt surprisingly calm considering what she was about to do. But then she was in her element. After all, she'd spent much of her life ducking and diving, using people as stepping stones to get ahead and discarding them once they were no longer of any use to her. Rex had served his purpose and now it was time to cut him loose.

She couldn't deny it had been an interesting ride though. It had even been fun at times. Looking round the cabin, she thought about the many long evenings they'd spent here talking and planning.

Now that was all going to come to an end. But then all good things did ultimately. That was life.

She noticed his deck of playing cards sitting on the table. Picking them up, she ran her fingertips over the well-worn edges of the box. She wondered if he'd be allowed to play cards in prison because that was surely where he'd be spending the rest of his life. She reflected that Solitaire was probably a good game to know how to play as she couldn't imagine the other inmates would want to be having much to do with him as a former policeman.

She had of course contemplated the possibility that the police might end up shooting him dead but that didn't bother her too much. So long as she didn't have to watch. As far as she understood, anything that happened would be taking place on the pontoon outside the catamaran hopefully well away from her.

Whether Rex ended up spending the rest of his days in prison, or whether he ended up being shot dead, he wasn't going to be in the position to exact much in the way of retribution for her betrayal so she wasn't too worried about having to change her identity or flee to some other country.

She hadn't really had the chance to give much thought to what she was going to do next, but now, as she sat there with the sunlight streaming through the blinds, she began to contemplate the new life that lay ahead of her and the exciting possibilities that it offered. She'd developed quite a flair for arranging contract killings and it seemed a shame not to take advantage of all the experience she'd garnered, not to mention the fact that it was an exceedingly profitable line of business. She was certain she'd be able to find another hitman to work with, although this time round she'd be sure to pick someone who wasn't afflicted with the same kind of complications that surrounded Rex.

Obviously before she embarked on any of that she had to fulfil her obligations to the police. But that would be straightforward enough. And then once it was all over she'd be free to do whatever she wanted.

Looking at her watch again, she saw that it was now two minutes past three.

She frowned to herself. That was unlike Rex. He was never late. She felt a faint ripple of foreboding. Did he sense that something was wrong? He did possess that uncanny ability to detect aspects of the environment that normal people couldn't.

She took out her phone and dialled his number again.

'Hi, where are you?' she asked, attempting to keep her voice casual and level.

There was a silence on the other end of the phone. She was suddenly aware of her heart beating strongly against the inside of her chest.

'Rex...?' she ventured.

Then he spoke, his voice conversational in tone. 'Do you remember that chat we had about scuttling the boat?'

'Scuttling the boat?' she asked, momentarily confused.

'About how I'd take it out into the middle of the ocean and deliberately sink it.'

She remembered the conversation... and what he was saying right now didn't bode well.

'You said you'd do it if everything went wrong,' she said.

Milena's throat felt tight. She suddenly felt claustrophobic inside this small cabin. The premonitory feeling that had nipped at her earlier now bloomed into full-blown dread.

'I never told you exactly how I would scuttle the boat, did I?' he said.

'I don't understand what you're saying Rex,' she stammered, attempting to stave off the enveloping fear that something was now awfully wrong.

He spoke softly with a cold finality. 'I thought you were my friend Milena. But I guess I was wrong.'

A paralysing realisation struck Milena. She had to get out of here now. Dropping the phone onto the sofa, she wrenched herself to her feet—

But it was too late.

45

The catamaran exploded sending a massive gout of flame into the afternoon sky followed instantly by a huge plume of black smoke.

Bailey and Stella reeled backwards as the windows of the office blew inwards under the force of the blast.

Lying on her back on the floor, covered in fragments of broken glass, Bailey blinked in shock, her ears ringing from the explosion. Glancing to her side she saw Stella lying next to her, a look of stunned bewilderment on her face.

Sitting up, attempting to shake off the disorientation, they both checked themselves for injuries. Apart from a few minor grazes, it seemed like they were both okay.

Staggering back up to the shattered window, they peered outside at the devastation which lay beyond. The luxury catamaran had been almost completely destroyed, the scorched remains of the distinctive dual hull sinking rapidly beneath the surface of the water. The explosion had wrecked most of the neighbouring boats and had scattered debris all across the marina. It seemed that most if not all of the windows of the surrounding buildings had been blown out and down by the dockside people were staggering around in a state of confused panic.

Stella immediately began shouting into her two-way radio, attempting to coordinate with the other teams to try and ascertain the extent of any casualties, civilian or otherwise.

Watching the tip of the catamaran's hull disappear completely beneath the water, a painful sense of guilt descended on Bailey at the knowledge that Milena had been killed in the blast. There was of course absolutely no way that she could have survived it. They had sent her to her death – she'd put her neck on the line and she'd paid for it. Milena might have been far from innocent, but did she deserve to die for this?

At the same time came the galling realisation that Rex must have somehow twigged that they were lying in wait for him for surely it was he who had detonated this explosion. Once again he was one step ahead of them. But what did that mean for Bailey now?

Her sombre thoughts were interrupted as Stella turned to her with an ashen face. 'I am not looking forward to explaining this to the Commissioner.'

* * *

Standing in the dimly lit interior of the lockup garage, Rex put his mobile phone back in his pocket with a gratified smile. Over a year earlier, as part of his contingency plan to scuttle the boat should anything ever go wrong, he'd planted a substantial quantity of plastic explosives in the hidden compartments in the twin hulls of the catamaran. The explosives were attached to a remote detonator which could be activated by a simple text message sent from his phone.

With a little tap of his finger he'd blown Milena to pieces. And good riddance too. The life of a rat was worth nothing. Less than nothing. Shame about the boat though...

Now with Milena gone, he'd obviously have to change his working practices but he was confident he'd manage. There would always be people willing to pay money to have other people murdered, and with a skillset like his he knew there'd be no shortage of work.

Talking of which, he still had a job to finish. He still had to kill Bailey Morgan. Milena or no Milena, a contract was still a contract and his principles stood firm. Always finish the job. That credo had carried him this far, and if he was to strike out on his own, he needed to adhere to it more firmly than ever.

Much as he'd liked to have stayed around in Bailey's hotel room waiting for her to return so he could kill her, he'd decided that it would have been unwise to remain there just in case she called the police down on the place in the wake of the explosion on the boat. There was the slim possibility that she might have realised how he'd sussed the trap they'd set for him, and he didn't want to risk getting captured so he'd made his departure...

...but not before taking the opportunity to tamper with her suitcase. With any luck she wouldn't notice until it was too late. All he had to do now was pick up a few extra bits and bobs in order to ensure the job was completed before the trial on Tuesday.

And that was why he'd come to Hackney in East London, for it was here, located behind a grubby row of shops, that he rented this lockup garage in which he stored various tools of his trade along with a number of items that it would have been impractical to keep on the boat. He'd been renting the garage for a while now and Milena knew of its existence but she didn't know where it was so he hadn't been too concerned about the police finding it.

Rooting through the garage, he began to select the items that he required for this last stage of his plan. As he did so he reflected upon his ongoing duel with Bailey Morgan. He had to admit, she'd proved to be a wily adversary, but he sensed that she'd just played the final move in her endgame... and it had failed. It was now his move, and Rex had the very strong feeling that he would win.

* * *

Sitting in the back of a stationary ambulance at St Katharine Docks, Bailey winced as the paramedic pulled a splinter of glass from a cut on her scalp.

Stella, who was standing by the open back door of the ambulance, was surveying the aftermath of the explosion with a bleak look on her face.

She sighed heavily. 'Well I suppose we should at least be thankful that no one was actually killed.'

'Apart from Milena,' Bailey reminded her.

'Of course,' said Stella quickly catching herself. 'Apart from her. Most regrettable.'

Although no one else had died in the blast, the flying glass and other debris had caused a large number of minor injuries to both members of the public and the police officers involved in the operation, and the tactical firearms team who'd been concealed in the yacht close to the explosion had been lucky to escape with their lives.

'What a total fiasco,' muttered Stella, shaking her head disconsolately. 'There'll be an inquiry of course. Lots of questions to be answered. And the Met will no doubt be hit with a whole load of lawsuits from all the injuries.'

'We came so close,' whispered Bailey, feeling a burning frustration and disappointment at the way things had panned out. 'I feel like we had him in our grasp. How did he know it was a trap?' The thought had been plaguing her ever since the explosion.

Stella shrugged. 'It doesn't matter now. The Commissioner told me that this operation to catch Rex is terminated. It's got out of hand. We can't have London turning into some kind of personal battleground between him and you. We cannot risk further civilian casualties. The Met's PR machine is already working overtime to try and come up with an explanation for this debacle. They're trying to pass it off as a gas explosion.'

'So what about Rex?' asked Bailey. 'He's still out there. He still has to answer for all the murders he's committed. And he's probably still looking for me. After all, the trial is going ahead as planned on Tuesday and from what I know of him, he'll do his utmost to kill me before that date.'

Despite the fact that Milena was dead, Bailey still had to assume that she was a target. From what she understood about Carl Freeman and the man he had become, he would pursue her obsessively until he caught up with her and killed her for she knew that his psychotic resolve was a lynchpin of his very identity.

'We're going to have to rethink our whole approach to catching him,' said Stella. 'But for the time being, between now and the trial on Tuesday, you'll have to sit tight in a safe house. It's only a few days away.'

'And after that?' demanded Bailey. 'I've got the feeling that he's not going to give up hunting me even if he does miss the deadline of the trial date.'

Stella fixed her with a cheerless look. 'There are solutions in place to address your long-term security.'

Bailey's heart sunk. 'You're talking about witness protection, aren't you? I don't fancy having to give up my job to spend the rest of my life living under an assumed name in some godforsaken bit of the UK. I'd have to move away from everyone I know, including my mum who needs me more than ever now that my dad's no longer around. And I'd be looking over my shoulder all the time wondering if he might eventually manage to track me down.'

'I feel your pain Bailey but there's not a lot I can do about it right now. We will catch Rex one of these days, I can promise you that, but in the meantime you're just going to have to be strong and hold out until we do.'

46

Bailey sat at the wooden dining table in the living room of the safe house feeling bored and a bit glum. She'd just eaten lunch with two of the protection officers who'd been assigned to protect her, and she was now wondering how to spend the rest of the afternoon.

It was Sunday the sixth of October, the day after the debacle at St Katharine Docks. They'd driven her straight to the safe house from the docks with a stop via her hotel to pick up her belongings. When she'd been checking out of the hotel the receptionist Ravi had told her that he hoped she got well soon. She'd been a little puzzled as to why he thought she'd been ill in the first place, but with her mind caught up with bigger things, she hadn't bothered to ask him to explain. Now though, as she sat in the seclusion of the safe house, she reflected on his comment with mild perplexity.

The safe house was located in the Oxfordshire countryside, tucked away in the woods down a narrow winding country lane. It had taken them just over an hour to drive there from London. Bailey knew the police had safe houses all over the country in all manner of locations and in her case, given that Rex was likely to be in London, they'd thought it best to place her somewhere outside of the metropolis, but not too far away seeing as she had to be in court on Tuesday.

Bailey supposed the safe house was kind of quaint. It was a slightly dilapidated little cottage with stone walls and exposed ceiling beams which sat in a clearing in the woods at the end of a long driveway and it probably would have made a nice countryside getaway were it not for its vaguely sinister connotations.

Sitting at the dining table with her were two burly protection officers, Ron and Barry. Two further protection officers, Ian and Keith, were currently sitting in an unmarked BMW X5 parked at the end of the driveway by the turnoff to the country lane that had brought them here. All four of them were dressed in plainclothes and armed with Glock nine-millimetre pistols in shoulder holsters, and all of them looked more than capable of performing the task they'd been assigned to do.

'Look on the bright side,' said Ron, rubbing his red beard. 'At least you're getting a bit of nice country fresh air. London is so polluted.'

'Yeah that might be so,' said Bailey, 'but the countryside's definitely a lot chillier.' She pulled on her suede-fringed cowboy jacket. The recent warm weather seemed to have disappeared to be replaced by a distinct autumnal chill, and it didn't look like the authorities had deemed it worthwhile to install double glazing in this particular safe house. 'Aren't you guys cold?' she asked, eyeing their rolled-up shirt sleeves.

They both looked at each other and shrugged. She guessed they were hardier than she was.

'Do you want me to switch the central heating on?' said Barry gesturing with a meaty hand in the direction of the boiler.

'Nah, I'm sure I'll survive,' she said.

She yawned and wondered what to do to pass the time. She'd spent most of the morning refreshing her knowledge of the

Benvenuto case and rehearsing her testimony for the trial which was now only two days away. A new Senior Crown Advocate had been appointed to the prosecution team and was himself currently under armed guard. Talking to him on the phone earlier that day, they'd discussed the possibility of her providing her testimony by video link from the safe house, but they'd both ultimately decided that her physical presence in court would make more of an impact on the jury in terms of securing a conviction against Benvenuto. More than ever, Bailey was determined to see him go down for as long as possible. The only thing that frustrated her was that she knew it was unlikely that they'd ever be able to prove that he'd hired Rex; they might have had a chance of doing so were Milena still alive and cooperating with them, but that opportunity had died with her.

Standing up from the dining table, Bailey stretched and walked into her bedroom to get her book of cryptic crosswords out of her suitcase. She wanted to take a break from the legal work and she'd always found cryptic crosswords a good way to take her mind off her concerns.

Walking back into the living room, she sat back down at the dining table, opened up the book and began to do one of the puzzles. Ron and Barry both observed her idly whilst she chewed on the end of her biro trying to work out the answers.

'Stuck on the answer?' said Ron, peering over at the book. 'I'm good at crosswords you know.'

She smiled thinly at him and read out one of the clues. 'Look inside the cat last seen on the map.'

Ron and Barry both looked at each other, confounded.

'What kind of crossword clue is that?' demanded Barry.

'It's a cryptic crossword,' said Bailey.

Barry rolled his eyes. 'Those things do my head in.' He stood up. 'I'm going outside for a smoke.'

'Those fags will be the death of you, mate,' remarked Ron.

'Bah!' replied Barry with a dismissive wave of his hand as he left the living room and walked out into the hallway, the front door slamming shut a few moments later.

Bailey raised her eyebrows hopefully at Ron. 'It's five letters,' she said.

Ron's brow crumpled as he tried to think of the answer. 'Look inside the cat last seen on the map...' he murmured, tapping his lip with his finger.

Bailey mulled over the clue. The key with cryptic crosswords was to think laterally. The answer hit her a few moments later. She clicked her fingers. 'Got it.'

'Oh yeah?'

'Atlas.'

'Atlas?' Ron looked puzzled.

'Yeah. "Look inside" is telling you what to do with the rest of the clue. If you look inside it you see that the actual answer is right there in front of you – the last two letters of "cat" and the first three letters of "last". The "map" part tells you what you should be looking for.'

Ron stared at her with awe and shook his head in wonderment. Licking her lips she began to write the letters of the answer into the crossword. But then her pen ran out before she was able to finish. She sighed in frustration and shook it but it still didn't work. It was definitely out of ink. Then again it was a cheapo complimentary pen she'd picked up from the Royal City Hotel so she wasn't exactly surprised.

'Got a pen?' she asked.

Ron shook his head. She then remembered that she kept one in her suitcase. Standing up, she wandered back into the bedroom and knelt down by her suitcase and unzipped the passport pocket. It was a small pocket on the outside that she rarely used, but she always kept a spare biro in there for easy access in case she needed to fill out any travel-related documents when she was on the plane or in the airport.

Slipping her hand inside the pocket, she rummaged round for the biro but instead her fingers closed round an item she didn't recognise. She pulled it out with a frown.

It was a small black oblong item made of plastic, around the size of a matchbox. Studying it in the palm of her hand, she couldn't work out what it was or how it had got there. She was pretty certain she hadn't placed it there herself. In fact she'd never seen it before in her life. An unsettling feeling came over her.

Holding it in her hand, she paced back into the living room, the sense of consternation growing inside her.

'Ron?' she said.

He looked up. 'Yeah?'

'What's this?' She placed the little black box on the table in front of him. 'I found it in my suitcase.'

He picked it up and examined it curiously. 'Looks like some kind of tracking device. One of those GPS trackers that you can put in your car so you can find it if it gets nicked. Connects to an app on your phone. Quite handy so I've heard.'

A cold spidery chill crawled over her scalp. She realised that Rex must have placed it there. She stared down at the tracker with horror as her mind frenetically joined the dots. The only opportunity for Rex to put the GPS tracker in her suitcase would have been if he had somehow gained access to her hotel room.

'Oh my God,' she whispered.

Ron's eyes widened. 'You think...?'

'He knows I'm here,' she said.

Ron stood up sharply. Pulling the gun out of his shoulder holster, he drew back the slide, loading a round into the chamber, and thumbed off the safety catch.

With his other hand he picked his two-way radio up off the table to communicate with the two officers sitting in the car at the end of the driveway. He pressed the 'push-to-talk' button on the side of the radio.

'Sierra Mike three-six, Sierra Mike three-six from November Golf two-one, over.'

Bailey knew that Sierra Mike three-six was Ian's call sign. November Golf two-one was Ron's call sign.

Silence. Just the hissing of static. Ron tried again, this time calling Keith's call sign.

'Whisky Bravo seven-nine, Whisky Bravo seven-nine from November Golf two-one, over.'

Nothing. Just more empty hissing of static. They weren't answering for some reason.

Ron swallowed, glancing at Bailey with a grim look on his face.

'Try Barry,' she urged.

He clicked the 'push-to-talk' button on the radio. 'Echo Lima four-four, Echo Lima four-four from November Golf two-one, over.'

The radio hissed static.

'Barry's not answering,' muttered Ron. He stepped over to the front window and pushed the corner of the net curtains aside with the barrel of the Glock. Bailey watched him nervously as he peeked outside. Her heart was beating hard all of a sudden, and a horrible dread twisted her guts for she knew that something was very wrong. Rex was here, she was sure of it. He had found her.

'Can you see anything?' she whispered, her throat constricted with tension.

Ron shook his head. 'Everything looks the same as normal.'

Going up to the window, Bailey peered through the net curtains. The clearing outside the front of the cottage was completely empty apart from the Skoda Octavia belonging to Ron and Barry which was parked around ten metres away, exactly where they'd left it after arriving. The BMW X5 belonging to Ian and Keith was situated at the far end of the winding driveway and thus obscured from her vision by the surrounding trees.

'I'm going to check outside,' said Ron, his voice low and urgent. 'Stay here.'

'Be careful,' whispered Bailey.

Holding the gun, Ron stalked out of the living room into the hallway and opened the front door. The deceptively tranquil sound of birdsong filtered in from the sun-dappled woods outside.

'Barry?' he asked, peering round.

No answer.

Bailey watched tensely from the hallway as he took several steps out in front of the cottage. Holding his gun at the ready, he slowly turned to scan the immediate environment.

'Barry?' he repeated in a slightly louder voice. 'Are you there?'

THUNK.

Ron stiffened suddenly. Bailey gasped. His head appeared to have been impaled by some kind of metal rod with a feathered flight at one end and a pointed tip at the other, now glistening with blood. Bailey realised that it was a crossbow bolt.

She stared at him aghast. 'Oh Jesus...' she muttered.

Ron staggered back and forth in an odd jerky motion, his eyes wide, an expression of surprise fixed on his face, and then collapsed on the ground, the gun falling down next to him with a clatter.

For a few frozen moments, Bailey stared in shock and horror at Ron's dead body. Swallowing hard, she pulled herself together. If she was to survive there was no time to lose.

She eyed the gun lying on the ground, her heart hammering in her chest. It was only about three metres away, but it was out in the open and she'd be exposed if she tried to get it. Having never undertaken firearms training, she had very little idea how to use a gun properly, but even so, it would be better than nothing against a hitman armed with a crossbow. She just had to try and retrieve it safely.

She crouched down just short of the front door and began to crawl forwards out of the house, her arm extended towards the gun.

THUNK.

A crossbow bolt whizzed past her to embed itself in the wooden doorframe centimetres from her head. She scuttled back into the house and slammed the door shut, reaching up and bolting it.

She was panting hard, adrenaline surging through her system, as she tried to get a sense of her predicament. It looked like Rex was concealed somewhere in the woods just beyond the edge of the clearing that the cottage sat in. He was armed with a crossbow, at the very least, and it looked like he had managed to kill all four of her protection officers. She felt nauseous at the thought that he had killed four men just to get to her. She couldn't believe she'd been having a conversation with two of them barely a few minutes earlier and now they were dead.

She had to do something. And soon. Retreating back into the living room, Bailey picked her iPhone up off the dining table and dialled Stella's number with shaking fingers.

It went to answerphone.

Bailey cursed as she waited for the bleep to leave a message.

'It's me. Bailey,' she gasped breathlessly. 'Rex is here. He's found the safe house. He's killed the protection officers and he's going to kill me. Get here soon.'

She terminated the call.

The next thing to do was call 999. The local police would be able to provide more immediate relief, although just how long it would take them to get here was another question.

Keeping an eye on the front window, she dialled 999 and calmly explained her situation to the operator, trying not to let panic overwhelm her. She could hear the operator tapping away in the back-ground, recording her details.

'What's the address?' asked the operator.

Bailey realised she didn't know the actual address of the safe house. However she knew that the Advanced Mobile Location functionality in her iPhone would send the GPS coordinates of her phone to the 999 call centre. All iPhones and Android phones now possessed the functionality, but not all emergency service control rooms had been enabled to accept it as it was a relatively new technology. She just prayed that it had in the case of this particular control room.

'I don't know the address,' said Bailey. 'But can you see my location? Are you getting my GPS coordinates?'

'Ah yes I can see your location,' said the operator.

A rush of relief went through Bailey.

She tied up the call and then rung off, thrusting the iPhone into the pocket of her jacket. Having explained that Rex was armed and dangerous, she was expecting firearms units to arrive in the very near future. She knew that even in relatively rural areas like this, emergency response times rarely topped twenty minutes.

The question was whether she'd be able to last here that long because right now Rex was no doubt looking for a way to get into the cottage and kill her. The problem she faced was that there were too many points through which he could enter the building – the front door and the back door, plus all the various windows – and she couldn't cover all of them at the same time.

Realising that she needed some kind of weapon with which to defend herself, she ran into the kitchen. She spotted a knife rack. It only had one knife in it. She pulled it out. It was a small paring knife. She huffed in frustration. That wasn't going to be much of a match against a crossbow and whatever other weapons he probably had with him.

Fuck. What was she going to do?

Standing there in the kitchen, panting heavily, her mind raced as she tried to think how to 'awaken' him for she knew her only chance of salvation was to somehow reconnect with the real Carl Freeman. The psychologist had said that with the right emotional trigger it was possible to snap someone out of a fugue. But what could that trigger be?

Running back into the living room, she went to the front window, keeping to the far edge of the window frame so as not to make a target of herself. Easing the window open, she took a deep breath and called out of the window into the woods.

'You're a policeman!' she shouted. 'Your name is Carl Freeman. Detective Sergeant Carl Freeman.'

Silence. Nothing but the sound of the birdsong and the rustling of the wind in the trees. She swallowed, her mouth dry.

'You have a brother called Toby,' she shouted. 'You have a wife called Bridget. You have a son called Jack.'

Nothing.

She trawled her mind for everything she knew about him, all the information she'd gleaned from Toby, from Bridget, from his personnel file.

'You grew up in a little village called Timbleheath in the North Wessex Downs,' she shouted. 'You attended Timbleheath Primary School. Then you went to St Christopher's Comprehensive School in Newbury. You left there with three A-levels to go and study Geography at the University of Southampton. After leaving university you spent a year travelling and working in Australia. And then when you came back you joined the Metropolitan Police. You're a police officer Carl! A police officer!'

Silence.

Had she done it? Had she woken him up?

47

Crouching in the bushes holding his crossbow, Rex observed the cottage and considered Bailey's words with a resigned shake of his head. People often got like this when they knew their end was near. They started babbling. Just as she was doing now.

Her words, of course, meant nothing to him. They were just the desperate bleats of a hunted creature trying to cling onto its last few moments of life. He'd encountered this kind of situation before and he was used to people saying the most delirious things in a vain bid to preserve their existence.

Him, a police officer? What a ridiculous assertion.

A wife and son? Pathetic.

Did she really think that spouting this bullshit would make a blind bit of difference?

He smiled grimly to himself. The end was close now. His mission was almost over.

After planting the GPS tracker in Bailey's suitcase, Rex had picked up the crossbow from the lockup garage in Hackney and had then stolen a car in order to drive here. He'd parked the car some way further down the country lane so he could make the final approach on foot for added stealth.

The crossbow was a Barnett Wildcat – powerful and fast, with a draw weight of 195lbs and the ability to fire bolts at 320 feet per second. Attached beneath the stock of the crossbow was a quiver containing bolts tipped with 100 grain broadhead tips designed specifically for hunting large game.

A crossbow was the connoisseur's hunting weapon of choice, much better than a gun in his opinion when stalking prey in the wild. It allowed for silence and long-range precision, unlike his pistol which was noisy and only accurate at short range. And there was something refreshingly old-school about hunting with a bow and arrow. It instilled that crucial element of sport which he relished so much.

Rex scanned the front of the cottage through the crosshairs of the 4x32mm telescopic sight that was fitted to the top of the crossbow. He was pretty sure Bailey was alone in there now. From his observations, he'd worked out that there were four protection officers with her, all of whom were now dead.

The two coppers in the car had been easy to kill. One of them had gone to urinate in the bushes. It had been the last piss he'd ever taken. Rex had shot him with the crossbow mid-stream. The other one had been sitting in the car with his arm leaning out of the open window. Rex had put a bolt through his throat leaving him to choke to death on his own blood.

He knew Bailey probably would have called for some form of backup by now. Not that it would do her any good because Rex knew exactly how to flush her out of the cottage before any kind of help arrived.

* * *

Bailey hovered tensely by the window of the cottage clutching the small paring knife, wondering if her words had made any impact on Rex. How would she know? It wasn't like she could go out and ask him.

She would just have to wait here inside the cottage for the emergency services to arrive, but knowing that he was potentially closing in on her right now, every second she waited seemed like a dangerous eternity.

There was a smashing sound. She spun round, her heart in her throat. It had come from one of the ground floor bedrooms. Was he trying to get in?

She tightened her grip on the small paring knife, more aware than ever of just how inadequate it would probably be against him. And as for her jiu jitsu skills, she doubted she'd be able to get close enough to use them on him before he managed to kill her.

Standing there rigid with apprehension, she frantically debated what to do. Should she lock herself inside the bathroom? Would that give the emergency services enough time to get here? But being trapped in a small room at his mercy... it didn't really seem like any kind of option at all.

She sniffed the air. There was a distinct smell of burning. With a jolt of horror, she realised that he was trying to smoke her out of the cottage. She ran forwards into the bedroom from where she'd heard the smashing noise to see flames licking up the curtains by the smashed window. Fuck. He'd set the place alight.

Momentarily paralysed, she gaped as the fire rapidly consumed the curtains, spreading up the wall across the wooden ceiling beams. There was no way she was going to be able to put that out. She knew that on average it took five minutes for a house to be consumed by fire, but she knew smoke inhalation became a serious hazard much sooner than that. It was imperative that she got out of the cottage right now... which was exactly what he wanted her to do. As soon as she walked outside he'd pick her off with the crossbow.

Feeling the heat on her face, she turned and ran desperately back into the living room. And then she spotted the car keys on the sideboard. They belonged to the Skoda Octavia that was parked about ten metres in front of the cottage. Snatching up the keys, she realised that if she could just get to the car in one piece, there was a slim chance that she could escape Rex by driving out of here.

The only question was which part of the cottage was he covering with the crossbow? She'd have to take a gamble as to which exit to leave by.

Smoke was now filling the house, making her cough and causing her eyes to water. She didn't have much time. Running through into the kitchen, she went to the back door and twisted the door knob, easing it open. Peeking outside, she saw the trees and bushes swaying gently in the breeze but she couldn't detect any visible sign of Rex. Taking a deep breath, she braced herself to be impaled by a crossbow bolt, and stepped outside.

But nothing happened. She sagged momentarily in relief. But there was no time to dawdle. Keeping tight against the exterior wall of the cottage, she tip-toed round the side of the building, staying in a low crouch, trying to form as small a target as possible.

As she rounded the corner of the cottage, she gasped and jumped back in shock as she came up against Barry's lifeless body. He was pinned to a tree a metre or so away, a crossbow bolt protruding from his chest. The cigarette he'd been smoking was lying at his feet still smouldering.

Crouching in the shadow by the side of the cottage, Bailey eyed the Glock pistol in Barry's shoulder holster. It would be better than the paring knife surely. Dropping the paring knife on the ground, she darted forward, unsnapped the retention strap of the holster and pulled out the pistol. It felt heavy and unwieldy in her hand.

Mimicking what she'd seen Ron do, she awkwardly drew back the slide to load a round into the chamber and then flicked off the safety catch. Holding the gun in front of her with her finger on the trigger, she edged forward until the Skoda Octavia came into sight.

She saw then that the tires had been slashed. Rex had already anticipated this kind of manoeuvre on her part. She cursed silently to herself. But so saying, she knew it didn't matter if the tires were flat. So long as she managed to get the car started, she'd be able to drive on the wheel rims for a fair distance, hopefully for long enough to get away from him.

The fact that Rex hadn't shot her yet told her that he was covering the cottage from the other side. But if she was to make it to the Skoda Octavia, she'd have to cross around ten metres of open ground where she would be in his sights. She'd just have to stay low and make a run for it.

Holding the gun in one hand, she quietly pulled the car keys out of her pocket with her other hand. Taking a deep breath, she broke cover and sprinted towards the car pressing the unlock button on the key fob as she did so.

The car's lights flashed and it emitted a loud bleep as it unlocked.

Powered by a huge surge of adrenaline, she propelled herself across the uneven ground in a low crouching sprint.

Nine metres.

Eight metres.

Seven metres.

Six metres. Almost there.

THUNK.

The crossbow bolt hit her in the upper right arm, the impact spinning her round and completely knocking her off-balance. She crashed to the ground. The gun flew out of her hand somewhere into the bushes and the set of car keys skittered across the ground underneath the car.

She lay there completely disoriented for a moment. Blinking in shock, she twisted her head to see that the crossbow bolt had penetrated right through the muscle of her right bicep. It was about half a metre long, its razor-sharp triangular tip glistening with her blood. A second later, the pain hit her with a burning nauseous throb, spreading through her arm all the way up to her shoulder and through her whole body.

And then she saw him. Stepping out of the undergrowth, holding the crossbow, he began to walk in her direction. She froze in fear, momentarily transfixed by the sight of him striding towards her, the cottage burning behind him, flames licking out of the windows.

He stopped a few metres from her, assessing her with his cold dead eyes. He started to re-cock the crossbow, lowering it down to place his foot in the stirrup to give himself the leverage to draw back the bowstring. Snapping into action, she realised she had less than a second to try and save herself.

She knew she wouldn't be able to retrieve the set of keys from under the car before he came over and killed her. And as for the gun, she had no idea where in the bushes it had fallen exactly.

The only option was to flee. Now. Into the woods. She knew he was an expert tracker but she had no choice.

She wrenched herself to her feet, emitting an involuntary gasp of pain at the wound in her arm. Staggering forwards, she set off at a run into the woods, the branches of the trees welcoming her into the talons of their embrace.

* * *

Rex calmly placed a bolt into the barrel groove of the crossbow and nocked it against the bowstring. A small smile crossed his face as he watched Bailey stumble into the woods.

The chase was on.

She didn't stand a chance out there. But then she hadn't really had much of a choice. She couldn't have gone back into the burning cottage and she would never have got the car started in time.

No doubt she was now scurrying away through the trees hoping to find some place to hide from him. Well, she could flee all she wanted. It wouldn't do her any good. He was a professional hunter and this was what he did for a living.

If there was one thing he was good at, it was reading the natural environment. He didn't know quite why he was so good at it, but it seemed to come instinctively to him, as if it had been instilled in him from an early age.

Utilising those special powers of observation, he now scanned the woods to try and ascertain which direction she was travelling in. He noticed a bird suddenly fly up from the top of the trees to his left, its black wings flapping, distinct in the light blue sky. It had been disturbed by something. And he knew it was most likely her who'd disturbed it. Angling himself in that direction, he pressed on after her.

* * *

Bailey pelted through the woods, zig-zagging through the trees, trying to put as much distance between herself and Rex as possible. She knew the police would find her in the woods sooner or later, but until they did so her primary objective was to try and remain alive, and that meant keeping herself out of Rex's clutches for as long as possible.

It was autumn, early October, and the vegetation was consequently that much thinner, the ground already covered with an ample layer of dead leaves. And that concerned her for it meant that she had less means to conceal herself from him.

Halting for a moment, her breath coming out in ragged gasps, she looked one way and then the other. It all looked the same to her. Trees to the left of her. Trees to the right of her. Trees all around. She had no idea where she was heading. So long as it was away from him.

Having grown up in the London suburbs, Bailey had always felt somewhat out of her element when she was in the countryside and she had never felt it more so than now.

Looking down at the crossbow bolt in her arm, she felt assailed by faintness and nausea. The pain had subsided into an intense throbbing ache that consumed her entire right arm and rendered it more or less useless. She wasn't even going to think about pulling out the bolt – its razor-sharp triple-bladed tip would do more damage on the way out than it had on the way in. Better to leave it in there and wait for the paramedics to deal with it... if she managed to survive that long.

She took a deep breath and fought off the dizziness. She couldn't afford to faint now. That would be fatal. Swallowing hard, she pushed herself onwards.

Picking a direction in which it looked like the trees were growing thicker and thus could offer more cover, she once more resumed her flight, taking herself deeper into the woodland.

* * *

Rex glided through the woods, treading carefully and quickly, fast enough to move with the rapidity required by a pursuit, but not so fast as to trip and injure himself, or, more importantly, to impede his powers of observation.

Bailey's trail would be fresh, and seeing as there was no strong wind or rain to obscure her signs, he was confident that she'd be easy to follow.

He scanned the undergrowth, searching for anything that looked out of place. A shadow or a silhouette, or a colour, or a glint of something unnatural, or a sudden movement of some sort, or anything where the natural state of the environment had been disturbed in any way.

He noted a displaced rock, dark wet soil on its underside where it had been upended, the colour change in the earth catching his eye. It had been moved very recently, woodlice still scuttling round it in panic. She'd probably kicked it aside as she'd passed.

A short distance further along he came across the indentations of her footprints, the dead leaves crushed into the patterns on the soles of her trainers. Going by the scuffed edges of the marks and the distance of her stride he could tell that she was running. Good. She was scared which meant she'd be clumsier which meant she'd leave a more noticeable trail for him to follow.

Buoyed by the conspicuousness of her spoor, he pressed on. At times the footprints disappeared, but he was able to detect other less obvious clues that she'd passed through. Clumps of moss dislodged from a tree. A spider's web broken, the fine strands hanging loose in the breeze. Blades of grass bruised and bent in the direction of her travel.

She was an urban creature, unused to the countryside. He could tell that much by the obvious trail that she was leaving behind her. And the deeper she went into these woods, and the longer she spent here, the weaker and more vulnerable she would become.

Stopping by a large fern, he noticed a glistening droplet of blood dribbling along the leaf. He dabbed at the spot of blood with his forefinger. Putting his finger in his mouth, he tasted her blood, savouring the distinctive iron tang. It was something a primeval hunter would have done, and he did it now for the same reason – to inhabit her as his prey.

He felt a visceral thrill. This was what he lived for. The hunt. It was pure sport and he'd happily have done it for free.

'I'm coming for you Bailey,' he whispered.

* * *

Bailey pushed on harder through the woods, painfully aware of all the noise she was making. Fallen twigs and pieces of rotten wood snapped underfoot as she sprinted through the trees but she had no time to watch where she was treading.

Stopping to look round, she realised she had no idea where she was. The trees stretched off into a knotted labyrinth in all directions. She was totally lost. But she knew he was in these woods with her, like the Minotaur, drawing inexorably closer.

She thought back now to his brother Toby and what he'd told her about their childhood growing up in the countryside, about their father who'd been a gamekeeper, who taught his sons how to track and hunt game and how Carl had particularly excelled at those things. Bailey knew that even in a fugue state Carl still would have retained those innate skills and, as Rex the hitman, he was no doubt making good use of them right now. She was at an acute disadvantage, but there was very little she could do about it.

She took out her iPhone and switched it to silent mode. If Stella called her back she didn't want the sound of the ringtone to give away her location. Putting it back in her pocket, she thrust herself onwards... and promptly tripped on an upturned tree root. She fell to the ground, her left ankle twisting awkwardly.

'Shit!' she gasped, tendrils of pain shooting up her leg.

She struggled to her feet but found it excruciating to put any pressure on her left foot. She must have sprained her ankle. This was not good. Limping along desperately, her right arm hanging uselessly by her side, she held onto the trees for support with her one good hand, the rough bark scraping the flesh of her palm.

She realised with a horrible black sinking feeling that she wasn't going to be able to go on for much longer like this. Sooner rather than later she'd have to stop and make some kind of last stand against him... and she wasn't looking forward to it.

* * *

Rex halted, went down on one knee and cocked his head. Holding himself completely still, he listened intently for anything out of the ordinary.

There was the gentle rustle of branches in the soft breeze... The intermittent chirping of a distant bird...

And then he heard a distinct snap as a branch broke. Then a further crackle of vegetation being pushed aside. It was her of course, blundering through the undergrowth with nary a thought for all the noise she was making.

Peering through the trees ahead, he saw the spindly upper branches of a sapling wobbling abnormally and surmised that she was probably holding the base of the tree for support. It made sense if she was wounded and struggling to make progress. He estimated her distance at being no more than a few hundred metres ahead of him.

Standing up, he proceeded forwards in an upright crouch, the loaded crossbow cradled in his grip. He was now in the final stages of the hunt. This was the part known as the stalk. And the key thing about the stalk was to remain unseen until the last moment.

Weaving fluidly through the trees, he closed in for the kill.

* * *

Exhausted now, Bailey staggered from tree to tree, her sprained ankle sending an agonising spike of pain through her with every other step that she took.

Somewhere in the distance she heard sirens and realised that the police had reached the safe house. But it was too late now. There was no way she'd be able to limp back there without Rex intercepting her and killing her.

Realising that she couldn't go on any further, she collapsed in the shadow of a large elm tree, falling down amongst the knobbly roots at its base. She'd reached the end of the road. If he was coming for her, this was where he'd find her... and this was where he'd kill her.

She knew she was beyond defending herself now. She no longer possessed the strength or capability to. There would be no final stand. A small part of her still clung to the slim hope that maybe this murky recess at the foot of the tree was enough of a hiding place for him to miss her. But another part of her instinctively knew with a fatalistic certainty that someone of his proficiency would ferret her out sooner or later.

The thought of death filled her with morbidity. Her thoughts went to her father. Soon she'd be joining him on the other side... not that she believed in any kind of afterlife. She thought about her sister Jennifer and how she wished she'd been able to know her better. And she thought about her poor mother who would be all alone once she was dead.

Lying there in the darkness of the shadows in the lee of the elm tree she gritted her teeth and stared through the foliage and waited for him to arrive.

* * *

Moving through the trees, Rex listened to the sound of the faraway sirens and smiled to himself. By the time they got this far into the woods he would have long melted away through the trees, leaving nothing but Bailey Morgan's corpse for them to find.

He registered the faint cool breeze blowing against his face. He was downwind. Good. It was always better to approach the quarry with the wind blowing in your face as he was right now. That way their scent, and the sound of their movements would be carried to you, and conversely, yours would not be carried to them.

He stopped stock still and slowly lifted his face, sniffing the air, detecting the unmistakeable scent of Bailey Morgan. He recognised it from the clothes he'd smelt in her flat. He now also smelt the mint flavour of the toothpaste on her breath... the chemical whiff of the antiperspirant she wore... the metallic aroma of the blood leaking from her open wound. And prevailing over all else was the sharp acrid tang of her fear.

She was very close now. All alone. A wounded animal separated from the herd.

Snaking rapidly through the undergrowth, he dodged from tree to tree, taking advantage of contours in the ground to cloak his approach.

And then through the leaves ahead he spotted her lying amongst the gnarled roots at the base of a large elm tree, the arm of her suede-coloured jacket soaked red with blood from the crossbow bolt protruding from her bicep.

Finally. At long last he could finish this job. But then he'd never doubted for one minute that he wouldn't.

48

Lying immobile in the shadow of the elm tree, the knobbly roots digging into her back, Bailey peered hard into the woods trying to discern if and when he might appear.

Remembering her phone, she put her hand in her pocket to check it to see if Stella had called her back. In her mad flight through the woods, with her phone being on silent mode, Bailey knew she probably wouldn't have noticed any incoming calls.

But just as she was reaching into her pocket, something caught her eye. A brief silhouette of something hopping from tree to tree. The motion was less like a human and more like some kind of spectral animal flicker. She froze. A shiver of fear went through her. She blinked and looked again but it was gone. Once more there was only vegetation.

And then suddenly he was standing over her, seemingly having materialised out of nowhere.

Carl Freeman. *Rex.*

She looked up at him, meeting his gaze. There was nothing there. Just an empty madness. A smile came over his face. Pure satisfaction. Triumph.

He levelled his crossbow at her. She thought about closing her eyes but then thought better of it. Staring back at him defiantly, she waited for him to pull the trigger. She'd long wondered what the face of death would look like when it finally came for her and this was it. An insane undercover cop. It seemed like a weird form of poetic justice.

But then... the fingers of her left hand, still in the pocket of her jacket, registered the presence of another item just beneath her phone. It was small. Made of metal. Rectangular in shape. At first she couldn't work out what it was. Then, like a jigsaw piece clicking into place, she recognised it.

The little music box.

The one that had belonged to Jack Freeman, Carl's eight-year-old son. The one he'd given her to give to his father.

She'd forgotten all about it. All this time it had been sitting unnoticed in the pocket of her suede-fringed jacket.

A last-ditch crazy nugget of an idea occurred to her.

Her grimy blood-covered fingers closed round it just as Carl was focusing the triple-bladed tip of the bolt right between her eyes.

A brief quizzical flash crossed his features as she pulled the music box from her pocket, but it was gone just as quickly, as his finger began to tighten on the crossbow's trigger.

With shaking fingers and a wince of pain, she swiftly transferred the little music box into the palm of her disabled right hand, just managing to hold it steady, and with her left hand she began to crank the tiny handle. It immediately began to emit a metallic tinkling noise, the bell-like chords eerily loud in the quietness of the woods.

The noise coalesced into the distinctive melody from the song 'Over the Rainbow'.

And as soon as it did...

Rex suddenly froze, his forefinger paused on the cusp of pulling the trigger.

Gazing up at him, Bailey saw that something had changed in his eyes. Something had lifted.

* * *

She swallowed tensely, continuing to turn the handle of the music box whilst staring intently at him trying to determine if she'd finally succeeded in snapping him out of his fugue.

He looked round, bewildered, as if he didn't know where he was or why he was here in the middle of the woods. Peering down at the crossbow in his hands, he frowned like he couldn't work out why he was holding it.

And then he looked down at her, staring back up at him as she cranked the handle of the music box.

'What am I doing here?' he said. He examined her with a look of concern. 'Who are you? Why are you lying on the ground? You're bleeding! Are you okay?' He peered at the crossbow bolt in her arm, then down at the crossbow he was holding. A shocked expression came over his face. 'Did I do that to you?'

A massive and profound wave of relief swept over Bailey. She'd done it. She'd finally woken him up. And not a moment too soon.

The music box he'd given to his young son as a birthday present had possessed enough of an emotional association to break the fugue. The trigger had been the sound of that particular tune played in that particular tinkling manner.

It now struck Bailey that, like Dorothy banging her head and entering the world of Oz, Carl had been living in his own version of Oz – that dark messed-up world of Rex. But now, like Dorothy at the end of the story, Carl had emerged from Oz and was back in Kansas... or rather, the English countryside.

Fairly certain that Rex was gone and Carl Freeman was back, she tentatively ceased turning the handle of the music box.

'Hello Carl,' she said. 'It's good to see that you're back with us.'

'Do I know you?' he asked with a puzzled frown.

She shook her head. 'My name is Detective Constable Bailey Morgan.'

'You're a police officer,' he murmured in surprise.

'Yes,' she said. 'And so are you.'

He nodded slowly. 'Yes that's right. My name is Detective Sergeant Carl Freeman.'

Bailey nodded slowly. That was the right answer.

'Do you know why you're here?' she asked, nodding at the woods round them. 'Do you know why I'm here?'

He frowned and scratched his head. 'No... now that you mention it, I... uh... I can't seem to remember...'

Casting her mind back to the psychologist's explanation of fugue states, Bailey recalled that once a person emerged from a fugue, they remembered nothing from the time they'd spent within the fugue. Carl appeared to remember nothing of what he'd just been doing in his incarnation as Rex.

'What's the last thing you remember Carl?' she asked gently.

He frowned. 'I remember being in my car. I was driving along. I was on my way to a meeting. It was part of an undercover operation I was working on.'

'You were going to meet someone called Jack Wynter.'

'Yes. That's right. I can't talk about it though. It's confidential. You know how it is with undercover deployments.'

Bailey nodded in understanding.

His face screwed up in anguish. 'But I... just before that, I was at my house... I...'

She tensed, aware that he was reliving the traumatic memory that had plunged him into the fugue in the first place. For a horrible moment she wondered if it would once again cause Rex to take over. But it didn't. Clearly that initial experience had been a one-off triggered by his heightened state of stress at the time.

'But you forgot your lucky rabbit's foot, didn't you?' she said gently.

He stared at her, befuddled. 'How did you know that?' he whispered.

'I know a lot about you Carl. More than you realise.'

'What's going on?' he asked. 'Why am I here? Why are you here?'

She observed him with a mixture of sympathy and pity. First a high-level undercover cop. Then a professional killer. Now he seemed like a lost little boy.

'You had a breakdown Carl,' she said. 'You underwent a severe mental episode.'

'When did that happen?'

'That was three years ago, Carl.'

'Three years ago?! What have I been doing since then?' He looked down at the crossbow he was holding, then at her wounded arm. A horrified expression settled on his face 'Have I done bad things? I don't remember.'

She swallowed. This wasn't going to be the easiest subject to broach. And now probably wasn't the best time to do it.

'You've done some questionable things, Carl,' she said, thinking painfully of the horrible fate that her friend Emma had suffered at the hands of Rex, not to mention Jeremy Westerby and all the other people he'd murdered over the course of his existence. 'But we can talk about all that later. Best thing for now, is if you put down the crossbow.'

He hesitated a moment then meekly laid the crossbow down on the ground. She breathed a sigh of relief.

'You need to come with me now, Carl,' she said. 'Help me up.'

She held out her hand and he took it and pulled her to her feet. Wincing as her sprained ankle sent pangs of pain shooting up her leg, she put an arm round his shoulder for support.

She held out the music box. 'Here, Carl. Your son Jack wanted me to give this to you.'

Taking it from her, he examined the small device, his face breaking into a tender smile of recognition, his eyes suddenly aglow with love and wonder.

'Jack,' he murmured. 'My boy. My little munchkin.'

He looked up at Bailey with an expression of profound gratitude. 'Thank you,' he whispered.

And then together they began to limp back through the woods in the direction of civilisation.

* * *

It was a long slow walk out of the woods. Bailey leaned against him all the way, feeling the lean steely strength in his muscles. It was ironic that this man who just a short while earlier had been hell-bent on exterminating her was now patiently helping her.

Getting back to the safe house was fairly straightforward. They just headed towards the large plume of black smoke which was intermittently visible in the sky through the treetops.

On reaching the edge of the clearing in which the cottage stood, Bailey saw that there were a number of emergency services vehicles, including several police cars and a police van, parked on the driveway leading up to the burning cottage. The cottage itself was now completely consumed by fire, the roof having collapsed inwards, flames and smoke towering up from within. Even from her relative distance, she could feel the heat on her face as it crackled and burned.

Standing by the vehicles were a number of black-clad

policemen armed with MP5 submachine guns. She glanced up at Carl with concern. He was observing them uneasily.

'Are they here because of me?' he asked, sounding worried.

'Don't worry Carl,' she said. 'I won't let them harm you.'

Much as she knew that the man next to her had been responsible for committing some terrible deeds, including the murder of a good friend of hers, she knew she couldn't allow him to be shot dead, however politically expedient that might be for the Met's top brass. They would be killing Carl Freeman, not Rex. She was determined to see Carl Freeman pay for the crimes of Rex but only in a way that took fair account of his strange mental condition.

'Walk behind me with your hands up,' she instructed.

Disengaging herself from him, she took out her warrant card and held it up in front of her. She limped slowly forward towards the emergency vehicles, with Carl following closely behind, his hands above his head. There was some shouting and commotion as they got noticed, and a number of armed officers started to run towards them, fanning out, pointing their guns at them and shouting at them to stop.

'I'm a police officer!' shouted Bailey. 'We're unarmed. There's no need to shoot.'

The two of them halted as armed officers surrounded them, their submachine guns levelled at Carl, their fingers poised on the triggers, their faces tense and scared.

Bailey recognised a familiar figure striding towards them. Stella was wearing a bulletproof vest and had a Glock nine-millimetre pistol strapped to her thigh. Holding up her hand to signal the police to remain as they were, she walked right up to Bailey and Carl.

Her gaze flickered over Bailey with concern, taking in the crossbow bolt sticking out of her bleeding arm. 'Thank God you're still alive Bailey,' she said. 'We thought you were in there.' She

gestured at the burning cottage. 'We'll get you to a medic immediately.'

She eyed Carl suspiciously, her right hand hovering by the butt
of her Glock.

'This is Detective Sergeant Carl Freeman,' said Bailey. 'He's
come back. He's woken up. Rex is no longer with us.'

Bailey hoped that by stating Carl's real name and rank in the
presence of the armed police officers, they would be less likely to
shoot him on the spot.

The armed officers swapped uncertain glances, looking to Stella
for a cue to action. Stella gave Bailey a brief daggers glare. If there
had been any possibility of a convenient execution and cover-up, it
was now much less feasible. Stella turned her attention back to
Carl, peering intently into his face. He looked back at her
anxiously.

'Detective Sergeant Carl Freeman...' she murmured.

He nodded obediently.

'...I am arresting you for murder,' she continued. 'You do not
have to say anything. But, it may harm your defence if you do not
mention when questioned something which you later rely on in
court. Anything you do say may be given in evidence. Do you
understand?'

She nodded to one of the armed officers. Lowering his submachine gun, the officer took a set of handcuffs from his utility belt
and clamped them round Carl's unresisting wrists.

Bailey relaxed a little. It looked like Carl's physical safety was
now relatively assured. Not that it was much consolation for him,
for he was standing there looking completely shell-shocked and
utterly confused.

'Murder?!' he exclaimed. 'Who did I murder?'

Stella stepped aside to let him see the black body bags being
loaded into the ambulances parked in the driveway.

'You killed four men today,' she said. 'Police officers. Some of them had families. You've killed a lot of people, Carl. Both men and women.'

Carl looked stunned, totally aghast. 'I... I killed them...?'

Stella nodded gravely. Bailey watched him sadly. She could see that he wasn't coping too well with the revelations.

Stella continued. 'You've been working as a contract killer, Carl. You've been murdering people for money.'

'But... but... I don't remember,' he protested. 'I don't remember any of it.'

'Tell that to the judge,' said Stella with a hard look on her face. 'Maybe he'll believe you. Even if he does, I think you'll still be going to prison for a very long time. I'm afraid there's no way out for you Carl.'

'What are my family going to think?' he said hoarsely. 'My wife? My little boy? He'll know I'm a murderer.' He turned to face Bailey, his face twisted in anguish. 'I'm not a murderer.'

Bailey regarded him sympathetically. She empathised with his torment, but there was nothing she could do to help. It was something he was just going to have to come to terms with. She realised now that this was the real punishment that he would face, more so than any prison sentence. For the rest of his life he would have to live with this terrible knowledge of what he'd done.

The armed police led him away towards the vehicles. Bailey watched him walk away, his head bowed. He was a broken man.

She suddenly felt weak and dizzy, the pain from her arm, and also now her ankle, returning stronger than ever.

'We need to get you to a medic right now,' said Stella, offering Bailey her arm. Bailey took it and together they walked slowly towards the emergency vehicles.

'I'm glad you got my message,' said Bailey. 'How did you get here from London so soon?'

'Helicopter. Took less than half an hour.'

Up ahead of them, Carl was standing compliantly next to a police van, surrounded by armed officers, his hands cuffed in front of him, ready to be transported to wherever they were going to take him.

As they walked past him, he looked up at Bailey, his eyes wide and mournful. 'Detective Constable Bailey Morgan?' he said.

Bailey stopped. 'Yes?' Accompanied by Stella, she limped a little closer to him until they were barely a metre apart. She wasn't scared of being this close to him as she knew now that he wouldn't harm her.

He took a deep shuddering breath, as if he was forcing back some emotion. 'Tell Jack that I love him.'

A strange twinge of foreboding went through Bailey. There was something disturbingly final in his tone.

With the speed of a cobra he suddenly whipped forward and, with his cuffed hands, yanked Stella's Glock from its holster on her thigh, and in the same fluid movement he drew back the slide and flicked off the safety. He now had a loaded gun in his hands.

Bailey watched agape, everything happening before her brain had even had time to send a message to her body to react.

Stella's mouth dropped open in shock, her hand going to her empty holster eons too late. The retinue of armed police officers clambered to point their submachine guns at him. But by that point he had grasped Bailey's shoulder, spun her round and pulled her across himself as a human shield.

The two of them stood there backed up against the police van. He had one cuffed hand gripping the back of her collar, holding her tight against him, and the other cuffed hand clutching the Glock with the barrel pressed up against the base of her skull. With her wounded arm and sprained ankle, she was in no position to throw him off.

Standing there as he pointed the gun at her head, Bailey realised with a gut-wrenching horror that she had made an awful misjudgement. Rex hadn't really gone. He was right here standing behind her pointing a gun at her head and he was going to finish the job, even if it meant dying in the process.

The armed police pointed their guns at him, shouting at him to drop the weapon and let her go, but Bailey knew they couldn't get a clear shot at him because she was in the way. Stella gazed into Bailey's eyes with a torturous expression, knowing that she was about to see Bailey's brains blown out.

Carl leaned in close so Bailey could feel his hot breath on her neck.

'Just remember,' he whispered in her ear. 'Tell my boy that his dad loves him.'

BANG.

The report of the gunshot was deafening at close range. Bailey's hearing shut down completely. In front of her Stella and the armed officers silently shouted in alarm.

For a second Bailey wondered if this was what it felt like to be shot through the head. But then she realised that he had let go of her.

She staggered forward and turned round to see that he was lying crumpled on the ground, his eyes staring sightlessly up at the sky. A large chunk of his skull was missing and his blood and brains were dripping down the white side of the police van. In his hand-cuffed hands he still clutched the Glock pistol with which he'd shot himself.

49

Standing at the kitchen island, Amy Benvenuto poured some olive oil into a bowl for the vinaigrette that she was making for the salad that she, her husband and their two daughters were going to eat for dinner as an accompaniment to the spaghetti bolognaise that was currently simmering on the stove.

It was Sunday evening and Charlie was in the living room and the girls were upstairs. Amy was absently watching the news on the small TV in the kitchen but not really paying much attention to it due to the fact that her mind was preoccupied with worrisome thoughts about Charlie's trial which was taking place the day after tomorrow. Not only that, the things she'd overheard him saying on the phone about having people killed had been gnawing away at her, and the more she raked over his words, the more uneasy she felt in his presence. Even though she tried to conceal her disquiet from him, she sensed that he too knew that something was up between them.

Mixing the vinaigrette round with a small spoon, she glanced up at the TV to see that it was currently showing an extended piece focusing on organised crime in the capital and the lawlessness and violence it entailed.

The journalist was interviewing a woman whose husband had recently been murdered. Apparently he'd been a top lawyer for the Crown Prosecution Service and his death was suspected to be linked to his work combatting organised crime. His widow was well spoken and middle class, not unlike Amy herself, and for that very reason Amy found herself watching the TV with a little more interest than before. She watched sympathetically as the woman tearfully described how she'd come back from a West End musical with their two children to find her husband brutally murdered in his study. Amy's heart went out to the poor woman as she listened to her describe the gruesome scene that had confronted them when they'd returned home.

Hearing footsteps behind her, she glanced round to see that Charlie had just entered the kitchen. He stopped and stared at the TV, then went to pick up the remote as if to change the channel. Amy pulled it away from him. 'I'm watching it,' she said. 'It's interesting.'

'I miss Jeremy so much,' the woman was saying. 'And so do the kids. They're going to have to grow up without a dad.'

Amy shook her head sadly. Then she noticed the woman's name which was displayed in the bottom corner of the TV screen.

Louise Westerby.

The name rang a bell.

Westerby.

Where had Amy heard that name before?

She studied the TV with a perplexed frown as she tried to remember the context in which she'd heard it. And then an awful sinking feeling overcame her as she remembered exactly where she'd heard the name Westerby.

She slowly turned to look at her husband. He was standing

there on the other side of the kitchen island observing the television with a closed expression on his face.

She swallowed nervously, her heart thumping hard in her chest. The urge to say something swelled up inside her and she was unable to repress it any longer. She mustered up her courage and took a deep breath.

'That woman's husband is a lawyer called Jeremy Westerby,' she said in a small voice.

He turned his head to fix her with a stony stare. A cold shudder went through her but she forced herself to continue nonetheless.

'I overheard you talking on the phone the other day,' she stammered. 'When you were out in the garden. You were talking about Jeremy Westerby on the phone. You were talking about him being "out of the picture", about "one less lawyer the better". I remember now. That's what you said.'

His face twisted into a disbelieving grimace. 'You were listening to me?' he growled.

'I couldn't help it,' she said. 'You left my phone in here. I thought you needed it to talk to your lawyers. I thought you'd forgotten it so I took it out to give it to you but then I couldn't help overhearing what you were talking about.'

'That was a private conversation,' he said, his voice low and dangerous. 'It was none of your business.'

'You were talking about having people killed!' she said, her voice going up an octave. 'You had Jeremy Westerby killed, didn't you? That's what you were saying on the phone. You paid money to have him murdered, didn't you? It was something to do with your court case.'

'Keep your voice down!' he snarled. 'Or the girls'll hear.'

'Tell me the truth!' she demanded. 'Did you have him killed?'

He watched her coldly. But he didn't deny it. And she could see now in his eyes the blackness that lay in his soul. Whether this evil had been there from the first time she'd met him, or whether it had developed subsequently, it was something that she only now saw properly and she knew for certain in her heart that he had been lying to her all these years and that all those allegations against him were most probably true.

'I did nothing of the sort,' he said dismissively.

'You're lying to me!' she said. 'You've been lying to me all along.'

'I'm not lying,' he insisted, attempting an expression of hurt. 'I can't believe you think I've been lying to you.'

'How could you do something like that?' she demanded. 'How could you murder an innocent man? Those kids don't have a dad any more! Do you realise that?'

He let out a frustrated exhalation and was silent for a few moments.

'It was for the best,' he growled. 'I was only thinking of you and the girls.'

She felt dizzy at his confession. Everything seemed to be spinning round her all of a sudden.

'So you did do it!' she gasped. 'You're a criminal! That's what you are. The police are right about you, aren't they? You are a drug trafficker. You're a murdering drug trafficker.'

'It's made us all this money, hasn't it?' he said, making a sweeping gesture with his arm at the luxury kitchen. 'Don't be so ungrateful! You and the girls have a good life because of me.'

She was gripped by an uncharacteristic fury at her husband. 'I would never have married you if I'd have known it would come to this! I didn't sign up for this!'

They stood there facing off against each other on opposite sides of the kitchen island, an unbearable tension hanging between them. And then his face formed into that charming smile that he was so good at giving her. But right now, in her current state, all Amy saw was a grotesque and failed approximation of something that was supposed to be human and warm... and she was repelled by it.

'I love you,' he started. 'I've always loved—'

'I'm going to call the police,' she stated.

The smile instantly dropped off his face, his eyes widening in alarm and his mouth dropping open slightly. He straightened up, his bulky figure suddenly growing large and threatening.

She gulped and shrank a little, cowering in his shadow. He was much bigger than her and she was suddenly glad that they were separated by the kitchen island. That whisper of fear she'd felt ever since overhearing him on the phone now bloomed into a full-blown dread that he might physically harm her. After all, she knew now that this was a man to be legitimately afraid of... a man who was capable of having people killed.

'Now don't do anything stupid Amy,' he warned.

'I draw the line at murder,' she said hoarsely and went to pick up her phone which was lying on the top of the kitchen island just in front of her.

He made a grab for it, lightning fast... but not quite fast enough, his large hand swiping on empty space, knocking the bowl of vinaigrette off the worktop. The bowl shattered on the tiled floor, the contents splashing all over the place.

Clutching her phone in her hand, she dodged round the kitchen island to try and get away from him. He mirrored her move in an attempt to cut her off so she twisted round to dodge the other way, her petite nimble form a shade quicker than his heavy bulk. He spun on his heels to try and catch her but put his foot in the vinaigrette on the kitchen floor. Slipping in the oily mixture, he lost his balance, crashing forward, his head slamming into the hard edge of the granite worktop.

She froze in horror as he slumped to the floor. He lay there with his eyes closed, a dark pool of blood forming on the white tiles beneath his bald head.

'Charlie!' she gasped. 'Oh my God Charlie!'

A cold heavy panic seized her. What had she done?! She dropped to her knees next to him and shook him by the shoulder.

'Wake up Charlie! Please wake up!'

50

It was the eighth of October. There was a chill edge to the air in Green Park and the ground was covered in a thick layer of fallen leaves. Sitting on a bench in the park, Bailey turned up the collar of her coat and contemplated that it really did feel like autumn now. Her right arm, bandaged and in a sling, still throbbed painfully whenever she moved it; her ankle, although still tender, had at least improved to the point where she could limp from place to place, albeit slowly.

As she observed the ducks paddling round in the nearby pond, she reflected that Charlie Benvenuto's trial would have been taking place today at Southwark Crown Court. However, she'd received a phone call from the CPS the previous day informing her that the trial was no longer going ahead and that the prosecution against Benvenuto was being discontinued. That was because Benvenuto was dead.

Apparently he'd fallen over in the kitchen of his house during the course of an argument with his wife. He'd banged his head, slipped into a coma, and died in hospital a few hours later from a subdural haematoma – bleeding on the brain.

The news had left Bailey both shocked and surprised and it had left her unsure how to feel. On the one hand she felt robbed of the opportunity to bring Benvenuto to justice. But on the other hand she also felt relieved that he wouldn't be calling out any more hits on her. She couldn't say that she felt particularly sad at his demise although she did feel sorry for his poor wife who apparently was devastated by what had happened.

Feeling her mobile phone vibrating in her pocket, she pulled it out to see that it was Stella calling her. She answered the phone.

Stella sounded in a buoyant mood. 'How are you doing Bailey? How's the arm?'

'It's fine thank you, although I won't be playing tennis any time soon.'

Stella laughed. 'Where are you now?'

'I'm in Green Park watching the ducks.'

'Oh? Er... that's nice. Well, anyway I just wanted to let you know that I caught up with senior management and debriefed them on the entire Rex affair, from start to finish.'

'Yes?'

'And they're generally pretty pleased with how it all turned out, despite the disaster at St Katharine Docks. In their eyes the whole Rex problem has been solved rather neatly with his suicide... which is why they're willing to overlook my negligence in letting him get hold of my weapon. The Met press office put out a statement this morning. It said that following a dedicated pursuit by members of the police, Rex was cornered and took his own life rather than face capture... which is more or less true. And it said that he so far remains unidentified. There will obviously be an inquest, but I'm sure that senior management will ensure that any cracks or inconsistencies are conveniently papered over.'

'A cover-up?' mused Bailey dryly. 'That doesn't really surprise me. But just remember, the man who killed himself wasn't Rex. It was Carl Freeman. I'd woken him from his fugue, and when he saw the situation for what it was, he couldn't see any other alternative apart from suicide. For someone as conscientious and principled as he was, the shame and the guilt were just too much to bear. We mustn't forget that he was an honourable man who stayed true to the police and to his family right through to the very end.'

'We won't forget him,' said Stella. 'Leaving Rex unidentified means that Carl Freeman's memory remains untarnished just as he would have wanted it to be. On his service record he's still the highly decorated cop who died in the line of duty three years ago. Sure, a few of us know the dirty truth, but as police officers, we're bound by law to confidentiality, and I don't doubt that senior management would jump to prosecute anyone who chose to leak something that damaging.'

'And his family?' asked Bailey. 'What about them? If anyone's entitled to know the truth, it's them.'

'What good would it do them?' said Stella. 'Surely it's better if they remember him as a police officer and a dad rather than as a hitman who killed a whole load of people before blowing his brains out?'

Bailey sighed. She was struck with a sense of sadness about what had happened to Carl Freeman. He'd made the ultimate sacrifice in a high-stakes game, but although his death was inextricably linked to her decision to wake him from his fugue, she knew that if she hadn't have done so she would be dead right now.

By means of atoning for her complicity in his death, Bailey intended to fulfil his final request. He'd asked her to tell his son that he loved him and she wasn't going to let him down. It would involve telling Jack the truth about his father; and, after retrieving it from whichever police evidence room it was currently in, she'd return the little music box to him and explain how it had saved her life. He was of course too young to take it all on board right now, but she resolved to tell him at some point in the future when he was mature enough to handle it. And if it meant breaching the rules round confidentiality then so be it. It was the least she could do for Detective Sergeant Carl Freeman.

'I have to say, Bailey,' said Stella with an audible tremor of excitement, 'I have a strong feeling that there'll be some commendations heading our way in the very near future. For both you and me.'

Bailey smiled mirthlessly. She wasn't necessarily sure that she either wanted or deserved a commendation for what had happened to Carl Freeman, but she could see that it meant a lot to Stella who would no doubt consider it a useful feather in her cap on the way up the ranks.

'You deserve it Stella,' she said. 'Thanks for being there for me.'

Stella sounded delighted. 'I look forward to working with you again Bailey.'

Bailey said goodbye and hung up. Checking the time, she saw that Anthony would be along shortly. He worked just nearby which was why they'd chosen Green Park as a meeting spot. As mutual friends of Emma's, they were going to talk about Emma and discuss the arrangements for her upcoming funeral.

Turning her head, she noticed Anthony walking along the path towards her. He smiled and waved at her. She smiled and waved back.

On seeing him approaching, she felt an unexpected rush of affection for him. She was glad they'd decided to meet. As he got closer, she thought to herself that he was better looking than she remembered. Who knows, maybe they would end up together after all.

ACKNOWLEDGMENTS

Caroline Ridding, my editor, for her characteristically excellent suggestions on how to improve the manuscript, and her supreme patience and willingness to ensure that it was of a publishable standard.

All of the team at Boldwood Books for their brilliant hard work in transforming the book from a manuscript into a fully-fledged novel, and for marketing it to the wider public.

Dorie Simmonds, my agent, for her shrewd advice and professional support, as well as her marvellous enthusiasm in discussing new ideas and her perpetual readiness to provide feedback on my work.

Dr Lucie Goddard for her fascinating neuropsychology insights which, along with Alan J. Parkin's books on human memory, proved to be extremely useful. I take full responsibility for any mistakes or inaccuracies that may have arisen around these elements of the story.

Claire, my wife, for being so supportive, and for taking the time to read the story not once, but several times. Without her ideas and encouragement it would have been a lesser book.

In terms of research, when it came to understanding the techniques and principles of tracking and stalking, I found *The Complete Guide to Tracking* by Bob Carss to be a most informative read.

MORE FROM CARO SAVAGE

We hope you enjoyed reading *Hunted*. If you did, please leave a review.

If you'd like to gift a copy, this book is also available as an ebook, digital audio download and audiobook CD.

Sign up to Caro Savages's mailing list for news, competitions and updates on future books.

http://bit.ly/CaroSavageNewsletter

Jailbird, the first instalment in the Detective Constable Bailey Morgan series, is available to order now.

ABOUT THE AUTHOR

Caro Savage knows all about bestselling thrillers having worked as a Waterstones bookseller for 12 years in a previous life. Now taking up the challenge personally and turning to hard-hitting crime thriller writing.

Follow Caro on social media:

 twitter.com/CaroSavageStory

 instagram.com/carosavage

 bookbub.com/authors/caro-savage

ABOUT BOLDWOOD BOOKS

Boldwood Books is a fiction publishing company seeking out the best stories from around the world.

Find out more at www.boldwoodbooks.com

Sign up to the Book and Tonic newsletter for news, offers and competitions from Boldwood Books!

http://www.bit.ly/bookandtonic

We'd love to hear from you, follow us on social media:

facebook.com/BookandTonic

twitter.com/BoldwoodBooks

instagram.com/BookandTonic

Printed in Great Britain
by Amazon

75884525R00200